**"TURN ON** the television!" he shouted at her.

"What?" she said.

"They blew up the White House," he said.

All the channels were showing the same pictures: the White House with a gaping hole in the south wall of the West Wing, people in suits and people in uniforms, emergency vehicles all around. Reporters explaining that all air traffic was grounded so they couldn't give aerial shots—thank God, she thought, that's all we need, the sky around the White House cluttered with choppers—and promising that as soon as they could get confirmation they'd tell us who died.

Because people had died. That much they knew. . . .

**AND THEN** there was the video clip—sold to the highest bidder?—on CBS and then picked up by everybody else (but with the CBS logo in the corner—captalism continues!) taken from a car on the eastbound lane of Independence Avenue, where it bridged the Tidal Basin. The footage showed the terrorists on the asphalt of the westbound lanes just past the retaining wall of the Tidal Basin, and two rocket launchers.

The camera was shaking—obviously a digital snapshot camera with only a short video capacity. But there were pops of gunfire and some of the terrorists turned to fire . . . almost right at the camera. Was this tourist insane? He should be down inside his car, not vidding the whole thing.

Then a dark shape moved right in front of the camera in a blur of motion. A man in a suit. But with a weapon. And then another, only in dress uniform. And a voice saying, "Get down inside your car!"

Of course the camera stayed where it was.

*Pop. Pop. Pop-pop-pop.* One of the terrorists went down. Another. One of the launchers was knocked out of alignment and tipped over. But the other one fired and then the video ended.

Mark pushed a button on the remote and things started rewinding.

"What are you doing?"

"Rewinding," said Mark.

"This is all a tape?"

"It's DVR, Mom," he said, like she was kind of dim. "We've had this for two years now. You can rewind anything if you haven't changed the channel in between."

"But I want to hear what they're saying."

"Mom," said Mark. "Why do we have to listen to *them* when we can *see*?"

And then he added, softly: "I think it was Dad."

# EMPIRE

## ORSON SCOTT CARD

TOR®

A TOM DOHERTY ASSOCIATES BOOK
NEW YORK

This is a work of fiction. All of the characters, organizations, and events portrayed in this novel are either products of the author's imagination or are used fictitiously.

EMPIRE

Copyright © 2006 by Orson Scott Card

All rights reserved, including the right to reproduce this book, or portions thereof, in any form.

Edited by Beth Meacham

A Tor Book
Published by Tom Doherty Associates, LLC
175 Fifth Avenue
New York, NY 10010

www.tor.com

Tor® is a registered trademark of Tom Doherty Associates, LLC.

ISBN-13: 978-0-7653-5522-5
ISBN-10: 0-7653-5522-1

First Edition: November 2006
First Mass Market: Edition: December 2007

Printed in the United States of America

0  9  8  7  6  5  4  3  2  1

*To Cyndie and Jeremy*
*for finding the balance*
*between the law and the life*
*and for sharing Victor and Cataan*

# CONTENTS

# EMPIRE

# ONE

# CAPTAIN MALICH

Treason only matters when it is committed by trusted men.

**THE TEAM** of four Americans had been in the village for three months. Their mission was to build trust until they could acquire accurate information about the activities of a nearby warlord believed to be harboring some operatives of Al Qaeda.

All four soldiers were highly trained for their Special Ops assignment. Which meant that they understood a great deal about local agriculture and husbandry, trade, food storage, and other issues on which the survival and prosperity of the village depended. They had arrived with rudimentary skills in the pertinent languages, but now they were reasonably fluent in the language of the village.

The village girls were beginning to find occasions to walk near whatever project the American soldiers were working on. But the soldiers ignored them, and by now the parents of these girls knew they were safe enough—though that didn't stop them from rebuking the girls for their immodesty with men who were, after all, unbelievers and foreigners and dangerous men.

For these American soldiers had also been trained to kill—silently or noisily, close at hand or from a distance, individually or in groups, with weapons or without.

They had killed no one in front of these villagers, and in fact they had killed no one, ever, anywhere. Yet there was something about them, their alertness, the way they moved, that gave warning, the way a tiger gives warning simply by the fluidity of its movement and the alertness of its eyes.

There came a day that one of the villagers, a young man who had been away for a week, came home, and within a few minutes had told his news to the elder who, for lack of anyone better, was regarded by the villagers as the wisest counselor. He, in turn, brought the young man to the Americans.

The terrorists, he said, were building up a cache of weapons away to the southwest. The local warlord had not given his consent—in fact, he disapproved, but would not dare to intervene. "He would be as happy as anyone to be rid of these men. They frighten him as much as they frighten everyone else."

The young man was also, obviously, afraid.

The Americans got directions from him and strode out of the camp, following one of the trails the shepherds used.

When they were behind the first hill—though this "hill" in most other places would have been called a mountain—they stopped.

"It's a trap, of course," said one of the Americans.

"Yes," said the leader, a young captain named Reuben Malich. "But will they spring it when we reach the place where his directions would send us? Or when we return?"

In other words, as they all understood: Was the village part of the conspiracy or not? If it was, then the trap would be sprung far away.

But if the villagers had not betrayed them (except for the one young man), then in all likelihood the village was in as much danger as the Americans.

Captain Malich briefly discussed the possibilities with his team, so that by the time he gave his orders, they were all in complete agreement.

A few minutes later, using routes they had planned on the first day, before they ever entered the village, they crested the hill at four separate vantage points and spotted the armed men who had just entered the village and were taking up many of the positions surrounding it that the Americans had guessed they would use.

The Americans' plan, in the event of such an ambush, was to approach these positions with stealth and kill the enemy one by one, silently.

But now Captain Malich saw a scene playing out in the center of the village that he could not bear. For the old man had been brought out into the middle of the sunbaked dirt of the square, and a man with a sword was preparing to behead him.

Captain Malich did the calculations in his head. Protect your own force—that was a prime concern. But if it were the only priority, or the highest priority, nations would keep their armies at home and never commit them to battle at all.

The higher priority here was the mission. If the village sustained any casualties, they would not care that the Americans saved them from even more. They would only grieve that the Americans had ever come at all, bringing such tragedy with them. They would beg the Americans to leave, and hate them if they did not go.

Here were the terrorists, proving that they were, as suspected, operating in the area. This village had been a good choice. Which meant that it would be a terrible waste to lose the trust that had been built up.

Captain Malich took his own weapon and, adjusting wind and distance, took careful aim and killed the swordsman with a single shot.

The other three Americans understood immediately the change of plans. They took aim at the enemies who would be able to take cover most easily, and killed them. Then they settled down to shooting the others one by one.

Of course, the enemy were firing back. Captain Malich himself was hit, but his body armor easily dealt with a weapon fired at such long range. And as the enemy fire slackened, Malich counted the enemy dead and compared it to the number he had seen in the village, moving from building to building. He gave the hand signal that told the rest of his team that he was going in, and they shot at anyone who seemed to be getting into position to kill him as he descended the slope.

In only a few minutes, he was among the small buildings of the village. These walls would not stop bullets, and there were people cowering inside. So he did not expect to do a lot of shooting. This would be knife work.

He was good at knife work. He hadn't known until now how easy it was to kill another man. The adrenalin coursing through him pushed aside the part of his mind that might be bothered by the killing. All he thought of at this moment was what he needed to do, and what the enemy might do to stop him, and the knife merely released the tension for a moment, until he started looking for the next target.

By now his men were also in the village, doing their own variations on the same work. One of the soldiers encountered a terrorist who was holding a child as a hostage. There was no thought of negotiation. The American took aim instantly, fired, and the terrorist dropped dead with a bullet through his eye.

At the end, the sole surviving terrorist panicked. He ran to the center of the square, where many of the villagers were still cowering, and leveled his automatic weapon to mow them down.

The old man still had one last spring in his ancient legs, and he threw himself onto the automatic weapon as it went off.

Captain Malich was nearest to the terrorist and shot him dead. But the old man had taken a mortal wound. By the time Malich got to him, the old man gave one last shudder and died in a puddle of the blood that had poured from his abdomen where the two bullets tore him open.

Reuben Malich knelt over the body and cried out in the keening wail of deep grief, the anguish of a soul on fire. He tore open the shirt of his uniform and struck himself repeatedly on the chest. This was not part of his training. He had never seen anyone do such a thing, in any culture. Striking himself looked to his fellow soldiers like a kind of madness. But the surviving villagers joined him in grief, or watched him in awe.

Within moments he was back on the job, interrogating the abject young betrayer while the other soldiers explained to the villagers that this boy was not the enemy, just a frightened kid who had been coerced and lied to by the terrorists and did not deserve to be killed.

Six hours later, the terrorist base camp was pounded by American bombs; by noon the next day, it had been scoured to the last cave by American soldiers flown in by chopper.

Then they were all pulled out. The operation was a success. The Americans reported that they had suffered no casualties.

**"FROM WHAT** one of your men told us," said the colonel, "we wonder if you might have made your decision to put your own men at risk by firing immediately, based on emotional involvement with the villagers."

"That's how I meant it to appear to the villagers," said Captain Malich. "If we allowed the village to take casualties before we were on the scene, I believe we would have lost their trust."

"And when you grieved over the body of the village headman?"

"Sir, I had to show him honor in a way they would understand, so that his heroic death became an asset to us instead of a liability."

"It was all acting?"

"None of it was acting," said Captain Malich. "All I did was permit it to be seen."

The colonel turned to the clerk. "All right, shut off the tape." Then, to Malich: "Good work, Major. You're on your way to New Jersey."

Which is how Reuben Malich learned he was a captain no more. As for New Jersey, he had no idea what he would do there, but at least he already spoke the language, and fewer people would be trying to kill him.

# TWO

# RECRUITMENT

When do you first set foot on the ladder to greatness? Or on the slippery slope of treason? Do you know it at the time? Or do you discover it only looking back?

**"EVERYBODY COMPARES** America to Rome," said Averell Torrent to the graduate students seated around the table. "But they compare the wrong thing. It's always, 'America is going to fall, just like Rome.' We should be so lucky! Let's fall just like Rome did—after five hundred years of world domination!" Torrent smiled maliciously.

Major Reuben Malich took a note—in Farsi, as he usually did, so that no one else at the table could understand what he was writing. What he wrote was: America's purpose is not to dominate anything. We don't want to be Rome.

Torrent did not wait for note-taking. "The real question is, how can America establish itself so it can *endure* the way Rome did?"

Torrent looked around the table. He was surrounded by students only a little younger than he was, but there was no doubt of his authority. Not everybody writes a doctoral dissertation that becomes the cover story of all the political and international journals. Only Malich was older than Torrent; only Malich was not confused about the difference between Torrent and God. Then again, only Malich actually believed in God, so the others could be forgiven their confusion of the two.

"The only reason we care about the fall of Rome," said Torrent, "is because this Latin-speaking village in the heart of the Italian peninsula had forced its culture and language on Gaul and Iberia and Dacia and Britannia, and even after it fell, the lands they conquered clung to as much of that culture as they could. Why? Why was Rome so *successful*?"

No one offered to speak. So, as usual, Torrent zeroed in on Malich. "Let's ask Soldier Boy, here. You're part of America's legions."

Reuben refused to let the implied taunting get to him. Be calm in the face of the enemy. If he *is* an enemy.

"I was hoping *you'd* answer that one, sir," said Malich. "Since that's the topic of the entire course."

"All the more reason why you should already have thought of some possible answers. Are you telling me you haven't thought of any?"

Reuben had been thinking of answers to that—and similar questions—ever since he set his sights on a military career, back in seventh grade. But he said nothing, simply regarding Torrent with a steady gaze that showed nothing, not even defiance, and certainly not hostility. In the modern American classroom, a soldier's battle face was a look of perfect tranquility.

Torrent pressed him. "Rome ruthlessly conquered dozens, hundreds of nations and tribes. Why, then, when Rome fell, did these former enemies cling to *Roman* culture and claim *Roman* heritage as their own for a thousand years and more?"

"Time," said Reuben. "People got used to being under Roman rule."

"Do you really think *time* explains it?" asked Torrent scornfully.

"Absolutely," said Reuben. "Look at China. After a few centuries, most people came to identify themselves so completely with their conquerors that they thought of themselves as Chinese. Same with Islam. Given time enough, with no hope of liberation or revolt, they eventually converted to Islam. They even came to think of themselves as *Arabs*."

As usual, when Reuben pressed back, Torrent backed off, not in any obvious, respectful way that admitted Reuben might have scored a point or two, but by simply turning to someone else to ask another question.

The discussion moved on from there into a discussion of the Soviet Union and how eagerly the subject peoples shrugged off the Russian yoke at the first opportunity. But eventually Torrent brought it back to Rome—and to Major Reuben Malich.

"If America fell today, how much of our culture would endure? Most places that speak English in the world do so because of the British Empire, not because of anything America did. What about our civilization will last? T-shirts? Coca-Cola?"

"Pepsi," joked one of the other students.

"McDonald's."

"IPods."

"Funny, but trivial," said Torrent. "Soldier Boy, you tell us. What would last?"

"Nothing," said Reuben immediately. "They respect us now because we have a dangerous military. They adopt our culture because we're rich. If we were poor and unarmed, they'd peel off American culture like a snake shedding its skin."

"Yes!" said Torrent. The other students registered as much surprise as Reuben felt, though Reuben did not let it show. Torrent *agreed* with the soldier?

"That's why there is no comparison between America and Rome," said Torrent. "Our empire can't fall because we aren't an empire. We have never passed from our republican stage to our imperial one. Right now we buy and sell and, occasionally, bully our way into other countries, but when they thumb their noses at us, we treat them as if they had a right, as if there were some equivalence between our nation and their puny weakness. Can you imagine what Rome would have done if an 'ally' treated them the way

France and Germany have been treating the United States?"

The class laughed.

Reuben Malich did not laugh. "The fact that we *don't* act like Rome is one of the best things about America," he said.

"So isn't it ironic," said Torrent, "that we are vilified as if we *were* like Rome, precisely because we aren't? While if we *did* act like Rome, *then* they'd treat us with the respect we deserve?"

"My head a-*splode*," said one of the wittier students, and everyone laughed again. But Torrent pushed the point.

"America is at the end of its republic. Just as the Roman Senate and consuls became incapable of ruling their widespread holdings and fighting off their enemies, so America's antiquated Constitution is a joke. Bureaucrats and courts make most of the decisions, while the press decides which Presidents will have enough public support to govern. We lurch forward by inertia alone, but if America is to be an enduring polity, it can't continue this way."

Even though Torrent's points actually agreed with much of what Reuben believed was wrong with contemporary America, he could not let the historical point stand unchallenged—the two situations could not be compared. "The Roman Republic ended," said Reuben, "because the people got sick of the endless civil wars among rival warlords. They were grateful to have a strong man like Octavian eliminate all rivals and restore peace. That's why they were thrilled to have him put on the purple and rename himself as *Augustus*."

"Exactly," said Torrent, leaning across the table and pointing a finger at him. "Of course a soldier sees straight to the crux of the matter. Only a fool thinks the turns of history can be measured by any standard other than which wars were fought, and who won them. Survival of the fittest—that's the measure of a civilization. And survival is ultimately determined on the battlefield. Where one man kills another, or dies, or runs away. The society whose citizens will stand and fight is the one with the best chance to survive long enough for history even to notice it."

One of the students made the obligatory comment about how concentrating on war omits most of history. At which Torrent smiled and gestured for Reuben to answer.

"The people who win the wars write the histories," said Reuben dutifully, wondering why he was getting this sudden burst of respect from Torrent.

"Augustus kept most of the forms of the old system," Torrent went on. "He refused to call himself king, he pretended the Senate still meant something. So the people loved him for protecting their republican delusions. But what he actually established was an empire so strong that it could survive incompetents and madmen like Nero and Caligula. It was the empire, not the republic, that made Rome the most important enduring polity in history."

"You're saying America needs to do the same thing?" asked Reuben Malich.

"Not at all!" said Torrent, acting out a parody of horror. "God forbid! I'm just saying that if America is going to ever *matter* to history the way Rome does, instead of being a brief episode like the Sassanid or Chaldean empires, then it will be because we spawn our own Augustus, to rule where right now we only buy and sell."

"Then I hope we fall first," said Reuben Malich. He knew as he spoke that he should have confined this comment to his Arabic notes. This was the trap Torrent had led him into, by showing him respect; yet, knowing he was being exposed and would surely be cut apart for it, he could not hold silence—because if he did, the other students would be sure this soldier longed for empire, just as Torrent apparently did. "America exists as an idea," Reuben said, "and if we throw out that idea, then there's no reason for America to exist at all."

"Oh, Soldier Boy, you poor lad," said Torrent. "The American idea was thrown out with Social Security. We nailed the coffin shut with group rights. We don't *want* individual liberty because we don't want individual responsibility. We want somebody else to take care of us. If we had a dictator who did a better job of it than our present system, then as long as he pretended to respect Congress, we'd lick his hands like dogs."

The whole seminar recoiled from his words, though not because they thought he was wrong; it was because he sounded like some kind of neo-conservative.

"Again," Torrent reminded them, "I'm not advocating anything, I'm only observing. We're historians, not politicians. We have to look at how polities actually function, not how we wish to delude ourselves into thinking they ought to function. Our short-term politics trump long-term national interests every time. Can't fix Social Security, can't fix the tax structure, can't fix the trade deficit, can't fix outsourcing, can't fix *anything* because there's always campaign money involved, or demagoguery that blocks the way. Between the NRA and the AARP, you can't even do things that vast majorities already agree need to be done! Democracy on this scale doesn't work, it hasn't worked for years. And as for that American idea, we flushed it away with the Great Depression, and *nobody misses it*." Then he grinned. "Except maybe Soldier Boy."

**PRINCETON UNIVERSITY** was just what Reuben expected it to be—hostile to everything he valued, smug and superior and utterly closed-minded. In fact, exactly what *they* thought the military was.

He kept thinking, the first couple of semesters, that maybe his attitude toward them was just as short-sighted and bigoted and wrong as theirs was of him. But in class after class, seminar after seminar, he learned that far too many students were determined to remain ignorant of any real-world data that didn't fit their preconceived notions. And even those who tried to remain genuinely open-minded simply did not realize the magnitude of the lies they had been told about history, about values, about religion, about everything. So they took the facts of history and averaged them with the dogmas of the leftist university professors and thought that the truth lay somewhere in the middle.

Well as far as Reuben could tell, the middle they found was still far from any useful information about the real world.

Am I like them, just a bigot learning only what fits my worldview? That's what he kept asking himself. But finally he reached the conclusion: No, he was not. He faced every piece of information as it came. He questioned his own assumptions whenever the information seemed to violate it. Above all, he changed his mind—and often. Sometimes only by increments; sometimes completely. Heroes he had once admired—Douglas MacArthur, for instance—he now regarded with something akin to horror: How could a commander be so vain, with so little justification for it? Others that he had disdained—that great clerk, Eisenhower, or that woeful incompetent, Burnside—he had learned to appreciate for their considerable virtues.

And now he knew that this was much of what the Army had sent him here to learn. Yes, a doctorate in history would be useful. But he was really getting a doctorate in self-doubt and skepticism, a Ph.D. in the rhetoric and beliefs of the insane Left. He would be able to sit in a room with a far-left Senator and hear it all with a straight face, without having to argue any points, and with complete comprehension of everything he was saying and everything he meant by it.

In other words, he was being embedded with the enemy as surely as when he was on a deep Special Ops assignment inside a foreign country that did not (officially at least) know that he was there.

Princeton University as an alien planet. Reuben Malich as the astronaut who somehow lost his helmet—and spent day after day gasping for air.

He had to acquire the iron discipline of the soldier who works with the government—the ability to stand in the same room with stupidity and say nothing, show nothing.

The real danger was not losing his temper, however. For in the second year of his studies, he realized that he was beginning to treat some of the most absurd ideas as if they had some basis in truth. It was Goebbels in practice: If you tell the same lies long enough and loudly enough, even people who know better will despair and concede the point.

We are tribal animals. We cannot long stand against the tribe.

Thank heaven he could go home to Cecily every day. She was his reality check. Unlike the ersatz Left of the university, Cessy was a genuine old-fashioned liberal, a Democrat of the tradition that reached its peak with Truman and blew its last trumpet with Moynihan.

It was part of the insanity of their marriage—the reason his father kept asking him, right up to the wedding itself, "Do you have any idea what you're doing?"

Because not only was Reuben committed to conservative values, he was also a Serbian by ancestry and upbringing—an Orthodox Christian with a native knowledge of the language of Serbia because his parents made sure of it.

And Cessy was Croatian—Catholic, yes, but also of the tribe that Serbians hated more than any. Once Serbs and Croats had been the same people. But the Turks had long ruled Serbia, while Croatia was sheltered within Catholic Austria-Hungary. What did Croats know of oppression and suffering? And when the Nazis came, they collaborated with the conquerors, and the price of their perfidy was paid in Serbian blood.

Nobody forgot things like this in the Balkans. Such injuries were nursed generation after generation. So when Reuben came home from Ohio State with a *Croatian* girl, and then left her with *his* family while he went off to begin serving his ROTC obligation to his country, his parents were appalled.

She won them over completely. It was hard to believe that anyone could get past Father's cast-iron hatred of Croats, but Cessy had insisted that she'd do just fine, now go off and be a soldier for a while. And when Reuben came home on leave the first time, it quickly became clear that not only did his family like Cessy, they liked her a lot more than they liked Reuben. Oh, they said they still loved him best, but he knew it was just to make him feel better. They *adored* Cessy.

And that was fine with him. "You should be our U.N. ambassador," he told her on that first leave. "You could get Hutus and Tutsis to be friends. You could get Israelis and Palestinians to hug and kiss. Hindus and Muslims, Hindus and Sikhs, Shia and Baha'i, Basque and Spaniard—"

"Not Basques and Spaniards," she told him. "That dates back to when there were still mastodons in Europe. That's practically like Cro-Magnon versus Neandertal."

"I want our babies to be as smart as you and as tough as me," he said.

"I just want them to *look* like me," said Cessy. "Because having daughters that look like you would be cruel."

Their daughters did look like Cessy, and their sons had Reuben's lean, lithe body, and all in all, their family life was perfect. That's what he came home to every day from school; that was the environment in which he studied. That was his root in reality that kept calling him back from the brink of getting seduced into the fantasyland of academia.

Until Averell Torrent decided he wanted Reuben's soul.

**REUBEN HAD** been goaded by professors before. He goaded them by wearing his uniform to every class on the first day. They took it as a personal affront. Why shouldn't they? That's how he meant it.

Some of them simply ignored him the rest of the semester—until his coursework forced them to give him an A. Others declared war on him, but their ham-handed attacks on Reuben always backfired, winning him the sympathy of the other students as Reuben answered all the attacks with unflagging courtesy and quiet good sense. Many of the others would begin defending him—and, by extension, the military. Thus Reuben would quietly lose all the classroom battles for the hearts and minds of the students, but win the war.

With Torrent, though, as they worked their way through the ancient long-lived empires—Egypt, China—and the ancient republics—first Athens, now Rome—it became for the other students a class in watching Torrent and Reuben spar with each other. They weren't angry at Reuben—they knew that Torrent always initiated their long, classtime-consuming exchanges—but they still resented the fact that Reuben Malich had hijacked their only class with the great man.

Can't help it, Reuben silently answered their huffish attitudes. He calls on *me*. What am I supposed to do, cover my ears and hum loudly so I can't hear his questions?

Though he was getting tempted to do just that. Because what Torrent was saying about America and empire made perverse sense. While the other students sidetracked themselves into a discussion about whether Torrent's statements were "conservative" or "liberal," "reactionary" or "politically correct," Reuben could not shake off Torrent's premise—that America was not in the place Rome was in before it fell, but rather in the place where Rome was before civil war destroyed the Republic and led to the dictatorship of the Caesars.

So when Torrent had finally silenced the other students' attempts to put his remarks into one or another of present-day political camps, Reuben was ready to speak.

"Sir," he said, "if civil war is a necessary precursor to the end of democracy—"

"The façade of democracy."

"Then it means our republic, such as it is, is safe. Because we don't have warlords. We don't have private armies."

"You mean 'so far,'" Torrent said at once. "You mean 'that we know about.'"

"We aren't Yugoslavia," said Reuben—the most obvious example, for him at least. "We don't have clear ethnic divisions."

Again, a storm of protest from the other students. What about blacks? Hispanics? Jews?

They debated that for a while, but Reuben was determined to stay on track. "We can have riots, but not sustained wars, because the sides are too geographically mixed and the resources are too one-sided."

Torrent shook his head. "The seeds of civil war are always there, in every country. England in the 1600s—nobody would have believed that those pesky Puritans could provoke a Royalist versus Puritan civil war, and yet they did."

"So where do *you* think America might divide itself into two factions that could fight a sustained civil war?" Reuben demanded.

Torrent smiled. "Red state, blue state."

"That's cheap media graphics. You might as well say rural versus urban."

"I *do* say that. But the geographical division is still clear. The Northeast and the West Coast against the South and the middle, with some states torn apart because they're so evenly balanced."

"No one's going to *fight* over those differences."

Torrent smiled his maddening superior smile. "The rhetoric today is already as hot-blooded and insane and hate-filled as it was over slavery before the first Civil War—and even then, most people refused to believe war was possible until Fort Sumter fell."

"One thing," said Reuben. "One tiny thing."

"Yes?" said Torrent.

"The U.S. Army is absolutely dominated by red-state ideals. There are some blue-staters, yes, of course. But you don't join the military, as a general rule, unless you share much of the red-state ideology."

"So because the red-staters control the Army, you think there can't be a civil war."

"I think it's unlikely."

"Don't hedge on me."

Reuben shrugged. He wasn't hedging, he was specifying; but let Torrent think whatever he wanted.

"What if the White House were in the control of blue-staters?" asked Torrent. "What if the President ordered American troops to fire on American citizens who fought for red-state ideals?"

"We obey the President, sir."

"Because you're thinking you'd be called to fire on neo-fascist militia nut groups from Montana," said Torrent. "What if you were told to fire on the Alabama National Guard?"

"If Alabama was in rebellion, then I'd do it at once."

"If," said Torrent. "We just got our first 'if' from Soldier Boy. You would obey the President 'if.'" Torrent grinned in triumph. "Civil wars are fought when leaders find out what those 'ifs' are and exploit them. I would only shoot at my neighbor 'if.' And then a politician tells you that the 'if' has happened."

They all regarded Torrent in silence, waiting for the clincher that they knew was coming.

"The ideology doesn't matter. You're right, no one cares enough. So here's when you'll get ready to shoot your neighbor: When you're convinced that your neighbor is arming himself to shoot *you*."

Reuben well knew how that worked. Few Serbs, Croats, or Muslims in the old Yugoslavia even imagined they could go to war—the intermarriage rate was so high that it was obvious you could never sort out one group from another.

But all it took was a handful of nuts with guns shooting at you because your parents were Croats, even if you never cared. If they're attacking you because you're part of a group, then when you fire back, you do it as a member of that group. "You get forced onto one side or the other whether you want to or not," said Reuben, "once the bullets start to fly."

"The bullets don't even have to fly," said Torrent, nodding. "You just have to *believe* they're *trying* to shoot you. Wars are fought because we believe the other team's threats."

"Which suggests," said Reuben, "that wars are also lost because one side *didn't* believe until it was too late."

"There we have it," said Torrent, looking around triumphantly at the rest of the class. "Right here in this class, I have persuaded a highly trained soldier who hates the idea of civil war to *think* about the possibility."

The others laughed and looked at Reuben Malich with some mixture of mockery and sympathy. He had fallen into Torrent's trap.

Only Reuben knew better. Torrent was a serious historian. So was Reuben. Torrent was right. A civil war could be fought anywhere, if somebody had the will, the wit, and the power to pull the right strings, push the right buttons, light the right fires.

The class ran ten minutes over—which was common with Torrent, because nobody wanted him to stop talking. And after class, many lingered to talk to him about the papers they were writing. Everyone was terrified of his acid pen, firing volleys of savage criticism across their pages. They wanted to get it right on the first draft.

Reuben didn't care about grades, mostly because he earned A's in everything. So when class ended, he always left at once. Today, though, Torrent waved him over before he could leave. By staying, Reuben was blowing off Contemporary African Conflicts. But when a man like Torrent calls, you come because it matters what Torrent thinks about everything. Even you.

Finally they were alone in the room.

"Major Reuben Malich," Torrent said. "It's not so much that I like the way you think, it's that I like the fact that you think at all."

"We all think, sir."

"No, my good soldier, we do *not* all think. Thinking is rare and growing rarer, especially in the universities. Students succeed here to the degree they can convince idiots that they think just like them."

"The professors aren't *all* idiots."

"Grad school is like junior high: You learn to get along. That's half of who ends up in grad school in the first place—the suck-ups and get-alongs. You're only here because you were *ordered* to come. You'd rather be in the Middle East. Leading troops in combat. Yes?"

Reuben didn't answer.

"Very careful of you," said Torrent. "I have just one question for you. If I told you that the civil war I'm talking about were being planned right now, just how far would you go?"

"I'd do nothing to help either side, and anything to prevent it from happening."

"But those *are* the two sides, before the fighting starts— the hotheads on one side, the rational people on the other, trying to rein them in."

"Soldiers don't have the power to prevent wars, sir, except by being so invincible that no enemy would dare to engage."

"Are you willing to trust your life—the lives of your family—on that belief—that civil war is impossible?"

"Exactly, sir. I already trust my family's life to that belief. It's like an asteroid colliding with Earth. It certainly *will* happen, someday. But right now, there's no urgency about figuring out how to avoid it."

"And when an asteroid *does* come toward Earth, how will you know? See it yourself?"

"No, sir, I'll trust astronomers to let us know. And I know where you're going—you believe you're the astronomer who's warning us about a social and political collision."

"More like a weatherman, tracking the storm and watching it grow to hurricane strength."

"Standing in front of the camera in the rain, strapped to a lightpole?"

Torrent grinned. "You understand me perfectly."

"What are you proposing, sir?" said Reuben. "You *were* proposing something, right?"

"There are those who are trying to prevent the civil war.

People who are in a position to share key information, to keep dangerous weapons out of the hands of those who would use them to provoke this war that nobody wants."

"Working on a doctorate at Princeton isn't exactly a key position."

"But you graduate after this semester, *n'est-ce pas?*"

"And go back into the Army, sir. I already have my assignment, protecting American interests abroad."

"Yes, I know," said Torrent. "Special Ops. Nice work in that country-we-cannot-name."

Reuben had run into this before—people pretending to have inside information in order to try to get the information from him.

"I don't know what you're talking about, sir. I'm not in Special Ops."

"I think you were dead right to open fire when you did, and you should have gotten the Oscar for the way you wept over that dead old man."

So maybe he did know something. That didn't mean Reuben could trust him. "I'm not much of a weeper, sir."

"You'd be the first person ever to win an Oscar for a performance that actually saved lives."

"I believe you're trying to compromise me, sir, and I won't do it."

"Dammit," said Torrent, "I'm trying to find out if you'd be interested in a covert assignment to help hold this country together and prevent its collapse into pure chaos."

"And its passage into empire."

"*If* there were some way you could help in an effort to prevent civil war, to preserve the republic, such as it is, how far would you be willing to go?"

"I'm a major in the United States Army, sir. I will never do anything contrary to my oath."

"Yes," said Torrent. "Yes, that's what I'm counting on. You're a superb student, you know that. The best I've had in years. And I know people, within and outside the government, who are involved in quiet efforts to prevent civil war. You have *my* solemn oath that anyone who contacts you in my name will never ask you to do anything that would violate yours."

"I'll listen. That's all I promise."

"Then listen to this. The first test is whether or not you tell your wife."

"I tell Cessy everything that isn't classified. If you don't like that, count me out."

"What if the knowledge might get her killed?"

"Then I'd be sure to tell her. Because if somebody thinks I *might* have told her, they'll kill her whether I really did or not. So she might as well understand the risk."

"Glad to hear it," said Torrent.

"You are?"

"That was the test. If you'd betray your wife and do something like this behind her back, you'd betray anybody." With a grin, Torrent picked up his now-stuffed briefcase and left the room.

Reuben headed for his next class, hopelessly late, with his mind racing. He just recruited me. I don't even know what the conspiracy is, and he recruited me just by appealing to my intelligence, my loyalties, my desire to be in on the action.

The trouble was, this *did* appeal to him in all those ways and more besides.

He's got me pegged, Reuben realized. The only question remaining was: Is Torrent a good guy? If I join whatever clandestine work he's got going, will I be on the right side?

# THREE

# NEW BOY

Heroic love is to do what is best for the loved one, disregarding desire, trust, and cost. Unfortunately, it is impossible to know what is best for anyone.

**CAPTAIN COLEMAN**—Cole, to his friends—still wasn't sure whether getting assigned to Major Malich was the opportunity of a lifetime or the dead end of his military career.

On the one hand, as soon as Cole got the Pentagon assignment, high-ranking people started dropping hints that Malich was regarded as more than merely promising—war hero in Special Ops, brilliant in strategic and tactical thinking, with the only real question being whether he would end up his career commanding in the field or from the Pentagon. "You just got your wagon hitched to the right horse, Cole," said one general that dropped by his new office apparently just to tell him that.

On the other hand, he'd been in his new position for three days and he hadn't met Malich and couldn't find out from anybody where he was.

"He goes out, he comes back," said the division secretary.

"Goes where, does what?"

"Goes *away*," she said with a tight smile, "and eventually returns."

"Are you not telling me because you don't know, or because you don't trust me yet?"

"I don't know, *and* I don't trust you yet," she said.

"So what do I do while I wait for him to come back?"

"Is this your first time in the Pentagon?"

"Yes."

"Go out and see the sights."

"It's not my first time in DC," said Cole. "My parents took me to all the museums and I've already waited in line to see Congress and the Declaration of Independence and I've climbed the Washington Monument to the top."

"Then go to Hain's Point or Great Falls of the Potomac and say ooh and aah, and get on a bicycle and ride the W&O trail from Leesburg to Mount Vernon. Or stay here and I'll give you a whole box of pencils to sharpen."

"What are *you* working on while he's gone?"

"I'm the division secretary. I work for all the officers, including the Colonel. Once every two months, Major Malich gives me something to do. Other than that, I take messages for him and explain to his confused subordinates how they can kill time till he comes back so he can tell them nothing in person."

"Tell them nothing—you mean even when he's *here* he—"

"Why do you think you're replacing a good man who only stayed for one month? Who replaced another good man who lasted three months because Major Malich gave him a huge pile of scutwork assignments without ever telling him what they were for and then thanked him and left *him* to sharpen pencils?"

"So you don't expect me to stay."

"I expect you to grow old and die on the job here."

"What does *that* mean?"

"It means," said the secretary, "that I've given up trying to understand Major Malich's role in this building and I've also given up trying to help young officers who are assigned to him. What's the point?"

So here he was, three days later, with his pencils sharpened, having seen the statue of the giant at Hain's Point and the new World War II Memorial and the FDR Memorial and the Great Falls of the Potomac. Was it too soon to put in for a transfer? Shouldn't he at least meet Malich before trying to get away from him?

Cole could imagine Major Malich's arrival in the office.

"What have you been doing while you waited for me to get back," Malich would say.

"Waiting for you, sir."

"In other words, nothing. Don't you have any initiative?"

"But I don't even know what we're working on! How can I—"

"You're an idiot. Put in for a transfer. I'll sign it and hope that next time they'll send me somebody with a brain in his head and a spark of ambition."

Oh, wait. That wasn't Malich speaking. That was Cole's father, Christopher Coleman, who believed in only two things: That people named Coleman should have really long first names (Cole's was "Bartholomew") and that nothing his son did could possibly measure up to his expectations.

Malich probably wouldn't even notice Cole was there. Why should he? As long as Cole was doing nothing, it didn't matter whether he was there or not.

So Cole left his office and crossed the hall to the secretary. "What am I supposed to call you?" he asked.

She pointed to her nameplate.

"So you really go by DeeNee Breen."

She glared at him. "It's the name my parents gave me."

"I'm sorry to hear that," he said. "That's even worse than Bartholomew."

She didn't smile. This was going well.

"I need some information."

"I won't have it, but go ahead."

"Is Major Malich married?"

"Yes."

"See? You did know."

"Her name is Cecily. They have five children. I don't know the children's names or ages, but one of them is young enough to have been crying one of the few times Mrs. Malich called here looking for her husband and there's a family picture on his desk but I don't know how old it is so that doesn't help with the ages. The children are boy boy girl girl boy. Debriefing over, sir?"

Cole realized now that she did have a sense of humor— but it was so dry that it came across as hostility. So he made another try at winning her over with wit. "It's improper for me to discuss debriefing you, DeeNee Breen," said Cole.

She either didn't get the joke or it was a Pentagon cliché or she thought it was hilarious but chose not to encourage him.

"Miz Breen, I need to know the address and telephone number of Mrs. Malich."

"I don't have that information," she said.

"They don't give Major Malich's contact information to the division secretary? What if the Colonel wants him?"

"Perhaps I haven't made myself clear," she said. "Major Malich does not consult with me. He does not give me assignments. I take his messages and when he comes in to the office, I give them to him. I have never needed to tell him his wife's address and telephone number. No one else has wanted it either. Therefore I do not have that information."

"But you do have a phone book," said Cole. "And a telephone. And an imagination. And some of your time is supposed to be used in support of Major Malich's work."

"You don't even know what Major Malich's work *is*."

"But with your valuable assistance, Miz Breen, I *will* find out."

"From his wife?"

"Now you've connected the dots."

She reached under her desk and pulled out a phone book. "I have real work to do," she said. "Assignments that are urgently needed for the ongoing projects of officers who actually work here and know what they're doing. However, if you find out that information, I would be happy to record the results of your research so that I can answer this question for the next person to hold your fascinating position."

"You have a gift for sarcasm, Miz Breen." He took the phone book from her desk. "Please feel free to practice it on me whenever you want."

"It takes the fun out of it, if you give me permission," she said.

It took ten minutes to find out that Reuben and Cecily Malich lived in a housing development off Algonkian Parkway in Potomac Falls, Virginia.

Cecily Malich sounded cheerful on the telephone when he introduced himself as Major Malich's new subordinate. Or whatever his job description was supposed to be.

"He gets a captain again?" she said. "How interesting."

"It might be," he said, "if I knew anything at all. Such as when he's expected back in the office."

"Why, hasn't he been in lately?"

"I've been here three days and have yet to meet him."

"Interesting," she said.

"I don't even have enough information for my lack of information to be interesting," said Cole. "I hoped you could enlighten me about a few things. Like what we do here in this office."

"It's classified."

"But I'm cleared to know it."

"But I'm not," she said. It was nice of her to leave off the "duh."

"So you won't help me? I just want to make myself useful to him, and I don't know how I can do that if he doesn't come in to the office. I'm not sure he even knows that he has a new captain assigned to him."

"Oh, he knows," she said.

"He mentioned it?"

"No," she said. "But he makes it a point to know everything about the people who work with him, including the fact that they work with him. Believe me, he knows all about you and my guess is he specifically asked for you in this assignment."

That was gratifying, even if it was only a guess. "But what *is* the assignment?"

"I assume you already asked around the office."

"Nobody knows. Nobody *cares*."

"That's because he doesn't report to anyone they know."

"Who *does* he report to?"

"Well, clearly he doesn't report to me or you."

"Mrs. Malich, I'm drowning here. Throw me something that floats."

She laughed. "Come out to the house. I'm a cooky-baking wife and it's summer vacation. Chocolate chips or snickerdoodles?"

"Ma'am, anything you offer will be gratefully received."

**IT WAS** more of a house than Cole would have expected on a major's salary, though still hardly a mansion. There were four bikes on the front lawn, two of them tiny with training wheels, which suggested that the kids were home from some sort of expedition.

"No, I only have little John Paul here," she said, indicating the three-year-old who was studiously drawing something with crayons at the kitchen table. There were, as promised, chocolate chip cookies on a cooling rack.

"I just thought, with the bikes on the lawn . . ."

"The kids have been told to put their bikes away. Often enough that we refuse to remind them again. They know that any bike that is stolen from the front yard will *not* be replaced by us. So there they sit. Reuben will mow around them before he'll move them an inch."

"So he does come home often enough to mow the lawn."

She looked at him like he was crazy. "Reuben is home every night, except when he's traveling, and he's never gone for more than a few days. It's really been quite nice since he got this Pentagon assignment. It's a far cry from the days when he'd be gone sometimes a year at a time, with only a few messages."

"That must have been hard."

"I take it you don't have a wife," said Mrs. Malich. "Or you'd already know all about it."

"I'm Special Ops, like your husband," he said. "Not

much time for dating, and I couldn't imagine asking a woman I actually cared about to marry somebody who might be killed at any time."

"Yes, that's a hard thing. But husbands die of other things, not just bullets. It's a risk everybody takes when they marry—that the other person might die. Much higher risk that they'll cheat on you or leave you. So I chose to marry a man who will never cheat on me and never leave me. Yes, he might be killed at any time, but my odds of keeping him are still far higher than the national average. And now that he's working at the Pentagon, he's far less likely to come home covered with a flag. Instead he brings home whatever groceries I ask him to bring."

"So you call him during the day."

"Of course."

"But the secretary said—"

"I only call DeeNee when he has his cellphone off."

"Doesn't she have his cellphone number?"

"Of course she does. And he checks in with her frequently."

"But she said—she claims not to know anything about what your husband does."

Mrs. Malich laughed. "She's hazing you, Captain Coleman."

"Please just call me Cole. Or Captain Cole, if you have to."

"DeeNee is a superb secretary. My husband trusts her implicitly. In part because she not only never tells anybody anything, she manages to not tell them in such a way as to make them think she doesn't know."

"She's very good at that."

"But you, I take it, are *not* pretending when you say that my husband has not been in to the office in three days."

He nodded.

"That worries me."

"Oh, I'm sure it's because he's busy on something—"

"Captain Cole, I know he's busy on something. I know from the way he tells me almost nothing. Normally he gives me enough information that I won't worry. Like when he worked on counterterrorism in the District for a few months. He didn't tell me anything at all about it, specifically, but he did let me know that he was supposed to imagine ways that terrorists might go after key targets in DC, and I gathered that he was not just looking at high-profile psychological targets like monuments and such, but also at infrastructure targets and political targets."

Cole felt a surge of relief. So his new boss *did* do something that mattered.

"But you don't know which ones."

"I have a brain. I assumed he looked at bridges and other choke points for transportation. And opportunities to attempt assassinations. That sort of thing."

"I thought the Secret Service worked on protecting the President and Vice President."

"And there are plenty of people working on protecting Congress and the Supreme Court and other key personnel. You have to understand, I'm only guessing here, but I know my husband and I know what he's good at. I'm sure his assignment wasn't to protect the President, it was to figure out how to kill him despite the protections that are in place. Just as his assignment was probably to figure out ways a terrorist might bring Washington to its knees without having a nuke or poison gas."

"And he completed that assignment."

"From his sudden air of relief and cheerfulness back in February, yes, I believe he did."

"And now?"

"And now he doesn't even go to the office, but doesn't tell me that he hasn't gone to the office, but he's still coming home every night at the regular time, and he has a haunted air about him, so whatever he's doing, he hates it."

Cole finally realized what was happening here. "You didn't invite me to the house just to chat."

"No, Captain Cole," she said. "I'm worried about my husband."

"But I can't help you. I've never even met him."

"But you will," she said. "And when you do, you'll form your own conclusions about what he's involved with."

"I can't tell you anything that's classified."

"You can tell me whether I should worry, and how much."

"About his safety? Here in Washington?"

"No," she said. "I deal with my fears for his safety in my own way. That's not what worries me right now."

"It's that haunted look?"

"My husband is a patriot. And a born officer. He is not troubled by the things he does to defend his country. He has killed people, even though he's a gentle man by nature, and yet he does not wake up screaming in the night from combat flashbacks, and he doesn't lash out at the children, and he shows no sign of traumatic stress disorder. I know what he looks like when he's worried about his own safety, or when he's intense about fulfilling an assignment, or when he's annoyed at the stupidity of superior officers. I know what those things do to him, how it shows up in his behavior at home."

"And this is new."

"Captain Cole, what I want to know is why my husband feels guilty."

Cole didn't know what to say, except the obvious. "Why do husbands *ever* feel guilty?"

"That's why I haven't confided these worries of mine to anyone. Because people will assume that I'm assuming he's having an affair. But I know for a fact that this is impossible. He feels guilty. He's torn up inside about something. But it's something to do with work, not with me, not his family, not his religion. Something about his present assignment is making him very unhappy."

"Maybe he's not doing as well at it as he thinks he should."

She waved that thought away. "Reuben would talk about that with me. We share self-doubts with each other, even if he can't go into the specifics. No, Captain Cole, he is being asked, as part of his work, to do something he fears may be wrong."

"What do you think it might be?"

"I refuse to speculate. I just know that my husband has no qualms about bearing arms for his country and using them. So whatever he's being asked to do that he hates, or at least has serious doubts about, it *isn't* because violence is involved. It's because he isn't in full agreement with the assignment. For the first time in his military career, his duty and his conscience are in serious conflict."

"And *if* I find out, Mrs. Malich, I probably can't tell you what it is."

"My husband is a good man," she said. "It's important to him to be a good man. He has to not only *be* good, he has to *believe* that he's good. In the eyes of God, in my eyes, in his parents' eyes, in his own eyes. *Good.* What I want you to do for me is tell me if he's not going to be able to get through this project, whatever it is, believing that he's a good man."

"I'd have to know him very well to be able to assess that, ma'am."

"He asked for you to be assigned to him for a reason," said Mrs. Malich. "A young Special Ops hotshot—that describes you, yes?"

"Probably," said Captain Cole, shaking his head.

"He wouldn't take you out of the front line, where you're needed, if he didn't think you'd be needed *more* working for him."

That was logical, if Malich was indeed the man his wife thought he was. It gave Cole the reassurance he needed.

"Ma'am," he said, "I'll keep your assignment in mind. Along with whatever assignments he gives me. And what I *can* tell you, consistent with my oath and my orders, I certainly *will* tell you."

"Meanwhile," she said, "let me assure you that you do *not* have to keep secret from him any part of our meeting today. I certainly intend to tell him I met you and exactly what we talked about."

"Please don't tell him about the cookies I hid in my pockets," said Cole. "I know you saw me take them."

"I made them for you. Where you choose to transport them is entirely your affair."

ALL THE way back toward the Beltway on Route 7, Cole tried to make sense of Mrs. Malich's behavior. Was she really going to tell Major Malich about the assignment she had just given Cole? In that case, would Malich regard Cole as compromised somehow? Or would Malich simply give up and tell his wife what she wanted to know?

Or was there some game going on between them that was far more complicated than Cole could suppose? Cole had never been married or even had a girlfriend long enough to really think that he knew her. Were all women like this, and Mrs. Malich was unusual only in being so candid about her conniving?

Whatever it was, Cole already didn't like it. It was outrageous to be given an assignment by your commander's wife, though heaven knows it happened often enough when it consisted of moving furniture or running errands. Cole could see no way things could turn out that would not be detrimental to his career.

Had she been drinking? Was that it?

No, there had been no sign of that.

His cellphone went off.

"Captain Coleman?"

"Speaking."

"This is Major Malich. What does it mean when I get to the office and find you gone off somewhere?"

"Sorry, sir. I should be back within thirty minutes, sir."

"How many hours do you think you *get* for lunch?"

Cole took a deep breath. "I was visiting your wife, sir."

"Oh, were you."

"She makes excellent cookies, sir."

"Her baking is none of your business, Captain Coleman."

"It is when she offers me cookies, sir. Begging your pardon, sir."

"So what did she want with you?"

"I called her, sir. Since I couldn't learn anything about you or my assignment there at the Pentagon, I hoped to discover something about what you expected of me by talking to your wife."

"I don't like you intruding into my personal life, Captain."

"Neither do I, sir. I don't see that you left me a choice, sir."

"So what did you learn?"

"That your wife is so worried about you, sir, that she enlisted me to try to find out what your clandestine operations are." How far should he go with a new superior officer, and on a cellphone, no less? He plunged ahead. "She believes you're morally troubled about those operations, sir."

"Morally troubled?"

"I think the word she used was 'guilty,' sir."

"And you think this is any of your business?"

"I'm convinced that it's none of my business."

"But you're still going to do it."

"Sir, I'll just be happy to find out what we actually *do* in an office so secret that the secretary treats your subordinate like a spy."

"Well, Captain Coleman, she treats you like a spy because the last two clowns we had in your position *were* spies."

"For your wife, sir? Or for some foreign power."

"Neither. They were spying for people in the Pentagon who are also trying to figure out what I'm doing when I'm not in the office."

"Doesn't the Army already know what you're doing?"

There was a moment of hesitation. "The Army owns my balls and keeps them in a box somewhere between Fort Bragg and Pakistan."

Sometimes a non-answer was a perfectly usable answer. "It's a mighty big box, then, sir. This Army's got a lot of balls."

This time the pause was even longer.

"Are you laughing at me, sir?" asked Cole.

"I like you, Coleman," said Malich.

"I like your wife, sir. And *she* likes you."

"Good enough for me. Coleman, don't park. Don't even come to the Pentagon. Meet me at Hain's Point in half an hour. Do you know where that is?"

"It's a big long park, sir."

"At the statue. The giant. Half an hour."

Malich clicked off before Cole could say good-bye.

What was the phone call about? A test to see if Cole would tell him what his wife said? Or was Malich really angry at him for leaving? Why the meeting in the park as if they were trying to avoid bugs? And if secrecy was so important, why did they talk over unscrambled cellphones?

If I ever get married, thought Cole, would I have the guts to choose a woman as tough as Mrs. Malich?

And even if I did, am I the sort of man that a woman like that would choose to marry?

Then, as always, Cole shut down the part of his mind that thought about women and marriage and love and children and family. Not till I can be sure I'm not going back into combat again. No kid is going to be an orphan because I'm his dad and I ducked too slow.

# FOUR

# TIDAL BASIN

In war planning, you must anticipate the actions of the enemy. Be careful lest your preventive measures teach the enemy which of his possible actions you most fear.

**REUBEN SAW** Captain Coleman approaching, but showed him no sign of recognition. Coleman was supposed to be sharp—let *him* figure out which of the people near the tip of the island was his superior officer.

Instead, Reuben looked out over the water of the Washington Channel to Fort McNair, headquarters of the U.S. Army Military District of Washington. He knew that the soldiers working there took their job seriously. In the post-9/11 era that meant vigilance, trying to prevent attacks on the two most symbolically important cities in America—Washington and New York. He knew how they monitored the skies, the waterways. He knew about the listening devices, the camera scans, the aerial surveillance.

He also knew what wasn't being done. Weeks after he had completed his report, and still nothing had been done.

Bureaucracy, he thought.

But that was the easy answer. Chalk it up to bureaucratic maneuvering and red tape, and then nobody had to be called to account.

Reuben was tired of having responsibility without authority. Where was the leader who could get things done?

Truth to tell, this President had changed things. Without

ever getting a bit of credit for it, he had transformed the military from the cripple it had been when he took office into the robust force with new doctrines that had the enemies of the United States on the run.

On the run? No, backed into a corner. It was time for them to act if they were to continue to have any credibility. Reuben Malich knew what they needed to do. He even knew how they would probably do it. He had given warning, and so far, it seemed, no one was listening.

"Major Malich, sir."

Reuben turned to face the young man in uniform. Young? Twenty-eight wasn't young for a combat officer. But he was nine years younger than Reuben, and in those nine years Reuben had learned a few things. Combat could leave a man with scars; but running errands for players in the mind-numbing game of government aged him far more. At thirty-seven Reuben felt like he was fifty, an age that had long symbolized, to him, the end of his useful life. The age when he should get out of the war business.

Today. I should get out right now.

"Captain Coleman," he said. "Don't even think of saluting me."

"You aren't in uniform, sir," said Coleman. "And I'm not an idiot."

"Oh?"

"You had me meet you here instead of the office we both share because you think people are watching you. I don't know whether those people are inside or outside the Pentagon or the government, but we're here because you have things you want to tell me that you don't want any listening devices to overhear."

Good boy, thought Reuben. "Then you'll understand why I want you to face me directly and duck your head slightly downward."

As Coleman complied, Reuben unfolded a city tourist map and brought one side of it up between their faces and any observer elsewhere in the park.

"I guess this means I don't get a chance to look at the statue," said Coleman.

"It's big enough you can see it on Google Earth," said Reuben. "Cessy and DeeNee both tell me you're not an idiot, and now you've told me yourself. So I'm taking the chance of telling you what I'm actually doing. I will tell you once, and then we go about our business as if we were doing what I'm officially supposed to be doing, except you'll help me do the other thing *and* help me cover up my real assignment."

"All perfectly clear, sir."

Oh good. A sense of humor. "Officially I'm working on counterterrorism in Washington DC, with the particular assignment of trying to think like a terrorist. I suppose that I'm considered appropriate for this because I lived in a Muslim village in a country in which we don't officially have any soldiers. Never mind that the terrorists I'm supposed to be outthinking were all educated in American or European universities."

"So your assignment gives you a valid cover for traveling all over the Washington area," said Coleman.

Since that was what Reuben had been about to explain, he had to pause and skip ahead. "My real assignment is to carry messages to and conduct negotiations with various persons of the anti-American but officially non-terrorist persuasion."

"Are they non-terrorist?"

"They claim to be helping us counter the terrorists. Some of them might be. Some might not. I believe I'm probably being used to spread disinformation and sow confusion about American plans and motives."

"Which is why these people haven't been arrested."

"Oh, when the time comes, I doubt they'll be arrested."

Coleman nodded. "You bring them messages. Who gives them to you and tells you where to go?"

"I'm not at liberty to tell you that."

"So I guess I won't be picking up your mail."

"I can tell you this much. My assignments emanate from the White House."

Coleman whistled softly. "So he negotiates with terrorists after all."

"Don't suppose for a second that the President has any idea what I do," said Reuben. "Or that I exist. But I have verified for myself that my chief contact has complete access to the President and from that I conclude that I am an instrument of his national policy."

"And yet you hide from lip-readers with telephoto lenses."

Reuben refolded the map. "Let us look at Fort McNair."

Together they walked to the railing near the water and looked across the channel at the fort. "There it is, Captain Coleman. The home of the National Defense University and half the Old Guard. You know, the guys who dress up in Colonial Army uniforms to wow tourists and foreign dignitaries."

"Also where the Joint Force Headquarters of the National Capital Region is."

"Three weeks ago, I turned in—as part of my official duties—a report on likely targets in the Washington area and how I, if I were a terrorist, would attempt to attack them."

"I'm betting Fort McNair was not one of those targets."

"Al Qaeda doesn't give a rat's ass about real estate. They did that in zip-one, but all the terrorists who attacked commuter transportation in Europe and plotted to hit buildings and subways in the States are really just wannabes. Al Qaeda trains them and encourages them, but these are not Al Qaeda's own operations."

"You think they're through with symbolism."

"The way they see it, they can't afford to make any more empty gestures. And with all respect to those who died on 9/11, that was an empty gesture. It made us angry; it goaded us to a brief moment of national unity; it led directly to the fall of two Muslim governments and the taming of many more."

"They want to hurt us this time, not just slap us."

"They have only one target that makes any sense at all," said Reuben.

"The President," said Coleman.

They stood in silence, looking out over the water.

"So let me put this together," said Coleman after a while. "You came up with practical, workable plans to kill the President of the United States and turned them over to your superiors at the Pentagon. But you also fear that you're being observed even when you come out to the tip of Hain's Point, a city park where a bunch of schoolchildren climb all over the statue of a giant rising out of the earth."

Reuben waited for his conclusion.

"This spot is part of the plan?" said Coleman.

"Part of the best plan. The simplest. The surest. Oh, lots can still go wrong. But each part of it is well within the reach of any terrorist group smart enough to think of it—and disciplined enough to keep its mouth shut during the training phase."

"Not the clowns we've been catching."

"The clowns keep us busy and give us a sense of complacency. 'Our counterterrorism is working,' we tell ourselves. But we haven't come up against the big boys since 9/11. Since we routed them out of their hidey-holes in Afghanistan."

"Do you sail?" asked Coleman.

"No," said Reuben. "I leave that to the SEALs."

"I grew up sailing. My dad loved it."

Reuben waited for the moment of relevancy he was sure was coming.

"You learn to see the water's surface and notice things. For instance, we've got almost no breeze right now, hardly a ripple on the Washington Channel here."

"Right."

"But did your plan involve something underwater? Something that passed right through here?"

"Yes," said Reuben. "And therefore my plan suggested

that the Joint Force install additional listening, sonar, and imaging devices in the water of the channel."

"Which they haven't done."

"Which they haven't done *yet.*"

Coleman pointed toward the water only a few dozen yards from where they stood. "There's something under the water—there, there, there, and there. Maybe more farther out, but those four are the ones I can see."

Reuben couldn't see a damn thing.

"As a sailor, I'd be wondering if the disturbance in the tidal flow—it's a rising tide, for any landlubbers present— hid a sandbar. It doesn't, because all four of them are moving, slowly, with the tide."

"Inward. Toward the city."

"That's the way the tide goes, sir."

Reuben laughed. "So you're suggesting that right here, when I happen to be having an unscheduled meeting with my new assistant, is the exact time and place that they're launching exactly the attack that I planned for them?"

"Is there any reason why your presence here would confer immunity from attack?"

"I still can't see them."

"Sir, they're making decent progress toward the city. I've never seen dolphins stay under the water in such perfect formation while making so much disturbance on the surface above them. In case you were thinking it was really big fish."

Reuben pulled out his cellphone.

The bars kept going up and down, and the "Out of Service Area" message kept coming up, then going away.

Coleman had his cellphone out. It was showing the same thing.

"We're getting jammed," said Coleman. And without further warning, he dropped to the ground, fully prone. "Get down, sir!"

Reuben understood what Coleman believed—that some-one obviously knew they were there, and might start shooting at any time. "Do five pushups immediately. One-handed," said Reuben. "Then laugh like it's a joke."

Coleman did as he was told, then bounded back up to his feet, laughing. "You think they want us alive," he said.

"They don't jam cellphones when they plan to kill the caller," said Reuben.

"You're being set up," said Coleman. "You're the fall guy."

"They have a complete set of plans for this terrorist operation, written by me, and I'm right here at this site."

"Who knew you were coming here?"

"I always come here." Reuben started walking toward Coleman's car. "Get your keys out," said Reuben. "You're driving."

"I've watched the movies. I know how this plays out. My car is going to get shot up and wrecked and fall into the river, and *your* car will be fine."

"My guess is that my car won't start," said Reuben.

They kept up the casual walking until they were in the car. "Drive gently for a while," said Reuben. "How fast were those underwater things going?"

"Slow swimming speed," said Coleman.

"But this is the area where Fort McNair maintains listening devices."

Coleman drove around the curve of the point and started back up toward the ranger station.

"A little faster now," said Reuben. "If they're following my plan, then they'll switch on the submersibles and make a lot better speed the rest of the way up into the Tidal Basin."

"And we're going to intercept them where?"

"We're going to the ranger station to make some calls on land lines. And to get some guns and some guys who know how to shoot."

"So what's the plan?" asked Coleman. "They get out of the water, take off their scuba gear, and run across the Mall and attack the White House from the Ellipse? That area is so blocked off and guarded that they'll be dead before they get close."

"They get out of the water, they set up their rocket launchers just above the retaining wall at the inside of the Tidal Basin, past the Independence Avenue bridge."

"Rocket launchers," said Coleman, nodding.

"You can't see the White House from there—the Washington Monument is up on a hill, and the White House is invisible. So for the past couple of weeks, they've been practicing how many degrees to aim to the left of the monument in order to hit the White House. And they've got the range set to the micron. They probably know how to put one through any window in the White House that they want."

And they were at the ranger station.

They parked the car illegally and ran inside, ignoring the remonstrances of the park ranger who followed them in, shouting, "Intruders!"

Great. *Here* there was something approaching vigilance.

Reuben had his ID out and was flashing it to the security guard and then to the receptionist. "I would appreciate your close attention," he said, almost softly, though with a great deal of intensity. He didn't want them to be afraid, he wanted them to obey. "There is a possible attack on the White House coming out of the Tidal Basin at any moment. It will be a rocket attack. We need to notify the President to get low and get out. We need troops mobilized and sent to the Independence Avenue bridge at the Tidal Basin. And we need the best rifles you can muster with all the ammo you have at hand."

"Tell us where to go and *we'll* shoot," said the guard.

"We're Special Ops," said Coleman. "We know how to *use* them."

There was only a moment of hesitation. Then men began running. The bad news—but fully predictable—was that the receptionist said, "The lines are dead."

To which Reuben said, "Then somebody get in your ranger jeep and get to a building that still has a phone. The Holocaust Museum. *Not* the Jefferson Memorial."

The good news was that they were up-to-date weapons

that seemed clean and had plenty of ammo. Reuben and Coleman grabbed them and ran for the car. There was a ticket on the windshield. Coleman turned on the windshield wiper and after a few swipes it blew away as they drove back along Buckeye Drive and then under the 395 overpass. "Who had time to write us a ticket?" said Reuben.

"It was probably an envelope filled with anthrax," said Coleman. "That's why I didn't take it off by hand."

"No, don't turn there—we're not going to try to shoot from the Jefferson Memorial. The Independence Av bridge and the cars on it will block any kind of clean shot." Reuben directed him up to West Basin Drive as he checked to make sure both weapons had full clips.

"You realize this is Friday the thirteenth," said Cole.

"Screw you," said Malich.

They drove among the tourist cars until they came to Independence Avenue itself, which was completely blocked going toward the bridge, and had no traffic coming the other way.

They stopped the car and ran for it. Not that far along the bridge—but too far, if the terrorists had already made it out of the water long enough to have traffic blocked.

When Reuben and Coleman got onto the bridge, they saw two rocket launchers being set up simultaneously, while a guy with a protractor—a simple junior-high protractor!—was standing at a particular fence post and now was indicating where the launchers should be aiming.

Another guy—there were only the four in wet suits, as far as Reuben could see—was standing in the westbound lanes, which passed behind the retaining wall and did not go over the bridge. He was holding a sign.

"There's more guys than that," said Coleman. "Somebody cut those phone lines."

"I wonder what that sign says," said Reuben.

Whatever it said, it was enough to keep the drivers in place without much honking. And because of the blockage going that direction, traffic was stopped cold the other way, too. It would delay any military vehicles that might attempt to stop them. And delay was all they needed. With these guys, there'd be no escape plan. Though if they *did* happen to live long enough to get away from the Tidal Basin, they'd no doubt run to the Holocaust Museum and start killing Jews and Jewish sympathizers—which is what they would assume the Holocaust Museum would contain. Oh, yes—and schoolchildren.

Reuben knew they wouldn't get that far.

He and Coleman had line of sight. They got down, and—

And a bullet pinged into the guardrail.

So they dropped down prone and sighted under the rail. They both fired.

The guy with the protractor spun and dropped. A shoulder wound, probably, thought Reuben. "Were you aiming at him?" he asked.

"No," said Coleman. He'd been sighting on the guy with the sign.

"Then I must have been," said Reuben.

One of the boneheads in the car behind them had rolled down his window. "Is this, like, a war game?"

"This is not a drill," said Reuben calmly. "Get down inside your car as low as you can."

By now the guys with the launchers were lying flat, still preparing their launch. There was no clear shot at them.

The guy who had held the sign was firing at them. And Reuben and Coleman couldn't get to a different position, because now the shots hitting around them were pretty steady. The close ones were not coming from the guy with the sign.

"They're not trying," said Reuben. "Wherever their sniper is, he could kill us anytime."

"Just trying to pin us down," agreed Coleman.

"Shoot for the launchers themselves," said Reuben.

"I'm left," said Coleman.

But by the time he said that, Reuben was already firing at the lefthand launcher. Which their bullets knocked over. And by the time they corrected to aim for the other, the rocket had launched.

Reuben guessed that their sniper would be unable to resist watching for the explosion when the rocket hit. So he got up and ran to a different position and Coleman followed him, and there would be no last stand in the Holocaust Museum because they got all three of the remaining wet-suit guys . . . as they watched the column of flame and the plume of smoke rise above the grassy hill of the Washington Monument.

"Either they hit the White House or they didn't," said Reuben. "We've got that sniper to catch."

"He was shooting from over to the left of the World War II Memorial," said Coleman.

"And you can bet he's got a car."

Their pursuit of him ended quickly. *Now* the choppers were coming in and military vehicles were jouncing over the lawns and here was Reuben in civilian clothes carrying a rifle and so he had to stop for a conversation. It wasn't long—Coleman's uniform helped—and soon there were soldiers and choppers in pursuit of the sniper. But what kind of pursuit was it when nobody knew what he looked like, what he was driving, or where he might be going next?

"Did any of those clowns from the ranger station get a message to you, or did you just come when somebody reported shooting?" said Reuben.

"The choppers went up," said the lieutenant, "when the cellphones started jamming."

"And you didn't send them to the Tidal Basin?" asked Reuben.

"Why would we do that?" asked the lieutenant.

Which meant that indeed, no one knew about the plans that Reuben had drawn up. Except, of course, the terrorists who had followed them.

There was nothing useful to do now except get to the top of the hill and see where the rocket had landed.

It had taken out half the south façade of the West Wing.

"Where was the President?" asked Reuben. He was talking to himself, but by now the lieutenant, who had climbed the hill with them, was talking over a military wavelength.

"At least twenty," the lieutenant repeated. "Including the President, SecDef, the Chairman of the Joint Chiefs."

How strange. For the death of a village wise man, Reuben had been able to keen and wail in grief. For the death of a President he respected and admired, he didn't have a tear or even a word. Maybe because he knew the old man in that village, and he didn't know the President, not personally.

Or maybe because Reuben hadn't drawn up the plans that killed the old man in the village.

Not that Reuben didn't feel *anything*. He felt so much that he was almost gasping. But it wasn't grief. It was resolve. Gnawing at him. He would *do* something. There must be something he could do.

The lieutenant turned to them with a face like death. "They got the Vice President, too."

"He was in the same meeting?" said Reuben, incredulous. "They're never supposed to be in the same place."

"His car was broadsided by a dump truck and pushed into a wall. He was crushed."

"Let me guess," said Coleman. "The Secret Service killed the truck driver."

"The truck driver blew himself up."

Reuben turned to Coleman. "They've got a source inside the White House," he said. "How else would they know what room the President would be in?"

Coleman touched his elbow and Reuben allowed him to lead them away from the lieutenant. "At least you know it wasn't timed solely to coincide with your being at Hain's Point," said Coleman. "That was just a bonus for them."

"The question is, do I go public about the plans I submitted, so the FBI can start trying to trace the leak?"

"Love those headlines: 'Presidential Assassination Planned in Pentagon,'" said Coleman.

"Or do I sit tight and let the Pentagon quietly set me up as the scapegoat?"

"Either way, your career is over," said Coleman. "Sir."

"You sure lucked out with *this* assignment," said Reuben.

"Hell of a first day on the job, sir," said Coleman.

Then it was time to stop pretending this wasn't tearing them up.

"We've been under fire together," said Reuben. "My friends call me Rube." He knew that Coleman probably wouldn't be able to bring himself to use the nickname. Not with a superior officer.

"My friends call me Cole."

The lieutenant coughed. "Sirs, I'm being asked to bring you in for debriefing. I believe those are your bullets in the bodies down there, right?"

"Well, technically not our bullets," said Reuben. "They were borrowed weapons." He was still in the black humor of combat.

So was Cole. "We did aim the weapons from which they were fired, and we did pull the triggers."

"Are they all dead?" asked Reuben. "We were under pressure and moving, and I'm afraid we probably shot to kill."

"They were strung with grenades," said the lieutenant. "They weren't going to be taken alive."

"Lucky thing we didn't hit any of the grenades," said Cole, "or there'd be no body left to identify."

There was the unmistakable sound of several grenades going off in series down by the Tidal Pool.

"Bastards!" shouted the lieutenant. Then he ran down the hill toward the chaos of mangled bodies and screaming survivors.

"They booby-trapped themselves," said Reuben, sick at heart. "Apparently killing the President wasn't enough."

"You didn't plan all of this," said Cole. "You couldn't have planned for a White House insider."

"But I did," said Reuben. "I said they either had to have a devastatingly powerful weapon, or reliable intelligence— not only about whether the President was in residence, but also exactly where he was inside the building."

"Yes, but putting that in the plan doesn't give them the

resources," said Cole. "They can't just magically say, Alakazam, and they've got a White House source."

But there *was* a guy in the White House who knew all about Reuben and his projects. "I thought I was on two different assignments," said Reuben. "One from my day job at the Pentagon, one from my White House guy."

"Shit," said Cole. "They were working you from both ends."

# FIVE

# WRECKAGE

If you wait to take action until you are certain of the enemy's position, strength, and intentions, you will never act. Yet to act without knowledge is to plunge forward into a trap (if your enemy is aggressive) or waste your strength on meaningless maneuvers (if your enemy chooses to avoid you).

**"WHILE THE** lieutenant is busy, I have an errand to run," said Major Malich. "You can come with me or not."

"Do I get to know where?" asked Cole. And because he thought that made him sound like a little kid on a car trip, he added, "I promise not to ask if we're there yet." Then he winced. This wasn't the time for attempts at ingratiating humor. He wished he knew Major Malich better. They'd just been in a firefight together, but Cole still had to worry about what impression he was making.

Malich turned away from him. "They're going to want to debrief me. That will tie me up for about a week, and by that time, whoever's trying to screw me will have me fully screwed. So I need to climb the screw and find out who's driving it. Before I get locked in a room somewhere."

Cole got it. "So let's go."

Cole dropped his borrowed weapon and Malich did likewise. They began jogging up the hill. When they neared the crest, they broke into a full run, though with Malich in a suit and Cole in uniform, they weren't in the right clothes for running—especially the shoes.

Military and emergency vehicles crowded all the available streets around the White House, and survivors were gathering and being triaged and treated on the south lawn. But to get there, there was the little matter of a huge crowd of stunned tourists being held at bay by a cordon of soldiers, none of whom would have either the authority or the inclination to decide to let a couple of midlevel officers come prancing through.

Near the bottom of the hill, Malich veered left to angle toward Constitution Avenue, heading away from the mess just south of the White House grounds. Cole caught up with him and as they ran side by side, Malich explained. "If we go around by way of New York Avenue and State Place, we can try to get in at the southwest gate."

As it was, they had to flash ID and do a little bullying even to get *to* the southwest gate, and when they got there the MPs on duty weren't inclined to converse.

"Get the hell away from here, sirs," they were told politely.

Major Malich took a step back and saluted. Confused, the MP saluted back.

"Soldier," said Malich, "you're doing your job. But my job is counterterrorism, and somewhere in that wreckage is the man to whom my information about the terrorists who did this must be reported. If he's dead, I need to know that so I can take this information elsewhere. If he's alive, then he needs to have it and he needs it now. And I can't tell you that information, soldier, because I would then be court-martialed, which would be the end of a glorious career." Then he smiled.

"Yeah, well what about *my* career if I get my ass kicked for letting you in after I was told *nobody* gets in?"

"But they didn't mean it," said Cole. "You know if one of the Joint Chiefs showed up he'd tell you to let him through the damn gate and you'd do it."

The MP sighed. "I have a feeling this was only the first of many urgent stories I'm going to be told today." But he let them through.

Which was when the real chaos began. The policy to admit no one was a good one, Cole saw at once. There were quite a few injuries, and even more weeping and hysteria and catatonia and pacing and panicky conversations and people just standing there clutching briefcases or stacks of file folders, and nobody seemed to be in charge.

"Maybe if you call his name," suggested Cole.

"Not a chance," said Malich.

"Why not?"

"I don't know his name."

"You're kidding."

"We didn't meet here," said Malich. "And he told me *a* name, but I have to assume that it wasn't real."

"Then how do you know he even worked here?"

"Because he arranged for me to meet the National Security Adviser at another location and the NSA confirmed that I was, indeed, working for someone who reported to the President."

"Okay, that would be convincing enough for me," said Cole.

"I'm not actually an idiot," said Malich. "You have to go to a little trouble to get me dancing on the end of a string."

"You think this guy is the one set you up?"

"If he didn't come in to the White House today, then I'll know something," said Malich. "If he is but he won't talk to me, then I'll know something else."

"What would it mean if he isn't here? That he knew to stay away?"

"No, that he *isn't* the inside guy for the terrorists. Whoever it is had to be able to tell them, to the minute, where the President was inside the White House. I get the feeling this guy isn't in the loop on the President's daily schedule. He'd have to be in position to observe."

And then the look on Malich's face told Cole that his White House guy *was* there. He was one of the briefcase clutchers standing in the shade of some shrubbery. A little on the heavy side, his hair a little thin, he was sweating like crazy and looking both furtive and miserable. In fact, he looked so guilty that it convinced Cole that he couldn't have been involved with the terrorist incident, because this guy didn't have a secret-keeper's face.

When he saw Malich and Cole approaching, he at first looked scared, but then visibly relaxed and stepped out to meet Malich with a handshake. Malich introduced Cole but didn't say the White House guy's name.

The White House guy only nodded at Cole, then turned to Malich. "Send him away."

"Captain Coleman was at my side today as we took out one of the two rocket launchers aiming at the White House."

"Gee," said the White House guy snidely, "you mean it could have been worse?"

Malich was suddenly in the guy's face, holding him by the belt so he couldn't back away. "I'm in the mood to kill assholes today," said Malich quietly. "Try not to be one."

"What do you want? Why are you here?" asked the guy.

"I've been all over this town, all over the world, delivering messages, negotiating sales, all to help the counterterrorism cause," said Malich. "But those two rocket launchers—they looked an awful lot like the kind of launchers I arranged to purchase for a Sudanese rebel force to help them counter the superior artillery of the pro-government militias."

"Everybody buys from the same merchants," said the guy.

"Not good enough," said Malich. "This hit took place under my nose. I was right there when the submersibles came up the channel and headed into the Tidal Pool."

"They killed the President," said the guy. "And you think it's about *you?*"

"It's about beheading the United States of America," said Malich. "But they used my plan, and I want to know where you fit into this."

"*Your* plan?" The man seemed genuinely puzzled.

"My assignment in the Pentagon. My day job—when I wasn't running around for you. Think up ways that a smart enemy might strike inside Washington, with the President as target." Malich gestured toward the White House. "This was what I came up with."

"That's just . . . that's sick. You think the people you gave your plan to, *they* did this? Our own military?"

"Information can pass from hand to hand, and most of the hands might be innocent. But someone knew I created that plan, and they were glad to have me close by when the attack was launched. Though probably they didn't want me as close as I got."

"But didn't you say you killed the guys?"

"I got there too late. If I hadn't had Cole here with me, I would have been even later. He's the one who saw there was something under the water. And somebody cut the phone lines and jammed cell reception on Hain's Point so I couldn't get word to the White House in time."

"Yeah, well, it wasn't me, I was here, I was in a meeting, and then there's an explosion and I only have time to get back to my office and get these files before they have us out here on the lawn. If you think I had something to do with this, then you've got your head up your ass."

"Did you know where the President was when the explosion took place?"

"They don't check with me," said the guy. "Don't you get it? I'm not in charge of things. I'm an aide to an aide. I'm a *flunky*. They tell me, get these messages delivered, get these arms bought using this account and get them delivered to that group and by the way, use this guy, this Malich guy, as your messenger. I don't know anything about you."

Today of all days, Cole couldn't be sure of anything, but this guy was believable enough. And it made sense. If something really ugly was going on, there'd be people pulling strings on other people pulling other strings. Everything kept at six removes from the actual conspiracy.

Malich seemed to believe him, too. He let go of the man's belt.

But Cole needed to know something, too. "Show me your White House ID," he said.

Annoyed, now that he didn't have to be quite so afraid, the guy pulled out his ID and held it up for Cole. The name was Steven Phillips. And when Malich caught a glimpse of it, he was really pissed off. "You mean that was your real name all along?"

"I never said it wasn't!" protested Phillips.

"You said you couldn't show me ID because then I'd know your real name."

"That was before I was sure I could trust you," said Phillips.

"So you'd rather use the National Security Adviser as your ID badge?"

"By then I didn't think you'd believe me unless I hauled out the big guns."

"So the NSA does this for you all the time?"

"He's my boss."

"And is he the one who got you to use me as your errand boy?"

"No." But the expression on his face said yes.

"This is not the time for more secrets," said Cole quietly.

"He didn't run it," said Phillips. "But he introduced me to the guy who gave me the stuff for you to do."

"And who is that?" asked Malich.

"*He* wouldn't tell me his real name or show me ID. That's how I got the idea of doing that with you. I'm so stupid. If my work for him had anything to do with *this* . . ." He waved a hand toward the damaged south wall of the West Wing.

"I'm giving you an assignment right now," said Malich. "Find out his name. Or at least find his face. Or at least give me a damn good description of exactly what he looks like and exactly where you met and every assignment he gave you that you *didn't* use me for."

"And why would I do that?"

"Because, Mr. Steven Phillips, whoever controlled you probably has something to do with killing the President, and since they're setting me up to take the blame for it, and you're associated with me, your ass is on the line right along with mine."

"They're setting you up?" Phillips seemed to think this was a ridiculous idea.

"I can bet that when they trace these guys back to some miserable fleabag rental they'll find a convenient copy of my report, with my name attached, and it'll be the exact copy that I provided, so my fingerprints will be on it."

"Why would they do that?"

"To make it look like the U.S. Army was behind the assassination of the President of the United States. And if they tie you to it as well, then what does it look like to the media? To the public? A Republican Party hack—that would be you—and a gung-ho officer in Special Ops provide the plans and the weapons to the terrorists who assassinated the President."

So Malich's secret work for Phillips dealt with the weapons trade.

"Who would believe *that*?" said Phillips.

"The public will eat it up. I can see the op-ed headlines now: 'Prez Not Right-wing Enough for Red Staters.' "

All of a sudden Phillips was crying, but fiercely. "They can't say that," he said. "I loved that man. He was the best President—"

"They *can* say it. They *will* say it. They're *dying* to say it. If they can paint this whole thing as a vast right-wing conspiracy, you think they'll hold back because it makes no sense?"

Phillips got control of himself. Dabbed at his eyes with a Kleenex from a little packet in his pocket. "So what does this mean, if your paranoid fantasies turn out to be true? That this was all a *blue*-state conspiracy? That's just as ridiculous."

"I agree," said Malich. "But these terrorists had to have somebody inside the White House to tell them which window to shoot their missile through. They got my plans that were turned in to the U.S. Army. Don't tell me that Al Qaeda had moles planted so long ago that now a bunch of dedicated Muslim fanatics somehow made it through security clearances into positions where they could provide all that."

"I'll get you what I can," said Phillips. "I'll talk to the NSA."

"And when you do," said Malich, "give the information to Cole here, as well as emailing it to me."

Cole tried not to show his surprise. Malich trusted him that much?

No, it wasn't that. Malich expected to be arrested. Held where he couldn't get to his email, where he couldn't be contacted by anybody. He expected Cole to keep on digging to find out the truth. That wasn't something you assign to a newly appointed subordinate. That's something you assign to a friend.

Cole repeated his cellphone number and email address to Phillips until the man could recite them back cold, because Malich forbade him to write anything down. "You think I want somebody to be able to get the information from your dead body that will allow them to track down Cole?" asked Malich. Which terrified Phillips—perhaps *not* the most tactically sound idea, Cole supposed, since Phillips could decide just to go to ground rather than keep investigating. But he had to assume that Malich knew his man. Sort of, anyway.

They made their way back through the southwest gate, past the same MPs, past the emergency vehicles and military vehicles and the cordon of soldiers that were now completely surrounding the White House. Cole finally asked, "Even if you're arrested, you know they can't convict you of anything."

"I'm not afraid of being convicted," said Malich.

"What, then?"

"I'm afraid of Jack Ruby."

The guy who assassinated Lee Harvey Oswald before he could be tried. The guy who made sure that the tough questions about the Kennedy assassination could never be answered.

Yeah, Cole understood that. In fact, it seemed the most likely thing to happen. That, or an unexplained "suicide" in a park somewhere. "Boy, I'm sure glad I got this assignment," said Cole.

Malich stopped and spoke to him earnestly. "You can get out right now if you want. It's dangerous and I had no right to assume you'd help me."

"I wasn't joking. I'm glad I got this assignment. What if you got some desk jockey? What if you got somebody who didn't know how to shoot to kill?"

"Right now I need somebody who can help me find out the truth."

"Oh," said Cole. "You mean you *want* a desk jockey."

"I want you."

Then, because the Metro was shut down at the moment and automobile traffic in the District was at a standstill, they headed for the Roosevelt Bridge to walk over into Virginia. Fortunately, it was a cool day for June in DC. They wouldn't quite die of the heat.

Cole thought wistfully of his air-conditioned car in the parking lot near the FDR Memorial—but it was evidence, so even if traffic had been moving, he couldn't have taken it. And thinking of evidence reminded him of those two borrowed rifles with both their fingerprints all over them. Cole figured he could pretty much rule out denying that he was there.

There were a lot of other pedestrians streaming onto the Roosevelt Bridge. Usually pedestrians wore jogging clothes. Now they were in suits, or women walking miserably on high heels.

At times like these, people rethought their dependence on cars. Started wishing they could live in an apartment in the city and walk to work. Then, when the crisis passed, they'd see how far those apartments were from grocery stores and movie theaters, and how old and rundown they were, and even those who went to the trouble of looking at rentals were stunned at how little you got for the money, and pretty soon they were back behind the wheel again.

But these pedestrians staggering across a bridge devoid of automobile traffic except for the occasional military ve-

hicle meant something else, too. They were a victory for
the terrorists.

Weirdly, though, it was a defeat for them as well, Cole
realized. All the oil money that funded them—if we no
longer burned oil for transportation, if we really became a
pedestrian world, then what would the whole Middle East
be but a waterless wasteland with way too many people to
feed themselves?

But that's what these diehard Islamists wanted. For the
whole world to be as poor and miserable as the Middle
East. For us all to live the way the Muslims did in the good
old days, when the Sultan ruled in Istanbul. Or earlier,
when the Caliph ruled from Baghdad, fantastically wealthy
while the common people sweated and starved and clung
to their faith. And if it meant reducing the population of the
world from six billion to half a billion, well, let eleven-
twelfths of the human population die and Allah would sort
them out in heaven.

What the terrorists aren't counting on, thought Cole, is
that America isn't a completely decadent country yet.
When you stab us, we don't roll over and ask what we did
wrong and would you please forgive us. Instead we turn
around and take the knife out of your hand. Even though
the whole world, insanely, condemns us for it.

Cole could imagine the way this was getting covered by
the media in the rest of the world. Oh, tragic that the President was dead. Official condolences. Somber faces. But
they'd be dancing in the streets in Paris and Berlin, not to
mention Moscow and Beijing. After all, those were the
places where America was blamed for all the trouble in the
world. What a laugh   capitals that had once tried to con
quer vast empires, damning America for behaving far better than they did when *they* were in the ascendancy.

"You look pissed off," said Malich.

"Yeah," said Cole. "The terrorists are crazy and scary,
but what really pisses me off is knowing that this will make
a whole bunch of European intellectuals very happy."

"They won't be so happy when they see where it leads.

They've already forgotten Sarajevo and the killing fields of Flanders."

"I bet they're already 'advising' Americans that this is where our military 'aggression' inevitably leads, so we should take this as a sign that we need to change our policies and retreat from the world."

"And maybe we will," said Malich. "A lot of Americans would love to slam the doors shut and let the rest of the world go hang."

"And if we did," said Cole, "who would save Europe then? How long before they find out that negotiations only work if the other guy is scared of the consequences of *not* negotiating? Everybody hates America till they need us to liberate them."

"You're forgetting that nobody cares what Europeans think except a handful of American intellectuals who are every bit as anti-American as the French," said Malich.

"You think we'll do it?" said Cole. "Bottle ourselves up and let the world go to hell?"

"Would it be any better for us to get really pissed off and declare war on all of Islam?" said Malich. "Because we've got plenty of Americans who want to do *that,* too, and we don't have the President anymore to hold them back."

"I have a terrible feeling," said Cole, "that some turban-wearing Sikhs are going to die today in America, and they've got *nothing* to do with this."

They reached the end of the bridge.

"It's weird," said Cole. "I always feel like when I get to Virginia, I'm back in the United States. Like DC is a separate country. And not just DC. Maryland along with it. Like the Potomac is the boundary line between the country I love and a foreign country where they hate me because of this uniform."

"Plenty of patriots in Maryland and points north," Reuben reminded him. "Plenty of good soldiers come from there."

"Can't help how I feel about crossing this river. I know it's crazy."

They headed uphill into Arlington.

"You know who I hate today?" said Malich. "This isn't like 9/11, when they exploited the loopholes in our open society, and we didn't see it because of pure clumsiness. These terrorists today couldn't have done what they did without the active cooperation of Americans who were in positions of trust."

"At least you know Phillips didn't have anything to do with it," said Cole.

"Phillips? That lying sack of shit?" said Malich. "I don't believe anything he told me. Just an aide to an aide? Yeah, if you think of the NSA as an 'aide.' He's running an operation out of the White House and he knows way more than he's telling me."

"Then why did you have me give him my email and cell number?"

"Cole, they can get that in four seconds if they don't already have it. By making him memorize it, maybe I convinced him that I trust him. At least a little."

They stopped at a drugstore and Malich bought four disposable cellphones and ten ten-minute cards for them. He gave one of them to Cole and they memorized each other's numbers. Except that Malich wouldn't let him memorize the one he was activating right at the moment. "No point," he said. "I'm throwing it away when this card is up. This is the last time I'm calling known numbers, but I still can't keep this phone."

Malich called his wife. It was brief. "You go ahead and visit Aunt Margaret without me," he said. "I'll get up there as soon as I can. I love you, Cessy." Then he ended the call.

"So you're sending her into hiding?" asked Cole.

"No, she's just visiting her Aunt Margaret in New Jersey. We lived with her for a while when I was going to Princeton."

"I thought it was a code."

"I'm assuming our phone is tapped. If Cessy and I had some code, that would imply she's part of my conspiracy."

Cole thought: Is there anything this guy hasn't thought

of? Oh, yeah—he didn't think of somebody passing his plans to the terrorists.

By then, Malich was calling numbers and leaving voice mail. Always the same message: "I always told you I was gonna take this job and shove it. Well, it's shoved. Drinks?"

"Now that *was* code, right?" asked Cole.

"My unit back when I was still in the field. These guys had my back a long time. We're going to meet later tonight near the Delta ticket area at Reagan. Want to come?"

"They don't know me."

"But they will."

"What if I was assigned to you by the very people you're hiding from? What if I report all this?"

"*Are* you spying on me?"

"No."

"Then stop trying to pick a fight with me. How's your Farsi?"

"Rusty. I didn't work with Farsi speakers in Afghanistan."

"Well, start thinking in Farsi, because that's what we use to converse when we get together in public places."

"Right now I'm barely thinking in English."

"Pardon me while I strip some cash out of my accounts."

They walked around Arlington, pulling max amounts out of five different accounts. "How paranoid are you, exactly?" asked Cole.

Malich handed him two hundred dollars. "You forget the line of work I was in and the kind of assignments I had. Always a chance I'd have to go to ground."

"So do you have a car with false registration hidden here in Arlington?"

"No such luck. I wasn't expecting to be on foot after the assassination of the President."

"Are we really walking all the way to your house?"

"I'd be surprised if I ever see that house again," said Malich. He sounded quite calm about it. He looked at his watch. "It stopped being my home about a minute ago, when Cessy and the kids left it."

"So where are we going?"

"Back to the Pentagon," said Malich. "On the Metro, if it's running again on this side of the river."

"Isn't that one of the places they'll look for you?"

"I have to debrief," said Malich. "So do you. They've got to know, on the record, exactly what happened. Most people in the Pentagon aren't in on the conspiracy. The good guys need to be able to fight, so they need information. Besides, if we go to the Pentagon and choose who to talk to, then some good people will know we're there. We won't just disappear."

Cole was suddenly aware of how uncomfortable his feet were. "Sure wish I'd known to wear different shoes today."

"And be out of uniform?" asked Malich. "Shame on you, soldier."

"I want to be in boots and camo," said Cole. "I want some bad guys to shoot at."

"So far today, we're the only ones who got to do that," said Malich.

"Ten seconds too late," said Cole.

"I try not to think of every shot that missed," said Malich. "Every step I might have been able to run a little faster."

"And if I'd driven faster—"

"Then we might have had to stop and explain things to some District cop and then we'd have gotten there even later," said Malich. "What happened, happened."

"And who we shoot at next, other people get to decide."

"Thank God for that," said Malich. "Thank God we live in a country where the soldiers don't have that burden, too."

# SIX

# WONK

Personal affection is a luxury you can have only after all your enemies are eliminated. Until then, everyone you love is a hostage,
sapping your courage and corrupting your judgment.

**CECILY MALICH** put the leftover cookies on the table for the
kids to discover as they wandered in and out during the
day. They did home school in the afternoons during summer vacation, but not on Fridays. Fridays were lazy days,
and that meant Mark was over at one of his friends' houses,
Nick was curled up with a book, slowly driving himself
blind with Xanth or Discworld novels, Lettie and Annie
were playing some madcap game in the back yard that
would leave them smelling like a compost heap, and John
Paul was dogging her heels. Except that he was down for a
nap right now so the house was silent.

And then he woke up and it wasn't silent anymore. He
was three and mercifully had toilet-trained himself fairly
early, so there was no diaper to change. J. P. got a cooky in
his booster seat.

The rest of the cookies disappeared in bunches as the
girls came in from the back yard and she sent them up to
the tub, where of course they would play almost as hard as
they had outside, but at least they had cookies in them to
renew their energy and guarantee full saturation of the
bathroom floor and walls.

It was only fair to bring a plate of cookies to Nick. It was a good thing that he was reading, even if she thought the books were deeply uninteresting herself. He shouldn't be deprived of his share of homemade cookies during his growing-up years. And she saved the last three cookies in a sandwich bag for Mark.

None for her, but that was fine. She didn't like chocolate. Never had. Now, if she had made snickerdoodles . . . but those took refrigerator time before you could bake them, so there was no way she could have gotten them made before Captain Cole showed up.

She wondered if she had done him any favors by telling Reuben that the boy looked like someone he could rely on. She knew that whatever Reuben was doing, it was dangerous and might be the kind of thing that would someday put him in front of a congressional committee like Oliver North back when she was a kid and watched CNN obsessively.

What kind of ten-year-old watched CNN? She was glad none of her kids was as strange as she had been. Such a loner. Didn't have any real friends till she was in high school and found a group of proud-to-be-geeks, though now they'd be called wonks. Who but a wonk like her would even be attracted to the studious young ROTC officer who wore his uniform every day as if he was just daring politically correct students to say something snotty. Which they did. And which he always answered with a surprised look and the same chilling little phrase. "I'm willing to die for you," he'd say, and then go back to whatever he was doing. How could they answer *that*?

He'd die for his country; and I spend my life taking care of his kids and making his life worth trying not to die.

She remembered those two glorious, hideous years as an intern and then a paid staffer in a Congressman's office, where she saw what went on behind the scenes, the stuff they never showed on CNN because reporters and cameras were never present when the real work was being done. It's not that her Congressman was corrupt—far from it. He was a squeaky-clean Mormon from Idaho who never drank or smoked and treated male and female staffers exactly alike.

But he knew how Congress worked—it drank campaign money and breathed publicity. He was an expert in finding and using both.

LaMonte Nielson. He had a conscience and strongly held ideas, but not for one second did he let that get in the way of making whatever deal would get things done and make him indispensable to other Congressmen. Now he was Speaker of the House. Not bad for a smalltown veterinarian who got bored with putting old dogs to sleep.

He had liked her. Gave her a job after her internship. Offered her a huge raise when she said she was quitting. But when she explained she was leaving to marry a soldier, he smiled and said, "That matters more in the long run than anything we do in this office. Go for it."

Today she might have been a senior aide to the Speaker of the House. Instead she was listening to J.P. in his booster seat at the kitchen table, babbling on about garbage trucks, his obsession of the moment. He was explaining the rules of recycling. She wasn't sure whether he could read yet or not. Could he really have memorized all this after getting one of the older kids to read the brochure to him?

Getting to know these kids was a lot more fun than getting to know a bunch of Congressmen and their aides. Negotiating with them about bedtime and videogame use was a lot more satisfying than wrestling with other wonks about what would and would not go into the legislation. Not just because at home she had all the power (she and Reuben, when he was home) but also because she could actually change things. Help them overcome their weaknesses. Help them discover and develop their strengths. Make them feel better when they felt bad. Rejoice with them when they were happy. Like Congressman Nielson said— this was what mattered in the long run.

Except . . .

Except she had to hide from the television. Whether it was CNN or, when Reuben was home, Fox News, she'd find herself filled with yearning—no, be honest, she told herself—frustration. Because things were happening and she wasn't part of it. All these years later, and she still had the disease.

The front door banged open and Mark ran into the kitchen yelling something. She was only half listening as she got his bag of cookies out of the fridge—he liked his cookies cold.

"Turn on the television!" he shouted at her.

"What?" she said.

"They blew up the White House," he said.

All the channels were showing the same pictures: the White House with a gaping hole in the south wall of the West Wing, people in suits and people in uniforms, emergency vehicles and military vehicles all around. Reporters explaining that all air traffic was grounded so they couldn't give us aerial shots—thank God, she thought, that's all we need, the sky around the White House cluttered with choppers—and promising that as soon as they could get confirmation they'd tell us who died.

Because people had died. That much they knew.

The information bled out, each bit savored and discussed till the next one surfaced. An apparent terrorist attack. One or more rockets launched from a distance. From the Mall, then from the Washington Monument, then from the Tidal Basin. That's the rumor that stuck.

And then there was the video clip—sold to the highest bidder?—on CBS and then picked up by everybody else (but with the CBS logo in the corner—capitalism continues!) taken from a car on the eastbound lane of Independence Avenue, where it bridged the Tidal Basin. The footage showed the terrorists on the asphalt of the westbound lanes just past the retaining wall of the Tidal Basin, and two rocket launchers.

The camera was shaking—obviously a digital snapshot camera with only a short video capacity. But there were pops of gunfire and some of the terrorists turned to fire . . . almost right at the camera. Was this tourist insane? He should be down inside his car, not vidding the whole thing.

Then a dark shape moved right in front of the camera in

a blur of motion. A man in a suit. But with a weapon. And then another, only in uniform. And a voice saying, "Get down inside your car!"

Of course the camera stayed where it was.

*Pop. Pop. Pop-pop-pop.* One of the terrorists went down. Another. One of the launchers was knocked out of alignment and tipped over. But the other one fired and then the video ended.

Mark pushed a button on the remote and things started rewinding.

"What are you doing?"

"Rewinding," said Mark.

"This is all a tape?"

"It's DVR, Mom," he said, like she was kind of dim. "We've had this for two years now. You can rewind anything if you haven't changed the channel in between."

"But I want to hear what they're saying."

"Mom," said Mark. "Why do we have to listen to *them* when we can *see*?"

And then he added, softly: "I think it was Dad."

The moment he said it, she knew he was right. Dad in a suit. And that was Captain Coleman in the uniform. Somehow they were at the Tidal Basin with rifles and they were shooting at the terrorists only they hadn't been able to get them all in time.

The video didn't prove anything. Everything moved too fast and blurred too much. But she knew it was Reuben.

"Again," said Mark.

"No," said Cecily. "Let me hear them talk. I have to know what they're saying."

A lot of babble about unidentified early responders and then some idiot talking head saying that the range had been quite short and these must not be trained soldiers because those weren't hard shots. Right, thought Cecily, not hard at the firing range, but damned hard when somebody was firing back at you and you were running from cover to cover.

Then the talking heads were interrupted by a bulletin

from the reporter standing just outside the White House grounds.

The President was definitely in the room where the rocket exploded, along with the Secretary of Defense and the Chairman of the Joint Chiefs.

Mark pushed another button and suddenly everything jumped on the screen. "What are you doing now?"

"Going live," said Mark. "We were a minute behind because of the replay."

"The President is confirmed dead," said a man inside a briefing room that she recognized immediately—it was in the Sam Rayburn Building. Why would he be in the Rayburn?

Because the White House briefing room wasn't available, of course. But . . .

There was Congressman LaMonte Nielson with his hand on the Bible. Raising his right hand. Why was he taking an oath of office?

"Apparently the Vice President was killed in a traffic incident only a few minutes before the rocket attack on the White House. I say 'incident' because it is hard to believe that this was an accident, a mere coincidence. By the time the President died, this country had no living Vice President. So the law of presidential succession is clear. After the Vice President, the Speaker of the House, and then the President Pro Tempore of the Senate, and—but here's the new President of the United States, just sworn in. President LaMonte Nielson. Most Americans don't even know his name, but he's all we've got right now."

His last words overlapped with Nielson's. Looking straight at the camera—Cecily remembered how hard it had been for him to learn how to do that steady gaze at the lens—he said, "Fellow citizens, our enemies have done a terrible thing today, and good people have been murdered. They clearly intended to strike a blow to our hearts, and they succeeded. But we still have—we *must* keep our heads. Our Constitution still works.

"I'm not the man anybody picked to be President. But I'll do my job, as will everyone else in government. Some emergency measures will be taken, but except as instructed by legal authorities, we urge you to go about your normal business. We do not know who did this. Do not jump to any conclusions. Do not show anger or hostility to anybody just because you think they might share the religion or the national origin or just *look* like whoever you *guess* might have done this. Let's add no tragedies to the ones we already face today.

"I join the rest of our nation in mourning for our President and Vice President and the other great public servants whose lives were taken today in service to their country. God bless the United States of America."

As the camera pulled back and the newspeople started judging the new President's short speech, Cecily could see that he was already surrounded, not just by the Secret Service, but by troops in full battle gear.

"Mark," she said softly, "don't tell the other children that we think Dad might have been under fire. Not till we know something for sure."

"Okay, Mom," said Mark.

From his voice she knew he was no longer just shocked. He was crying.

"Stay here, please," she said to him. "I'm going to get the other kids."

A few minutes later they were gathered in the living room on their knees. None of the prayers she knew seemed adequate. She struggled to come up with the right words to add to the prayers the kids all knew. Ultimately, it all came down to the same thing that LaMonte Nielson— President Nielson—had said. God bless the United States of America.

And then Nick added, "And God bless Daddy and all the soldiers."

"Amen," said Cecily. But then she hastened to add, "But as far as we know, Daddy's all right."

"But it's a big war now," said Nick. "It has to be."

Go about your normal business, LaMonte had said. But what was her normal business now?

She sat the kids down and explained about presidential succession. She told them about her time working for La-Monte Nielson. She talked about the slain President.

"You didn't even vote for him, Mommy," said Lettie. "Mark said so."

"Your father voted for him," said Cecily. "And even though I didn't, he was still our President, and he did the best he knew how to do for our country. It's a terrible thing, not just for him but for all of us, all Americans. By killing him, they were trying to hurt us all."

But after a while, she ran out of words. The girls were too young to really understand it all well enough to stay interested. She let them go back to their room and play quietly. "Indoor rules," she said.

Mark and Nick, though, stayed with the television, watching CNN. Cecily knew the footage at the Tidal Basin would come back on. She knew that at some point, some one would tell the names of the men who were firing at the terrorists. But she couldn't very well forbid them to watch history unfold. And she couldn't stay and watch with them, because J. P. needed her attention.

And because she might break down and cry from sheer frustration and fear if she didn't keep herself busy. So with J. P. playing on the kitchen floor, she fumbled around the cupboards looking for something to prepare for dinner that might keep her busy for a few hours.

The first call came from DeeNee Breen. "As far as we know," she said, "Major Malich was not injured in any way. Nor was Captain Coleman. But it's confirmed that they were the ones who fired at the terrorists and disabled one of the launchers. At the moment their location is unknown but I can't imagine they won't make their way here as quickly as possible to be debriefed. Or somewhere."

Cecily thanked her and then went in to tell Mark and Nick that yes, it *was* their father and his new assistant who were in the video, firing at the terrorists.

"So . . . Dad's, like . . . a hero," said Nick softly.

"Honey," said Cecily, "your dad's a hero about forty times over. But yes, he did all he could. But I also know he's very sad right now that he wasn't able to stop both rockets from firing."

"They thought the bodies were booby-trapped," said Mark. "Of the terrorists. But it was just the rocket in the launcher they didn't fire at the White House. Somebody touched it and it launched into the ground and blew up and killed a bunch of guys."

"But not your father," said Cecily. "Or DeeNee would have known. They would know if he was hurt and she would have told me. So he's okay."

Mark looked relieved. But Nick—she could never guess what *he* was feeling. Privately, Reuben called him Stoneface, because he just took things in. She had worried when he was four that he might be autistic or suffer from Asperger's. But no, not at all, he was just a quiet kid who kept things to himself. Like now. Did he believe his dad was safe? Or did he not care? Or was he a seething mass of fear and none of it showed? The mystery child.

But she wasn't going to try to get through to him right now. What would "success" consist of? Nick erupting in tears? Oh, he'd thank her for an achievement like that! "Yes, Oprah, my mother was never happy unless she could get me to cry." Child-rearing today was so complicated. You always had to think of what they'd say on television later.

DeeNee called again to find out if she knew anything about Reuben's whereabouts. And then she started getting calls from friends who wondered if it could possibly have been Rube in those videos from the Tidal Basin. "I don't know," she said. "It looked like a blur to *me*. No, I don't know where he is, but he could be anywhere, you know how his job is." Of course they *didn't* know how his job was, but what could they say, anyway?

And then came the call from Reuben.

She said hello, not recognizing the number on caller ID, expecting it to be another curious friend.

She knew Reuben's voice at once. "You go ahead and visit Aunt Margaret without me," he said. "I'll get up there as soon as I can."

"Reuben, what—"

But he talked right over her. "I love you, Cessy." And then the connection was gone.

He had warned her back when this most recent assignment began that there was a strong chance their phones would be tapped all the time. By both sides. So they had longstanding telephone discipline—play along with whatever the other one is pretending.

The game was this: Apparently they were planning a trip to Aunt Margaret's in West Windsor, New Jersey. Though Reuben's tone was cheerful, the cryptic nature of his instructions told her a great deal: He wanted her and the kids out of town. And it wasn't just because the press would hound them as soon as his identity was known—he would have explained that openly over the telephone. Something was seriously wrong.

And her job, now, was to trust Reuben.

She went into the living room and knelt down in front of the two boys. She beckoned them to get their faces close to hers, so she didn't have to talk loudly to be heard above the noise of the television.

"That was Dad," she said. "He's fine. But he asked us to do something. We're getting in the van and we're driving to Aunt Margaret's. I need you two older boys to pretend that we've been planning this trip for a long time, and the only thing different is that Dad will be coming along later. If the girls don't play along, don't argue with them. I'll help them pack and you guys pack your own stuff. Three days' worth of clothes, plus Sunday clothes, plus swimming trunks, plus a couple of books and maybe DVDs and the PSP and the Gameboy Nintendo thing—the DS."

They looked at her gravely and Mark nodded. Nick

didn't nod, but when Mark got up, so did Nick, and they padded out of the room together.

It was packing for J. P. that took the longest, but it was as if they had rehearsed for such a move for years, it went that smoothly. They were backing out of the driveway only half an hour later.

They went out Route 7 and crossed the Potomac above Leesburg. The bridge was packed and it took almost two hours to get past the bottleneck—hardly a surprise, since all the Washington bridges were closed and this was the first bridge open to the public. After that it was still slow going, so it wasn't until after dark before they pulled into Margaret's driveway. Aunt Margaret had the front door open before they were out of the minivan.

"Your soldier boy called," she said. "He's being debriefed and everything's fine."

But she and Aunt Margaret both knew that nothing was fine. The President was dead, Reuben had shot some of the assassins, and he had sent his family out of town in a rush and without explanation. In some ways it was worse than when he had been in Special Ops. At least in the field, Americans were all on his side. He had support. But for all she knew, he was in serious trouble and couldn't count on anybody.

Except her. He had assigned her to take care of their children. As long as he knew his kids were safe, then he could face anything else with courage. Her own dreads and worries had to be set aside. She had a job to do, and she was going to do it well.

# SEVEN

# TEAM

The great irony of war is this: While war is the ultimate expression of mistrust, it cannot be waged without absolute trust. A soldier trusts his comrades to stand beside him and his commander to lead him wisely, so that he will not be led to meaningless death. And the commander trusts his subordinates and soldiers to act with wisdom and courage in order to compensate for his own ignorance, stupidity, incompetence, and fear, which all commanders possess in ample measure.

**REUBEN WAS** being followed—but that's exactly what he expected. By the time he was through a long debriefing—three different interrogation teams—it was nearly dark.

The real question was *which* group was following him—the FBI, the Army, or the CIA. Maybe all three. Or—always possible—some other agency within Homeland Security. How many parking places should he look for when he got to Reagan National? He wouldn't want to inconvenience them.

Reuben could hardly blame them for expending resources on following him. What else did they have to go on? The bodies of the terrorists would undoubtedly have no information on them; it might be days before anyone came forward with information about rooms they occupied. And in all likelihood they would be far more disciplined than the 9/11 terrorists had been—there would be no notes, no letters, no convenient ID that might lead to an easier trace.

The only thing they had was Reuben himself—with poor Captain Coleman being interrogated just as thoroughly in another room, by his own teams of debriefers. He had told Cole to answer everything, thoroughly and fully. Including as much as he wanted to of Reuben's conversation and actions afterward, and all their speculations about why things might have fallen out as they did.

"Tell the truth," said Reuben. "We want these guys to get the terrorists. Of course they'll suspect me, and if we pretend we don't know that I'll be suspected, the more they'll think I have something to hide. We'll answer this weird conspiracy with pure truth, so that they never have a moment where they can say, Here's what you said, but here's what we know you actually did. They'll never catch us in a lie. Clear?"

Reuben had followed his own advice. While he didn't tell them anything about his activities for Steven Phillips, that was because they were highly classified and his interrogators did not have clearance for it. "If Phillips tells me to go ahead, then I'll happily tell you everything." They understood and accepted this—the fact that he told them Phillips's name was in itself a sign of extraordinary cooperation on his part, since he really shouldn't have told them even that much. "But we're all on the same side, here, and I'm not going to let foolish red tape keep you from finding out what you want to know." Holding back Phillips's name would have been foolish red tape, with the President and Vice President dead; but keeping his actual activities secret until he was cleared to divulge them was not foolish—it was essential. These guys interrogating him were just as faithful about sticking to protocols, or they wouldn't be in their positions.

After they decided to call it a night, Reuben went to his office, which he assumed had been searched, and then to the little coffee room, where, inside a brown lunchsack labeled "Keep your hands off my food you greedy bastards—DeeNee," he reached under a sandwich and took out his newly acquired cellphones. If they had been thorough enough to find these, they must already be convinced of his guilt and he wasn't going to accomplish anything anyway.

Now Reuben was heading from the Pentagon to the airport—not much of a drive, and probably the one that would make his followers the most worried. He could imagine cellphone speed-dial buttons getting pressed and teams being mobilized. "Stop him before he can board a plane, but otherwise just keep him in sight," they told each other.

But the followers could take care of themselves. It was the men he wanted to meet with whose response he wanted to see. They hadn't foreseen anything like what was happening, or even that he would try to assemble them. But he *had* once told them, jokingly, that if they ever had to save the world, he'd give them a call and meet them at the Delta ticket counter at Reagan National. Just a joke.

But guys in Special Ops didn't forget things—they were trained to memorize things so they could debrief accurately later. They would remember.

Remember, but . . . do what? Would he really find a miniconvention of extraordinarily fit men in civilian clothes standing around waiting for him?

No. They would have recognized him on the TV news. They would know that his call to them had something to do with the assassination, and the cryptic nature of his message, along with the context of the old joke—saving the world—would prompt them to call each other. Maybe one of them would meet him there. Maybe none.

He didn't even get to the Delta ticket counter before they made contact. Lloyd Arnsbrach stepped onto the escalator just in front of him. "South of the border restaurant in town center," he said—in Farsi. If he had said "Rio Grande Café in Reston Town Center," the words "Rio Grande" and "Reston" would have been easy enough to understand for any English speaker.

And since there was nobody within earshot, that must mean that Lloyd—"Load," they had always called him— believed that they were being overheard—either a big-ear listening device or a bug planted on Reuben's clothes.

"You're being followed," continued Load in Farsi. "Get on the toll road on the hill of spring"—which meant Spring Hill. "We'll make sure you have a clear mile, so get off the toll road immediately."

When they got to the top of the escalator, Load headed off in another direction from the Delta ticket counter.

So all that was left for Reuben to do was go and buy a ticket on the DC–New York shuttle for tomorrow. If asked—and he would certainly be asked—it was his intention to fly up to join his family tomorrow on their spur-of- the-moment visit to Aunt Margaret.

It was late enough in the evening that there weren't many ticket buyers, which would make it harder for his fol- lowers to remain unobtrusive. But they were apparently pretty good at what they did—he didn't see anybody with that agentish look of studied nondescriptness. It would be surprising if they didn't have somebody near enough to hear what he said. But then, they could count on being able to ask the ticket agent what he had said—those federal badges were so helpful.

Or . . . and this is something he should have thought of before . . . they might very well have planted a bug in his clothing. So they were just sitting in a van somewhere, lis- tening. Or everything was getting piped into somebody's iPod earphone.

And it wouldn't have made any difference if he had stopped in his office and changed clothes. They would have bugged the uniforms he kept there. Or if they didn't they were idiots and he preferred to think the assassination of the President was not being investigated by idiots.

He got back to his car and practically had to force him- self not to glance around to see if he could spot any of the tails. Of course they knew he was Special Ops and had been doing clandestine work for the NSA, so of course he'd guess that someone was following him. But looking around would make him seem, not curious, but furtive, as if he had something to hide. And since he did have something to hide, and was about to make it obvious that he did, the last thing he wanted to do was signal them that he was watching out for watchers.

What twisted thinking. Will they guess that I guessed that they'd know I'd assume they were there? But that was part of the training of Special Ops, especially if you were going to be in country on a longterm assignment. You couldn't take anything at face value. You constantly had to think: How will this action look to them? How will they interpret what I say and do? How should I interpret what their words and actions say about what they believe about me? On and on, never achieving certainty, but getting closer. If you got close enough, you succeeded in your mission. Not so close and you failed. Way not close and you died.

The George Washington Parkway was open again, as were the bridges, and traffic from the District was still flowing out in a much-delayed rush hour. Reuben patiently stayed with the stop-and-go traffic. Getting onto the Beltway southbound took forever, but he stayed with it to the Chain Bridge Road exit, then went around Tysons II till he could get under the toll road overpass and enter the onramp at Spring Hill. There were only two tollbooths there, and sure enough, the human-manned one was being tied up by a guy who had apparently dropped his money and was out of his car looking for it.

Reuben didn't recognize him, but he didn't expect to. His team would have their own networks of friends who could be called on to fill assignments they didn't necessarily understand. "It's connected with the current national emergency, and it's a good guy we're helping." That would be enough.

He tossed his coins into the basket and moved on through. In his rearview mirror he caught only a glimpse of the driver behind him—who also apparently threw his coins on the ground and had to get out of the car to get them.

The tollbooth operator would have a story to tell tonight. "Two idiots at the same time! It's a wonder we can even field an Olympic team, when these people can't hit a two-foot-wide basket that's a foot from their car."

Of course, if the guys following him were any good, they already had somebody waiting on the toll road to pick up the tail, but he'd be off by then.

When he got to Reston Town Center he wasn't sure how to proceed—surely they wouldn't all be sitting at a big table eating guacamole.

He didn't get a chance to see the inside of the restaurant. As he pulled up past McCormick and Shmick he spotted Mingo—Domingo Camacho—who crossed the street in front of him, pointing once at the parking garage across the street. Reuben made the left turns to get up into the garage and kept going up to the third level, where Mingo stepped out from the elevator area just in time to stop him. A car pulled out of a parking place as if on cue—because it *was* on cue—and Reuben pulled his car into the spot.

Mingo put his fingers to his lips and walked to the passenger door. Reuben rolled down the window and through it, Mingo handed him the shopping bag he was carrying. Chino shorts, T-shirt, flip-flops.

Reuben slid past the gearshift and changed clothes in the passenger seat. He thought of keeping his briefs on but decided against it; and that was apparently what Mingo had thought as well, because when he got the clothes out of the bag, there were briefs among them. Everything his size. These guys were good. Thank heaven he hadn't gained any weight since his Special Ops days. This was where the endless workouts paid off. Reuben was determined never to be one of those sad fat officers who no longer even pretended to live in a battle-ready state.

If he stayed in the service long enough to be a general.

If he stayed alive and out of prison.

With his clothes completely changed, he put the cellphones into his new pockets, put his keys above the visor, and locked the car. It would be easy to open the car later, with the codepad on the door.

He walked with Mingo, still wordless, to a car parked in a handicapped stall. But these guys had been so thorough that a legal-looking handicapped tag was hanging from the rearview mirror. It probably *was* legal, given how pathetically easy it was to get those tags these days.

Mingo pointed to the rear passenger seat, where Reuben lay down on the floor as Mingo closed the door behind him, then got in front and drove. Reuben didn't try to look and see where they were going—trust meant you didn't expose your face in order to second-guess the route.

That didn't mean Reuben could turn off the part of his brain that automatically counted turns and estimated distances. When he figured they were on Route 7, heading back toward Tyson's Corner, Reuben finally spoke.

"Am I supposed to stay down here till we get where we're going?"

Mingo picked up his cellphone from the cup holder in the center console, flipped it open, and only then answered Reuben, so that if someone saw him talking they'd think it was on the phone. "Safer, don't you think? We go to all this trouble, it'd be pretty dumb to have one of your tails spot your big happy white face just by chance."

"Destination?"

"Play along, Rube. I want you to guess."

"Not a restaurant where we have a waiter who can overhear us. But a place where it's okay for a bunch of guys to gather around and talk in Farsi. So that means something like a Starbucks or a bookstore with a café in it. We're on Route 7 so I'm betting on the Borders across from the Marriott in Tyson's Corner."

"Shit," said Mingo.

"Is that a good shit or a bad shit?"

"Bad."

"How much you lose?"

"Just a dollar, but you know Benny. 'Never bet against the Rube.'"

"Is that what he says?"

"I wasn't betting against *you*," said Mingo. "I was betting that Benny's plan sucked so you'd think of a better one and assume that's what we'd do."

"Good plan so far," said Reuben. "But I have one more man to bring to the party." From the floor of the van he called Cole and spoke only a single sentence, in Farsi: "Borders on Route 7 in the Corners now." Couldn't say "Tyson's Corner" because "Tyson" didn't translate.

Not that the people tailing him wouldn't already have gotten a Farsi translator after Load's words to him in the airport. So if Cole had been careless, or somebody had opened DeeNee's lunch in the break-room fridge, this would bring his tails right back on him, and implicate everybody else in whatever conspiracy they supposed him to be part of. But you had to take some risks, or you might as well pull a Saddam and hide in a hole somewhere till you were arrested and put through a show trial.

They got to the Borders and soon had taken over two tables and eight chairs in the coffee shop.

Speaking quietly in Farsi, Reuben quickly explained how his own plan had been used to kill the President. Cole arrived—in civvies, mercifully—and Reuben introduced him around.

But Cole had to know more than just names. "Were you a team once? I mean, in-country?"

"We've all been in the same team with Rube, one time or another," said Arty Wu. "But that was long ago and far away."

"We're his *jeesh* now," said Mingo.

Cole knew his Arabic, even when the word was dropped into the midst of Farsi. "His army?"

"His little tiny army," said Load. "Because he's our hero."

"We're guys who trust each other," said Reuben.

"And were really good at killing bad guys," said Drew.

"So we gave our club a scary Arabic name," said Babe.

"Cole, tell them about the meeting we had outside the White House," said Reuben.

If Cole wondered why Reuben, who knew more, was having *him* make the report, he didn't show it. Cole's Farsi was okay—good enough, and now and then when he struggled somebody would supply a word. The idea wasn't to impress them with his language ability. They needed to hear Cole's voice and see that Reuben trusted him, despite having met each other only today.

"My family is with Aunt Margaret Diklich in West Windsor, N.J.," said Reuben in Farsi. "Unless I can think of a better plan, I'm driving up there tomorrow, because by now the FBI or whoever's tailing me knows I have a ticket to La Guardia. I have no plans beyond that, except that I'd like to not be arrested while I'm trying to find out who gave those plans to the terrorists and what their goal really is."

"You mean you don't think it stops with killing the President and Vice President?" asked Arty Wu. "That's kind of like Al Qaeda's idea of nirvana right there."

"I don't think the *terrorists* planned anything more than what they did today, no," said Reuben. "But the people using them have to have something more in mind. Surely we didn't have Steven Phillips inside the White House and whoever 'shared' my plans from inside the Pentagon acting out of a desire to see the President and Vice President dead. I'm assuming that these Americans did this with some goal in mind that has nothing to do with Al Qaeda."

"Destabilization," said Cole, in English. He continued in Farsi. "But that's obvious."

"Yes," said Reuben, "but we believe in saying the obvious. We're not here to impress each other with our guessing ability. Except for Benny and Mingo."

Benny raised an eyebrow, and Mingo handed him a buck.

"What we're looking for," said Drew Linnie, who was now a professor at American University, "is what they plan to do next, so we can be there first and catch them with their pants down."

"An image both colorful and vaguely gay," said Babe Austin.

"*Cui bono?*" asked Cat Black, who was a lawyer. "If America is in chaos, who benefits?"

"Showing off by speaking Latin," muttered Load.

"We can rule out LaMonte Nielson," said Reuben. "Cessy knows him and he's a decent guy. Besides, I have a feeling nobody in their right mind would consider being President right now a 'benefit.'"

"Nielson's going to have this big sympathy thing for a few minutes," said Cat, "but it's not likely to translate into a lot of support. He could never have been elected President, and he's too conservative not to be a lightning rod."

"Assassinations aren't enough to really destabilize the country," said Load Arnsbrach. "We've had them before and the country goes on."

"We've had unelected Presidents before, too," said Benny.

"One, anyway," said Load.

"So, we're all political geniuses here," said Cat. "Anybody else figure that this is only Step A?"

"I think," said Cole, "that Step B is Major Malich, here. I think that the people who gave the info to the terrorists didn't care if the assassinations worked or not—the fact that Al Qaeda or whoever it was succeeded might even appall them. The *purpose* was to set up Major Malich."

"Reuben," Reuben corrected him.

"Rube." Mingo corrected his correction.

"I think to find out who did this, we need to look at Rube," said Cole—it was clearly painful to break protocol like that—"and see who would benefit from having him put on trial for betraying his country and conspiring to assassinate the President and Vice President."

"You mean Rube, specifically, or Special Ops war hero Major Reuben Malich, symbolically?" said Arty.

"It'll be Rube, specifically, who goes to jail," said Cat.

"So if Rube takes off running," said Benny. "Or hides. Anything that makes him look guilty. They win. From that moment on they don't need him alive, because he's guilty in the public mind. In fact, he's more useful to them dead. Because nobody will feel much urgency about clearing the name of a dead man."

"Assume that's the plan," said Drew. "Rube is painted as part of the conspiracy and then he's dead. Excuse me for the hypothetical fatality, Rube."

"I'm checking my pulse," said Reuben.

Drew went on. "What, exactly, could anyone do with Rube's death?"

"Discredit the right wing?" offered Mingo.

"I'm not that right-wing," said Reuben. "My wife's a Democrat, for pete's sake."

"You don't have to *be* an extremist to be *called* one," said Mingo. "Hell, you're a soldier, man. Look at you. The poster child for the anti-war image of the mighty Aryan warrior."

"I can't help being an incredibly good-looking Serb in perfect shape," said Reuben.

"For an old fart in his forties," said Benny.

"I'm thirty-seven," said Reuben.

"An old thirty-seven, though."

"Look," said Cole, "we still aren't *there* yet. What can you do with the image of a red-state warrior who planned the assassination of the President? You can't win an election with it—the President was a red-stater and his successor is too. Who's in favor of presidential assassinations? How can you win elections on the basis of being anti-assassin? Who's your opponent?"

Only now did Reuben put it together. "Who said anything about winning elections?"

"Well, what else?" said Mingo.

"Maybe it's not my being a red-stater. Maybe it's about my being Special Ops. The elite of the Army. Maybe it's an attack on the military."

"The p.c. crowd attacks the Army all the time," said Load dismissively. "They've never let go of the Vietnam-era baby-killer slogan."

"Yes, but sane people ignore them. Not now," said Reuben.

"This still isn't it," said Drew. "Nothing in this justifies such a monstrous act."

"Al Qaeda—" began Cat.

"They're in the monstrous-act business," said Load. "It's the other guys. The American guys. Why would they go after Reuben, the Symbol of Militariness? Why discredit the Army in such a drastic way?"

Babe slumped farther down in his chair. That meant that he was about to say something he thought was important. Sometimes it even was. "I don't think we're going to find out what they mean to do with Rube until they do it."

"But then he'll be dead," said Arty.

"Since we won't let anybody kill him," said Babe, "what I mean is this: We have to see how the story is spun, and who does the spinning. Then we'll know what they set him up for."

"So we do nothing?" said Cole.

"Not at all," said Babe. "What we got to do is, don't give them *anything* to work with. And meanwhile, we spin back. Or, I guess, Rube spins back."

"Nothing for them to work with," said Reuben. "So you mean I shouldn't go to Jersey? Nothing that could look like I'm hiding?"

"No, I mean you should talk to the press first," said Babe.

"About what? All my work was classified."

"How long do you think that'll last, once they start leaking about how you came up with the plans?" said Babe. "How classified do you think any of this shit will stay when the investigation turns ugly and political?"

"It's a crime to reveal classified information."

"That became irrelevant the second your classified information was used to kill the President," said Babe. "Besides, just the fact that you met with us here, that's *already* enough for the press to infer a conspiracy."

"Babe's right about that," said Load. "The fact that he

ditched a tail is probably enough. Shows a guilty conscience, right, Cat?"

"You watch too much *Law and Order,* Load," said Cat.

Cole laughed in disbelief. "Come on, are you saying
Major Malich should hold a press conference?"

"No," said Babe. "You got to announce those in advance
and the feds can shut you down. I think that right now,
while he's still not being tailed, we get his ass over to *The
Washington Post.*"

"Why *The Post*?" said Reuben. "Why do I have to go to
the people who are most dying to destroy me?"

"Because *their* story will get picked up and used everywhere," said Babe. "Even if they mock you for it, your
statement that somebody deliberately set you up to take the
fall for this will resonate with people. *Then,* if somebody
kills you, it *will* backfire on them. A lot of people will believe that someone killed you to shut you up."

"I don't *want* to find out what people believe about why
I was murdered," said Reuben. "This is a really disturbing
conversation."

"If they don't think it will help them, there's no reason
for them to kill you. Tell it all to *The Post.* Name all the
names you can." Babe grinned. "I'm in p.r., and I'll tell you
what I'd tell Brad Pitt and Russell Crowe—don't wait for
them to tell the story on you, you tell it on them first."

"*They're* not your clients," said Arty.

"I didn't say they were," said Babe. "Rube's nowhere
near as pretty as they are. Though I *will* say he's almost as
manly."

Which is why, at eleven o'clock at night, Reuben found
himself in a conference room at *The Washington Post,* with
his whole team around him, as he and Cole sat there to be
photographed and questioned by the reporters and editors
working on the assassination story.

"We're not answering questions for the first while," said
Reuben. "I'm just going to tell you exactly what happened,
including some classified stuff whose classification got

blown all to hell. But I'm getting set up, and I at least want my story out there to compete with the lies that are going to be told about me."

They didn't like it that he wanted to be in control of the interview.

"Just listen to what I have to say and then decide whether it was worth getting out of bed for."

The lead reporter on the story was Leighton Fuller. He was their top political reporter, and he also had his own weekly column in which he had already killed every idea the President had ever had. Though he never admitted they actually rose to the level of being called ideas.

"I don't see what this is about," Leighton said. "You're a hero, you tried to save the President. Who's trying to set you up?"

"Okay, I'll pretend I'm answering your question," said Reuben. Then, with Cole affirming or correcting or supplementing him all the way, he told about the day's events. Including how on his own Reuben would never have seen the signs of the submersibles.

And at the end, Reuben explained about the manuscript of his plan for assassinating the President. "If they find my fingerprints on the copy the terrorists worked from then you'll know something important."

"What will we know?" asked Leighton.

"I never touched the final report with my own hands. The division secretary delivered it electronically to the printing office and they printed it and bound it and she delivered it around. I wasn't making a point of not touching it, I just wasn't in the country when I finished it and emailed it to DeeNee. If my fingerprints are on it, then it's a rough draft. One of the ones I hand-carried to people for comment."

"Which people?"

"The division secretary is putting together the list."

"Can I have it?"

"No. I'll turn it over to the FBI. But I want you to know it exists in case it gets ignored there."

"You do realize how paranoid you sound," said Leighton.

"Yes, sir," said Reuben. "And if they never do any of this stuff I'm anticipating, then I'll have to agree with you. But which of *you* would have been paranoid enough to think the President and Vice President might be killed within minutes of each other—that the President could have been blown up right through a West Wing window?"

"I'll give you this," said Leighton. "You two are the only people who even tried to stop this assassination when there was still time to have a chance to stop it. I didn't like this President, but I didn't want him dead. He was the *President.* So you've earned a fair hearing on your completely wacko account. Does everybody understand that?" Leighton looked at his editor. "I don't want us to screw around with the headline or the captions to paint this guy as guilty." He turned back to Reuben and Cole. "Unless we get evidence confirming that you really did collaborate with terrorists."

"Of course you'll get evidence like that," said Cole. "It's being planted even as we speak."

"Evidence that satisfies *me,*" said Leighton. "I don't think you're crazy, Major Malich, and you've proven you've got brains and guts. The way you tell it, this is all part of a larger plan. And if you're right, do you know what that smells like to me?"

They didn't.

"It smells like war. Somebody wants America's military to be humiliated and demoralized before the war."

"Who?" asked one of the other reporters. "Who's going to dare to attack us?"

"I guess we'll find out when they're through crucifying Major Malich," said Leighton.

One of the editors spoke up. "Leighton, it looks to me like these guys are just trying to use us to spin the story."

"Everybody tries to use us to spin the story," said Leighton contemptuously. "And when we like them or their cause, we follow their spin. I don't know if I like these guys. But I also don't know but what they're telling the truth. So my story is going to report their claims neutrally. Then we'll see who jumps on it."

"Or on us," said the editor. "I don't know if I'm going to be able to let them use us this way."

"That's honest enough," said Reuben, getting up. The other soldiers also rose to their feet. "We'll go to the *Washington Times,* then, and hope the truth seeps out somehow."

Several of the reporters laughed nervously. Leighton grinned. "You're right—telling the *Times* isn't a leak, it's seepage."

"Thanks for coming back to the office so late at night," said Reuben. "Now I've got to go wake up the *Times.*"

The editor looked annoyed. "We want the exclusive. That's what you promised us."

"We wanted a fair hearing," said Reuben. "You're already planning to spin it against me." He headed for the door.

Load said, in Farsi, "Can't we bruise them a little bit, as long as we've got them all in the same room?" Reuben's team laughed.

Reuben had to walk past Leighton to get to the door. Leighton winked at him. "You watch," he said. "You'll have your fair hearing."

Reuben paused and studied Leighton's face. He didn't know this man. Did the popularity of his column give him so much power at the paper that he could override his editor? Or did he simply trust in his powers of persuasion? Or . . . was he lying right now, to keep Reuben from going to the *Times*?

Reuben made his guess, and bet his future on it. When he and Cole and the rest of the team got back to their cars, he told Mingo the combination to the keypad on the door of his car back in the Reston Town Center parking garage. "The keys are above the visor," he said. "I need to take your SUV, if you don't mind my borrowing it."

"I made some modifications," Mingo answered. It took him only a few minutes to show Reuben where the weapons and ammunition were hidden.

"I hope I don't need this," said Reuben. "I'll surrender before I shoot at Americans."

"So you're not going to the *Times*?" said Cole.

"I'm betting on Leighton," said Reuben. "But in the long run, we know it's going to go against me. Because they'll have evidence. And they'll have some Jack Ruby wannabe waiting for me."

"That's why I'm coming with you," said Cole.

"Then we really will look like a conspiracy."

"We're going to look like one anyway," said Cole. He glanced around at the other guys. "Heck, we *are* a conspiracy. We're plotting to save your life and your name."

"I hope what we're doing," said Reuben, "is working to find out who killed the President and prevent them from hurting America any worse than they already have."

"Oh, yeah," said Cole as he got into the passenger seat of Mingo's SUV. "That too."

"Help me pull him out of there," said Reuben.

"No way," said Mingo. "He's Special Ops."

"He's a bad dude," said Cat.

"He might hurt me," said Benny.

Reuben was annoyed. "Why should two careers go down the toilet on this?"

"He's assigned to you by the Pentagon," said Drew. "It makes sense for him to stay with you."

"And we need him," said Babe, "to tell us the truth about whatever danger you might get into. Because we know *you'll* never tell us to come kick ass for you."

"It all depends on whose ass needs kicking," said Reuben. He pointed to Cole. "Right now, it's his, and you guys are worthless."

"Only because he's so strong," said Load. "And his American accent when he speaks Farsi is so bad."

"Let's go, sir," said Cole. "Let's get you to your family."

It was time, Reuben knew, to accept the fact that his friends might well see things more clearly than he did. He took Mingo's keys and got into the SUV.

"I'll never forgive you for making me drive a Ford," said Mingo.

Reuben closed the door and drove out of the parking garage.

# EIGHT

# COUP

All the common people want is to be left alone. All the ordinary soldier wants is to collect his pay and not get killed. That's why the great forces of history can be manipulated by astonishingly small groups of determined people.

**FOR COLE,** the bad thing about Reuben Malich having left for New Jersey was that it left him in charge of the office. That had been fine for the first couple of days, before Cole ever met Rube, because even though he didn't know anything, nobody ever called to ask him anything, either. Now he still didn't know anything, but the phone didn't let up.

Most of the people wanted to talk to Major Malich—old friends of his calling to congratulate him on stopping one rocket, at least. Cole would take a message with a promise to give it to him as soon as he saw him.

But the press callers were just as happy to talk to Cole and pump him with questions. The trouble is, Cole couldn't think of anything to tell them that couldn't be spun into an attack on him and Rube. The story in *The Post* had been more or less balanced—though a soldier like Cole was so used to the way the media treated the military that he heard a tone of snideness in everything they wrote. Still, Leighton Fuller had kept his word. Even the headline was balanced.

The questions Cole was getting now, however, were obviously designed to get him to say things that could spin against Reuben. Questions like, "How did you happen to be where you could see the underwater operation unfolding?" and "What exactly are the signs that you saw on the surface of the water? Why did you know to look for them?" and "Didn't you and Major Malich both qualify as sharpshooters? Why were you able to hit only one of the rocket launchers?"

To all the questions, Cole gave the same answers: "We're still in the debriefing process. We're not authorized to discuss this." To which they always replied, "But Major Malich talked to *The Post*!"

Like little children—they demanded that Rube and Cole be "fair" to the print and television newspeople, but there was going to be no attempt at fairness to them or the military they served.

Even as he thought this, he also knew that the questions were perfectly legitimate ones. And that the only answers he had were speculative at best. Why did they happen to be at Hain's Point when the terrorists scubaed by? Maybe they tapped into the phone conversation; maybe they'd been watching Major Malich and knew him well enough to predict he'd go there for a private meeting. Why did sharpshooters like them only hit one launcher? Maybe because they were working with unfamiliar weapons. Maybe because they didn't say, You take the left one, I'll take the right, so they both shot at the same one. Maybe because they were distracted by being fired on. Why did you kill all the terrorists so none were left to be questioned? Maybe because we were getting fired on and in the heat of battle it's hard to say, Let's just wound this one. Especially when you fear that they'll try to involve civilians if you let them live.

But the real answer, to question after question, would have been, "I don't know." The only thing he knew was, Rube was no actor. He had been furious that the terrorists got hold of his plan, desperate to stop them, devastated when the President died. Yet that was precisely the kind of thing that the press would never take seriously. Yeah, yeah, you felt "sure" that Rube didn't know what was going on. Let's have some *facts.*

The President was killed using a plan created by Major Malich. Major Malich was on the scene precisely when the plot unfolded. But you and he happened to hit only one of the launchers, so that the other one was still able to fire.

They weren't there. They couldn't know. All they knew was the collection of "facts" and the video footage from the guy in the car, and none of those showed the frenzy of being under fire, of being so wired with adrenalin you had no idea of the passage of time. Didn't they get it that it was a miracle they got even *one* of the launchers? Didn't they understand that it was a miracle they were able to get there, with weapons, as quickly as they did? Not for one second had Major Malich done a single thing to delay the operation to make sure the terrorists had time. And the terrorists got that rocket off with less than a second to spare. Nobody could *plan* for that.

Especially because Major Malich could not know that Cole would fail to hit the other launcher. He could not have planned on that. So if Rube had secretly wanted the assassination to succeed, it was a gross mistake bringing Cole along.

Unless, of course, Cole had been part of the assassination plot, too.

Only Cole knew he wasn't part of any plot. And he knew that if Rube really had been part of the assassination, then he screwed up big time letting Cole be present with a weapon when the assassination was unfolding. It was the kind of screwup that a leader like Rube would never, never make.

That's how Cole knew Rube was innocent of any intent to kill the President.

But that knowledge could not be conveyed to the press, particularly if somebody was juicing the process with leaks designed to incriminate Rube.

And me, thought Cole. Incriminate him and me.

Then there were the hang-ups. Ring ring, answer, click. Cole guessed those might have something to do with Major Malich's clandestine work. Phillips and his cronies. Either that or they were just making sure Cole was still in the office.

DeeNee was no help. She let all the calls through to him while *she* was running errands around the building. Cole had no authority to ask her for an accounting, but since Rube trusted her, Cole could only assume she was about Major Malich's business.

Those calls from friends in the Army. Which of them might be the one who passed along Rube's secret worst-case-scenario plan to the terrorists who proved that it was, indeed, the worst case?

Or was it?

Up and down the halls of the Pentagon, television sets were set to CNN, Fox News, MSNBC, C-SPAN. A lot of stuff about the funeral arrangements, sympathetic statements from world leaders who had vilified the President but now were officially regretful, human interest bits about the First Family and the Vice President's wife and children, and the families of the others who died.

But in the cracks there were the real stories: How surprisingly small a blip the assassination of the President made in the stock market. ("Is this a sign that the identity of the President is no longer a significant issue in the market? Or that LaMonte Nielson as President is somehow reassuring to Wall Street?") The identity of the terrorist group responsible. ("All the assassins identified so far entered the country legally and with no known ties to terrorists or to groups that sympathize with terrorists.")

And, now and then: "Questions continue to arise about why the two Pentagon officers, Major Reuben Malich and Captain Bartholomew Coleman, happened to be on the scene. According to a *Washington Post* story this morning, Major Malich actually worked on a hypothetical plan for assassinating a President that was eerily close to what the terrorists actually did . . ."

Bad spin. The public didn't like coincidences. They made up stories about coincidences without the media actually having to spell it out. In Europe, the media always told people what to think, and they thought it. In America, the press asked leading questions and framed things to point to what they wanted people to think—but they never actually said it outright.

That was Congress's job. And sure enough, the House Minority Leader was on camera saying, "Just because the dead bodies at the Tidal Pool were all Muslims from Arab nations doesn't mean that this was exclusively a foreign plot. In a White House populated with right-wing extremists, maybe somebody didn't think the late President was extreme enough."

And there was already a ghoulish online cartoon making the forwarded-email circuit. A drawing of the blown-out West Wing windows, with two cops looking up at it. One of them says, "At least we know it wasn't the Vice President." "Oh yeah?" comes the answer. "Maybe they got each other."

The thing that Cole couldn't let go of was the fact that maybe they were right. Not about him and Rube being complicit, but quite possibly about who the insiders were. There *were* no left-wingers in the White House to finger the President's location. And given the makeup of the military, the odds were in favor of it being a conservative of some kind or another who passed along Reuben's plans.

Meanwhile, Cole couldn't call anybody and actually talk about what was on his mind, since he could only assume that his phone was being monitored. And whom did he have to call? The only people he could trust, Reuben's friends, were not *Cole's* friends, not yet anyway.

He did call his mom, who was so proud of him for doing his best to stop the assassination, he was a real hero, he should get the Medal of Honor. He didn't have the heart to break it to her that he'd probably be hauled in front of a couple of congressional committees and have people accuse him of being part of the assassination plot. She'd find it out in due time.

So he let her talk about how brave and smart he was and how proud she was, and tried to answer in something like a natural way, knowing that the tape of the conversation might well end up being played over and over on the news at some future date. "Listen to how he talked with his mother, saying nothing about the suspicions already in the media. If he could lie to her this way, then how can we believe anything he says?"

And then there was a man standing in front of his desk. A two-star general.

Cole leapt to his feet and saluted, saying to his mother, "Got to call you back, Mom, I've got a general in the office."

"General Alton," said his visitor. "I don't think we've ever met, Captain Cole."

"Major Malich is out, sir," said Cole.

"I know," said Alton. "But I came to see *you*."

Generals don't come to your office to escort you to a court-martial—MPs do that. So what did he want? To hear the story in his own words?

"Interesting article in *The Post*. Your picture was in it, but not a single quote from you. All Malich's show?"

"It was Malich who wrote up the plans that the terrorists used, sir," said Cole. "I only got here a few days ago."

"And yet your ass is going to go through the wringer just like his," said Alton. The general looked Cole up and down like he was sizing up the prototype of a new weapon. "Do you eat, Captain Cole?"

"Yes, sir."

"Lunch?" asked Alton.

"I was thinking about it," said Cole.

"Anybody expecting you?"

"No, sir."

"Any urgent appointments this afternoon?"

"Unless they need more debriefing time, sir."

"Come with me, Coleman."

A half hour later they were in a Thai restaurant in Old Town Alexandria across the street from the Torpedo Factory. The whole way, Alton had kept up a low-key interrogation. Where were you raised? Any family? Was your father military? Good service record—what was your best assignment so far? It was what passed for smalltalk between a general who outranked almost everybody but God and a lowly captain who still had no clue what his assignment at the moment even was.

Only after they ordered did Alton start in on talk that didn't sound so small anymore.

"So how do you see this whole thing going down, Coleman?"

"Down, sir?" asked Cole. He wasn't playing dumb, he just wasn't sure what the general was asking.

"The public crucifixion of Major Malich, Captain Coleman, and the U.S. military."

"Oh, that," said Cole. "Well, I'd say it's right on schedule, sir. We're at the innuendo stage right now. I give it till tomorrow before the first calls for a congressional investigating committee surface."

"They're already calling for that," said Alton.

"I mean, a committee to investigate Major Malich and me, sir. In particular."

"And investigate the entire Army," said Alton. "You and Malich being there yesterday, that's going to cause the whole Army a shitload of trouble."

"Yes, sir."

"If you two hadn't had to be heroes, if you'd just driven away, your faces wouldn't be all over the news and you wouldn't be under suspicion for anything."

"That didn't seem like an option at the time, sir," said Cole.

"Damn straight," said Alton. "Not an option. You don't stand by and do nothing while your country is being assaulted and innocent people are getting killed. Well, more or less innocent people."

Cole didn't know where he was going with this.

"I didn't like our President much, to tell you the truth, Coleman. Didn't trust him. Thought he was a clown. A puppet of the SecDef, God rest his soul. A SecDef who thought he could transform military culture. The two of them, thinking you could wage war like they did it in Vietnam, one hand tied behind our backs. Boots on the ground, kicking down doors, that's what would have cleaned things up in record time! You can't subdue an enemy that doesn't believe you beat them! Not this namby-pamby stuff about going in and making nice-nice with the locals."

Cole didn't know how to answer. It was obvious Alton was one of the old school, one of the guys who had no use for the new doctrines. But Cole's whole military career was built on the new doctrines—small forces that get to know not just the terrain but the people, so that locals start helping you. And Cole believed in it—the idea that you toss out the enemy regime, but do it without alienating the people. Get them to see you as their liberators and protectors, not their conquerors and occupiers. But Alton liked it the old way. And Cole couldn't see a thing to be gained by arguing with him.

"It's useful to know the local language," said Cole.

"The only thing you need to know how to say," said Alton, "is 'Put up your hands or I'll blow your ass to hell.'"

Cole tried a little levity. "I can say that in four Middle Eastern languages, sir."

Alton shook his head. "New model Army. Pure bullshit. But I went along! Civilian control of the military! The Constitution! I believe in it, God help me but I do. The SecDef wants to cripple our Army and the President says to go along, then my job is to implement the emasculation. The *gelding.*"

"We did some things," said Cole softly, "that took some balls to do."

"I'm not talking about you! Or Malich! You did what you were trained and ordered to do and you did it brilliantly. You're the real thing. Alvin York, Audie Murphy. The guys who get it done. The five percent who actually do the killing and the winning."

Cole couldn't say what he was thinking: What is this about? Why did you take me to lunch? So you could have an audience for some meaningless tirade about our dead President?

"I'm in the Pentagon now, sir," said Cole. "I don't carry a weapon right now."

"That's the problem right there," said Alton. "It's not the boys in the field, not the ones who are eating sand and sleeping with camels and firing their weapons and getting blown up by roadside bombs. It's us in the Pentagon, us right here who got clipped and don't even know it. Shooting blanks, that's what we're doing. We signed on to defend the Constitution, and now they're knocking it down and blaming *us* for it. Specifically, you and Malich, but it's all of us they'll be crucifying, don't think otherwise."

"The Constitution is working well enough, sir," said Cole. "President Nielson was sworn in before the smoke cleared."

"President," said Alton contemptuously. "If I got taken short without a toilet I wouldn't even piss down that man's throat. He's a hack and everybody knows it. *He's* our commander-in-chief?"

"That would be what the Constitution says, sir," said Cole.

"Yes, well, that's fine, my point isn't that he's a bad guy, my point is that he's weak, and that's what they want."

"Who, sir?"

"The people who set you and Malich up," said Alton. "The people who made damn sure Malich was there at the scene—almost blew it, though, didn't they, because you and Malich came *that* close to wrecking their plan. They didn't know what a soldier could do, did they! Didn't know that suppressing cellphones and cutting landlines wouldn't stop you! Didn't know our boys know how to *improvise!*"

"Who are those people, sir?" asked Cole.

"The Left, Coleman, and you know it. The blue-staters. The latte-sipping assholes who took over this country by taking over the law schools so that everybody on the bench has been brainwashed into thinking that the *written* Constitution is nothing but modeling clay, you can shape it into anything you want and what they want is for it to be a nation where marriage between faggots and lesbians is sacred and you can kill babies right up to the moment they're born and who gives a shit whether the people vote for it or a constitutional amendment could ever pass! They learned with the ERA—you're too young to remember that, but I do—Equal Rights Amendment, they couldn't get it through the state legislatures, so they learned their lesson. No more amendments! Just take over the courts and make them the dictators. Make them tell us that the Constitution says the *opposite* of the words on the paper and then it will take a constitutional amendment to set things back to rights!"

Cole hated it when people talked like this. Because sure, he felt like this a lot of the time, but he didn't like hearing somebody say it this way. Angrily. Abusively. Cole might hate the way the courts decided stuff that was supposed to be decided by supermajorities of the citizenry, but he wanted it to be discussed and corrected reasonably.

The trouble with Alton was that he had generalitis, the inflammation of the ego that came from having everybody salute you and say yessir all the time. You started to think it was you they were saluting, and not the stars. You started to think you were smart.

And maybe Alton *was* smart.

"I can see your face, Coleman," said Alton. "I know what you're thinking. You don't like me talking plain. I'm not supposed to say 'faggot.' I'm supposed to call them 'fetuses,' not 'babies.' I'm supposed to sound reasonable, not like an extremist. But *they* don't play by those rules, do they! *They* can say any outrageous, offensive, name-calling bullshit they think of. They can label everybody that doesn't lift their skirts or spread their cheeks for them as some kind of extremist wacko, but if you name *them* for what they are, then that *proves* you're an extremist wacko. It's a catch-22, isn't it, Coleman? If you argue against them with any kind of passion, then you're not worth listening to. And if you *don't* argue with passion, nobody hears you!

That's why they get things all their way. Nobody yells back at them!"

Coleman thought of listing a few talk-show hosts who did plenty of yelling back, but decided that wasn't a conversation he wanted to have. He wished profoundly that he had told Alton he had an urgent appointment. It was too late to "remember" one now, though.

"There *is* a point to my diatribe, Coleman," said Alton. "My point is this: What is this left-wing conspiracy going to *do* with the death of this President? Because you know that's who did this. That's why they're going to such lengths to implicate you and some nameless right-wing conspirator inside the White House. They want to discredit the people who still stand for something. They want this country thrown into chaos and blame it on the Right, so they can force their agenda through. I don't know why they hated this President so much. He was their boy. Look what he did—amnesty for illegals, socialized medicine, molly-coddling defeated nations instead of *occupying* them—this President made FDR look like Barry Goldwater, he was so damn liberal. But never liberal enough for *them*. Because they're insane. They have to have *everything* fit in with their vision of utopia. They're going to make us live in hell, and if you don't *call* it heaven, then off with your head!"

"There's still a conservative majority in Congress, sir, and President Nielson—"

"They'll all jump through hoops once the media is done with them. You know they will! Because they've got no spine."

"Sir," said Cole, "I don't know why you're telling me this."

"I'm telling you this," said Alton, "because we're not going to let it happen. They killed the President and the Vice President and SecDef and six *fine* soldiers who were doing their duty for their country, and now they're going to blame the *Army* for it and use it as an excuse to take over even more than they already have."

"What do you mean, you're not going to let it happen?" said Cole. "Sir?"

"I mean exactly what I'm saying. This is a time of national emergency. Like the American Civil War. President Lincoln said it best. 'The Constitution is not a suicide pact.' Sometimes you have to suspend parts of the Constitution in order to save the whole thing. The left-wing courts have already thrown out half of it. In order to put those parts back, we have to take steps. The new President can still lead, but with the Army behind him, and without the media twisting everything into a pack of lies. You and Malich are not going on trial, Coleman. Not in a court martial, not in a civilian court, and not in the media."

"Are you proposing a coup?" asked Cole. He couldn't help looking around to see who was listening.

"I'm proposing to save America," said Alton, "and return it to the system that made us great. I'm proposing to bring it back from the ruins of the extreme left. I'm proposing to restore a country where it's not a crime to be a Christian, where criminals go to jail, where marriage is between a man and a woman, and where we aren't killing millions of babies every year. Eisenhower's America. And don't give me any crap about 'does that mean segregation again?' because this is a racially integrated Army and we're not bringing back any of that racism shit. That was a good change and we're keeping it. We're going to let women keep the vote, too, in case you were going to ask that."

"I don't know what to say, sir," said Cole. Because at this moment it finally dawned on him. This guy was serious. He was going to try to use the Army to take control of the government, impose martial law, stifle the media, and nullify fifty years of Supreme Court decisions—the ones he didn't like, anyway.

Alton had just laid out his agenda and if Cole said no, was that his own death sentence?

"Say what's on your mind, Coleman," said Alton. "You've got nothing to fear from me, no matter what you say. I know you're a good man, but I also know that many good men will disagree with what I'm doing. I'm restoring democracy, not eliminating it. Majority rule. When everything's back the way it's supposed to be, then they can arrest me and put me on trial and shoot me for all I care. I'll be proud to die for my country. As long as you don't actively fight against me—and I mean with weapons, not with words—then nobody's going to touch you. So speak your mind."

"It's treason," said Cole.

"Absolutely," said Alton. "The Left has committed slow treason. The country is being strangled by treason. But yes, we're committing treason, too. We're bringing the force of the military to bear. Like in Turkey, where the army keeps the wackos from turning the country into another Iran. We're stepping in to save the country, no matter what it costs us."

"It's the wrong way, sir. We need to find out the real conspirators and expose them."

"And put them on trial? Like O. J. was put on trial? Like the courts allowed the Clintons to steal FBI files and withhold subpoenaed documents from Congress and commit perjury and accept bribes and nobody was ever put on trial? Like that? The courts in America are the heart of the leftist conspiracy. Only regular Americans get convicted in those courts. Americans like you."

"I won't help you, sir," said Cole.

"Well, there you go," said Alton.

"I'll work against you, sir."

"Do your damnedest," said Alton. "But just like yesterday, you're already too late."

"Am I?" said Cole. "Didn't it occur to you that my debriefers probably planted bugs on me? On my uniform?"

"Of course they did," said Alton. "But all your interrogators are with me on this, Coleman. You still don't see it. What I'm doing—what *we're* doing—is an Army operation."

"No way, sir," said Cole. "There's no way the whole Army is behind you."

"They will be," said Alton. "I wanted you with us because you and Malich would be great on camera. War heroes. The guys who tried to save the President and are now getting framed for killing him. But we can still use your story—we just won't put you on camera."

"I'll go on camera against you," said Cole.

"And what?" said Alton. "Tell the world that you *did* conspire to kill the President? Since the story we'll be telling happens to be true, I don't know what you'd say."

"I'd say that you don't save the Constitution by tearing it up," said Cole.

"Say what you want," said Alton. "Nothing you say will be broadcast. No one will hear it. No one will read it."

And for the first time it dawned on Cole that much as he hated the media, he and Malich *had* been able to get some version of their story out there. Leighton Fuller believed them, or at least thought they might be telling the truth, and he gave them their public hearing, and his editors went along with it. It wasn't some Pentagon committee deciding what could be published. Cole knew something about military culture, and he didn't want the Army controlling the American news media.

He didn't even want the Army controlling the Army.

"Sir," said Cole. "This is an all-volunteer military. We're all citizens of a free country. We took an oath to support the Constitution, not destroy it. To obey elected civilians, not dictate to them. Most of us get pissed off by a lot of things going on in this country, but our weapons are meant to point at foreign enemies, not at American news editors and reporters. If you think the Army is going to follow along blindly, you're crazy, sir."

"Well, you know what they say," said Alton. " 'Soldiers want to get paid and not die. Civilians want to be left alone.' We'll pay the soldiers and we won't ask them to die. We'll leave the civilians alone."

"Except the reporters and the judges."

"They ain't civilians, son," said Alton. "They're the tyrants and traitors." Alton stood up. "We're done here," he said. "You've been brainwashed, but that's fine, no harm."

He put two twenties down on the table and led the way out to his car. "As for the Army," Alton said, "we've succeeded in retiring most of the top officers who would oppose us. All the stateside forces of any size are already under our control. And our public statements will not be as plain as what I've said to you. We've got our own media experts, Coleman. We know how to spin this story."

They got in the car and Alton's driver started back toward the Pentagon. "It's the nice thing about how the Left has emasculated America. Most people really will just sit back and let it happen. There just aren't that many real men left in this country. You watch—inside of a week, we'll have all the editors asking us when to jump and how high. America has been pre-adapted to live under a dictatorship, because we already do. All we're doing is trading in politically correct judges for dedicated soldiers."

All the way back to the Pentagon, as Alton went on talking, all Cole could think about was: He can pretend he's not going to kill me, but this is going to lead to bloodshed almost immediately. He can pretend that he doesn't care what I do, but I just went on an enemies list.

They pulled into General Alton's reserved parking space. Cole did not open his door. "Sir," he said. "This is all working out so well for you. You were so ready. So what I want to know is this. Was it you? The Army, I mean. Your group inside the Army. Was it you that gave those plans of Major Malich's to Al Qaeda?"

Alton's brisk, cheery attitude disappeared at once, replaced by true rage. "By God I swear to you we did not," he said. "We were preparing, yes—for the day when a leftist President was elected, determined to destroy the military. We weren't going to stand for it. But that was still many months away. This President was an idiot. But he kept the military strong. We didn't want him dead."

"I believe you, sir," said Cole. "But can you vouch for everybody else in your . . . group?"

"I can, son," said Alton. "I can indeed. We had nothing to do with this. It took us by surprise. But we do contingency planning in the Pentagon, Coleman. When shit happens, we're ready to deal with it."

"I've got another contingency for you, sir," said Cole.

"What's that?"

"The guys who really did get the President killed—doesn't it occur to you that they know about your group and your contingency plans and they pulled this off specifically to get you to do exactly what you're doing? So they'd have an excuse to go to war to save the country from *you*?"

"Maybe," said Alton, "but so what? We've got all the guns."

# NINE

# JOB OFFER

It is possible to be too much smarter than your opponent. If you give him credit for more subtlety than he has, he can achieve tactical surprise by doing the obvious.

**THEY MIGHT** as well have stayed home, for all the difference it made in the children's activities. Mark was the kind of boy who remembered the friends he made in Aunt Margaret's neighborhood the last time they came to New Jersey, so he was already out doing something with them. Nick was holed up in some corner of the back yard, reading; he read outdoors so Cecily wouldn't keep telling him to go out and play. Lettie and Annie were whooping around with some old clothes Aunt Margaret let them play with; Cecily only worried when she couldn't hear them. And John Paul was her shadow; he had apparently decided that she was better than TV, because he didn't have to figure out the channels to get entertainment from her.

Not a single reporter had got wind of the fact that they were there, so it had been worth the drive. She had discussed it with Mark and he knew not to tell anybody that it was his dad who tried to save the President—and also came up with the plan that the terrorists used. The other kids didn't see anybody outside the house. With luck, they could keep something like a normal life for a few days more.

Until Reuben started testifying. Because the hue and cry was already beginning in Congress. They loved to strut in front of the cameras, didn't they, and spout off about things they knew nothing about. "Why was a United States soldier ordered to think of ways to kill the President?" demanded a Senator who should have known better, because he was in on all the contingency plans as part of his duties on the Armed Services Committee. Didn't he know that the essence of defense was to anticipate the enemy's attacks and prepare to meet them? Of course he knew it. But the people back home wouldn't know it.

Besides, the nominating conventions were coming up soon. In the Republican Party the nomination was still up in the air—no clear candidate had emerged. LaMonte Nielson wasn't even in the running, but there would soon be a groundswell to nominate him so they could have the advantage of incumbency.

Whereas the Democratic candidate had it nearly locked up, barring a massive swing of the few uncommitted delegates away from her.

The Senator who was grandstanding was one of those who had a handful of delegates. Maybe he thought everything would break his way at the convention if he made enough noise at Reuben's expense. What did *he* care that he was trashing the reputation of one of the best soldiers in the Army? If it got him a single vote, it was worth it to him.

"Oh, we're angry today," said Aunt Margaret, who was sitting at her computer desk in the kitchen, scanning pictures out of food magazines.

"They killed the President, Aunt Margaret."

"And they're hinting that it's all your husband's fault."

"I don't want to talk about it."

"Good. Then you can listen. Do you think I haven't been watching the news? How they make such a big deal about the fact that Reuben is the son of immigrants from Serbia? Then they always show a map of Serbia with Kosovo and Bosnia in big letters, as if his family had something to do with the war crimes of Milosevic and his stooges. As if Reuben were some troublemaking Bosnian Muslim. And how they've all picked up on the fact that he speaks Farsi.

They just can't let that go. He takes notes in Farsi. He thinks in Farsi. One time, just once, they explain that it was part of his military assignment to learn Farsi. Then they keep reminding people about his fluency in speaking the language of Iran. Never mind that it's also the language of half of Afghanistan. But you're only angry because they killed the President."

"Aunt Margaret, when I was little I thought you were the coolest, smartest grownup in the whole world," said Cecily.

"That would be right," said Margaret.

"But I'm trying not to think about it."

"I know. That's why I'm trying to dig your head out of the sand."

"I'm just staying sane. That may not seem such a high priority to you because you've never bothered trying."

Margaret burst out laughing. "Oh, you are so ticked off today!"

"How do the wives of politicians stand it? All the terrible things people say."

"They're in the game. Besides, their husbands' people are usually doing the same thing to the other guy."

"Well, what can Reuben do? Nothing."

Margaret let that one pass in silence. For a long minute.

"Nothing?" she said. "Is that what that article in *The Post* was? Nothing?"

"A lot of good it will do."

"It spun pretty well. His story is out there. All the innuendoes from the news media, but his story is available and people don't have to believe what they get pounded with on CNN."

"So maybe it will do some good."

"So *he's* doing something," said Margaret. "And you're . . . hiding."

"Oh, for Pete's sake."

"Your uncle Peter is dead, dear. And he never cared about politics."

"He cared about it all the time."

"Yugoslavian politics, yes. American politics, no. The

body count was so much lower in America, it was hard for him to stay interested."

"Come on. Under Tito there *was* no politics."

"No national politics. Local got very intense. Anyway, we're not talking about my late husband the Serbian atheist, God bless him. Remember, you weren't the first in the family to marry a Serb."

"We were talking about how you think I'm supposed to do something instead of sitting here nursing an ulcer."

"That's not a nice thing to call your little boy John Paul."

"I don't work in government anymore, Auntie M."

"And all the people that you used to know, they died? They emigrated to Ireland or Morocco?"

"Nobody that I knew could possibly have had anything to do with this."

"But they could have something to do with helping you find out things that will help your husband. For instance, there was a Congressman you once worked for who just got a sudden job promotion."

"And if I call him right now—assuming I could even get through—he'd assume I'm asking for a job."

"So you tell him that you're not, you just want some help, you know your husband did nothing wrong."

"He knows my husband did nothing wrong."

"Does he? I didn't remember you were even married when you worked for him."

Aunt Margaret was right. In fact, the idea of trying to get Congressman Nielson—no, President Nielson—to help protect Reuben had already occurred to her, in a vague sort of way, but she always pushed the thought out of her mind because she didn't want to be the kind of person who suddenly calls somebody the minute he becomes President. Office seekers. Hire me, make me important, put me in the White House.

Besides, there was that White House switchboard to deal with. She'd be routed . . . somewhere.

Not that LaMonte was in the White House yet. He had officially said that the First Lady could take all the time she needed to vacate the White House. In fact, the rumored quote was, "I like the house I live in, and I can commute." But everyone knew that was a ludicrous idea—it put too much of a burden on the Secret Service, which was already humiliated by having failed to protect the last President.

So where was he? What happened to his staff? No way would he go anywhere without Sandy, the battleaxe who ran his office—and his staff, especially the young wet-behind-the-ears aides like she had been—as if they were prisoners who had just been brought back from an escape attempt. And Sandy might even remember her.

What was Sandy's last name? She'd always just been . . . Sandy.

"Where's the phone?" asked Cecily.

"Long distance? On *my* telephone? What, is your cell-phone out of batteries?"

"You're the one who wanted me to get involved."

"Right, *you* involved, *me* not paying for anything except the vast quantities of food your children eat."

"They don't eat vast quantities, you just *cook* vast quantities."

"I want them not to die of starvation like fashion models."

Cecily got her cellphone out of her purse and then dialed LaMonte's office number from memory. After all these years.

Except in the meantime he had become Speaker. So the number got her somebody else. That was fine. "I'm such an idiot," she said. "Can you give me the phone number of the Speaker's office?"

"Oh, I can give it to you, honey, but it ain't gonna do you much good," said the southern woman on the phone. "The Speaker isn't the Speaker anymore, sweety."

"But I'm not looking to talk to President Nielson," she said. "It's Sandy Woodruff that I want to talk to."

"Well, she's *with* him, of course."

"But somebody in their old office can get a message to her."

"By smoke signal maybe, but here's the number, I was

looking it up the whole time I was talking to you, in case you thought I wasn't."

"Since when do you have to look up the number of the Speaker of the House?"

"My Congressman is in the other party, sweety. We don't call the Speaker much."

"You *should* have," said Cecily, imitating her southern drawl. "He's always been such a dear."

The woman laughed heartily. "Well, you're a caution. Good luck on getting your call returned."

Cecily got through to the Speaker's office. It was answered by a flustered aide—or perhaps an intern. Somebody who was not deemed important enough to take along to the White House.

"Sandy isn't available," said the kid. "But I'd be glad to take a message."

"Cecily Malich," said Cecily. "Only when Sandy knew me I was Cessy Grmek. I will definitely have to spell that for you."

"Oh, no need," said the kid. Definitely an intern.

"That means you aren't writing it down, because I assure you, you cannot spell it."

A faint sigh. A scruffing among papers. Finally: "All right, I have a pencil."

"Cessy. C-E-S-S-Y. Grmek. G-R-M-E-K. Can you say it back to me?"

"Did you leave something out? What I have here looks like a bad Scrabble turn."

"Say 'Grrrr' like a bear. And then 'mek' rhymes with 'check.'"

The girl said it twice.

It had the desired effect. She could hear Sandy's voice in the background. "Cessy Grmek? I thought she was dead or got married." In a moment, Sandy was on the line. "What are you bothering us for, you office-seeking hanger-on?"

"I saw LaMonte on TV," said Cessy. "I think he's handling himself splendidly."

"Of course he is. I tell him every word to say."

"Listen, Sandy, my call is selfish, but I don't want a job."

"Too bad. Just the other day he said, 'Whatever happened to that girl with no vowels? How can this office run without her?'"

"He did not."

"But he would have, if I'd remembered to tell him to say it. Get on with your request, my dear. Remember that the President of the United States is not the Wizard of Oz. Chances are very good that you will not get your wish."

"I did get married, Sandy. And my husband is Major Reuben Malich."

It took a beat for Sandy to realize why she knew that name. "You're saying you're married to the Hero of the Tidal Basin?"

"The hero who is getting set up to take the fall for the assassination plot."

"You know what, Cessy? I think LaMonte will want to talk to you himself."

"No, I don't want to bother him."

"Your husband is the real thing, Cessy. Not that you aren't, of course. But he's a hero. Not just yesterday, but before. He's the kind of soldier they make movies about."

"I just don't want the movie to be *The Dreyfus Affair*."

"I don't get to see any of the new movies."

"It's an old one. Jose Ferrer."

"You're thinking of *I Accuse!* From Zola's famous article 'J'Accuse.' Jose Ferrer directed it, too. 1958."

"Sandy, your memory astonishes me."

"It's not the memory, it's the superb retrieval system. And I don't think President Nielson wants your husband to spend years of his life fighting a false charge of treason, either. What number are you at?"

Cecily gave it to her.

Then the conversation was over. She flipped her phone closed.

"Just as I thought," said Aunt Margaret. "The President himself is going to call back."

"She thinks he might," said Cecily. "But I think he won't."

"Then turn your phone off."

"Okay, I think he might."

"Are you going to tell him you switched parties?"

"I didn't switch parties," said Cecily. "I was a Democrat the whole time I worked for him."

"But not *much* of a Democrat."

"Moynihan worked for the Nixon White House and *he* was a Democrat."

"A Democrat with a dark, dark stain on his tie."

"I did a lot of good things with LaMonte. We got things done. Because he's a practical politician. And I knew how to talk to liberals without sounding like a doctrinaire Republican so I could make friends with key aides on the other side of the aisle."

"And then you gave it all up to have these beautiful babies," said Margaret. "Including the one who currently has nothing on from the waist down."

"I hope it's J. P. you're talking about."

"Short? Smeary face and butt and hands?"

"That would be the one." Cecily was out of her chair and in hot pursuit.

Aunt Margaret called after her. "Don't let him sit down anywhere!"

"Too late!" Cecily called back.

By the time J. P. was bathed and dressed and the carpet more or less cleaned up from the fudgesicle that he had set down and sat upon, it had been forty-five minutes. Her cellphone chimed.

"Don't you have a special ringtone for calls from the President?" asked Aunt Margaret.

"Hold please for the President," said a voice on the line.

And then: "Cessy, I didn't know that was your husband. I've watched that footage a half-dozen times and I think he and the other boy were splendid. Bartholomew Coleman, right? A captain. And your husband's a major. Brilliant record in the war. They're starting to tear at him already, aren't they?"

So Sandy had briefed him.

"I really called just to tell you—oh, this is silly, I'm just wasting your time—Mr. President, he's the—"

"LaMonte. Please. I'm not on Rushmore yet. There are forty guys ahead of me in line."

"LaMonte, Reuben Malich is the real thing. A true patriot. Unlike me, he really is a Republican. He loved the President. This is tearing him apart."

"I can imagine."

"I'm not just a loyal wife talking here. I just wanted to make sure you knew that whatever they say about him, whatever evidence got planted to incriminate him, he did not do anything wrong. He fulfilled a legitimate assignment. He did *not* pass those plans on."

"Oh, I'm quite sure of that," said LaMonte.

"What I'm asking is—stand by him, sir. Please."

"Let me tell you my dilemma," said LaMonte. "I'm walking into a White House filled with people chosen by the late President. They're used to regarding me as an obstacle to getting things done because they never understood that the Speaker isn't boss of the House the way the President is boss of the White House. But these people have been part of the administration. And one of them—at least one of them—pinpointed the President so that somebody could kill him."

"You've got trust issues. But my husband—"

"Don't jump to conclusions, Cessy. I don't have trust issues, I have a major world-class investigation going on around me here while I'm trying to transition into being President. Plus everybody's crying, which is understandable but doesn't help much. I need you here. I need somebody I can trust."

"I'm a Democrat, remember?"

"I know, and I need someone who knows that language, it's foreign to me."

"LaMonte, I'm flattered, I'm *honored*, but I have a family."

"I'll pay you a huge salary. We raised all the White House salaries last session and I promise you, you can afford to live in Georgetown if you want to."

"LaMonte. My parents already own a house in Georgetown, if I needed one. You can't lure me with money. You can't lure me at all. But as I said, I'm honored."

"Money can't seduce you? What about pleading? I can whimper and beg if you want. I learned how to do that in conference committees."

"You can't use me in the White House. My husband will be testifying before the congressional committee investigating the assassinations. And it won't be pretty. The last thing you need is, 'Major Malich, whose wife is an aide to President Nielson.' There *is* such a thing as bad publicity."

"Well, just for you, I'll wave my wand and make that all go away."

"If only," said Cecily.

"You'll see. We're going to have a very harmonious administration."

"Don't count on much of a honeymoon."

"Work for me, Cessy. Your husband won't hurt us, he'll help. He's a hero. You're the wife of a hero. Plus Sandy assures me you're the only aide she ever liked."

"She did not like me," said Cecily. "Not till I left."

She felt herself getting sucked into the vortex. She really did miss it. And to think of a White House in transition, under internal investigation, in desperate need of people who could concentrate, who could get things done—she knew she could do it. She had a knack for getting along with people. For isolating differences and making them seem small. She was good at the minutiae of making things happen in Washington. She wanted to say yes.

But she wanted even more to say no. The last thing Reuben needed right now was a wife with a sixteen-hour-a-day job. It had been her decision to stay home with the kids and she had made the right choice—for her and Reuben, anyway. With Reuben often gone for weeks and months at a time, the kids needed somebody who was an island of stability in their lives.

"We've got five kids, Mr. President. You know better than to try to take me away from them."

"Patriotic pep talk won't do it?"

"No, sir," she said.

"Well, I'll tell you what. The offer's open for a month. Change your mind before August, and you're in. Meanwhile, don't fret about your husband. Major Malich is going to have the full support of the White House and the Army. I guarantee that nothing bad will happen to him."

That was all she could ask for. And he had a lot to do. No time for small talk. She thanked him, said good-bye, and hung up.

"He tried to hire you," said Aunt Margaret.

"You heard my answer."

"I heard you considering it," said Aunt Margaret. "Hard thing to turn down, isn't it? In the White House, when the President knows you and trusts you, you get real power, yes?"

"Yes, I suppose," said Cecily. "Good thing I get all the power I want from bullying my children."

"He promised to help your husband, but you still look worried."

"I *am* worried," she said. "Why am I worried?"

"You're a Croat," said Margaret. "Nothing's ever so good but what it can all come crashing down, and Croats never forget that."

"Yes, what was your toast at our wedding? 'Every day that ends with you two still speaking to each other is a triumph over human nature.' "

"Or words to that effect," said Margaret. "And I was right."

"There's something. Wrong. It's . . . I don't like the way he promised he could make everything go smoothly for Reuben. If there's anyone on God's green earth who knows that Congress can*not* be controlled from the White House, it's LaMonte Nielson."

"Maybe he thinks he'll still have clout in Congress."

"No, he often said that the only President who ever controlled Congress was Johnson, and he did it by being a world-class . . . jerk."

"A tush flambé," said Margaret.

"And he can't control the press, either. They're going to try to kill Reuben's reputation and dance on the grave."

"He just got made President. He's feeling grandiose."

"He was never grandiose. But no, he was joking. Cajoling me."

"And yet you're still worried."

"I'm worried because Reuben is off the radar. Is he coming here? Is he going somewhere else to hide? Is he leaving the country? Is he on some kind of assignment? Is he arrested? Is he . . ."

The front door slammed open.

"Oh, be gentle with my ancient house!" cried Aunt Margaret.

"Dad's got a new car!" shouted Mark.

"He's here," breathed Cecily.

"Go help your father with his luggage," called Margaret.

"He doesn't have any!"

When Cecily got to the front door, carrying J.P., the garage door was already closing with Reuben and whatever car he was driving on the inside. So Cecily went back through the house and intercepted him at the inside garage door. They kissed and Reuben took J.P. into his arms and greeted the girls, who had already run downstairs. "Where's Nick?" he asked.

"Reading about strong-thewed women and bewitching men," said Mark.

"In the back yard," said Cecily.

Reuben gave everybody another hug and then went out into the back yard in search of his second son.

They gathered in the kitchen and Reuben gave them all a blow-by-blow account of his fight with the terrorists. Lettie and Annie were fascinated, but their reaction was most at the level of "Oh, gross," and "Did you see them after they were dead?" Mark wanted more details, but in reply Reuben reminded him that this story was not to be told outside the family. "If you tell anybody that your dad is Major Reuben Malich, *any* of your friends, pretty soon there'll be reporters outside the house and we won't have any peace."

Mark was disgusted. "I know that, Dad," he said.

Nick said nothing. He just watched his father. And listened. And took it all in. He was the one that worried Cecily. Nick built his life around imaginary heroes, even if the fantasy novels *were* supposed to be funny. And then look at the father he had—the real thing, the strong-thewed warrior, the hero. How could Nick ever measure up to *that* fantasy?

Nick was the one who would go into the Army, she thought. He'll think he has to in order to be a real man. Only the Army is not where he belongs. He needs to have time to himself. He needs a regular life. He needs to be surrounded by a gentle reality. Because he's fragile. Real combat would hurt him. He would get scars that would never heal.

Scars like the ones that gnawed at his father. You don't kill men without taking damage to your soul. Even when you're defending yourself and other people. Even when the bad guys are truly evil. And if you ever get to the point where it doesn't damage you to kill, then you've lost your decency. Thank God Reuben had never reached that point, and never would. But Nick—could he bear it, to have those wounds on his soul?

"So I'm on vacation for a few days," said Reuben. "Maybe longer."

"Two words," said Mark. "Atlantic City!"

"You are way too young to scope out babes, Mark," said Reuben.

"I said that *once,* Dad. As a *joke.*"

"I don't care what you said. I know how I've seen you look."

"Yeah, well, have you seen how they *dress*?"

"You're ten. That's way too young for you even to care."

And on they went. The war talk was over. But the kids lingered. Dad-time was precious. And it wasn't often he actually told them about what he did as a soldier. They didn't need that knowledge. It would only frighten them when he was away. This time, though, Cecily knew that he had to tell them, because they were going to hear the negative stuff, and they had to know the story the way it really happened.

After a while, the girls dragged their father upstairs to look at whatever insane project they were working on together—Lettie always had a project, and Annie always ended up being chief assistant who never, ever got her way on anything, and they ended up yelling and crying and then going right back to the same project because Annie would rather be miserable and oppressed *with* Lettie than free but alone.

Mark went with them because he was Mark and had to be with people who were doing something. J. P. went with them because Reuben was holding him. Which left Cecily alone at the kitchen table with Nick.

"What are you thinking?" she said. "If it involves ice cream, I think the answer is there are still two fudgesicles that J. P. didn't smear all over his body."

Nick ignored the offered ice cream—not a surprise. He was mostly indifferent to food. "The king is dead," he said. "Long live the king."

"What?"

"You asked what I was thinking," said Nick. "Somebody killed the President, and all anybody can think about is, How does this benefit me?"

"I'm not thinking that way," said Cecily.

"No, 'cause you and Dad are thinking about how it's going to hurt you. They're saying things that make Dad look like he was maybe part of the assassination instead of the guy who tried to stop it."

"It's how they sell papers."

"That's what I meant," said Nick. "See? The President is dead—how can we sell papers? The President is dead—how can I take advantage of it?"

"And you're nine years old, right?" asked Cecily.

"I know you think I read too much fantasy," said Nick, "but this is what it's all about. Power. Somebody dies, somebody leaves, everybody comes in and tries to take over. And you just have to hope that the good guys are strong enough and smart enough and brave enough to win."

"Are they?"

"In the fantasy novels," said Nick. "But in the real world, the bad guys win all the time. Genghis Khan tore up the world. Hitler lost in the end, but he killed millions of people first. Really bad stuff happens. Evil people get away with it. You think I don't know that?"

Our children are way too smart for their own good, thought Cecily. "Nick, you're absolutely right. So do you know what we do? We make an island. We make a castle. We dig a moat around it and we put up walls that are strong, made of stone."

"I guess you're not talking about Aunt Margaret's house," said Nick.

"You know what I'm talking about," said Cecily. "I'm talking about family, and faith. Here in this house, we're not trying to take advantage. Our family doesn't try to profit from the death of the king. Our family always has enough to share, even if we don't have enough to eat. Do you understand?"

"Sure," said Nick. "That's church talk. Because Dad has a weapon and goes out and kills the bad guys. He doesn't just hide in a castle inside a moat and help the poor and the sick."

"Your dad," said Cecily, "does not go out and kill the bad guys. He goes out and does what he's ordered to do, and the goal is to persuade the bad guys that they won't get their way by killing people, so they'd better stop."

"Mom," said Nick, "all you're saying is that our Army persuades them to stop killing people by being better at killing people than they are."

She slumped back in her chair. "Hard to reconcile that with Christianity, isn't it?"

"No it's not," said Nick. " 'Greater love hath no man than this, that he lay down his life for his friends.' "

"You *listen?*"

"I read."

"I just turned down an offer from the President. La-Monte Nielson. I used to work for him. I must have done a good job, because he wants me to come work in the White House."

"Are you going to?"

"No, I'm not. And do you know why?"

"Because of us?" said Nick.

"Because the best thing I can do to make this world a better place is to do a really brilliant job of raising you kids. And I can't if I'm not home to do it."

"If you worked in the White House," said Nick, "you might have been one of the ones they blew up."

"But I wasn't. And I won't be."

"They've got to be mad at Dad," said Nick.

"Who?"

"The boss terrorists. He shot their guys. He stopped one of their rockets. He almost stopped them from killing the President."

"I suppose they're a little bit mad at him. But they didn't expect us not to shoot back."

"They're not going to come here to kill us, are they?"

"No," said Cecily.

"In the movies, they always go after the hero's family."

"They do that because it's a Hollywood formula. To make the movie scarier so you'll keep watching for the whole two hours. In the real world, these terrorists don't care about regular people like us. They strike at big targets—like the World Trade Center and the President."

"And the Pentagon," said Nick.

"And soldiers in the field. We've always known that was Dad's job. But our house? Like I said—it's a castle."

Nick nodded. Then he got up and went to the fridge and opened the freezer compartment and took out a fudgesicle. "Want one?" he said.

"I don't like chocolate," Cecily answered.

"A creamsicle?" said Nick.

"Bring me one, you monster of temptation," she said.

He tossed her a creamsicle and kept the fudgesicle for

himself. "Do you ever wonder," he said as he unwrapped it, "what it would feel like to smear this all over your body?"

Cecily made the connection. "You didn't happen to say that to J. P., did you?"

"His fudgesicle was dripping all over his hand and he was getting all frantic about it."

"He was in the back yard?"

"He turns doorknobs just fine, Mom. Didn't you know that?"

"So you said, 'Wonder what it would feel like to smear this all over?' "

"I told him he was already halfway covered in fudgesicle, he might as well take his clothes off and finish the job."

"And you didn't think to watch him to make sure he didn't?"

Nick looked at her like she was crazy. "Why would I do that? It was *funny* watching him wipe his butt with a fudgesicle."

"Oh, yes," said Cecily nastily. "You read *comic* fantasies."

"What's the point of having a little brother if you can't talk him into doing stupid things?"

"Nick, please don't do that again. J. P. is not your toy."

"He's *your* toy. But aren't you supposed to share?"

"You know I'm very angry with you."

"Not *very*," he said, reverting to their old game.

"Very *very*," she said.

"Not *very* very very."

"Very *very* very very very very very veriver vy. Very," she said.

"You did that on purpose."

"I cannot say 'very' that many times in a row without stumbling."

"Come on, Mom, you speak a language that has no vowels."

"Croatian has vowels. We just don't need them in *every* syllable."

Then everybody trooped down from upstairs and the private conversation was over.

Cecily didn't get a chance to be alone with Reuben until dusk, when they went out and sat on the glider on the patio. Cecily told him about talking to the President and declining his job offer. Reuben told her about talking to Leighton Fuller at *The Post*. "And Cole telephoned me," said Reuben. "General Alton is planning a coup. Keep Nielson as a figurehead. Maybe it'll happen. Alton's always been a big talker. But there are people who see the world his way. Maybe he has support. Maybe people will go along with him."

"So what are you going to do about it?" asked Cecily.

"Keep my head down," said Reuben. "There are things that a major in the United States Army doesn't have the power to do. If they really do it, though, I'm resigning my commission. I signed on to serve the United States of America, not some committee of generals who think they have the right to decide how the country should go."

"It won't happen," she said. "It can't happen. That's . . . it's so Latin American. So *Turkish*. It doesn't happen *here*."

"Until it does," said Reuben. "Something else Cole said."

"What?"

"He quoted something General Alton said to him. Quoted to him. What he remembers Alton saying is, 'Soldiers want to get paid and not die. Civilians want to be left alone. We'll pay the soldiers and we won't ask them to die. We'll leave the civilians alone.'"

"That's pretty cynical. Does he really think people will give up freedom that easily?"

"Here's the funny thing," said Reuben. "That's not an old saying. Where I first heard it was at Princeton. Averell Torrent said it."

"Oh, yes, I forgot he was your professor there."

"He's a brilliant man, and a constant devil's advocate. I thought he had it in for me, and then he . . ."

"Recruits you."

"I'm not *sure* he got me the contacts that I've been working with. They never mentioned his name."

"But you assumed."

"Anyway, he said it twice in class—and it was in one of his books. You know me, that guaranteed I'd memorize it. 'All the common people want is to be left alone. All the ordinary soldier wants is to collect his pay and not get killed. That's why the great forces of history can be manipulated by astonishingly small groups of determined people.' "

"That's not *exactly* what Alton said to Cole. If Cole remembered it right."

"Cole's a memorizer," said Reuben.

"Like you."

"Word for word," said Reuben. "I think Alton has met Torrent. Or at least read his books."

"Of course he's met him," said Cecily. "Torrent is NSA."

"As of this morning," said Reuben.

"But he's been in the NSA's office for a couple of years."

"This may shock you, my dear, but the NSA staff and the top brass at the Pentagon don't get together every night and schmooze."

"But you think Torrent and Alton did?"

"I think Alton heard Torrent speak. About how America can't become an empire during its democratic phase. About how we've outgrown our democratic institutions. They need to be revised, drastically, but everybody has so much invested in the old system that nobody can build the consensus to change it. A Gordian knot. Time to slice through it if America is ever going to achieve its greatness."

"Not manifest destiny, manifest dictatorship?"

"I always took it as Torrent warning us about the movement of history. What lies ahead if we're not careful. But it's possible to hear him the wrong way—to hear what he's saying and think, Oh, good idea, let's do that."

"So you think Alton's been planning to move America away from democratic institutions for a while now, and this is just a pretext?"

"You don't build a coup overnight," said Reuben. "Here's the thing. Cole asked him outright if his group stole my plans and gave them to the assassins. Of course he said no. But Cole believes him. He thinks Alton isn't a good enough actor to sound so genuinely appalled at the thought."

"Do you know this General Alton?"

"I know *of* him," said Reuben. "I never actually served under him. Well, I guess technically I did, but never under his direct command. Layers, you know?"

"So you just have to take Cole's word for it?"

"Cole's a smart guy," said Reuben.

"But you still can't do anything about it."

"No," said Reuben. "But what I'm thinking is, Torrent is smart, he's charismatic. What if, by writing about the great forces of history, he's accidentally changed them? Like he said, they can be manipulated by astonishingly small groups of determined people."

"Like Alton's coup."

"Like whoever gave my plans to the terrorists. I don't think it was Alton. But that still leaves us trying to figure out who it is."

"What we need is the computer guy," said Cecily.

"Who's that?"

"In every mystery novel these days, it seems like the detective has some friend who can work miracles on the computer and find information nobody else can find. We need that guy. You call him up, tell him what you need to know, and in a little while he comes back with exactly the facts you need."

"When you say it like that, it sounds like a wizard from one of Nick's novels."

"I was thinking it sounded more like God," she said. "You pray, you get answers."

"Yeah," said Reuben. "You're right. We need that guy."

"Don't have him, though, do we?"

"All you got is me, and all I got is you."

"And Cole," said Cecily. "And DeeNee. And Load and Mingo and Babe and Arty and . . ."

"And not one of them can grant a miracle."

"But *I* know the President, and *he* promised we'll have one."

"That's why I was so smart to marry you."

Nothing was actually any better. But Cecily felt like it was better, sitting there on the glider with Reuben. When they were apart, she was perfectly competent and confident, but . . . there was something always at risk. Things could go wrong. When Reuben was there, she simply felt safer. He wouldn't let things get hopelessly out of hand. He'd put it all in perspective for her. The problems would all be somehow outside the walls of the castle, and inside, as long as Reuben was there, she was safe. The children were safe.

"Retire right now," said Cecily. "Come home and be with us always."

"Think Aunt Margaret will let us stay here?"

"I can't think why not. We're excellent company, and thanks to J. P. she's going to get a free carpet shampooing."

"I don't want to hear the story of that one," said Reuben.

"I don't want to tell it," said Cecily. "But Nick is involved."

"Has he taken to the dark side?"

"J. P. does whatever Nick suggests."

"I wonder," said Reuben. "Is that how J. P. got toilet trained so young?"

That had never occurred to Cecily before, but it was possible, wasn't it? Nick says something and J. P. uses the toilet forever afterward. "So he can use his powers for good as well as evil."

"We all can," said Reuben. "It's telling the difference that gets so hard."

# TEN

# FAIR AND BALANCED

If you always behave rationally, then reason becomes the leash by which your enemy pulls you. Yet if you knowingly make irrational decisions, have you not betrayed your own ability? The battlefield is not a place for actors, playing the role of this or that style of commander, for you can always imitate a worse commander, but never a better one. You must be yourself, even if your enemy comes to know your weaknesses, for you cannot pretend to have personal abilities and traits that you do not have.

**AS A** soldier, Cole had forced himself to learn to wait until an order was given. It wasn't that he didn't trust his commander to make the right decision. It's that he couldn't stand to do nothing.

As a boy growing up, he couldn't hold still, not even in church. It wasn't ADHD—he didn't fidget, and he could easily concentrate on the task at hand for hours and hours. It's that he couldn't stand not to accomplish something. Why *shouldn't* he clip his fingernails during a sermon? That way he'd hear the sermon *and* accomplish a job that needed doing.

His mother listened to his argument and answered with her typical "Interesting thought." But she heard him—she always heard him. That night at dinner she brought in a roll of toilet paper and, after taking her first bite, spooled off a section of toilet paper, lifted the back of her dress, and made as if to use the paper. Cole yelled at her to stop, to which she replied, "But this way I can chew my food *and* accomplish a job that needs doing."

"Not in front of *me!*" Cole said.

Out of his own mouth, he made her point for her.

So he learned to wait. And in the Army, he learned again. Nothing like live-fire exercises to concentrate the mind. He schooled himself to wait for many hours, for days. He learned to hide even the fact that he was waiting.

But that was war. He knew as soon as General Alton brought him back to the Pentagon that he couldn't do *nothing*.

He didn't even go back to the office. There was too much danger that Alton's reassurances about how nothing would happen to him were a scam. So easy to detain him— soldiers didn't have the rights of civilians against phony arrests. They could say he needed to be interrogated again. Then he'd disappear. When Congress subpoenaed him, the Army would tell them that Cole was on duty somewhere. And then his family would get word that he had been killed in action. His body would be produced with all the appropriate wounds.

How could he consider this kind of thinking paranoid? There was a general openly plotting a military coup. Cole's inclination and his sworn duty as a soldier and a citizen required that he do whatever was within his power to stop it from happening.

So he got in his car and started driving. CNN or Fox News? Atlanta or New York? On the one hand, CNN would be all too eager to hear about a right-wing coup-in-progress. On the other hand, Cole's purpose wasn't to inflame people against conservatives, it was to be heard by soldiers who might be tempted to cooperate with Alton's coup. And *those* soldiers regarded CNN as being almost as much of an enemy to the America they loved as NPR. They'd be watching Fox.

When he called Rube from the car to tell him about Alton, he couldn't quite bring himself to report where he was going and what he intended to do. He knew that was wrong. That it was stupid. *Why did I hide that information?* he asked himself. The answer was obvious—you didn't have to have a psych degree to figure out that he didn't tell Rube what he was doing because he fully expected Rube to order him not to do it. Or to talk him out of it by persuasion alone.

He thought of all the reasons why he shouldn't do it.

They won't believe it. So they won't broadcast it.

If they do believe it, they still won't broadcast it because Alton's people have already gotten to them.

If they believe it and broadcast it, I'll come across as a complete wacko. Especially if everyone denies everything I'm saying and the coup doesn't actually take place.

If they believe it and broadcast it and the coup happens, at best I'll be out of a job. At worst I'll be dead.

And it won't make a bit of difference to history whether I do this or not. It's a completely futile campaign. I'm wasting myself for nothing. I'm pulling the pin on a grenade just so I can fall on it. Either the coup happens or it doesn't, regardless of what I say now.

Yet he kept driving north, up I-95 to Delaware and then across the river into New Jersey and its ugly toll road that funneled you to New York City as if you were being flushed down a toilet.

He found public parking, mortgaged his firstborn child to pay for it, and then walked to 1211 Sixth Avenue—no, "Avenue of the Americas," as if the fancy name changed where it was located—and threw himself on the mercy of Fox News.

Army interrogators were trained never to reveal any reaction to what the person they were questioning might tell them. The reporters and producers who interviewed him tried to do the same, but they couldn't hide their skepticism. Until it finally dawned on somebody that he was one of the two guys in that Tidal Basin video they'd been running for the past twenty-four hours.

*Then* they loved him. Only they didn't know what to

make of his story. "We can't corroborate," said one of the producers, finally. "Nobody backs up your story."

"I'm not surprised," said Cole.

"The thing is, we can't run it as news unless we know we can stand behind it."

So it was all for nothing.

"What we *can* do, Captain Coleman, is interview you on the air. You're newsworthy because of what you and Major Malich did yesterday, trying to save the President and nearly succeeding. In that interview, you can tell the story of your meeting with General Alton. Then the news is not that there's going to be a coup, the news is that you *said* there was going to be a coup. We don't have to stand behind the truthfulness of what you say, we only have to stand behind the fact that you said it on the air."

"Okay." Cole knew that their interview shows were largely during the primetime hours. Who would he get? Greta Van Susteren? Hannity and Colmes?

"Bill O'Reilly wants you," said the producer. "It's the most-watched show on cable TV, so that's a good thing, right?"

"Right."

"Captain Coleman," she said. "I don't think you're lying. But I sure hope you're wrong."

"I hope so, too," he said. "Though if I am, I'll look pretty silly, won't I?"

"You got a lot of hero points yesterday. Even if you get a bunch of nut points tonight, they'll probably balance out."

"Am I going to be one of the guys O'Reilly goes after? Or one of the ones he treats sympathetically?"

"What, you think Bill tells *us* what he's going to say?"

"Come on," said Cole. "He talks from a script just like everybody else."

"Actually," said the producer, "that's just the talking points. Everything else, he makes up as he goes along. The thing is, Bill likes soldiers. He likes heroes. At the same time, he's going to be pretty skeptical of a claim that the Army's going to stage a coup."

"A small element within the Army is going to attempt it," said Cole.

"Like I said, you just stick to your story and tell the truth. I don't think Bill's going to hurt you. But he's going to give you plenty of chances to hurt yourself." She leaned closer to him. "Captain Coleman, here's the main law of TV interviews. Whoever gets mad, loses. Don't get mad. Don't even *show* anger."

Cole smiled at her. "Ma'am, you don't survive in the U.S. Army without being able to listen to stupidity for hours on end without showing the slightest reaction."

"Good," she said. "Because we're trying to get General Alton onto the program via a hookup in the Washington studio."

"He'll just deny everything."

"That's right," she said. "And he should have a chance to do it. Fair and balanced, remember?"

**IT WAS** Mark who told them that Cole was going to be on O'Reilly that night. He came home from a friend's house and charged into the living room, where Reuben was taking something like a nap on the couch. "The other guy's going to be on Fox tonight."

Still a little groggy, Reuben was sure he must have missed something. "Who's the first guy?"

"You are. The other guy, the guy who was shooting terrorists with you. He's going to be on *The O'Reilly Factor*."

Reuben made himself alert at once. "Okay. Thanks, Mark. You heard this at a friend's house?"

"His dad was watching Fox News when he got off work."

"But you aren't supposed to tell people—"

"Dad, I'm not supposed to tell them that you're *here*. They already know that you're my dad. It's too late for me to deny *that*."

They kept the TV on while they ate dinner—usually against the rules—but the promos for O'Reilly were neutral enough. Tonight Bill talks with one of the heroes of the fight at the Tidal Basin. Only as they got closer to the actual show did the promos start talking about "astonishing revelations" and then, in the last promo, "serious charges" against "high-ranking officers."

"Sounds like they got some corroboration," said Reuben.

"Sounds like they're hyping a TV show," said Cessy.

When Cole's segment came on, Reuben felt like leaving the room. He liked this soldier, he trusted him, but military people were notoriously bad on television. They kept their cool, yes, but they didn't let *anything* show. They usually came across wooden. Scripted, even.

Cole, though, looked like a real guy. With normal human emotions. At first O'Reilly got him talking about the fight at the Tidal Basin. And Cole told it clearly but humanly—it didn't sound memorized. He skipped around a little. And when he talked about how they didn't get the other launcher in time, he choked up and it looked genuine. "People call us heroes but it doesn't feel like that," said Cole. "It feels like mission failure."

"But it wasn't your mission," said O'Reilly.

"My mission is to defend the United States of America and its Constitution, sir," said Cole. "It was being attacked, and there was nobody else close enough to make a difference. Rube and I—Major Malich and I, we both keep thinking, what if we'd chosen a different target. Driven a little faster. Run harder. Shot sooner. One second, and maybe we could have stopped it."

"In my book you *are* a hero, Captain Coleman," said O'Reilly. "Heroes don't always succeed. They're the ones that try." Then he took a commercial break with the promise that there'd be more with Captain Cole after the ads.

"So far so good," said Cecily.

"He didn't go to Fox News to talk about the Tidal Basin," said Reuben.

When the show came back on, it wasn't just Cole on the screen. There was also an inset showing General Alton. "Joining us from our Washington studio is General Chapel Alton. Thanks for joining us, General."

"It's an honor to be on the program with Captain Coleman, sir," said Alton.

"Oh, right, like he doesn't know what Cole's going to talk about," said Reuben.

"It's television," said Cessy. "War by other means."

When O'Reilly turned to him, Cole briefly told about his lunch meeting with General Alton. Reuben liked the way he told it without anger, though a little bit of outrage did creep into his voice.

But then it was Alton's turn, and this guy was a pro. He showed no anger, either. In fact, he immediately apologized. "Captain Coleman is a great soldier. I took him to lunch because I wanted to get to know him better. I knew his service record, which is excellent. I'd seen the video that everybody else has seen."

"Did you say the things Captain Coleman tells us you said," O'Reilly asked him.

"I warned him about what the media was going to do to him. We've already seen some of it on several news programs. Things that certain members of Congress are saying. Why were these two soldiers there in the first place, armed, in a city park? And of course Major Malich had already broken protocol and told *The Post* about his having designed a similar contingency plan, so that was hitting the fan, too. I warned him about the turmoil he was going to face."

"Nothing about a coup? Stopping the media from casting aspersions on Captain Coleman and Major Malich?"

"In my effort to express sympathy with his predicament, sir, I'm sure I must have said things that Captain Coleman misconstrued. I'm sorry if I led him to a false impression about just how much support he was going to get. We believe in civilian leadership of the military in this country, period. I took it for granted that he would know that our support for him would stop at that line."

O'Reilly turned to Cole. "Well, Captain Coleman? What do you say to that?"

"Don't get mad," whispered Cessy.

"First," said Cole, "I have to correct one thing—Major Malich and I were not armed. After we realized what was happening, we *obtained* arms from the ranger station in the park."

"Don't digress, don't digress," murmured Reuben.

"No, it's okay," said Cessy. "He's establishing credibility."

"I'm glad to hear that General Alton now disavows any of the plans he described to me at lunch today. I urged him to do so at the time. But I can assure you, Mr. O'Reilly, that there was no mistake. General Alton was quite specific. He regarded the assassination of the President and Vice President and Secretary of Defense as a pretext for a left-wing assault on the Constitution. His plans were all designed to forestall that, he said. But they were quite specific."

While Cole was talking, Alton made the mistake of doing some eye-rolling. "Bad form, General," said Cessy. "Makes people dislike you. Makes people think you're lying."

There was a little more back and forth, with Alton showing a little anger—not much, just enough to weaken him.

"This is a guy who does congressional hearings," said Cessy. "I'm surprised he's letting it get under his skin."

"It's because he's lying," said Reuben.

"Oh, come on. Like they don't lie to Congress."

"They *spin* to Congress."

"Well, he's spinning this, too, isn't he? 'I'm sure it's just a misunderstanding.' That's fartspeak for 'I said it, you jerk, but you weren't supposed to tell.' "

" 'Fartspeak'?"

"That's what we called it on the hill," said Cessy.

But now Cole was speaking again. O'Reilly had just given his famous "I'll give you the last word" line, even though he usually said something after them so it wasn't last after all.

"I'm talking to all the soldiers who watch your show, Mr. O'Reilly. Remember, you're citizens first. Citizens of a country where the military doesn't decide things, the elected people do. If we break that rule they'll never trust us again. The country might be screwed up, but if you get an order to point your weapon at Americans who are just doing their job, don't obey that order. Point your weapon at the guy who gave it."

For a moment, O'Reilly was speechless. Maybe even breathless. "I pray to God nobody ever needs that advice in this country, Captain Coleman."

"Me too," said Cole.

And then they were off to more ads.

"Think Cole's gonna get his own TV show now?" said Reuben. "Like Ollie North?"

"He was great. Gave me chills."

"Yeah, but I got chills for another reason." Reuben pressed the rewind button on the DVR. "Watch Alton while Cole is making that last speech."

He waited for Cessy to see it, but she didn't. So he showed it again. "Look. He's enjoying it. See?"

"No, that's a supercilious smile. He's mocking it."

"Right, at the start. But now—see how it changed?"

"He was just tired of holding the expression."

"He's happy about something," said Reuben. "He just lost this interview. Cole owned it. Not that everybody believes Cole, but they believe him enough and dislike Alton enough that they're going to want to know about it—and Alton's happy."

"Because he thinks he won."

"You're probably right," said Reuben. "But like you said, he testifies in front of Congress and shows nothing. But here he rolls his eyes, he smirks. And then, when it's over, and he damaged himself, he's *satisfied*."

"What would that mean?"

"I don't know," said Reuben. "But I think we've been played."

"For suckers?"

"Like a violin."

"Why would somebody *possibly* want you to announce that they're planning a coup against the United States government?"

"It makes no sense," said Reuben. "But still. It's like

when you're face to face with a guy who might or might not have a gun under his robes or a bomb strapped to his body and you look him in the eye. You got to be able to read him. Alton reads wrong. That's all."

Cessy thought about it in silence for a while. Reuben had long since learned that if he filled such silences with talk, she would leave the room in order to be able to think, and then he wouldn't be there to hear whatever it was she thought of as soon as she thought of it.

"It's like what LaMonte said about how he could make this thing go away. It just didn't sound like him. There's something wrong."

"Maybe," said Reuben, "just maybe. It's not a coup. It's a grab."

"I'm sorry, your high-level military jargon just defeated me."

"A coup is where they arrest the President and replace him. But a grab is where the President is actually in charge of the coup, and he uses the Army to arrest everybody he thinks is a threat."

"No," said Cessy. "No, no, and no."

"Not possible?"

"Not LaMonte Nielson. Truly, Reuben. I know the man."

"Knew him. Back then."

"Core character. He's a very deft and ruthless politician, but he stays inside the lines. He loves the Constitution. He would never."

"Unless he thinks he's Abraham Lincoln and the country needs to have some of the lines crossed a little."

"He's President for barely a day and he's planning a military dictatorship?"

A new thought occurred to Reuben. "I hate to say what I'm thinking."

"I know what you're thinking and you may consider that this time I *screamed* 'no no no.' He had nothing to do with the assassination."

"Well *somebody* had something to do with it."

"Not him."

"Somebody really wanted LaMonte Nielson to be President."

"Or maybe somebody really wanted the President and Vice President dead and they didn't care who was next in line."

"LaMonte only became Speaker about three months ago, right?"

"There's been a lot of turnover at that job."

"How long do you think this assassination was planned?" said Reuben. "They had to drill those guys. They did not stop to think about anything. They had practiced hauling up the watertight cases and opening them and assembling everything. They knew down to the footstep where to place those launchers, exactly what angle to point them at. They did it like machines. How many months do you think they've been practicing that?"

"I don't know," said Cessy. "How long ago did you finish your plan?"

Reuben thought and couldn't remember. He opened his PDA and she scoffed. "Oh, come on, you can't be that paranoid."

"President's dead using my plan," said Reuben. "It's not paranoia."

"All right, I'll look up the exact date when the previous Speaker stepped down."

Reuben followed her to the computer. "March fourth is when I started showing around a draft that had the Tidal Basin plan in it."

"March tenth," said Cessy. "That's when the job came open. March thirteenth LaMonte got the nod."

"So he wasn't put in as Speaker of the House until they had the plan they'd use to make him President."

"No," said Cessy. "No."

"How do you *know*?"

She looked at him with defiance. "The same way I *know* that you had nothing to do with the assassination plot, even though you wrote the plan they used, even though you're always gone on mysterious trips and late-night meetings and you can never even hint what you're doing. Do you want me to trust that instinct or not, Reuben?"

It took him aback. It hadn't occurred to him that it might actually be hard for her to be certain of him. *He* knew he had nothing to do with the assassination—not deliberately, anyway—but when he thought of how all his activities must look to her, it said something that she believed him. Why *should* she believe him?

Would *I* believe me, if I didn't know what I know?

He put his hand on her cheek. "Trust it," he said. "And I'll trust your instinct about LaMonte Nielson, President from Idaho." He forced something like a laugh. "It's really kind of like *Mr. Smith Goes to Washington*. Farm boy makes good."

"No," said Cessy. "LaMonte is the consummate insider. He's no Jimmy Stewart. But he doesn't cheat. And he doesn't kill. And he liked the President. Liked him before he was elected. LaMonte is solid."

"And yet it was *you,* not me, that made the connection between Alton's attitude and what Nielson said to you on the phone."

"You haven't yet thanked me for turning down the coolest job I will ever have offered to me."

"I thought you already had the coolest job."

She pursed her lips.

"You mean doing meals and dishes and errands isn't *cool?*"

"It's the most important job in the world. That's why I turned down the *coolest* job in order to keep doing this one."

Reuben's cellphone rang. One of the new ones. "Cole," he said to Cessy. And then into the phone he said it again. "Cole."

"Please tell me I didn't completely screw up," said Cole.

"No, you did great," said Reuben. "Kept your cool. Just enough fervency to show you care. Guys out there who might be wavering about joining this coup, I think you might have persuaded some of them not to do it. Maybe a lot of them."

"Or maybe I started some mutinies. Maybe people will die."

"People do what they do," said Reuben. "What you did was remind them of honor."

"Yeah," breathed Cole. "I didn't know for sure they were going to have General Alton on until right before."

"Well, if you'd bothered to call me first, I could have told you, of course they'd offer him a chance to answer you. Talking heads are bad television, nose to nose is good television."

"Sure, but I didn't think he'd do it. If you could have seen him yesterday! It's like he's a different guy. What a liar."

"Yeah," said Reuben. "But which one was the lie?"

Silence for a long time.

"You think I was being set up?"

"Why should I be the only one?"

"Now that I think about it," said Cole. "He was so over the top. It's like he studied the right-wing fanatic playbook. He even said 'faggots.' "

"And dykes?"

"No. I guess he drew the line somewhere. He played me? You really think so? But why?"

"I don't know. I don't know if he played you, and if he did I don't know why. But one thing's for sure. The assassination of the President was a terrible thing, but it is not causing so much confusion that there's any excuse for the military to seize power. If there *is* a coup, it's just a naked grab for power. In fact, if there's a coup, then we can almost count on it that whoever carries it out, that's who gave my plans to the terrorists. That's who tipped them off about the President's location."

"So it was a right-wing thing," said Cole. "Like Oklahoma City."

"Yeah, well, the Left had the Unabomber, though nobody ever seems to remember that his logic sounded just like Al Gore preaching about the environment—crazy as a loon, but full of all kinds of internal politically correct logic."

"Wackos on both sides."

"One man's wacko is another man's prophet."

"Meaning one man's Hitler is another man's Churchill."

"Except Churchill never thought up death camps."

"You know what I meant. There really are good guys and bad guys. But before they have a chance to show you what they do with power, it can be hard to tell them apart."

"Cole," said Reuben. "Where are you staying tonight?"

"I haven't even thought about it."

"Unless you're independently wealthy, you can't afford to stay in Manhattan on a captain's pay."

"Hell, I can't even afford to park my car."

"So come on out to West Windsor. I'm handing the phone to Cessy to give you directions from the city—she's been coming here all her life, she knows the route better."

Cessy took the phone. "He's just lazy," she told Cole.

As she gave him the directions, Reuben walked back into the living room. He had paused the program on Alton's face.

"What's your game, General Alton?" he said. "Are you that dumb? Or are we?"

# ELEVEN

# GROUND ZERO

The great breakthrough in human evolution, the one that made civilization possible, was the discovery that two alpha males could form intense bonds of ur-brotherhood instead of the normal pattern of fighting till one is dead or driven away. It is the story of Gilgamesh and Enkidu—a man will plunge into hell for his friend. Thus the male DNA is tricked into sacrificing itself to the benefit of unrelated DNA; story triumphs over instinct; the monogamous civitas triumphs over the patriarchal tribe. Instead of one alpha male reproducing his superior genes over and over again, a far higher proportion of males reproduce, even though some die in war. All because human males learned how to trick themselves into loving each other to the point of suicidal madness.

**WHEN COLE** got to Aunt Margaret's house, with Cessy guiding him in on his cellphone like an instrument landing in the fog, it was after nine o'clock and all the news channels were full of stories of rumors of a coup, or stories of rumors that the rumors of a coup were a smokescreen to justify a right-wing—or, depending on the station, left-wing—takeover.

"I think," said Aunt Margaret to Cole, "that you managed to upstage the funerals of the President and Vice President. And the Secretary of Defense might as well not have bothered dying, for all the attention they're paying to him."

Cole was eating leftover pasta salad—Aunt Margaret specialized in main-dish salads in which she substituted fresh mozzarella cheese for whatever meat the salad called for. Cole was eating it like he had just discovered food. Still, he took a moment to swallow and then answer. "I'm sure if he'd had it to do over, he'd have skipped that White House meeting."

Mark and Nick were still up, sitting at the entrance of the hall, where they probably hoped not to be noticed by the adults in the kitchen, because if they were noticed they would doubtless be sent to bed. But Mark couldn't help laughing, as much because of the way Cole said it right after swallowing and with a forkful of salad still in midair.

Cessy turned on them. "Bed," she said.

"*I* didn't laugh," said Nick.

"I'm not sending you to bed for laughing," said Cessy.

"She's sending you to bed because you're young," said Cole. "Being young is an eighteen-year prison sentence for a crime your parents committed. But you do get time off for good behavior."

Nick *did* laugh at that—Mark just looked at him like he was weird. But they obeyed and left the room.

"Thanks for subverting our parental discipline," said Reuben to Cole.

"They're just going to listen from the door of their room," said Cole.

"They're obedient children," said Cessy.

"Big and terrible things are happening in the world," said Cole. "If *you* were a kid, would you really be so obedient you wouldn't sneak a way to listen to what the grownups are trying to protect you from knowing about?"

"No," said Cessy. "But I'm not a kid, I'm a mother, and I don't want them to know."

"You don't think it'll scare them worse not to know what's going on?" asked Cole.

"People without children always know how to raise them better than their parents do," said Aunt Margaret. "I speak from experience. I never had kids of my own."

"None of my business," said Cole. "Really good salad."

Reuben looked at Cessy. "We trust Mark not to tell his

friends I'm here, and that's the only secret that has bad consequences if they tell it."

"I don't want them to be frightened," said Cessy.

"I don't want them to be frightened either," said Reuben. "So let's let them come back in."

"You're not the one who wakes up with their nightmares."

"Is that a no?"

"That's a vote. You have the other vote."

"Is that permission?" asked Reuben.

"Grudging permission, full of possible I-told-you-sos."

"Good enough for me." Then, without raising his voice even a bit, he said, "All right, boys, you can come back."

The scampering of feet began instantly.

Cole grinned, with flecks of basil on his teeth and lips. Cessy handed him a napkin.

"See," said Cole, "when I go home, my parents *still* send me out of the room when they discuss things."

"You're the baby of the family?"

"Yep," said Cole. "They still call me Barty." And before Reuben could call him by that name, Cole raised a hand. "They're the only people *alive* who call me that."

With the boys back in the hallway and Aunt Margaret stirring fresh raspberries into the soft homemade ice cream she had in the freezer, they got down to business.

It seemed perfectly natural for Cessy to take charge, because she was the one who had more experience inside the Washington bureaucracy. Not that Reuben and Cole hadn't dealt with bureaucracy for years in the military, but that was on the Pentagon side, where people actually did what they were told, more or less.

Cessy laid it out on paper. A chart showing:

The terrorists, the unknown person who gave Reuben's plans to them, the unknown White House staffer who told them when the President would be in that room, the unknown person or persons who suppressed cellphones and cut landlines at Hain's Point and who fired at Reuben and Cole from the trees.

General Alton and his coup conspiracy—represented by

a dotted line, because it might exist and it might not, and if it did exist it might be connected with the assassination and it might not.

President Nielson, who might or might not be connected in some way to Alton and his perhaps nonexistent conspiracy.

And, of course, Reuben, Cole, and Reuben's jeesh.

"Who benefits?" asked Cessy.

"Define 'benefit,'" said Reuben. "I mean, usually you think money or power or sex or vengeance. Plenty of people hated the President. The media aren't covering it, but the Internet is full of blogs and pictures talking about people openly celebrating the assassination—like fireworks and signs and riding around honking horns."

"Yes, but those idiots didn't have access," said Cessy.

"But there might be people who feel the way they feel who *did* have access."

"Working in a Republican White House?" asked Cessy.

"A housekeeper. A clerk. It didn't have to be somebody who agreed with the President's politics. There's no ideological test for White House custodial staff. Or the Secret Service, for that matter."

"It was Clinton the Secret Service guys hated," said Cole.

"*Some* Secret Service guys," said Reuben.

"You're not seriously suggesting this, are you?" asked Cessy.

"I just think there are too many people who think a dead President is, in this case, a good idea. They might be people who think they just saved America from the death of freedom. I mean, think of the rhetoric that's been flying around Washington for the past years. Hate hate hate. Most dangerous President ever. Constitution crumbling. All our sacred rights and values being thrown away."

"Or being restored," said Cole.

"Exactly," said Reuben. "I think we have to look at this in the context of the run-up to a civil war. There are two sides that see the world so radically differently that they truly believe that anyone who disagrees with them is evil or stupid or both. In that context, you really do find people who are willing to kill. Or help those who want to kill. I can imagine somebody telling himself—or herself, because we're keeping an open mind here—telling herself that yes, she's helping terrorists, but *this* time it won't be innocent office workers and firemen and cops in the twin towers, this time it'll be the one who's causing all the trouble, it'll be the source of evil himself."

"So what you're saying is that we can't look at motive," said Cessy.

"There are too many motives. Too many reasons why someone would want to help kill the President."

"Then how do we find them?" asked Cessy. "The conspiracy is real enough."

Cole raised his hand off the table. Just a little wave, since he felt like something of an interloper, interrupting these two. After all, he'd only just met them yesterday. Though it had been a pretty full thirty-six hours. "Um," said Cole, "why is this our job? I mean, isn't the FBI working on this?"

"Are you sure the FBI has no elements within it that were part of the conspiracy?" asked Cessy. "Nothing to conceal?"

"Hey, I'm just saying," said Cole, "this isn't what we know how to do. There are hundreds of people, *thousands* of them, who are all trained at this."

"We have an extra motive," said Reuben. "All those people are being fed a lot of evidence that points at me. And after your performance on TV tonight, I'm betting there's a lot of evidence pointing at you, now, too."

"*If* General Alton is for real," said Cessy.

"So if we leave it up to those investigators, who are under enormous pressure to come up with answers *now*," said Reuben, "then the answer they're going to come up with is me. And maybe *us*."

"And don't forget," said Aunt Margaret cheerfully, "that your wife was once a well-beloved member of the *new* President's team."

"She's right," said Cessy. "People who are looking for conspiracy seize on every single coincidence and make something of it."

"Yeah," said Cole, "but isn't that exactly what we're doing?"

"Sure," said Reuben, "with the difference being that we don't consider ourselves possible suspects."

"So our guesses will be better than theirs," said Cessy.

"So why are you letting people interrupt you?" said Cole. "Go on. Go ahead."

Cessy patted his hand. "It was a good question," she said. Then she turned back to Reuben across the table from her. "If we can't use motive to narrow the list of suspects, then what do we use?"

"Means," said Reuben. "Opportunity. Connections."

"A whole lot of people in the White House *could* have known where the President was."

"But they would have to have been alone, out of earshot of anybody else for at least a few minutes during the time between the decision to hold the meeting in that particular room and the time the rockets hit."

"The decision?" asked Cole. "Do they issue a go order right then? What about timing it so you're on Hain's Point? Was that part of the choice?"

"Meeting rooms change unpredictably," said Cessy. "I think that's standard policy in the Secret Service. Ever since they tried to kill the first President Bush in Kuwait back in . . . whenever."

"But the meeting was expected to be a long one, right?" said Cole. "I mean, you don't bring *that* group together for a meeting and then adjourn in fifteen minutes. You have a long agenda."

"So the terrorists could have gotten the go from their White House contact when the meeting actually started," said Cessy.

"How far from the point where the scuba tanks went into the water till they got to the Tidal Basin?" asked Reuben.

"We don't know where that point was," said Cole.

"Couldn't have been in the channel. That's right in front of Fort McNair and Anacostia Naval Base and Bolling Air Force Base, for pete's sake," said Reuben.

"So we need to find out the capacity of those scuba tanks and how much air was left in them," said Cessy, "in order to find out how much time elapsed between their going into the water and reaching the Tidal Basin."

"And that tells us the timeframe in which the White House contact had to be alone to make his call," said Reuben.

Again Cole raised his hand a little. "I don't mean to cause trouble here."

"Which means 'I don't want you to be mad at me for causing trouble,'" said Aunt Margaret. But her smile was encouraging. It seemed she had taken it upon herself to encourage Cole to contribute and stop apologizing for it.

"Somebody's already figuring this out and we don't have the resources to do it ourselves," said Cole. "Who do *we* have inside the White House?"

"Yesterday, we had nobody," said Cessy. "Today we have . . . oh, nobody much . . . only the *President*."

Mark laughed at that. Reuben almost said something sharp to him, but he saw that Nick had already clapped a hand over Mark's mouth and Mark was letting him, which meant Mark agreed that Nick was right that he should shut up, and anyway, it was Reuben who had insisted the boys should be able to listen.

"More to the point," said Cessy, "we have Sandy Woodruff."

"Whose role is completely undefined," said Reuben. "Which means that the existing White House staff is going to circle the wagons to freeze her out."

"Or suck up to her outrageously because she has the President's ear and can help them stay," said Cessy.

"Oh. That's right. Different rules from the Pentagon."

"And then the other question—who had opportunity to get your plans," said Cessy.

"It all depends on finding out which version was

planted—which DeeNee is working on—and then she'll know who had their hands on it and can start finding out where it got before it vanished," said Reuben.

Cessy smiled at him very, very sweetly. "Unless it was DeeNee who handed it over to them."

"Not a chance."

"Not to them directly," said Cessy. "But to the person who gave it to the person who gave it to the person."

"You don't know DeeNee," said Reuben.

"Like you don't know LaMonte?" asked Cessy, still smiling.

"Exactly like that," said Reuben. He was not smiling. "We have to trust somebody or we might as well get out of the country and try to hide somewhere."

Then he remembered the boys sitting there listening. "I was making a point by exaggeration," he said to them. "We're not leaving the country."

"If we do," said Mark, "I want to go to Disney World."

"*I* want to go to Xanth," said Nick.

"Xanth is imaginary," said Cessy. "And Disney World is *in* the United States."

"I didn't know that either," Cole said to Mark.

"Shut up, boys," said Reuben. "I mean that in the nicest possible way." He turned back to the table. Cole had his hand over his mouth. What a time for him to be sucking up to the boys. But then, maybe that was precisely what was needed. Some reassuring humor. An adult ally. Maybe Cole was helping.

"May I interject a comment from the cook and landlady?" asked Aunt Margaret as she set out dishes of raspberry ice cream. There were two extras. She snapped her fingers at the boys and they took seats at the table.

"You may," said Cessy, "since everybody else's mouth is going to be full."

"Mine already is," mumbled Cole, barely intelligible with his spoon held between his teeth.

Mark started to hold his spoon between *his* teeth. Nick pulled it out and put it into Mark's ice cream. Again Mark peacefully accepted an action that would normally have caused a fight.

"My observation is," said Aunt Margaret, "that you can't figure out a single thing from this point on until you hear from Sandy and DeeNee, whoever they are, and *they* can't find anything out until the start of the business day tomorrow. Reuben has had only a short nap since the night before the assassination, and Cole has just given a speech to twenty million people."

"In O'Reilly's dreams," said Cessy.

"Go to bed," said Aunt Margaret. "Go to sleep. I'll tuck you in. Things will be *just* as bleak and hopeless in the morning. Isn't this good ice cream? My secret is lots of hydrogenated fat. I buy it in large lots from doctors who do liposuction."

"Delicious," said Nick.

"Gross!" said Mark.

**FIVE IN** the morning, still dark, Reuben woke up and couldn't get back to sleep. Quietly, so he wouldn't waken Cessy, he got up and looked for whatever Cessy had thrown into a suitcase for him to wear. There wasn't a lot of choice. Fatigues or civvies. It was Sunday. He should wear a suit and go to Mass with Cessy and the kids. But that would entail a lot more noise. He could change clothes later. For now, he put on fatigues.

Downstairs in the kitchen, he found that Cole had made the same choice. "I see you decided you wanted to be in uniform today."

"A choice I made years ago," said Cole. "You caught me. I was prowling for leftover ice cream."

"There's never leftover ice cream in Aunt Margaret's house," said Reuben. "Can't sleep?"

"I woke up thinking I heard something. I had visions of a team of ninjas surrounding the house and climbing up the walls onto the roof like in *Crouching Tiger*."

"Were there any?"

"I did a circuit of the house. No alarm system—I checked *before* I opened the door."

"Any ninja footprints on the walls?"

"Nothing. But there was a newspaper wrapped in plastic sitting in your driveway. And there I was in my jockeys, holding the paper, wondering if the door had locked automatically behind me."

"Had it?"

"Yes, but it was incredibly easy to pick," said Cole.

"I shudder to ask, but with *what?*"

"It was still partly open," said Cole. "I was joking."

"Not much to do in West Windsor, New Jersey, at 0515 on a Sunday."

"You know what I want?" said Cole.

"For Christmas?"

"For this moment. I want to get in a car and drive to the city and look at Ground Zero. It's Sunday, it's five in the morning, there won't be traffic. We can be there and back before church, right?"

"Easily," said Reuben. "But I don't think you'll see what you want to see. It's not a rubble heap or even an excavation anymore. They're building something appalling on the site, aren't they?"

"I don't know how far they've gotten," said Cole. "But even if it's a Starbucks now, I want to tread that ground. Or at least look at it. Imagine the towers. Remember them. The media has forbidden us to remember the falling towers—they don't allow us to see the footage. It's like their slogan is, Forget the Alamo. I'm tired of being obedient to their decision to keep us blind."

"Let me get the keys to Mingo's SUV."

"Not my trophy car?" asked Cole. "Oh, wait—Mingo's has been mod-oh-fied."

"Mingo's isn't registered to you or me," said Reuben. "For all we know, there's an APB out on our vehicles."

"It has *nothing* to do with his arsenal?"

"If we hadn't had to scrounge up weapons at Hain's

Point," said Reuben, "the President would still be alive. So maybe yeah, maybe I want to have the weapons with me. But if somebody does try to arrest us, I'm not fighting. I didn't train as a soldier so I could kill Americans."

**THE HOLLAND** Tunnel took them into the city not far north of where the World Trade Center used to be. The traffic was heavier than Cole had expected, and the city was already full of life.

"How does anybody *sleep* here?" asked Cole.

"Air-conditioning," said Rube. "It lets them close their windows and it makes white noise to help them not to hear the street. Plus, you get used to it."

"So you've lived in the big city?" asked Cole.

"Not this big city, but I've spent a lot of time here, and a lot of other big cities, too."

"In your real life, or on that secret assignment from the White House?"

"Which I now doubt had anything to do with the White House," said Rube. "I think they've been playing me all along. I don't know why I set off their use-this-guy alarms, but I think they marked me years ago."

"And probably had a GPS on your car already, eh? So they didn't have to tail you to find out if you went to Hain's Point?"

"I'm more paranoid than that," said Rube. "You think I didn't scan my car regularly? I was doing weird stuff. Weapons systems. Parts delivery. Working out financial transactions in remote locations."

"Laundering money?"

"I didn't think of it that way, but probably, yes."

"But you're not going to tell me anything specific."

"There's still a chance I was working for the good guys, and this stuff is so classified it can't be classified."

"They trusted you."

"To be a world-class fool," said Rube. "But it's nice to be trusted."

There was actually on-street parking here and there.

Rube took a spot and parallel-parked forward. "NASCAR trained," said Cole.

"NASCAR drivers always double park. For quick getaways." He locked the car using the remote. But Cole noticed that Rube still checked the locks visually. "I figured maybe there are closer parking places, but maybe not, and we're extremely physically fit so walking won't hurt us."

"We do have government-issue shoes," said Cole. "So we're using up taxpayer money."

"They pay for your shoes?" asked Rube.

"At Defense Department rates. So the left shoe is two hundred bucks, and the right shoe, which has to be separately requisitioned, is five hundred."

Cole appreciated the fact that Rube chuckled. Cole knew it wasn't really a good time to be making stupid jokes, but they also couldn't brood about the assassination and the worries ahead of them—they had to keep their minds clear. Concentration was important, but so was distance. Maybe if they could laugh a little, they'd see more clearly.

And maybe Cole was so nervous himself that he couldn't keep from cracking wise even when it was completely inappropriate. *Especially* then.

They didn't make it to Ground Zero. They were still walking on Barclay Street when they heard an explosion. Then a siren. Then small-arms fire. Single shots. Then automatic weapons fire. Not a set of sounds you'd expect from ordinary criminal activity. The cops didn't carry automatic weapons. And this sounded big. Cole knew that this was something too big for a couple of off-duty off-assignment Special Ops veterans to take on when the only weapons on them were pens and keys.

"I want to go back to Mingo's car now," said Rube.

They started back up the street. Broke into a jog at the same moment.

And then heard a loudspeaker behind them.

"We are not your enemies. We are fellow Americans here to protect your city from the unconstitutional government in Washington. Stay off the streets and you will not be hurt."

They turned around to see what kind of vehicle was playing the recorded announcement. To see just what kind of evasive action they needed to take.

It was not a vehicle. Or maybe it was—there *could* be a human inside it. But it looked like a robot, about fourteen feet high, like a ball on two legs. It gave no sign of noticing them. Until they started to move. Then it zeroed in on them, started striding purposefully toward them, though it was still a hundred yards away.

Cole stopped. So did Rube. "Motion detectors?" asked Rube.

"Or a guy inside who just spotted us on his screen."

"Or both."

The loudspeaker sounded again. "Go inside. The streets are not safe."

"So the message can change," said Rube.

"I don't want to go inside," said Cole. "I want to get a really big gun and see what it takes to destroy that wonderful machine that's here to protect me from the unconstitutional government in Washington."

"I think that thing looks awkward and slow. Let's see if we can outrun it."

No further discussion was needed. They turned and ran.

"Stop and you will not be hurt. Stop and you will not be hurt."

They did not stop.

"Stop now or you will be fired on."

Cole glanced back over his shoulder. The machine had just kicked up into a higher gear.

"It's faster than we are," said Cole.

"It's faster than we *were*," said Rube, and he nearly doubled his speed.

So the major hadn't gotten out of shape during his desk-jockey days. Cole had a hard time catching up to him.

Gunfire began. The warning repeated.

"Blanks so far," said Cole.

"Those weren't blanks," said Rube. "It was a recording of gunshots."

"You know what that thing reminds me of?" said Cole.

"*The Empire Strikes Back*," said Rube.

"I was thinking *War of the Worlds*."

"Yeah, but those were computer-graphics bullshit. Why do they think two legs will make a thing like that work better than tracks?"

"If we're still talking," said Cole, "we're not really running fast enough."

They sped up again as the live bullets began striking around them. The corner of Greenwich Street was on their left, a couple of steps away.

"Not a recording now," said Cole.

"So do we try for Murray Street or settle for Park Place?"

"You pick *now* to play Air Monopoly?"

The thing turned the corner behind them sooner than they had expected. It fired immediately.

"The warning message apparently ran out," said Rube.

They dived between parked cars, then kept low as they moved along the sidewalk.

A car just behind them blew up. The blast knocked them off their feet.

Cole was up at once. Rube was maybe a little bit slower. It might have had to do with him being blown into a fireplug.

"You okay?" Cole asked.

"That is the ugliest girl I ever kissed," said Rube. He was okay enough to keep running.

They made the corner of Park Place just as the tank-on-legs lined up with the sidewalk so it could shoot them without having to go through cars to do it. The bullets tore up the concrete of the sidewalk and Cole felt little bits of concrete spatter the back of his head. It would be hell getting them out by himself. He hated to pay the deductible to have an emergency room do it. It's times like this, he thought, when it would be really nice to have a wife. *Cecily* will pull all the concrete bits out of *Rube's* head.

The things that run through your head when the fear of death comes on you, thought Cole.

They were nearly at the corner of Broadway when the thing rounded the corner and started shooting at them again.

"What kind of threat . . . do we pose?" said Cole between breaths.

"Plenty of civilians . . . would act like this," said Rube, also panting. "Shoot anything . . . that runs . . . bad order . . . collateral . . . damage."

"Maybe it's . . . cause we . . . run too . . . damn fast," suggested Cole.

"Maybe it's . . . our uniforms," said Rube.

Cole had forgotten they were wearing uniforms.

He saw a deeply recessed doorway and dodged into it.

Rube joined him but didn't like it. "We'll just be . . . pinned here," he said. "When it comes . . . up the street."

"If it's just a machine," said Cole, "it won't see us . . . and it might retarget."

"That would be a really . . . stupid program, too," said Rube.

"So maybe the guys who . . . built this are really stupid."

They heard the thudding of steps on concrete, coming closer, echoing off the buildings of this street.

"Okay, so they're not that stupid," said Cole. "Sorry."

"It's on the sidewalk," said Rube.

The door behind them opened. A terrified Chinese woman looked at them.

Rube didn't hesitate. He shoved the door open wider, picked up the woman, and carried her farther inside as she shouted in Chinese. Cole followed and slammed the door behind them. They were inside a narrow Chinese restaurant.

"Does this place have a back door?" Rube demanded.

The woman only continued screeching in Chinese. A terrified old Chinese man came through a curtain, carrying a shotgun. Rube, who still had hold of the woman, dragged her down as Cole also hit the floor. The shotgun went off, blasting right where they—and the Chinese woman—had been standing.

"This guy is crazy," said Rube.

"He also just called that walking tank." Cole was up and running around and over the tables. The Chinese man tried to aim the shotgun at him. Just before he fired, Cole leapt high and the shot passed under and between his legs. Then Cole was on the guy and came up with the gun. Rube was already running after him, dragging the woman.

An explosion blew the door open. They dragged the Chinese couple deeper into the restaurant.

"How much ordnance does that thing carry?" asked Rube.

"I don't want to find out just now," said Cole. "I want to find out later, in a nice safe lab."

"Is there a back door?" Rube asked the Chinese man, who wasn't screaming like the woman was. But the Chinese man only pointed to the safe and said, "No money, no money!"

Cole shouted at the woman in Cantonese. He had guessed right. She was from China proper, or at least Hong Kong—not Taiwan. "Back door?"

She pointed.

"Big gun coming!" he shouted in what could only be terrible Cantonese. He had only been two months into the language course when he got the assignment to work with Rube. "Get upstairs! Hold still! Don't talk! Shut up!"

That had to be enough. They had to get out. And he thought he saw them out of the corner of his eye, fleeing up the stairs to a higher story.

The mechanical outside was firing a virtual sheet of bullets through the windows. They went through the kitchen wall like it was paper. Which it probably was. Cole and Rube were already at the back door. Which had a crash bar and a big red ALARM WILL SOUND sign on it.

"Gee, we might wake up the neighbors," said Rube. Then he pushed on it.

The door opened. The alarm went off. They went out on their bellies as bullets continued to slap against the door and the bricks of the back wall of the kitchen.

Then the door closed behind them. The shooting continued but at least now they could hear themselves think.

They were not in an alley. New York City didn't believe

in alleys. That's why they had to put their garbage right out on the street. Like a weird kind of window display—come, look what we throw away from this store. Don't we have attractive garbage? Don't we use an incredibly cheap grade of plastic bag?

"There's no way out of here," said Rube.

"Yet," said Cole. He was already trying doors. Rube checked around the other way. They met in the middle of the opposite side of the courtyard. All were locked.

"These people are so *paranoid*," said Cole. He headed for the lowest window. It was barred, of course, but there were loose bricks in the courtyard from somebody's unfinished remodeling job. Cole started slamming a brick into the bars. They weren't all that strong. They could probably be pried out of the wall. Rube had found a two-by-four and was prying on the other side.

A shotgun blast tore through the window. Fortunately, it missed both Cole and Reuben.

"I thought privately owned guns were illegal in this city!" shouted Cole.

"They had one hell of a shotgun salesman come through here, I guess."

Cole shouted into the window. "The city is being attacked. We're United States Army! Look at our uniforms!"

A woman's face appeared in the shattered window. They both stood out from the wall, showing ID and letting her look at their uniforms.

"Who's attacking!" She had some kind of foreign accent, maybe Spanish, but her English was nice and clear.

No time to explain. "Aliens!" shouted Cole.

The door swung open so fast it rebounded off the wall and almost shut again. Cole and Rube pushed through it. "We need to get out onto Murray Street," said Rube. "We need to get to our weapons."

She ran ahead of them, praying in Spanish as she went.

"Stay indoors," said Cole.

*"No va fuera,"* said Reuben. *"No entra la rua! No mira la rua!"*

The woman nodded as she fumbled with the keys and finally got the front door open.

Cole started looking for Mingo's SUV. Only when Rube pushed the button on the remote did Cole realize that the SUV was directly in front of him.

"I planned it this way when I chose our parking place," said Rube.

"It's a miracle from God and *you* want to take credit?" said Cole.

By now they were both inside the SUV with the doors closed.

"Want to try to run for it in the car?" said Rube.

"Did you see what it did to that parked car back there?" said Cole. "I want to see Mingo's arsenal!"

"He won't have a grenade launcher, more's the pity," said Rube.

"I'd be happy with a World War II bazooka."

Rube pulled out an M-16A2 rifle. "You want this? Or there's an M-4."

"How the hell did Mingo get an M-4 for private use?" said Cole.

"You want it or not?" said Rube.

"Duh," said Cole, reaching for the weapon he knew best, the M-4.

"And maybe I'll take the Minimi."

"You didn't tell me there was a machine gun when you offered me my choice."

"Too late, no takebacks. Here's an M-9 for you and an M-9 for me."

Cole took the offered pistol and then they started sharing out ammunition.

"When did you learn Chinese?"

"They were starting to train me for the *next* possible war."

"They guessed wrong," said Rube. "*This* is the next possible war."

"*Now* you tell me. When did you learn Spanish? Special Ops is planning for a war with Colombia?"

"That was high school Spanish. And some college Spanish. And look. An M-240. Forget the Minimi. I want the heavier bullets."

"Against tanks?"

"I'm betting the mechs aren't armored like a tank," said Rube. "Too heavy for those legs to hold up."

"They're big and new and maybe the people who made them have a new way to repel bullets, too."

"Here's a belt of grenades for you," said Rube, "and a belt for me. You take the Minimi if you want it so much. Just don't load yourself down with too much weaponry."

"Yes sir," said Cole. "Look who's talking, sir. Yours is ten pounds heavier than mine."

"Where's our friend?" asked Rube.

"From the sound, still shooting at the Chinese restaurant."

"Or at something," said Rube. "Us again in a minute."

"What's our objective, sir?" asked Cole.

Rube laughed. "Good point, Captain. No, we will not seek confrontation. Our objective is to get the hell out of New York City before the tunnels are sealed off."

"My guess is that unless these guys are complete idiots, the tunnels were sealed off and emptied first thing."

"They'd seal off the bridges, too," said Rube. "And the tunnels are closer."

"But there are buckets and buckets of water above them," said Cole.

"And just as much water way, way, way below the bridges. And most of the bridges lead to Long Island."

"On *24*, Jack would find a helicopter he could commandeer."

"On *Smallville*, Clark would take a mighty leap and jump over the Hudson River." Rube clicked a clip into place on his pistol. "Ready to go?"

"Holland Tunnel, sir?" asked Cole.

"And we *do* stop and help local defense forces wherever it looks like we could make a difference," said Rube. "My guess is that it'll mostly be cops, and these things are going to tear them apart. Against this, New York isn't prepared to defend itself."

"Do you think it really is Americans attacking the city?"

"Yes," said Rube. "Because I can't think of any foreign country that would be dumb enough to try to attack the U.S. like this."

"So Mingo's weapons—we're going to be shooting at Americans."

"*They're* shooting at uniforms," said Rube. "That means they're trying to destroy legal authority. And we're sworn to defend it."

"Plus, they shot at us first," said Cole.

"So when you know you can't win, you save your army," said Rube. "Our proper course is to get as many fighters as possible out of this city to a place where they can fight again."

"I think we can do this and still get to church, don't you?" said Cole.

They put their hands on opposite door handles. "Ready?" said Rube.

"Mingo is going to be so pissed we left so much of his arsenal behind," said Cole.

"Mingo's going to be happy he had what we needed. If this *is* what we needed."

"Let's find out," said Cole.

They opened their doors and dashed for the buildings on the other side of the street. Even though no mech was in sight, they kept low as they moved along the sidewalk.

Cole was surprised to realize that he was more excited than scared. He knew what to do. He'd done it before. So much better than trying to figure out politics. Even though mistakes in a street battle did kill you faster. At least you knew at the end of the day whether you were alive or not.

# TWELVE

# HOLLAND TUNNEL

There are hard wars and easy wars. It's easy to conquer a country whose people hate their own government more than they hate the invaders. It's hard to fight a war when your army knows that back home, their families are rooting for the other side.

**IT MADE** sense to dodge the mechs wherever possible. But the sound of shooting and explosions drew Reuben. It was a part of who he was. It's not that he felt no fear of danger—quite the contrary. When he knew of danger, he had to approach it in order to weigh it, to see how much of a threat there was. And it was more than that—he had to eliminate it if he could. He knew what he could do, when it came to combat. He knew that few other people could do it. With Cole beside him, they might be able to do what any number of men with police training could not do.

And there were the bodies. Riddled with bullets, they lay half in, half out of squad cars, all wearing uniforms. Most of them New York's finest, but one was simply a doorman to an apartment building, lying out in the street because, apparently, he had not obeyed an order to stop.

"Not one civilian," said Cole.

"Except the doorman."

"In uniform. Nobody in civilian clothes."

"It's summer," said Reuben. "We could do this in our underwear."

"They're trying not to kill civilians," said Cole. "Same rules of engagement as we use. They really are Americans."

"Using weapons that aren't in the American arsenal. In *anybody's* arsenal," said Reuben.

"You think these were developed by Iran? North Korea?"

No need to answer. They both knew that Iran and North Korea might have nukes, but that they were copied from existing devices. These things required original work. "Russia?" asked Reuben. "China?"

"Possible, but not practical. What could they hope to accomplish?"

"But who could afford to develop this?" asked Reuben. "How many of them are there? Are other cities getting hit right now? And again, how do you occupy New York City? How do you defend this island against the Marines when the counterstrike comes?"

"Best we can hope to find out right now," said Cole, "is just what these things are and how they work."

"Bring one down," said Reuben, agreeing with him.

"Open it up and drag out the guy."

"Or the computer chips."

"Or the trained squirrels," said Cole.

"That means we've got to go toward the noise," said Reuben.

"Weren't we already?" asked Cole.

They rounded a corner and found, not a mech, but three squad cars and about two dozen cops along with a couple of plainclothes guys who were clearly in charge. One of them spotted Reuben and Cole and at first signed for them to get off the street. Then, as Reuben and Cole began to jog toward them, the police officer realized that they were U.S. Army, not civilians.

"Thank God!" the cop shouted. "The Army's here."

"Sorry," said Reuben. "It's just us two. Major Malich. Captain Coleman."

"Sergeant Willis," said the plainclothes guy, introducing himself.

"We need to get one of these mechs down to ground level so we can open it up and see how it works," said Reuben. "Unless you already know."

"Our bullets don't even bounce off," said Willis. "It's like they eat them and spit them back at us."

"They can't have an infinite supply of ammunition in there," said Cole.

"We're planning to run squad cars at them and try to trip them up," said Willis.

"One at a time?" asked Reuben. "All from the same direction?"

Willis looked a little crestfallen. "I guess that makes us the dumb movie cops who don't know what we're doing."

"You're not trained for war," said Reuben. "Leave one squad car here, but have the doors open and make it look abandoned. As soon as the mech passes, *then* the driver comes out of hiding and drives out behind the thing. Meanwhile we get the other two cars coming from cross streets. Maybe it can't shoot all three at once."

"And maybe it can."

"Meanwhile," said Reuben, "Cole and I will run up alongside it and try to get on top. Don't waste bullets shooting at it. Just keep it busy. And if you have a way to keep the cars driverless, that's fine with me. But with or without drivers inside, they've got to run right at the thing."

A cop at the corner was already shouting. "It's coming!"

"With me or not?" asked Reuben.

"Better than my plan," said Willis.

Reuben and Cole rode in different cars, back around blocks to get into position for the ambush—if you can count a bunch of third-graders jumping a grown man as an ambush. In the car, the cop who was driving was clearly scared. "The announcement they run—it says they're Americans, right?"

"By birth, maybe," said Reuben. "They're criminals right now. Traitors. They're aiming at cops. Trying to wipe out authority."

"Yeah, well, I don't have any weapons that'll hurt these things."

"Maybe the car will."

"And maybe I'll get my ass blown up."

"You could get it shot off on a drug bust, too," said Reuben. "But there's no point in all you guys dying to defend against an enemy you can't beat."

"A couple of us are thinking, we should just give up."

"Do you see any way for that thing to take a prisoner?" asked Reuben.

The guy didn't say anything.

"What I think," said Reuben, "those things are here to kill cops. When the cops are dead, then they own the city. So once we get this sucker on the ground and take pictures and whatever piece we can carry, you guys come with us and get out of New York. Live to fight another day."

"I got family here," said the cop. "Brooklyn, anyway."

"When the Army or the Marines come back in to retake the city," said Reuben, "they'll need people who know every street and every building. We need you guys in Jersey, not dead on the streets here."

The cop nodded. Reuben knew that having a purpose could make all the difference.

The mech must have passed by the apparently-abandoned squad car, because when it was in midblock, the car pulled into the intersection behind it. Reuben had only just reached the corner, and he could already see the thing swiveling to shoot at the car.

So he ran out into the street, pulling the pin on a grenade as he went, and threw it as close to between the mech's feet as he could, without overshooting it. The idea was to get the mech to turn back around and face this way.

It worked too well. The thing didn't just turn, it began to run, big leaping clumping steps, straight toward Reuben, firing as it went.

He ran toward the parked cars, though he knew they provided no shelter, and hit the ground. Meanwhile, he could hear the squad car behind the mech picking up speed. He also heard the cars hidden on the side street behind him gun their engines.

The mech saw the trap at once but didn't even try to dodge out of the way. It simply jumped onto the hood of one of the cars and stepped over it. The drivers braked and the collisions were minor. But from behind them, the mech started shooting at all three cars. The drivers had their doors open at once, but before they even emerged, Reuben was running at the thing. He could see Cole coming at it from the other side.

If the mech saw them it gave no sign. Which might mean the operator knew there was nothing that two guys could do from the outside.

Reuben didn't need to say anything to Cole as each of them climbed up a leg. No vulnerabilities where the legs joined the body of the thing. How inconvenient that they hadn't provided a nice place to put a grenade that would blow it apart.

There also were no handholds to grip in order to climb around and get on top. The thing was designed for combat, and they'd anticipated the obvious moves.

It was Cole who came up with an idea. He gripped the mechanical leg tightly and swung his over to brace his feet against the leg Reuben had climbed. Reuben understood at once, and did the same, so his feet were pushing against the mechanical leg Cole was holding.

As soon as the mech started to take a step, Reuben and Cole both pushed the legs apart as hard as they could. That way its foot would come down in an unpredictable place. Everything depended on how well the software that controlled the walking process was able to respond.

The answer was—pretty well. But not well enough. It staggered and lurched, and while it took all Reuben's strength to hang on, they knew now that it was worth continuing. On the next step, they pushed again, and the machine staggered again.

And now another car—a civilian car this time—came

straight for them from the side street. The mech tried to swivel toward the car, but again Cole and Reuben pressed the legs apart and its shots missed.

Since the mech was facing the car now, more or less, the car hit both legs just as Reuben and Cole were swinging down and away. They let go in time, though, hit the street and rolled.

The mech was on the ground. But it was prepared for that and was already using a slender armlike projection from the center of the body to push itself up to its knees. Not fast enough, though. There was already a cop on top of it, and he held out an arm to Reuben to help him get up.

The hatch on the back had to be the entry point, either for a living operator or for the mechanics who worked on the machinery inside. There was a keypad that allowed entry by combination. Instead, Reuben slapped an adhesive patch on the keypad, and then stuck a grenade to the patch and pulled the pin. "Jump!" he yelled to the cop.

They both jumped.

Another car hit the mech's legs just as the grenade went off. Again it was down, and this time the entry door, which was facing straight up, had no keypad, just a hole with a bunch of broken wiring.

Inside the hole, Reuben quickly discovered, was a button that looked to him like it ought to be an emergency release. He couldn't get his finger down inside. But a pistol bullet went through the gap and into the button just fine.

Now the entry panel could be pried off, though it still wasn't easy.

One cop was standing directly over it when it came free. The explosion evaporated him.

The inside of the mech was nothing now but a mass of debris.

"Was it manned?" asked Cole.

Reuben wasn't sure he could tell. "No body parts inside," he said. "But they might have been burnt up. Vaporized. It's big enough for a man, but maybe they use the space for ammo. That's what blew."

Willis was at the base of the thing looking up. "Did you learn anything?"

"Something," said Reuben. "As much as we're *going* to learn. Sergeant Willis, I want to take your guys out of this city right now."

"Our duty is here."

"Your duty is to guide our guys or the Marines when they come to take this city back," said Reuben. "And that means right now your job is to stay alive and get off this island."

Willis might have taken a long time making the decision, except that four mechs appeared at the ends of all four streets. "Shit," he said. "They know we got their boy."

"This way!" shouted Cole. He had already done *his* duty, which was to look for avenues of escape.

In this case, that meant running down the subway stairs at the corner.

"Cover me!" shouted one of the cops, and a couple of them started shooting at the mech coming up the street toward the subway stairs.

"There's no 'cover me'!" yelled Reuben. "They don't care about our bullets! Just run and get down there!"

Only one man was hit on his way to the subway—hit bad enough that Reuben dragged away the cop that was trying to go back to drag the body with him.

"Are the subways running?" Reuben asked Willis.

"All stopped," said Willis. "And all entry points to the city closed from the other side."

"What about the third rail—powered or not?"

"I don't know," said Willis.

"Then let's not touch it," said Reuben. "We want to get to the Holland Tunnel," he said. "Which way?"

"The subway doesn't go there."

"But do we go this way or that way to get to the next station? Or the one after that? Or is there some way up to the surface *not* at a station?"

"Not that I could get us into," said Willis. "This way."

They dropped down to the track level and ran, the emergency lighting barely illuminating the tracks enough to see where to plant their feet.

Reuben pulled out his cellphone. No bars. "Am I getting no signal because I'm below ground, or because the signals are jammed?"

"We've got cellular all the way through the subways," said Willis. "So it's jammed."

"Too bad," said Reuben. "I was going to call in air support."

"I can't believe they're not already here."

"The Air Force may not know yet. It's what, six-thirty in the morning? If nobody in New York can call out, has it even been reported?"

"You can't keep something like this a secret!" said Willis.

"Not forever. But for an hour, maybe you can."

They came to another station. "No," said Reuben. "They'll be waiting at this one. They can move at least as fast above as we can down here. Keep going."

They went on to the next. And the next. Now they were beyond the Holland Tunnel. They'd have to backtrack.

They ran up the stairs to the surface and immediately ran for a side street so they were out of the view of the avenues. They were lucky. No mechs in place to observe them.

"If they had five hundred of these things," Reuben said to Cole, "they could scan the whole city. They don't have that many. Not even close."

"I'm not surprised," said Cole. "What do you think it takes to build one of those? Two million? Six?"

"Real costs or Pentagon costs?" asked Reuben.

"Microsoft costs."

"These are not a Microsoft product," said Reuben.

"Developed in secret, though."

"Yeah, but they don't lock up."

Willis knew the objective and he knew the streets. He'd never been a soldier, but he was a commander, and a good one. His men followed him without argument. So did

Reuben and Cole. You follow the guy who knows what he's doing.

When they got to a bunch of concrete barriers near the entrance to the tunnel, that stopped being Willis and started being Reuben and Cole.

There were no mechs guarding access to the tunnel. But there were a half-dozen men in space-suit uniforms. Helmets that covered their whole heads, even their faces.

"I bet those helmets are transparent from their side," said Cole.

"With a heads-up display and automatic targeting and heat-source tracking," said Reuben.

"And Tetris," said Cole.

"Got to kill these guys," said Reuben. They had no way to deal with prisoners. They needed stealth. "Except maybe the last one, for interrogation."

"Body armor for sure."

"Which I bet their own weapons can pierce."

"They only have to be able to pierce *ours*."

"Let's not make these guys into supermen. Armor's heavy and hot. If it's really secure, with no gaps, these guys are dead on a hot June day like this is gonna be." Reuben pointed toward one. "Yours. Try not to make a lot of noise."

"They're probably transmitting to each other constantly," said Cole.

"So . . . not even a gurgle," said Reuben.

It was a matter of stealth. And stealth meant patience as well as silence. No sudden movements that would catch the peripheral vision of any enemy soldier who had them even slightly in his field of view.

He tried to imagine who might be inside those suits. New guys who had never fought before? Or vets from the Middle East, fed up with the government and eager to use their training to overthrow it? Was he going to face some X-Box geek from Seattle or a killing machine from Fort Bragg?

Something in between. He had instant reflexes—the moment he felt Reuben's hands on him, he started to move. But he hadn't spotted Reuben coming. A killing-machine soldier would never have left so much of his field of view unattended for so long.

Because by the time Reuben's hands were on him, it was already too late for the guy. He turned to the right, so Reuben turned his head sharply to the left and he dropped like a rock.

But inside that helmet, he might have said, "Hey." Or something.

Or maybe not. Because the other guys didn't show any alarm. Cole also got his man silently.

Not so lucky with the next guy. Reuben didn't know whether it was his guy or Cole's who gave the alarm, or maybe just a chance observation, but nobody was standing still to get their neck broken. But they weren't shooting yet, either. Reuben still needed a silent weapon. The Uniball pen he always carried.

Reuben got his man down on the ground and put a knife into his throat under the jaw of the helmet faceplate. It took some wiggling to get the artery. The two remaining guards were shooting now. No doubt calling for reinforcements.

Reuben called to Willis and the cops. "Fill your hands, you sons of bitches!"

Whether they got the movie reference or not, they understood the order and began firing. The bad guys' body armor was good, but it wasn't perfect. Reuben wasn't sure that any of the cops' bullets felled either of the remaining tunnel guards—he knew that he got one of them with his M-240 and Cole was certainly firing the Minimi, so he probably got the other.

Before the firing even stopped, Reuben had one of the helmets off a dead enemy soldier, and was stripping the body armor. "Go ahead!" he shouted to Willis. "If it's our guys on the other end, identify yourselves and for pete's sake tell them we're coming!"

"And if it isn't?"

"Then hide if you can and wait for us and our weapons."

Cole was also stripping material off another soldier. "Cole!" shouted Reuben. "Take a thumb! We want to know who these guys are, not just what they're wearing!"

It was grisly work. But they had to know what they were up against. Criminals? Ordinary civilians? The FBI needed a chance to make an ID.

Reuben knew they were done scavenging when they could hear the thud, thud of approaching mechs.

The cops were already out of sight down the tunnel. "I wonder if they'll come down the tunnel after us," said Cole.

"I've got a helmet and vest," said Reuben. "You drop the ones you got. Keep the pants and the weapon."

They each dropped their version of what the other was keeping, and ran on, that much lighter.

The cops just weren't in Special Ops shape. They caught up with them before they reached the midpoint of the tunnel.

"Don't leave us behind!" one of the uniforms shouted.

"Shut up," said Willis.

"Not leaving you," shouted Reuben. "Setting up a rear guard."

There were no cars in the tunnel. Reuben and Cole set up in recesses in the tunnel wall, one well behind the other, on the opposite side. As the cops jogged and panted past them, Reuben called out. "Leave a relay chain to tell us when you get to the end so we know when to pull back!"

Willis gave a thumbs-up and kept jogging. Up the slope now. Steeper and steeper.

"There's a lot of water over our heads," called Cole.

"Shut up and keep bailing," said Reuben.

After the cops had had enough time to get well up the tunnel, Reuben left his position and moved back to one farther up than Cole's. He was just turning to get in place when they heard the thuds. Lots of them. The mechs were in the tunnel.

"What did we decide our bullets were worth against those mechs?" called Cole.

"Get back here," called Reuben. "No stopping now!"

The rear guard only made sense if they could slow down the enemy. If it was all mechs, then Reuben and Cole would die for no purpose. The mechs were fast. But for a few moments, the curvature of the tunnel would protect them.

When they got to the end of the tunnel, they were met by National Guardsmen who obviously expected them. Thanks, Willis.

"Commander?" asked Reuben.

Twenty steps on, Reuben was greeted by a young captain. "You know what you're doing?" Reuben asked.

"Two tours in Iraq," said the captain. "I've been under fire and gave back."

"You have any artillery?"

"Tanks are almost here."

"Don't do anything till they get here unless you got AT-4s or SMAWs."

"AT-4s, sir. Never used them under fire, though," said the captain. "Didn't face many tanks when I was in Iraq, and the actual teams are raw."

"Now the training pays off," said Reuben. He pointed left and right. "They got armored walker things, mechanicals. Might be manned, might not. They can't be hurt by small arms fire. Minimis and M-240s can get through the body armor on the soldiers, though." He held up the pieces to show. "Don't expose yourselves. The mechs shoot at uniforms."

"Here they come," said the captain, pulling him along toward cover.

Not that they could see anything. But the sound was deafening. How many mechs were down there?

As the mechs came toward the mouth of the tunnel, Reuben checked out their assets. Two AT-4s, one on each side of the roadway. The National Guard had placed themselves well. They might never have been under fire, but they weren't untrained and their leader knew what he was doing.

Meanwhile, Cole was getting Willis and his men to move back farther, completely out of the way. They were useless now, an asset for later that needed to be protected. Cole obviously understood that even if everybody here at the tunnel mouth was killed, the New York cops still had to survive and tell what they'd seen. Cole had even given Willis the body-armor pieces he had scavenged.

Reuben needed to get rid of his own. "Can you spare a guy?" Reuben asked the captain. "These armor pieces need to get back to somebody who can study them and figure out who the hell made them and what we can do against them."

In a moment he was handing the pieces to a young corporal. "Wait," said Reuben. He dug the bloody thumb out of his pocket and handed it to the kid. "Don't puke, just get this to the FBI for fingerprinting. Think of it as spent ammunition that needs ballistics done on it."

The corporal gulped once, pocketed the thumb, and took off running, carrying the armor pieces.

The mechs were emerging from the tunnel now, still in shadow but clearly visible.

"Any time now," Reuben said to the captain.

"Any points of vulnerability?"

"These ain't death stars," said Reuben. "Just hit square on the body. If you get lucky, they blow up real well. They're full of ammunition."

They got lucky.

The first two rockets hit. The two mechs blew up.

I have to tell Mingo what he needs to put in his next arsenal, thought Reuben.

The National Guardsmen were cheering. But the captain was yelling at them. "Keep firing, you boneheads, there could be a hundred of them!" There were already four more visible.

"How many MT-4s you got?" asked Reuben.

"We're National Guard stationed in Jersey," said the captain, "what do you *think*?"

"Does that mean less than ten?"

"That means two more."

"Then fire them as if you had a hundred," said Reuben.

The captain signaled again for them to shoot. Two more hits. Two more scores, though one of the mechs did *not* blow up completely, but fell over and did not try to get up.

The other mechs turned around and ran back down the tunnel.

This time the captain didn't try to stop the cheering.

A couple of guardsmen started running down toward the blown-up mechs.

"Don't go near them!" shouted Reuben. "They might be booby-trapped! You'll get blown to hell!"

The guardsmen stopped. Again, good discipline.

Reuben and Cole made their way down to the one that hadn't blown up. They played the same routine with the back panel. Only they didn't pry the lid off after blowing the keypad and shooting the button.

The hatch came off by itself.

A man's head emerged. He saw the situation—Cole and Reuben with their weapons pointed at him—and ducked back inside.

"Come out and surrender!" demanded Reuben.

He was answered by a single gunshot inside the mech.

"Shit," said Cole.

Reuben ran for the hatch. The man inside had put a pistol in his mouth and fired. But there was less mess than Reuben would have expected. "I think he missed," he said. "Help me get him out."

It was awkward, but finally they each got an arm and pulled him through the hatch. He had shot into his mouth but the barrel had been pointing the wrong way. The bullet had apparently gone up through the roof of his mouth and through his left eye. There was a furrow in the forehead and the skull was open, showing brain. But the guy wasn't dead, even though he was definitely unconscious and his left eye was destroyed, along with his palate and cheekbone.

They dragged him up toward the waiting guardsmen. "Medic?" Reuben asked.

"Ambulance on its way," said the captain. "I called for it when we set out for the tunnel."

"Good man," said Reuben. "Major Reuben Malich," he said. "The guy with me is—"

"Hell, I know who you are, I own a TV. My name is Charlie O'Brien. I'm honored to meet you."

Two things happened while they waited for the tanks to arrive. First, a couple of jets approached Manhattan from the south, flying low. The guardsmen started cheering, but when the jets got close to the Statue of Liberty, the pilots lost control of their aircraft. The jets veered off. One of them hit the water flat on its cockpit; the other smashed through Liberty's gown and then dropped like a rock into the water.

"Tell them not to send any more jets," Reuben said to the captain.

"What *did* that?" said the captain. "I didn't see an explosion or anything."

"A death ray," said Reuben. "Or avian flu," said Reuben impatiently. But the captain wanted a straight answer. "My guess is, a highly focused electromagnetic pulse. F-16s are shielded, but if you can get past it and screw up the electronics, they can't fly. Get on your damn radio and tell them no more jets."

The second thing was, Captain Charlie O'Brien heard something over the radio and turned to Reuben. "I'm supposed to put you guys under arrest."

Reuben looked at him sternly. "That's politics, Charlie. You saw me come out of that tunnel. You saw me and Cole bring along a bunch of New York City cops. We took down four mechs together and you saw me pop the hatch and pull out that poor bastard. I will debrief to you and you can pass that information along. But whoever wants me under arrest is part of the same group that killed the President and Vice President."

"Who?" said Charlie. "Who's doing this?"

"They're Americans," said Reuben. "And anybody could

be on their side, working inside the government, against the Constitution."

"They aren't terrorists?"

"Definitely not," said Cole, who was with them now. "They're the opposite. They were killing all uniforms, but leaving civilians alone wherever possible. Warning them to stay off the streets. These guys mean to occupy and govern New York, not terrorize it and run away."

"Are we under arrest?" asked Reuben.

"Hell no," said Charlie. "But they said they were sending choppers to pick you up. So take my car—it's a Ford Escort back up the road, just press the remote and see which lights come on." He handed Reuben the keys.

"You're going to be in deep shit about this," said Reuben. "I can't take your car."

"Take it and I'll make them *eat* their shit," said Charlie. "We were down there with infantry before those cops started coming up the tunnel. I know which side you're on."

"I don't even know what the sides are yet," said Reuben. "This could be a right-wing militia group that picked New York to punish the capital of pansy left-wing weenies. Or it could be a left-wing militia that went for New York because they think they've already got the hearts and minds of the citizens."

"Whoever they are," said Cole, "they've got a really cool weapons designer and they're willing to blow their own brains out rather than be captured."

"Get to my car and go," said Charlie. "I didn't get the message till you were already gone."

# THIRTEEN

# PASSWORDS

How much responsibility do you bear for the ill uses others might make of your ideas? Almost as much as the responsibility you bear if you fail to speak your ideas, when they might have made a difference in the world.

**REUBEN STAYED** off the toll roads on the way back to Aunt Margaret's house. Too easy to stop traffic for an ID check. Besides, they'd be transporting troops northward. The toll road would be blocked up for miles.

"It probably isn't right to take Charlie O'Brien's car all the way to West Windsor," said Cole. "But I don't see us riding a bus back, either."

"It's wartime," said Reuben. "We'll mail him the keys and tell him where to pick up his car."

"I keep running my head into a brick wall here," said Cole. "How could weapons like this be developed without any intelligence service knowing about it?"

"Easier than you think," said Reuben. "Defense Intelligence is mostly looking abroad for weapons development and manufacture. If they have a key guy in the FBI who knows what *not* to pass upward to his superiors, or who can steer agents away from the right direction, you could probably do it in some out of the way place in this country."

"They had to transport those mechs to New York."

"On trucks painted with the ABF logo so nobody looks twice at them."

"There are inspection stations."

"It's all about money and true believers," said Reuben. "Most of the people in the know are true believers in the cause. They don't talk. And those who aren't true believers are paid a lot of money, and they don't know much anyway."

Cole pushed SEEK on the radio to find a broadcast station running news.

They were all running the news. But it was still scattered. Some kind of disturbance in New York. Two downed jets. Firing reported. All landlines and cellphones silent. Rumors of aliens, of military convoys heading north through New Jersey, warships sailing toward New York, Marines getting ready to land, National Guard troops called out in New Jersey, New York, and Connecticut.

And, oh yes, preparations for the funerals of those who died on Friday the Thirteenth.

"Great. That's how they're going to refer to the assassination of those good men," said Reuben. "Friday the Thirteenth. As if their deaths were simply a stroke of bad luck."

"This is what you were doing, isn't it," said Cole. "Working with weapons sales and development. You *know* how weapons systems are hidden and how they're found."

"I think I was their patsy all along," said Reuben. "I've been going over shipments and contracts. I was tracking some, I was carrying out others. Bidding, buying, selling, passing money to third parties to pass along to fourth parties. They told me I was fighting terrorism, helping penetrate organizations. But I think I may have shipped some of this stuff to the staging areas."

"They did this using government budgets?"

"I don't know whose money I was using. I was a middle man. An errand boy. I had to be smart because sometimes the assignments were dangerous. Guys who'd rather take what you delivered *and* keep the money, which meant killing me. Sending me helped assure that things didn't get ugly."

"How did you prevent it?"

"I recognized the problems going in. If it looked bad, I

aborted the mission. Phillips joked that that's why I was getting the big bucks—for knowing when to walk away from the deal."

"Big bucks?"

"It was a joke," said Reuben. "I drew my salary, period."

"I bet you were a good boy and didn't keep any records."

"I wasn't that good. Encrypted files on my PDA."

"What's your password?"

Reuben couldn't believe he asked. Then he realized Cole was right. "I guess we've got a new system of classification now. Top Secret. Eyes Only. Coleman Only."

"You could have died today," said Cole. "They could arrest you or kill you at any time. You need that PDA out of your possession and someone else needs to know the password. If you think it has evidence."

"I never even told Cessy my passwords," said Reuben. "To protect her."

"It only protects her against a rational enemy," said Cole. "An irrational one won't believe she doesn't know it till she's dead."

"I think these guys are trying to play by some version of American rules."

"Those bullets pouring into the Chinese restaurant at us didn't know who was behind those walls."

"Maybe they had software that recognized our faces. Maybe getting us was worth some collateral damage."

"Password," said Cole.

"And maybe you've been my shadow the past few days just so you could get that password before you kill me," said Reuben. "Maybe you're working for these clowns. They accepted that you might have to kill a few of their guys to earn my trust. You get my password, then you take my PDA and kill me. I don't know you, Cole."

"No, you don't," said Cole. "For a minute there you trusted me, though."

"I did."

"How's it working out so far?" asked Cole.

"I asked for you to be assigned to me," said Reuben. "Then again, I chose from a list. They provided the list."

"We don't know who *they* are," said Cole. "But hang on to the PDA for a while yet. I'm not going to try to force the issue. It's foolish. But I understand the paranoia."

"Thank you," said Reuben. "I still trust you, Cole. I'm taking you home to my family."

"I know," said Cole.

"They didn't know where we were, but they'll figure it out," said Reuben. "Where else would I have gone on the Jersey side of New York City? A little research and they'll be at Aunt Margaret's. Maybe before we even get there."

"So let me out before we get too close," said Cole. "So they don't get us both."

"I keep the PDA at home, or I'd give it to you right now."

"But not the password."

"No, not the password. You'd be my off-site storage."

"Who's trying to arrest us?" said Cole. "Is it the guys who just invaded New York—the ones who are working inside the government to subvert it? Or is it the good guys, who figure it can't just be coincidence that we keep showing up right where the crisis is?"

"All that planted evidence," said Reuben. "They can't ignore it."

"*Is* it just coincidence we keep showing up?"

"It's only happened twice," said Reuben. "First time, they watched us. Not coincidence. Part of their effort to pin it on me. On an American soldier. But today—no, they had no way of knowing we'd decide to take a five A.M. drive to Ground Zero. They certainly weren't going to time this invasion to fit our whims. The second day after the assassinations. Still within the time of maximum chaos. Who's in charge? Nobody's established the chain of command again. What will this President want? How long will he wrestle with the problems before he acts? Ideal time. Nothing to do with us."

"Except that I don't care who did this," said Cole. "They

were killing cops. They were killing uniforms. They may think they're saving the Constitution, but they're saving nothing. It's all about imposing their will on unwilling people."

"But Cole," said Reuben. "Don't you understand? When you have the Truth, then anybody who opposes you is either ignorant or evil. You rule over the ignorant and you kill or lock up the evil. Then you can make the world run according to your perfect Truth."

"On the Left and the Right," said Cole. "Same thing."

"The English Civil War," said Reuben. "On one side, Divine Right of Kings, patriotism, the status quo, the cool long-haired Cavaliers. On the other side, the Puritans, guardians of God's word, short-haired, Bible-carrying perfectionists. Most people couldn't care a rat's ass either way."

"The Puritans had Cromwell."

"So they won. For a while," said Reuben. "But as soon as they had power, they started trying to enact their program. No Christmas, no sports, can't twitch on Sunday, lives of unrelenting work and prayer. No playing, no plays even. No bear-baiting. No heresy tolerated, and that includes the familiar trappings of religion. Ten years of that and the people were ready to bring back the kings—even if they *might* have Catholic sympathies."

"So you're saying that people will get sick of the excesses of whichever group of perfectionists just took over Manhattan."

"Eventually," said Reuben. "But that doesn't mean they can get rid of the Puritans that easily. Cromwell died without a strong successor. Castro flat out didn't die. Hitler and Stalin were too ruthless to be overthrown. Pol Pot just killed everybody. Whenever the fanatics take over, it's a crapshoot whether you can ever get rid of them, at least without a long and bloody struggle, or decades of oppression. Generations."

"So you're saying you have *limited* optimism about the future."

There was nothing to say to that. They drove in silence

for a while as they took some back roads to avoid sirens and Cole studied the state map that Charlie O'Brien carried in his car.

Reuben knew Cole was right about the password to the PDA. The information on there might be the key to finding out where these weapons originated. There was that series of shipments that were going to the Port of New York, ostensibly for overseas shipment. But what if they only got to the port and sat on the dock waiting for the command to take over the city? The trouble was, Reuben wasn't sure where the shipment originated. Again, it *seemed* much of it was coming from the Port of Seattle. But did that mean it came from overseas, or somewhere else on the West Coast, or maybe it originated in Washington, or maybe it was paperworked out of Washington but in fact was shipped from Mexico. For all he knew.

Still, it was a start, that link to Seattle. *If* he really had helped to arrange shipment eastward.

These bastards, plotting to take over New York City, and using government money to pay for it and government agents to handle the paperwork and payments.

Could Phillips possibly be clean? There he was in the White House. He had to be the one who notified the terrorists!

No, no, Reuben told himself. No leaping to conclusions. If they were smart—and so far they've been smarter than me—they'd never have the same guy working on shipments of weapons *and* serving as the inside guy to tip off the terrorists. They'd use two different people.

Two people inside the White House, betraying what was supposedly the most fanatically conservative presidency in history, to hear the Left talk about it—or an endemically corrupt, power-hungry government no matter who was in power, to hear the Right talk about it.

And who inside the Pentagon? It was time to call DeeNee and find out if she knew anything yet.

She wasn't at the office, of course. Or maybe she was—on a Sunday with New York under attack, everybody would be called in. He called her cellphone anyway. She answered on the second ring.

"Hope I didn't interrupt anything," said Reuben.

"I got the preacher to hold the prayer till I'm off the phone," said DeeNee.

"Not really, right?"

"Where are you?" she asked.

"Not in Washington," said Reuben. "If you don't know—"

"I know," she said.

"What do we know?"

"Well, we know you're supposed to be under arrest near the Holland Tunnel," she said, "and there's a guy standing here telling me not to say this."

The phone was apparently torn out of her hand as she said the last few words. A man came on the line.

"Do you realize how guilty you're making yourself look?" Reuben recognized the voice of one of his debriefers.

"I was in New York looking at Ground Zero," said Reuben. "One of their pod monsters started shooting at me. Some cops and I got the sucker down on the ground and looked inside. Then I got a dozen or so cops *out* of the city and helped plug the Jersey side of the Holland Tunnel. There I pulled a semi-living soldier out of one of the mechs for later interrogation. I also saved the body armor and personal electronics of one of their ground troops. And you want to *arrest* me for something you know damn well I tried to *prevent*?"

There was silence for a moment.

"Hell, Malich, I don't want to arrest you, but that's the orders we're getting."

"Getting from where?" said Reuben. "Doesn't it occur to you that the same people who gave my plans to the terrorists might be the people who are ordering you to arrest me?"

"Major Malich, you know as well as I do that it's possible to be a hero *and* a traitor. Benedict Arnold was."

"Not on the same damn day," said Reuben. He turned the phone off.

"Probably talked too long," said Cole.

"They already know I'm in Jersey."

"I'd throw away that phone."

"And lose all my speed dial numbers?" Reuben tossed it out the window. "This is getting expensive. I wish I had some of the budget these guys had to build the mechs."

"I thought they were pod monsters."

"One is the brand name, the other's the generic. Like Coke and soda pop."

"Or heroin and smack. I noticed how you made yourself the lone ranger. I did this, I did that."

"Trying to keep you out of the discussion."

"Yeah, like the cops will forget there were *two* Army guys helping them."

"I can't stand to share credit," said Reuben. "Live with it."

Reuben came toward Aunt Margaret's house from the north and parked the car two streets away. "Keeping your weapons with you?" he asked Cole.

"I'm not taking a piss without my weapons, sir," said Cole.

"Just don't yank the clip out of the wrong one," said Reuben.

"I'll keep that in mind, sir." Cole got out of the car.

Reuben drove on to the house.

Nobody waiting out in front. No news vans. No police cars. No military vehicles. No unmarked black cars with guys in suits.

So maybe the guys who were after him weren't perfect.

Or maybe they just didn't care enough right now to make him a top priority, compared to, say, conquering New York.

When he went into the house, Cessy greeted him with a hug. She had been crying. "Where were you?" she said.

"I don't think we can make it to Mass this morning," he said.

"You were there, weren't you. You and Coleman, you had to go into the city, didn't you?"

"We didn't know this was invasion day," said Reuben. "But we got out alive. Now we've got to get out of here.

They know we're in Jersey, it doesn't take a genius to think of checking the homes of known relatives."

"Who's after you?" she asked.

"I don't know. There's an order from the Pentagon to arrest me. But I don't know if it's the good guys, who are fooled by the phony evidence planted against me, or the bad guys, hoping to use that as an excuse to get their hands on me and shut me up for good. Where are the kids?"

"I confined them to their rooms. Mark and Nick are entertaining the girls and J. P."

Aunt Margaret came in dangling keys. "Take my PT Cruiser."

"We won't all fit," said Reuben.

"You aren't taking the kids," said Margaret. "Don't be insane. People are shooting out there. This is a nice little house in a nice little town in the Garden State. But the two of you are very smart. You need to get away from the kids to keep them safe."

"In your PT Cruiser."

"I have your nice SUV. Where's the one you borrowed to come here?"

"In the city," said Reuben. "I don't want to leave the kids."

"Neither do I," said Cessy.

Her cellphone rang. "I guess it's not you," she said.

She said hello and then listened. Then she said "all right" about five times and hung up.

"That's one hell of a cold-call salesman if you just bought new carpet," said Reuben.

"That was Sandy. LaMonte wants us to meet with him."

"Us? You and me?"

"And Captain Coleman. Where is he? He's all right, isn't he?"

"He walked the last couple of blocks in full battle gear. In case this place was surrounded."

The doorbell rang. Aunt Margaret opened it. "You have blood on your uniform, young man."

"I had a cut thumb," said Cole. He held up his Minimi. "In a neighborhood like this, I feel like a little kid playing army men. Can I come in?"

"*May* I come in is more proper," said Aunt Margaret, opening the door wider to let him pass. "But it's rude to correct people's grammar, so I never do."

**THE PT** Cruiser didn't like going faster than 65. At 70 it started trembling.

Then again, Cessy didn't like driving faster than 65 anyway. And she was driving. Cole was sitting behind the seats with the shelf over his head. They looked like two nice citizens on their way to or from church. Unless you looked closely and saw all the weapons on the floor of the back seat. And the guy in the back with the machine gun.

Aunt Margaret was taking the kids to the home of some very good friends in Hamilton. "Good Croatians," she said. "They'll not breathe a word. And I'll stay with the kids the whole time." She was only driving Charlie O'Brien's car as far as Lawrence, and her friends were picking her up there. She'd mail Charlie's keys to him and tell him where to get the car. "I feel like a spy," she said.

"You should feel like a refugee," answered Cessy.

But it still tore her apart to leave the kids behind. And she could see that even though Mark was as manic as ever and Nick as quiet, they were scared. There was terrible stuff happening on the news, and their own parents were right in the thick of it, and now they were going into hiding. The girls, of course, were irritated that Mom and Dad were leaving them, but they had no clue about the outside world. They'd be fine, she was sure of that. Fine fine fine.

"I thought I turned down that job in the White House," Cessy said.

"Well," said Reuben, "technically, since the President isn't in the White House . . ."

Cessy wished she could have heard the discussions when LaMonte told them he wasn't going to Camp David or any of the known locations. "Since we don't know whom we can trust," LaMonte would have said, "we can't vouch for our security anywhere."

"Some political adviser was bound to say, 'It'll look like you're in hiding. It'll cause confusion and make you look bad.'"

"I'm not running for anything right now," LaMonte would have said. "And the country doesn't need another dead President right now."

But . . . why Gettysburg?

"Gettysburg?" she said out loud.

"It's an appropriate place," said Reuben. "He's not moving the whole government there, just himself and enough aides to keep communications going. Lots of parkland. A good buffer. Relatively easy to maintain reasonable security."

"Plenty of places for people to sneak past checkpoints," said Captain Coleman from the back.

"Symbolically," said Reuben, "it's the place where the last Civil War we had broke its back. And it's close to Washington. He can come back whenever he wants."

"Also lots of motels for his staff," said Captain Coleman.

"And since the visitors information office is closed most of the time, it won't really interfere with park operations," said Reuben.

Cessy explained to Captain Coleman. "He's still irritated that we got there after six on a summer day and they were already closed. Three more hours of daylight. This was two years ago, remember."

"I just don't understand why government has to be run without reference to what people actually want and need," said Reuben.

"People want so many different things," said Cessy. "Some people want visitors' centers open late. Other people want lower taxes."

"Other people want to take over a city here, a city there."

"Oh look," said Cessy. "Aunt Margaret has XM. We can listen to the news."

Reuben turned on the system and went straight to Fox News. They listened for a while. No mention of attacks on any city other than New York. Lots of speculation about the death ray that brought down the F-16s. Speculation about what city would be next. Speculation about casualties in New York. Experts talking about how long New York could last without trucks bringing in food and fuel. Other experts talking about how many businesses would be shut down because their workers couldn't get into the city tomorrow.

Speculation on foreign powers that might take advantage of the present situation. Speculation about foreign powers that might be behind all of this. Was this a terrorist takeover? What would the United States do if Manhattan was being held hostage? What were the diplomats at the United Nations going to do?

Eventually, though, some answers started coming through, in an endless succession of news bulletins. It came from the United Nations, where a group of diplomats from Germany, France, and Canada were allowed to take off in a helicopter and go to Kennedy, where they held a press conference. The Canadian ambassador did most of the talking, and most of what he said came from documents provided him by the invaders.

"The military force that took over Manhattan affirms that not one civilian has been harmed."

"What a lie," said Coleman. "We saw one dead doorman with our own eyes."

"They call themselves the Progressive Restoration. They declare that Progressives won the popular vote and the electoral vote for President in 2000, and only flagrant vote-stealing by the radical Right kept the duly elected President from taking office."

"Please say they're not bringing back Al Gore," said Reuben.

"Shut up, please, boys," said Cessy.

"Since stealing office, the usurpers trampled on the Bill of Rights, involved the United States in illegal and immoral foreign wars, destroyed the environment, oppressed minorities of every kind, imposed their brand of Christianity on the whole country, stifled scientific research, ran up huge deficits, and flaunted—I'm sure they mean flouted—"

"He's correcting their grammar now," said Reuben.

"Flouted world opinion and international law, and brought the world to the brink of disaster."

"They didn't mention Zionism," said Coleman. "What are they thinking?"

"Now the radical right wing, which dominates the U.S. Army, has planned and carried out the assassination of their own President and Vice President as the first step toward imposing full-fledged dictatorship on the United States. Only this national emergency prompted the Progressives to take action in defense of freedom against the totalitarian Christian and Zionist agenda."

"They were saving it up for last," said Reuben.

"The Progressives have liberated New York City, they say, as the first step to restoring Constitutional government to the United States."

"All they have is Manhattan," said Coleman.

"They are not interested in war with the illegal government, but they are prepared to defend New York City against any attempt to impose hegemony over the city. They encourage the U.N. to remain in New York City and affirm that it will be protected and all diplomatic rights respected. They have petitioned the city of New York to recognize the Progressive Restoration as the acting government-in-exile of the United States of America and they invite all other cities and states in the United States to recognize the Progressive government and no other as the legitimate government of the United States."

The official announcement was over. Reuben reached over and turned down the press questions. "So it was the Left," he said.

"But it could have been the Right," said Cessy.

"And it could very easily turn into a war between the wackos of one side and the wackos of the other," said Reuben. "We saw it in Yugoslavia. People were getting along fine, Serbs and Croats, Christians and Muslims. But when the wackos started shooting, you either had to shoot back or die. Not wanting to fight didn't protect you. You had to choose up sides."

"There weren't any sides today," said Coleman. "Just uniforms and non-uniforms."

"The whole leftist philosophy is about rejecting authority," said Reuben bitterly. "And replacing it with an even more rigid list of forbidden ideas. The only difference is that the Progressive thought police won't wear uniforms."

"Stop it," said Cessy. "Like I said, it could have been the right wing, and then the thought police would carry Bibles."

"Let's not do this now," said Reuben.

"But you *were* doing it," she said. "You're married to a liberal, Reuben."

"Not an insane one."

"Most of us are not insane. Just like most conservatives are like you, reasonable people. You warn us how it could turn into a war just like Yugoslavia, and then you start condemning the other guys like their ideas don't matter."

"I was, wasn't I," said Reuben. "I'm just so angry. They killed the President."

"Really? All the Progressives of America, all the liberals, they got together and plotted to kill the President?"

"But they're *glad.*"

"No. You're wrong. The sick ones, yes. The sad, miserable, mind-numbingly self-righteous ones, sure. But most of them are in shock. They didn't do it and they didn't want it done. They didn't ask for anyone to invade New York, either."

"But they'll let it stand, won't they?"

"They might. Or they might enthusiastically join this Progressive Restoration. That's what they're counting on, aren't they? That people will flock to their banner. And if *we* start talking and thinking the way you were talking and thinking just now, Reuben, then we'll end up *driving* them to the Progressive banner. So stop it!"

Reuben looked out the side window.

"Reuben," said Cessy. "I think the great American achievement of our war against terror was that we did it without having to hate all Arabs or all Muslims or even all Iranians, even though they're financing it now. We stayed focused. We waged a war without hate."

"Except for the Americans who hated *us* for fighting it."

"Do you hate them, Reuben? Enough to kill them?"

He shook his head. "You're right," he said. "Completely right. But they're tearing apart my country. They're killing guys like me because we volunteered to defend it. You can't expect me to stay calm."

"When it's all over," said Cessy, "I want you to come home as Reuben Malich."

"Me too," said Reuben. "I will." And then he turned again toward the window and Cessy realized that he was crying, his forehead resting on his right hand, tears dropping straight down from his eyes onto his lap. "I killed a man with my bare hands today," he said. "And another with a knife. And another with a spray of bullets. I cut off a guy's thumb."

Cessy had nothing to say to that. She knew that was the kind of thing a soldier had to do. If he hadn't done it, he'd have been found and killed. He got other men out of the city alive. He helped stop the mechs at the Jersey end of the Holland Tunnel. And that's how jobs like that are done— with force. Force unto death.

But she couldn't say, There there, that's all right. It wasn't all right. It was a terrible thing. It had to be done, and because he and Coleman were the ones who knew how, it had to be done by them.

Steering with her left hand, she hooked her right hand through the crook of Reuben's left arm. She slid her hand down the inside of his arm, pulling it closer until she was holding his hand. She squeezed. He squeezed back. But he still cried.

In the back, Coleman had brains enough to keep silent.

On the radio, the press conference and commentary

went on and on, almost too soft to hear now. A constant background of commentators pooling their ignorance but coming, bit by bit, closer to the conclusion that a second American revolution had begun, if you viewed it one way, or a second civil war, if you looked at it another.

"What did that professor of yours say?" Cessy asked softly.

"What?"

"At Princeton. That one professor. What's his name? Torrance. No, that's a city in California."

"Torrent."

"About the fall of Rome. How civil wars in the Roman Republic led to the foundation of the empire."

"Oh, yeah, I bet Torrent's happy now," said Reuben. "He's getting all the chaos he could ask for."

"He really is the same guy they just made National Security Adviser, right?"

"Yes," said Reuben. "He was already a top adviser to the NSA. Adviser to the adviser. Now that Sarkissian is Secretary of State, they bumped Torrent up to NSA."

"If Congress approves him."

"Oh, that's one thing President Nielson's got for sure—a rubberstamp Congress. Time of national emergency and all that."

"Maybe not," said Coleman from the back.

"So . . . *will* Torrent be happy?" asked Cessy.

"No, of course not. I just meant—he just said that before America could truly be great, we had to—have a crisis that would end the republic and bring about—no, he can't be part of this."

"Why not?"

"He didn't *advocate* it," said Reuben. "He just . . . but the way he talked . . . somebody could get the wrong idea. Somebody with a little megalomaniac in him could decide to try to act on Torrent's theory. Fulfill his prophecy."

"So it might be a bunch of his former students doing this?"

"All it would take is *one* former student in the group. Or just somebody who went to a speech of his. He used to lecture all over the place. I don't know if this Roman Empire thing is in any of his books. Wouldn't that be a weird situation to be in? National Security Adviser to a President who's fighting a civil war caused by somebody following *your* theory."

"Kind of like having the President assassinated by somebody using your plan," said Coleman from the back.

"Yeah," said Reuben. "Like that."

Silence for a while. Then Reuben said, "Zarathustra."

"What?" asked Cessy.

"I'm telling Cole. The password. To my files. 'Zarathustra.' And then when the software tells you that you're wrong, type in 'Marduk.' " He spelled it.

"You're so paranoid you doubled your password?" said Cessy.

"Hope I never need to use them," said Coleman.

"I've got to trust somebody. And if I die, I don't want that data lost."

Cessy shook her head. "Ancient gods of Iran and Iraq."

"Zarathustra was a prophet, not a god," said Reuben.

"They sacrificed children to Marduk, didn't they?" said Cessy.

"You're thinking of Moloch."

"Gods of war, either way," said Cessy.

"But not *my* God," said Reuben. "I don't take *his* name in vain."

I hope we can learn to forgive our enemies, thought Cessy. I hope God forgives us for daring to decide that we know when it's right to kill.

But if men like my husband weren't willing to kill in defense of civilization, then the world would be doomed to be ruled by those who were willing to kill in pursuit of their own power.

I'll explain all that to God on judgment day. I know he's just waiting for me to clarify the matter.

If he sends these good soldiers to hell for killing the enemies of their country, then I'll go with them.

# FOURTEEN

# GETTYSBURG

You don't know who a person is until you see how he acts when given unexpected power. He hasn't rehearsed for the part. So what you see is what he is.

**COLE WAS** sure that not since July of 1863 had there been so many soldiers in and around Gettysburg. And they were in combat gear—this was an armed camp. They started running into military checkpoints at the crossroads at York Springs, and then four more times before they got into the town itself. The first time it took some argument before they were allowed to keep their weapons.

Standing outside the car, Cole tried to keep his temper with the young MP who insisted on disarming him. "This morning I fired these weapons at the enemies of the United States who were attacking us on our native soil. I killed at least one enemy soldier with it. What has *your* weapon done today, soldier?"

But it was Cecily Malich's call to her former boss, Sandy Woodruff, that led to their getting passed through the other checkpoints without delay and fully armed.

The President was installed at Gettysburg College, which for the moment was the seat of the executive branch of the government of the United States. Cole and the Malichs were sent to a motel that would have been a lovely surprise in a village in the mountains of Iran, but which Cole's family would have disdained on any of their cross-country trips.

Rooms were at such a premium that Cole finally had to get in the face of the officious young clerk making the assignments and explain, "I'm not their son," before he gave way and assigned them separate accommodations.

"Good job of making yourself memorable," Rube said to him before they disappeared into their room.

Cole only had a few minutes to unpack and use the bathroom before there was a knock at his door. MPs had been sent to escort them—this time definitely unarmed—to the President's office.

It made Cole vaguely disappointed that when he actually got to meet a President of the United States, it was only the stand-in, not the real one. LaMonte Nielson was a little shorter than Cole, and seemed nice enough and intelligent enough as he came forward to greet them. But he also looked just a little surprised to see them. A little too grateful that they had answered his summons. You're the President, man! Of course we came! But Cole kept his reaction to himself. He'd done enough exasperated talking today. Especially considering that he was only in this room out of courtesy. It was Rube and Cecily that the President wanted to talk with. Cole was there just to have his hand shaken and get the official thanks of the President for his heroic actions in the face of yadda yadda yadda.

Only there wasn't any yadda. Nielson asked them to sit and then half-sat on the edge of the college president's desk and said, "The city council of New York met today in emergency session and voted by an overwhelming margin to recognize the Progressive Restoration as the legitimate government of the United States of America."

"Under duress?" asked Cecily.

"U.N. witnesses say there was no threat from the Progressive Restoration."

"Except their troops all over Manhattan," muttered Reuben.

"That's only the beginning. San Francisco, Santa Monica, San Rafael—I can't remember all the Sans in California that have passed resolutions recognizing the Progressive Restoration."

"But those have no legal force," said Cecily.

"I'm sure the Supreme Court would agree with you. The Attorney General certainly does. But so what? Progressive state legislators in California, Oregon, Washington, Vermont, Massachusetts, Hawaii, and Rhode Island have all declared their intention to demand a quick vote in those legislatures. There are others calling for plebiscites in Minnesota, Wisconsin, New Hampshire, Connecticut, New York state, Maryland, and Delaware. Let the people decide, they say."

"They'll fail," said Cecily.

"Probably," said President Nielson. "Probably the first motion will fail. Oh, and needless to say, all over the South and Midwest and Rocky Mountains there are political leaders demanding the immediate suppression by force of any political unit that goes over to the Progressives. Rural and suburban legislators in many of the states in question have been . . . fervent, let's say . . . in their opposition to any movement to switch allegiance. But you see my predicament."

"Is the Army loyal?" asked Cecily.

"Think about what you're asking," said Nielson. "Loyal? Of course. Willing to fire on Americans who do not fire on them first? What an interesting question. Wouldn't it be better if we could avoid fighting?"

"There's already been bloodshed," said Reuben. "And they killed first."

"Fort Sumter," said Nielson. "And if I were Lincoln, I'd issue a call for 75,000 volunteers. But we don't have such a clear Mason-Dixon line. The red-state/blue-state thing is actually deceptive. If you look at recent elections on maps of the counties, you'll find that it's an urban versus suburban and rural split. Even southern states show metropolitan areas as blue more than red."

"But that's the black vote," said Reuben.

"Oh good," said President Nielson. "Let's make it a racial war as well as a philosophical one. But here's the point. The New York City Council has legalized this invasion after the fact and now declares the armed forces of the Progressive Restoration to be the police and defense forces of the entire city, not just Manhattan. Under those circumstances, if we attack or occupy any part of New York City, are we liberating or invading? When we fire on their armed forces, are we killing traitors or shooting down New York cops?"

"I know who the New York cops are," said Reuben. "They killed as many of them as they could find."

"It's public perception. They've played this beautifully. I have to admire it, even as it makes me want to weep for my country. They provided arms, plans, and information to terrorists so they could behead the country. Our strongest leadership wiped out in a stroke. Then they set up a rightwing coup to establish martial law and abrogate the Constitution during this time of emergency." Nielson sighed and looked down at his shoes.

"A phony coup," said Cole.

"Oh, yes," said Nielson. "General Alton came into my office and told me that he and a large number of officers were ready to implement my order to establish martial law. He didn't call it a coup. He was handing it to me. But I was so naive and so—what's the word I want?—yes, so *stupid* . . . that I didn't even recognize the veiled threat—that martial law would be declared anyway, with or without me. I was new at this. I was frightened. I was not well advised." Nielson walked around behind his desk and finally sat in the president's chair. "If it had not been for your broadcast, Captain Coleman, I would have announced martial law at nine P.M. yesterday. The President's writers—oh, they would be mine now, wouldn't they—were scrambling to write an appropriate speech. I was just about to read the final draft when Sandy came in and told me to switch to O'Reilly and listen to one of the soldiers who tried to prevent the assassinations.

"You reminded the soldiers of their duty. You reminded me of mine. I finally saw what Alton was doing. As God is my witness, it was never my intent to throw out the Constitution. I thought it was hanging by a thread, and I could save it." He chuckled bitterly. "You don't save it by cutting that thread."

"You didn't make the announcement," said Cecily. "That's what matters."

"It's more than that," said Nielson. "I remembered how Alton talked. Thinking back on it, it was crazy. A paranoid version of conservative principles. It should have been obvious. It was like a parody, the Left's version of the Right. But you see, I was a Congressman from Idaho. The people who fund my campaigns talk like that. It's the looniest ones who pony up the most, sometimes—ideology opens the pocketbook. I'd been hearing their lunacy for so long that it didn't sound irrational to me anymore. I was used to madness.

"Well, so is the Left," he continued. "The wackos on both sides have controlled the rhetoric for so long that the Left really thinks they're right when they call simple mistakes 'lies' and openly-arrived-at decisions 'conspiracies.' That city council in New York, if you said to them, 'Will you secede from the United States and bring the full wrath of the U.S. military down on your city?' they'd say no. They'd say *hell* no."

"Actually," said Reuben, "this is New York you're talking about. They'd say—"

"I know what words they'd use," said Nielson, smiling tightly. "But I don't use them. Look, these Progressives, they're playing it smart. Keeping the tempo up. They undoubtedly already had people on the council, ready to drive things forward. It's not a coincidence that there are legislators and city councilors in all the blue states, calling for their city or state to get on the bandwagon. I think they've already counted the votes while we were napping. I think tomorrow morning we'll find that Washington or Oregon, maybe even California, officially ceases to recognize me as

President of the United States. If I had declared martial law last night, I think it would be a dead certainty that they *all* would. Because I would be out in the open as a tool of the insane faction of the extreme right wing."

"Are you saying," said Reuben, "that you intend to do nothing?"

"I intend to proceed carefully," said Nielson. "The New York City Council has declared that their borders are peaceful—and open. Everyone who works in the city is invited to come to work tomorrow, and apart from some reconstruction work and traffic problems because of the damage caused by . . ."

He picked up a paper on his desk and read from it. " 'Caused by the illegal resistance of reactionary forces' . . . apart from that, it should be business as usual. But any attempt to restrict access to New York City will result in sudden, harsh retaliation. 'We will defend ourselves.' "

Reuben shook his head. "You can't let this stand. If you let people go to work, if you let trucks in with food and fuel—"

"If I don't, then I'm starving perfectly good Americans as part of my fascist conspiracy to force theocratic antienvironmental—I can't do their rhetoric very well, but you know what I mean. Remember the propaganda that Saddam got from the embargo, even after we were supposedly letting humanitarian aid get into Iraq."

"You're going to let public relations determine the course of this war?" asked Reuben.

"Spoken like a soldier," said Nielson, not unfavorably. "But as my advisers—*my* advisers *now*—point out, it's already a public relations war. It's about winning the hearts and minds of the people. If we leap in with guns blazing, we might win—and we might not, because those jets they knocked down yesterday have the Air Force generals wetting their pants—but what do we have? A huge portion of our population will believe that they are now an oppressed and conquered people. We will *prove* that the Progressives were right, and guess who wins the election this fall?"

"You think people would vote for the very people who tried to break this country apart?"

"But they *aren't* breaking it apart," said Nielson, smiling sarcastically. "They're simply restoring government by the principles that the American people voted for in 2000, and which have been suppressed for all these years by the evil right-wing conspiracy. This is not the American Civil War. It isn't one region against the other. There are no boundaries. What kind of war can we wage if we have no secure areas? How can we tell, looking at the local populations, who is for us and who is against us? Who is a supporter and who is a saboteur? And then consider collateral damage. And then consider the way most of the media is playing this. Oh, they cluck their tongues about those bad people who took over New York, but their stories are full of admiration for the chutzpah of it—and for the high technology, and for the 'peaceful approach' they're taking now. Naturally, everybody is calling for negotiations. I've had so many messages from European governments begging me to negotiate I could paper these walls with them."

"Now we know how the Israelis feel," said Cole.

"Except we'd have to build about a hundred fences to separate the red from the blue," said Reuben.

"Not to mention," Cole added, "sorting out which soldiers are actually *from* the cities in rebellion."

"Now you understand," said Nielson.

"So why did you bring us here?" asked Cecily. "Surely not for more advice."

"What I need," said Nielson. "What the country needs. Is proof. Proof of this conspiracy. And I think you have it. Major Malich, I think you were set up. But I hear you can identify who leaked your assassination plans if you have the copy the FBI found in the terrorists' apartment."

"I think I can, yes sir," said Reuben.

President Nielson lifted a file folder from his desk. "This is a copy of the one we found. The original had your fingerprints all over it."

"Anyone else's?"

"Your secretary's. But no others. Which is one of the reasons the FBI is suspicious of it. Did the terrorists wear gloves when they handled the paper?"

"It should have the prints of the leaker, too, and everyone who handled it before him," said Reuben.

"From this we conclude that it went to the leaker first," said Nielson. "And the leaker didn't want to risk smearing or covering your prints. So *he* wore gloves as he copied it, and then bagged the original so no new fingerprints would get on it."

"I wish I could tell you just by looking at it," said Reuben. "But it's DeeNee who knows which version is which and where they went first."

"I urge you to call her."

"The last time I did, she was closely supervised by people who thought it was urgent that I be arrested."

"Arrested? Who gave that order? I specifically told them *not* to arrest you."

They all knew what that meant.

"It's a strange time to be President," said Nielson. "Nobody knows who's on which team. It will sort itself out eventually, but right now I need proof of who it was in the Pentagon who conspired to kill the President and lay the groundwork for this Progressive Restoration nonsense."

Cecily laughed harshly. "This gets worse and worse. Because if you do start laying off people just on suspicion of being Progressive sympathizers, your opponents in Congress *and* the press will screech that you're imposing an ideological test on government employees."

"It's why we need proof. Even if you have to go to the Pentagon to get it, Major Malich."

"Can I choose and arm a team of my own choosing?" asked Reuben. "I'll also need a letter of authorization from you. Giving me supreme authority over all personnel whose obedience I require in pursuing my assignment. Because I have to be able to tell any general who stands in my way to get lost."

"I'll also detail two Secret Service agents to accompany

you," said Nielson. "The Secret Service has always prided themselves on protecting even people they despise."

"Do you have any idea yet who it was inside the White House?"

"One of the household staff," said Nielson. "She hasn't shown up for work. We believe she's in hiding. But fellow staff members say she was bitter about her son's injury in Iraq three years ago. He lost a hand. She blamed the President. I suspect if we do find her, she'll be dead before we arrive. Maybe she didn't know she was triggering an assassination. But maybe she did. The people who can hurt us are the ones that we trust."

"Why did you need *me*?" asked Cecily.

"You mean apart from the fact that I need somebody who can speak the language of the Left and help me translate my statements into neutral rhetoric?"

"I already turned you down for that job."

"I was hoping you could do some clerical work for me," said Nielson. "Immediately after his arrest, Steven Phillips, an aid to the NSA, provided us with his few scraps of notes about illegal arms trading that was being run out of the White House. Since some of this work was done by your husband, I thought you might have a vested interest in finding who was sending what to whom. Especially since Phillips was happy to tell us that he knew nothing much at all, it was completely Reuben Malich's operation."

"So, *was* Phillips part of the conspiracy?" asked Cole.

"No, he's just a bureaucratic weasel," said Reuben.

"Actually, the jury's still out on that question," said Nielson. "Not about whether he's a weasel—his weaselhood is self-demonstrating."

They all laughed. Only partly because he was President.

"There are better people than me to conduct this investigation," said Cecily. "I have children to take care of."

"I'm not asking you for a career decision, Cecily," said Nielson. "Or a lifestyle choice. The people I can trust who are also capable don't really make up that big a list." He leaned across the desk. "For your country, Cecily Grmek."

"Malich," she corrected him.

"I'm asking the idealist who used to think she could turn me into a liberal if she found just the right piece of data to pass along to me."

"The kids aren't that far away," said Reuben. "After things settle down a little, maybe we can bring them here."

"Besides," said President Nielson, "Major Malich will be reporting directly to me. On this and all his future assignments. If you're here, you'll see a lot more of him."

Cecily nodded, but Cole could see she was still torn. We all make sacrifices in wartime, he said to himself silently. But he wasn't married; he wasn't a father. It was easier for him. His mother would miss him if he was gone. His father was already dead. His siblings—they got along fine. It wouldn't disrupt their lives if he died. But for Cecily and Rube, it wasn't like that. With both of them gone, their children would be parentless for a while. Temporary orphans. Never easy on kids.

Like it wasn't easy on Cole when his father died. And they had plenty of warning on that. Cancer. Months of chemo. And then the news that it hadn't done the job, it was just a matter of time. They were able to say good-bye. Able to see how the disease wasted his body and tore him apart inside until he was ready to go, and death came as a relief. That was hard enough on Cole, knowing his father loved him, hearing him say, several times, I'm proud of you, Barty, keep making me proud.

Dad couldn't help going. Reuben is under orders. But Cecily feels like she has a choice. So . . . if she abandons her children for a while, does that make her *worse* or nobler?

Glad I have my life, thought Cole, as he did so often. Rather my life than anyone else's that I know of.

"As for you, Captain Coleman," said the President.

"Oh, I'm going with Reuben," said Cole, without thinking who he was talking to.

"You are?" asked Nielson.

"I'm in his team," said Cole. "I'm his number two. Whether he likes it or not. I was *assigned*."

"I was thinking of reassigning you. We need a military spokesman with your—"

"Mr. President, you wouldn't take a fighting machine like me and waste me in front of cameras, would you? You need to watch *First Blood* again and think of me as being about as articulate as Stallone."

"Rambo couldn't have said the sentence you just said," Cecily said.

"You said Major Malich could choose his own squad," said Cole. He looked to Reuben for support, half expecting him to say, Obey your commander-in-chief.

"He's right, Mr. President. I need him more than you do."

"Then he's yours. This meeting is adjourned."

As they came out of the President's office, there were several people waiting to get in. Sitting on a wooden bench, not looking eager to enter, was a slender man of perhaps thirty-five, who looked like he played tennis a little, and swam a little, but mostly read books through those rimless glasses and wrote brilliant essays with those slender, graceful fingers. The poster child for what every professor wanted to grow up to be, and what every politician wished he could put on his posters. Cole had never seen him before, but couldn't take his eyes off him.

The tennis-playing professor rose to his feet and held out his hand to Rube. "Soldier Boy," said the professor.

"Professor Torrent," said Rube. "I go by Major Malich now."

So this was Averell Torrent, the young hotshot of the NSA's office who had just been nominated to be NSA as his boss bumped up. The Torrent whose essays on history had been all the rage a couple of years ago. Since he was a Princeton professor then, Cole had assumed it was History For Liberals, meaning that it would be elaborate explanations of why whatever the Republican administration was doing was wrong, complete with references to global warming and the need for negotiations under all circumstances. Therefore he hadn't read it. But Reuben knew him, and even if he was a little prickly about the "soldier boy" greeting, Rube was showing him deeper respect than he had shown to President Nielson.

"So the President has brought you aboard," said Torrent.

"Both of us," said Rube, including Cecily. Then he indicated Cole as well. "All three of us."

Torrent looked at Cole somewhat quizzically. "Very powerful sermon on Fox last night," he said.

"Thanks," said Cole. But he thought: It sounded to you like a sermon?

"We have some interesting new armaments that are being rushed out of prototype to meet these mechs," said Torrent. "I know you're a dirt-and-languages kind of soldier, but you have to love some of the new weaponry, Major Malich."

"You got something that will trip a two-legged tank?" asked Rube.

"We've got a foam that dries in two seconds and then won't let go. Basically, you glue them to the ground like gum." Torrent grinned. "Some of these geniuses in weapons development must be thrilled to have a chance to use some of this far-out stuff."

"As long as some of them didn't moonlight by coming up with the Progressives' weapons in the first place," said Rube.

"And magnets," said Torrent. "You lay them like mines, and anything big and metallic that passes within twenty feet is pulled toward it and can't get free. And grenades that are all shockwave, no flame. Hit one of those mechs with it, and everything comes loose inside. Lovely things."

"I'm glad our troops will have *something*," said Rube. "Have they figured out what shot down those F-16s?"

"A hyperpowerful EMP."

"That would suck up so much power the city'd black out," said Rube.

"They think it might be laserized, so you get a lot more clout for the kilowatt. Whatever it is, it wipes out the electronics that keep those planes aloft."

"So we're going to do what, go back to propeller planes?" asked Rube.

Torrent paused for a moment. "You know, that's not a bad idea. The jets hang back for air cover, and the little biplanes come on in, machine guns blazing. Like shooting down King Kong."

"Looks like you're having fun, Professor," said Rube.

"War triggers human inventiveness at its most brilliant, because if you don't win your wars, your civilization disappears."

"It's bad form to quote yourself," said Rube, smiling.

"I said that before?"

"Don't worry," said Rube. "Quoting Averell Torrent makes everybody look smarter."

Torrent clapped him on the shoulder and they moved down the corridor as Torrent disappeared inside the President's office.

"So you know Torrent," said Cole.

"Had three seminars from him in grad school."

"Is he too dashing to be smart and too smart to be so dashing?" asked Cecily.

"He's got more ego than a movie star," said Rube, "but unlike most of my former professors, he has the brains to back it up. He never served in the military but he has his own version of history that works better than most others, and he has an eye for strategy. President Nielson isn't wrong to seek his advice."

"But he irritates you," said Cole.

"He *works* at irritating me," said Rube. "I don't know what I did to get under his skin, but he rode me all the way through three seminars and gave me hell during my orals."

"How did he irritate you just now?" asked Cole. "Besides calling you 'soldier boy.'"

"He's got a severe case of Winston-Churchill-itis. Churchill was the genius of global politics, so Torrent has to be, too. Churchill went ape over every wacko bit of military tech that came up, so Torrent has to pretend he's a tech guy."

"He isn't?"

"No more than Churchill was. I don't know why I think

he's faking his enthusiasm. Maybe because a former advisor to the NSA wouldn't usually know that much about cutting-edge weaponry." Rube stopped and took Cecily by the shoulders. "Cessy," he said, "the stuff on my PDA will make your job easier. As soon as I get back, I'll give it to you."

"Give it to me now so I can get started," said Cecily.

"Everything's in Farsi," said Rube.

"The names and addresses?" asked Cecily.

"They don't mean anything without an explanation. I'll be back by noon tomorrow. I'll just pop in to the Pentagon, pull DeeNee and my files out, and then we're home."

"Then take a minute and copy it to another computer," Cecily insisted.

Rube hesitated. "Cessy," he said softly. "I don't know how the stuff on here will make me look. The minute I let a copy be made, it's out of my hands. Somebody can steal it. Somebody can leak it."

"Then leave the PDA with me," said Cessy. "I'll take better care of it than you can. There'll be no chance of it falling out of your pocket or getting bumped when another army of mechs walks into Arlington."

"There's information in it that I might need while I'm in DC," said Rube.

"You really aren't going to part with it for any reason, are you?" said Cessy.

"How do you think I kept it secure for the last two years?" he said with a sad smile. Then he kissed her. "Cole and I are going to haul now, Cessy. When you talk to the kids, remind them they have a dad and I love them."

"We love you too, Soldier Boy."

Cole saw that Reuben walked away grinning. "So it's okay if *she* calls you soldier boy?"

"I'm not in love with Torrent," said Rube.

# FIFTEEN

# GREAT FALLS

History is an omelet. The eggs are already broken.

**ON THE** way down US 15 to Leesburg with two Secret Service agents in the back seat, Cole and Rube debated about where they should stay. Neither Rube's house nor Cole's apartment seemed like a good idea, given that there were people who thought it was quite important to get them out of the picture.

The Secret Service guys voted strongly for a single hotel room. "We patrol the hall in shifts all night."

"That's not subtle," said Rube.

"If we meant to be subtle," said the agent, "would we dress like this and openly scan the crowds?"

"So the 'secret' part of your agency's name—"

"A holdover from the old days," said the agent. "We'd rather scare amateur assassins away. And make life very hard for any pros that might give it a try."

"You'd really take a bullet on purpose?" asked Cole.

"For the President," the agent said. "For you, I'll just subdue the guy who shot you so we can try him for the crime, and then call an ambulance."

"I wouldn't think to ask for more."

In the end, Rube and Cole shared one hotel room and the agents shared an adjoining one. Cole had argued for the Ritz-Carlton but they settled for the Tyson's Corner Marriott. It was expensive enough.

As soon as they were safely installed in the room and the agents had swept for bugs and other surveillance devices, Rube called DeeNee's home phone on his cell. Cole only heard Rube's side of the conversation, but it was clear enough. Rube ascertained that DeeNee still had access to all the files and that none of the office locks had been changed. Then he asked DeeNee to come to work at 0500 so they'd have less chance of being interfered with. "I don't want confrontations." She resisted, but finally agreed.

Then Rube called the other members of his team and set up a rendezvous for 0730 at the same Borders where they had met before. "But be up early," he said to each one of them. "Because if something goes wrong at the Pentagon, our rendezvous may change, time *and* place." Every one of them volunteered to come along to the Pentagon with them, but he turned them down. "If something goes wrong, if I get arrested and Cole, too, I don't want you guys caught up in it. I don't want them to know your faces. Besides, we have Secret Service protection."

Every single one of them commented that so had the President on Friday the Thirteenth. Every single time, Rube gave the same little smile.

They both showered before they went to bed, so there'd be no delays in the morning. By the time they were done with their showers, the agents showed up with the uniforms Rube and Cole should wear to work, and several other changes of clothes. They apparently had sent some flunky from the office to both their homes to pack for them.

So when they got to the Pentagon, they were crisply dressed in the right kind of uniform. Cole would rather have been wearing fatigues and body armor, but the idea this morning was to be relatively unobtrusive.

There was a discussion with the guards about the pistols the Secret Service agents were carrying. The Secret Service won, partly because of Rube's letter from the President. Orders from the President superseded the standing policy. The guards pointed out that Rube and Cole weren't the President. The Secret Service agents said to shut up and let them through.

Cole noticed that Rube didn't lead them on the same route through the building that Cole had always taken. There were about nineteen different ways to get from point A to point B in the Pentagon, none of them convenient. Cole memorized this one as an alternative route.

When they got to the office, DeeNee was already there, with files stacked in boxes. How early did *she* arrive, Cole wondered. He was happy to see that she had the same cold and sarcastic attitude toward Rube that she had toward him. It wasn't just that he was new—she talked to everybody that way.

"You know that everything in here has already been photocopied about three times. If they removed anything, I don't know. And I'm not helping you carry this out to your car."

"I never expected you to," said Rube as he picked up one of the two boxes.

Cole looked at the Secret Service agent nearest him and gestured for him to feel free to pick up the other file box. The agent looked at him coldly. Apparently protecting somebody did not allow for carrying boxes. Cole stepped forward to pick up the other.

"So you're on assignment from LaMonte Nielson?" asked DeeNee.

"We're going to prove that these Progressives planned and carried out Friday the Thirteenth," said Rube.

DeeNee bent over and opened a desk drawer. "Well, I can tell you right now who copied your assassination plans and kept the one with your fingerprints to use as evidence against you." There was a .22 pistol in her desk drawer. She pulled it out. Why was she showing them a weapon? Did she feel that some threat was imminent?

"*I* did it," said DeeNee. Then she stepped toward Rube and aimed straight at his left eye and shot him with the barrel no more than two inches away.

First Rube dropped the box of files. Then he followed

them to the floor. He never made a sound. He was dead the instant the bullet entered his skull. It did not come out. There was no functioning brain inside.

Cole realized that the Secret Service agents had started reacting the moment they saw the pistol in the drawer. They were only a split second too slow. They both fired simultaneously and *their* bullets knocked DeeNee halfway across the room.

Immediately two doors opened and men with weapons came into the office. One of the agents shoved Cole backward and down as they began shooting at the intruders.

But Cole was not going to leave without two things: the PDA and the car keys. So he lunged for Rube's body and got both of them out of his pockets. In the midst of doing it, in the midst of all the noise of gunfire, he heard one of the bad guys say, "PDA."

The agents were good at what they did. Neither of them was hit as they scooted out of the room through the still-open door. Cole didn't follow the route they had just taken to get there; his own normal route got them out of the corridor sooner. Because the bad guys weren't wasting any time in following him. Whether they cared about Cole was moot. They wanted the PDA.

As he and the agents raced down the stairs, one of them said, "They'll have somebody in the parking lot watching your car."

"How do you know?"

"Because *I* would," said the agent.

Nobody was shooting now—the gunfire that had already taken place had alerted the security guards, and they would instantly call for support. Soon enough the chasers would be chased.

Unless the security guards were in on it.

They weren't. But they weren't helpful, either. They saw the drawn guns of the Secret Service agents and had their own weapons out.

"We're Secret Service assigned to protect Captain Cole.

We're being pursued by assassins. They've already hit one of our men."

But while this explanation was still registering, the bad guys got into the hall and now the shooting began again. They hit one of the guards and one of the agents. The other agent and the other guards returned fire.

Between shots, the remaining agent hissed at Cole. "Get out of here while we keep them busy."

He was right. There was no reason for an OK Corral showdown, if Cole could simply get away. He broke for the door and headed for the car.

If there was somebody watching the car, they didn't shoot at him. Maybe they were waiting for Rube to come out.

As he started the engine and pulled out of the parking place, Cole noticed Rube's cellphone sitting in the cup holder. All the numbers he had called last night would be in its memory. Thank heaven Rube left it here. Thank heaven Cole hadn't thought of the cellphone back in the office and wasted time trying to find it along with the keys and the PDA.

As he drove—at a normal pace, because there was no obvious pursuit—he tried to make sense of it. DeeNee. Did they bribe her? Blackmail her? No. Her hand didn't even shake as she aimed the weapon. And she knew where to shoot to make a .22 lethal without fail. She had been trained.

She was a civilian employee. She never chose the military the way soldiers did. Maybe her nastiness to soldiers was because she hated the Army. Maybe she originally took the job because she needed the money. Or maybe she was a true believer who planned all along to bide her time until she could cause real damage to the evil U.S. Army.

Trust. Who else could have drawn a weapon on Reuben Malich without triggering an instant response. If his hands hadn't been full with the box she gave him, if he hadn't simply assumed that DeeNee meant no harm, she would never have gotten that shot off.

Oh, God! Rube is dead! He found himself gasping with the shock of it.

Then he heard the screel of tires behind him. Once again he went with the adrenalin and set aside his feelings. Survival first. Mission second. Grief next week, next month, but not now.

A van and a sports car—one pursuer with mass and the other with speed. He wasn't going to get away easily, not in a PT Cruiser.

His only hope for the moment was to get into traffic, where they'd find it harder to catch him.

Monday morning traffic. But still early. Barely 0530. Not enough cars.

So he made turns. Enough turns that he ended up on the bridge heading into DC.

But he didn't want to go there. His only help would be Rube's jeesh. They were planning to gather in Tyson's Corner.

He couldn't just turn around. These guys wouldn't hesitate to ram him if they saw him coming the other way. Besides, Cessy had complained yesterday about the PT Cruiser's lousy turning radius. If he tried, he'd just run into the concrete wall of the bridge.

He didn't want E Street or Constitution Ave. He took the exit leading toward the Rock Creek Parkway.

All the cars were coming the other way, into town. There *was* no park traffic at this time of day—nobody went to the zoo this early.

But as he got up into the park, there were joggers everywhere. A lot of them kept out of the way of traffic. But a lot of them thought that they had as much right to Cole's lane as he had.

I'm so clever, thought Cole. I'm taking a PT Cruiser uphill in order to evade pursuers.

Very quickly they were right behind him. They weren't shooting yet. But as the sports car slowed down to let the van pass, Cole could see the plan easily enough. A few bumps from that van, and the PT Cruiser would be in the creek, against the cliff, or wrapped around a tree.

He picked up the cellphone and pressed SEND. Nothing happened. It wasn't on. So he struggled to find the power button, and when there wasn't one, he pressed everything, one at a time, and held it down until finally one of them worked and the screen lighted up. *Then* he pushed SEND.

Meanwhile, he was trying to drive around oncoming cars—there were rather a lot of them, this was a major commuting route into the city—and joggers. He couldn't steer the winding road, hold the cellphone, and lay on the horn at the same time.

Where were the cops when you *wanted* to be arrested?

No. He didn't want cops involved. They'd gone to too much trouble yesterday trying to save the lives of cops for him to want any of them to die today.

Rube was dead.

Don't think about that. He pressed the cellphone to his ear with his shoulder and steered while pressing on the horn. The van came up behind him. He tried to swerve and nearly hit a runner. He hoped the guy was still on his feet and flipping him off instead of flat on his face torn up by asphalt.

It was Drew, the American University professor, who answered.

"Rube's dead," said Cole. "DeeNee shot him in his office. I'm alone, in his car. I've got his PDA. I know his password. I'm in Rock Canyon with two vehicles in pursuit, trying to ram me, and I don't know where the hell I'm going."

"I know the park," said Drew. "Stay on Beach Road. Way up the canyon you come to a place where Wise Road is a very, very sharp left. Take that turn. It gets you up to Oregon Avenue. Take that to Western Ave. There'll be traffic. You want traffic, right?"

"I *want* my mommy," said Cole. But it wasn't really a joke even though he meant it to be. "Rube's dead. I'm sorry. It came out of nowhere. We were holding file boxes."

"Shut up. I'll call you back in a minute. I'm calling the other guys. We'll try to get you some help."

Cole pocketed the phone in time to swerve sharply. There were weapons in the car. He hadn't thought to grab any when he got in. He reached behind him, fumbling to find *something*.

He was hit from behind. It nearly knocked him into a jogger, a woman, who screamed at him as he swerved and fishtailed. An oncoming car ran off the road. Sorry sorry sorry. Not my fault. He got control of the car. He also got his hand on a pistol. That was something. He felt better.

He opened all the windows in the car. No reason to deal with flying glass shards if he needed to shoot.

There was an intersection ahead, with a light. He laid on the horn, jabbing at it to warn people he was coming through. He could see the van behind him lay back, trusting him to have his own wreck.

Instead Cole braked sharply and swerved off the road to the right. The car stopped abruptly and the airbag would have smacked him except he already had the door open and was leaning far to the left. He released the seatbelt and rolled out of the car.

The van was still going too fast to stop, despite squealing brakes and the fishtailing. Fine. He didn't want the van. He wanted the sports car.

It was doing a better job of stopping. Cole didn't want the windshield broken. But the passenger window was already open. There was a rifle pointing out of it. What an idiot, to bring a rifle to shoot out of a car window. Maybe these guys were amateurs after all.

Cole stood, feet planted, two hands on the pistol. He fired once and shattered the hand of the man who had been holding the rifle.

The driver's door was already opening. Good. The moment the driver's head showed above the roofline, Cole shot off the top of his head.

Then he ran back around the PT Cruiser, yanked open the back door, pulled out Rube's M-240, and opened fire on the van, figuring that the bullets would easily go through the metal sides and the seats.

He scooped up Rube's Mollie vest because it held the ammo for the M-240 and the pistol. Then he ran to the sports car. The guy he had hit in the hand was halfway out of the car, holding a pistol—he had a pistol all along, the idiot!—but it wasn't his good hand and he hadn't practiced with it that way. Cole shot him in the face so the bullet wouldn't damage the car. He tossed the Mollie vest and the M-240 through the window and then ran around to the driver's side. He could see now that the driver's door of the van was open and there was a dead body draped down onto the asphalt.

He turned around as he went for the sports car's door. He could see two humvees coming up the canyon at a high speed. So they had already called for backup.

The sports car was still running. He swerved out around the van just as the light changed and civilians started trying to turn into the lane he was driving in. He held the pistol in his left hand and showed the weapon out the window. They stopped honking at him. He ran the light and didn't hit anybody.

Now he had some power going up the hill. The Humvees really weren't built for this.

But they were undoubtedly calling somebody else to intercept him. How many military people were involved in this conspiracy?

No. No, these humvees were regular soldiers. Loyal guys who had got a call through military channels. No doubt they had described Cole as a dangerous assassin who just killed an officer, a civilian employee, and shot or killed multiple agents in a shootout in the Pentagon. There was no way—there would be no chance—for Cole to identify himself to them and wave the letter from the President. Besides, he didn't *have* that letter. It was in Rube's pocket. Probably about to be used as evidence to embarrass President Nielson.

The cellphone rang. It was Drew.

"I'm on Oregon," Cole said immediately.

"Pass Western and then jog right on Wyndee, then left again. You're back on Beach but it isn't one-way. Turn left on the East-West Highway."

"I'm not in the PT Cruiser anymore," said Cole. "I'm now in a Corvette C6, black. I've got an M-240 and a pistol."

"Good," said Drew. "I was afraid you didn't know how to Rambo this."

"The point is I've got some speed now."

"Then when East-West splits, stay right and then turn right on Connecticut. It's the first big street. One more light and it cloverleafs onto the Beltway heading west, toward Virginia. If you see the Mormon temple you went the wrong damn way."

"I don't think I should try to get to that Borders."

"No, no. You can't stay on the Beltway long. It's going to be clogging up pretty bad and now that you've got speed, you want lonely side roads. But do you still want to meet up with us, or get up to Gettysburg?"

"I don't think I'll make it to Gettysburg without help," said Cole. "They've called in the Army against me now."

"Some of the roads are one-way the wrong way in the morning," said Drew. "Best route—take the MacArthur Road exit. Heading west. It curves around past the Great Falls Park and then it joins River Road, which is Maryland 190."

"You *know* these roads that well?"

"I'm looking at Google Maps on my laptop, what do you think? But I've driven all these roads. Stay on 190 a long way. Till you have to turn right onto Edwards Ferry Road, and stay on that up to 107. By then we should have Babe with you, he lives out that way. He'll guide you the rest of the way to a rendezvous on the Maryland side of the Leesburg bridge."

"If you think I memorized this—"

"Call me as often as you want. But I'm hanging up now to go get in my car. No more laptop. Sorry."

By now Cole was doing the ramp up to 495. Whereupon

he found himself stopped cold behind traffic waiting to merge, as the humvees came up behind him. There were a couple of cars between them and him, but these guys weren't going to stay in their lane or even in their vehicles.

Cole debated between getting out and commandeering somebody else's car, or betting on the gods of traffic to help him. He could imagine himself stuck with an M-240 on the side of the road, unable to shoot without hitting civilians, choosing between surrendering or running into the nice little jogging park where snipers could take him out at leisure.

The traffic gods came through. The car ahead of him moved. A couple of aggressive Maryland drivers fudged their way into traffic and things broke free. He checked the rearview mirror and saw that the first humvee left two of its guys behind and the second one didn't stop for them. They looked pissed off. That's what you get for leaving your transportation without first ascertaining the enemy's intentions and capabilities.

Except he was the enemy, and they were the U.S. Army.

Now he was moving with traffic, driving the Corvette into gaps so small that other drivers not only honked at him, it looked like they wanted to ram him. But he didn't show the pistol again. No reason to cause extra panic. He'd just look like an asshole in a sports car, which was exactly what people expected anyway. A normal day of driving in Maryland.

Now he had time to make another call. The one he hated worst. But he had to make it, not just because Cecily had a right to know, but because he needed her to get Nielson to help him from the other end. Call off this chase if he could.

He knew her cell number—he had memorized it, of course—and she answered on the first ring.

"Cecily," said Cole. "This is the worst call you'll ever receive in your life, but I need help desperately. So get near someone so they can take over this call if you can't continue it."

"He's dead," said Cecily.

"DeeNee shot him and he's dead. There is no hope that he survived."

"DeeNee . . ."

"She was working for them. She turned over the plans to the terrorists. Cecily, are you still with me? I'm being pursued by regular Army troops. I need the President to call them off. Can you do that?"

"Yes," she said. "Call off pursuit."

"I'm in a stolen black Corvette C6. The two humvees following me are to let me go and not follow me. No other pursuit is to be permitted. Do you have that?"

"I do."

"I'm sorry, Cecily. You know I'd have taken the bullet for him if I could have."

"Do you have the PDA?" she asked.

"Yes."

"Then get back here alive."

"Yes, ma'am."

"I'm at the President's door. Stay on the line if you can." He heard talking.

Then Nielson was on the line. "This is Cole?"

"Yes, sir. Major Malich is dead. The secretary set up a trap and she pulled the trigger on him herself. After I left the Pentagon I killed the first wave of pursuers—they were definitely rebels. But the guys chasing me now are regular Army. They've undoubtedly been told lies about who I am and what happened in the Pentagon."

"I'll take care of it, son," said Nielson. "That's what Presidents are for."

The connection broke. Cole ended his side of the call.

He had to give the humvee drivers credit. They did a good job of keeping in hot pursuit through traffic. Once he got on the open road, he could open up the Corvette and leave them in the dust.

Cole had no idea how long it would take Nielson to call off the chase. It would be so stupid to get killed—or to kill somebody else—during these minutes waiting for the word to filter down. Battle of New Orleans all over again.

MacArthur Road was packed coming toward him, but there was nobody going his direction. The trouble was, if he *did* overtake somebody, there was no way to pass on the left with all those cars. And, sure enough, he came up behind a farmer's stake truck and watched the humvees come up behind him.

But these guys didn't do any ramming. They stayed behind him, but didn't move in. Maybe they were on the radio right now.

Drew called. "Where are you?"

"MacArthur. Just past where Clara Barton splits off, but I'm stuck behind a farm truck. I think President Nielson might be getting the order down the line for them to leave me alone."

"Stay on the line and tell me if they back off. We can change your route, then. No reason to go to Leesburg if you aren't being pursued."

The humvees weren't tailgating him now, but they hadn't given up, either. "He was supposed to tell them not to follow me, but—"

The second humvee blew up.

"Somebody's shooting at the humvees," Cole shouted into the phone.

The humvee right behind him was swerving, taking evasive action. What was following it?

Cole saw a break in the oncoming traffic. Not enough of one for any sane person to pass, but whatever was shooting at the humvees probably just wanted them out of the way so they could get to Cole. He swung out and started around the farm truck as the remaining humvee also burst into flames and blew up.

The driver of the farm truck could see what was happening and even if he didn't understand the explosions, he did understand being passed by a madman. He pulled hard to the right. Meanwhile the oncoming cars slammed on their brakes and swung right. Cole barely made it through. Then he floored it.

At first the other drivers were cursing him. Then they

saw what was following Cole now. About a dozen one-man hovercrafts, looking like rocket-powered motorcycles, and at least two of them had anti-tank weapons mounted on the housing. They didn't actually have to overtake him. Even a Corvette C6 can't outspeed a rocket.

Fortunately, the road started curving, and there were cars trying to join the inbound traffic. Cole had to drive for his life, trying not to hit anybody while staying on a road that wasn't exactly designed for ninety miles per hour. At least there weren't any joggers. Oh, wait. Yes there were.

Apparently the greenery to the left was part of the Great Falls Park.

"Drew," said Cole into the phone. "The humvees are gone. Killed. They've got hovercycles with what looks like anti-tank weapons. MacArthur is curvy enough they can't get off a shot yet, but I've got to know what—"

"Look," said Drew, "this is real bad. If you stay on MacArthur it dead-ends in the park. You have to turn right on Falls Road to stay on track. And it runs straight as an arrow away from the park."

"These guys may be bastards, but they're still Americans and I don't think they want to hit civilians. Maybe they'll—"

"Bullshit," said Drew. "They'll kill anybody they want and blame it on you. And they'll mean it, too, because it's your fault for getting away."

"So what do I do?"

"Babe is heading toward you. I'm with Cat now, and he's calling him to tell him to hurry."

"Only if he's armed to deal with anti-tank weapons. Here's the turn for Falls Road. If I can make this turn without slowing down enough for them to blow me up . . ."

He made the turn. And immediately regretted it. Heading straight toward him, filling Falls Road from one side to the other, were six of the two-legged mechanicals they had fought in New York City yesterday.

"They've got mechs ahead of me," said Cole. Then he pocketed the phone and made a U-turn going way too fast.

In the movies these always looked cool. In real life, cars usually flipped and rolled. The Corvette acted like it was definitely considering the flip-and-roll. But American engineering was good enough this time that Cole didn't end up smeared on the asphalt.

Now he was headed straight back at the cycles, which were just rounding the turn from MacArthur. Cole deliberately wove back and forth so nobody could aim at him properly. Instead, they swung off the pavement. Didn't bother them at all. Hovercycles didn't need a paved surface. They only slowed down so they could turn around and follow him.

When he got to the MacArthur turnoff, he could have turned left, but soon enough he would run into the inbound traffic and not only would *he* probably die, several civilians would likely die with him.

Besides, he was getting a glimmer of another plan. A stupid, dangerous one. But that seemed to be the kind that was needed right now.

This was Great Falls Park. He remembered seeing it from the Virginia side. From the observation points on that side, he could see an observation point on the Maryland side. He picked up the phone as he went with all deliberate speed into the park.

"Drew, I'm back on MacArthur heading into the park."

"It's a dead end!"

"I'm going to cross the river at the park."

"You can't cross the river!"

"We'll find out, won't we?"

"People drown there. Not just some of them. Everybody who tries to hop the rocks."

"But I'm Ranger trained," said Cole.

"I don't care if you're a damned SEAL," said Drew.

"I'm a dead man if I stay in this car and on those roads," said Cole. "So this is my best chance."

"Then your chances suck, man."

"I'll deal with the river if you guys can lay down suppressing fire."

"Damn. It'll cost five bucks a car to get into the park."

"Shut up," said Cole. He ended the call and concentrated on driving.

The park entry booth loomed ahead. There was a car at the booth chatting up the ranger. Cole approached at top speed. The ranger saw him coming and ran out of the booth, yelling for him to stop. Cole didn't. He went around the booth on the other side. He didn't need the rearview mirror to know that the ranger was on the phone instantly, calling for whatever backup rangers called for. That was good. Because in a moment he would use that phone connection to tell whoever it was about mechs and hovercycles blowing through in hot pursuit.

For a crazy moment he thought about those two soldiers who had been left beside the Connecticut Avenue freeway onramp. That was the luckiest move of their lives, getting out of that humvee.

Cole didn't worry about parking nicely. He did take the Mollie vest and the M-240 because even though it was useless against the mechs, it would do fine against anybody who got out of a hovercycle.

He headed for the woods, at first on the path, but soon getting off it. He didn't want to get trapped at the observation point. And he wanted to improve his odds a little.

Sure enough, the bad guys tried to stay on their hovercycles along the path to the observation point. Only when they found he wasn't there did they stop, settle down to the ground, and get out. The mechs were probably still lumbering up the road. So it was Cole, his M-240, and now, by actual count, eight guys. Unless there were two others who had stayed behind and were now approaching on foot. Because his initial count had been ten. Had to remember the possibility that there were bad guys behind him.

The trouble is that a machine gun is best against massed troops. It isn't much of a tool for taking guys out one by one. And if he got close enough to use a pistol, they'd overwhelm him by sheer force of numbers.

But for the moment, as they were still getting out of their

hovercycles, they were massed enough. Cole set up the weapon and let fly. Short bursts, to husband his ammo, because there wasn't much.

He was pretty sure he put four of them down. Maybe disabled another. But from this moment on, the M-240 was useless. He had to get to the river, where sniper fire from Reuben's jeesh would be his only protection while he negotiated the river.

Getting to the edge of the cliff wasn't bad. Getting down the cliff face wasn't all that hard. And he really had tried to pick the point with the narrowest gap over the rushing water of the falls. From above, it didn't look too bad. From here, it looked impossible. Because the boulders didn't conveniently line up with two flat surfaces. Instead, they were rounded and jagged and even though he could easily make the jump, there was nothing he could be sure of gripping on the other side. So easy—so *likely*—to slide off into the water and get carried down the rapids, the pieces of his body eventually assembling in the smooth water downstream.

He heard the slap-plunk-whine of sniper fire from the Virginia side. The guys had gotten there, even at five bucks a car.

But that didn't guarantee that somebody on the Maryland side couldn't get off a round at him while he was exposed on the rock.

A quick prayer. And then a little aside to Rube: I don't know if they give angel status that fast, but if you can, look out for me here. I've got your PDA and Cecily needs it.

Nothing for it but a run and a leap. So he ran. And he leapt.

And even though he scrabbled a little on the rock, he was solidly on and there was nothing for it but to make a shorter leap and then one that was more like a step and now he was on the big center island.

It was rough going. But the guys were doing a good job of suppressing sniper fire.

And then suddenly they weren't.

Because it wasn't sniper fire. It was mechs. They were just *stepping* over the gaps that had been leaps for Cole. And the sniper fire from the Virginia side couldn't do a thing against them. They knew it. And since the bad guys also knew it, they weren't exposing themselves anymore. Let the mechs do it, they were no doubt thinking.

His cellphone rang.

He cowered in a depression in the rock, trying not to present a target to the oncoming mechs. Fortunately, the mechs weren't really designed to walk on terrain as rough as this rock. One of them even tripped. It was keeping them busy. But eventually they'd get where his hiding place no longer hid him, and then he'd be dead. "Hello?" he said into the phone.

"Any way to take those suckers down?" asked Drew.

"Either an AT-4 or two guys pressing the legs apart while two cars run into it."

"Nobody's willing to sacrifice their cars," said Drew. "But hold tight. We've got backup."

"From who? The U.S. Army doesn't know I'm on their side."

"Think, Cole," said Drew. "Our side doesn't have those mechs. Wherever we see them, it's okay to kill them."

It was only a few more minutes, and the Apaches came up the river. No focused-EMP weapon now—where would they plug it in? The mechs didn't even try to run away. As hard as it was for them to get as far as they had gotten, there was no going back. They aimed at the choppers but before they came in effective range, the missiles the choppers sent by way of greeting ended the conversation.

Cole got up and waved his thanks. He knew there was no way they could land on the island. It was safer for them to get out before the guys from the hovercycles—if there were any left—tried out their antitank rockets to see if they could bring down choppers.

So Cole was on his own getting to the narrowest place on the Virginia side.

Arty and Mingo had both climbed down to the nearest point. What, did they think they were going to catch him?

No. They had a rope.

He caught it. He tied it around himself, up under his arms. Mingo wrapped it behind his back and sat down and braced himself. If Cole fell in the water, they could haul him out, hopefully before he had been beaten to death on the rocks.

He jumped.

He landed.

Arty caught him by the wrist and Cole didn't even get wet.

Arty and Mingo helped him get up to the observation point.

"Good work," he said to them.

"You, too, sir," said Arty.

Drew was waiting up top. He made a point of turning off his cellphone. Cole held up his cellphone and ended the call, too.

"Does Cecily know?" asked Load.

Cole nodded.

Then he staggered to the railing and stood there, leaning on it, and trembled from the spent adrenalin, and then found himself crying, and he decided that it wasn't for the ordeal he'd just been through, and it wasn't for the fear, and it wasn't from killing a bunch of guys in Rock Creek Canyon and back on the Maryland side of the park.

"I only knew him for three days," he said.

"He makes an impression," said Load softly. One by one they each touched his shoulder. And the kind touches were enough to revive him. Calm him. He walked back with them along the path, around the ranger station, ignoring the civilians and rangers who were being watched over by a heavily-armed Benny.

"Thank you for your cooperation," said Benny. "I'm happy to tell you that the operation was successful. You can resume your normal activities." Then he joined them on the walk to their cars.

# SIXTEEN

# FINDING THE ENEMY

They also serve, who only sit and type.

**IT WAS** Reuben's PDA that got Cecily through the first month of widowhood. Recording the shipments and financial transactions, following the trails, searching for patterns, tracking corporate entities, passing along names and leads to FBI and DIA agents: It was a vast spiderweb, with Reuben's notes like dewdrops that reveal where the otherwise invisible strands must be.

It was an urgent task. And they were Reuben's notes. Reuben's words. It was his trail that she was following. All those days when he traveled on assignments he couldn't tell her about, all those trips abroad and in America, all those nights when she could see that he was troubled and yet knew he couldn't talk about it. Now he was telling her.

Meanwhile, Aunt Margaret brought the children down to Gettysburg and stayed with them. "I'm an old widow myself," she said. "I know how hard it is. You need the children near, and you also need to lose yourself completely in something that isn't your family. So here I am and here I'll stay while you save the world."

It wasn't the world Cecily was saving. It might be America. It might be herself.

But one thing was certain. It was not going to save Reuben's reputation. There was no way that he could have helped but see that something wrong was going on. Too much of what he did was within the borders of the United States. Most of the shipments seemed to go from port city to port city, so some illusion could be maintained that these weapons shipments were going overseas. But who would bring weapons from China or Russia to the United States in order to ship them to pro-U.S. partisan groups in Iran or Sudan or Turkmenistan? Reuben had to at least wonder if some or all of these weapons were meant to be used domestically.

Which was why he kept these notes on the PDA—and why he was so reluctant to give it into anyone else's hands. Because he knew something dangerous was going on and he was helping with it—yet he believed he was doing it for a President that he admired and trusted, and so he acted the good soldier and did the jobs he was assigned to do.

Yet if it turned out to be wrong, he would have the paper trail—well, the digital trail—that someone could use to track it all down. Reuben never needed records like this. He had trained his memory like a Jesuit. So he was deliberately creating evidence.

He knew he was only guessing about the integrity of the people he served. If he guessed wrong, then he was serving traitors, and he could not claim that it had never occurred to him. All he could do was make sure that the full confession was here. The evidence to unravel what he had helped them do.

If only he had talked to me, she thought again and again.

And most of the time she answered herself: What did I know? What would I have counseled? Of course, caution, yes—I'm the woman who set aside the political career to raise a family. I choose safety. That's what I do. But I also loved Reuben. Still love him. And I knew how unhappy he would be, to walk away from something that *might* have been in service of a cause, a President, he believed in.

So few seemed to believe in that President, and yet Reuben was sure that he was pursuing the right course. So *would* she have counseled him to give it up? To denounce it?

And . . . *could* he have given it up? It was clear *now* that he had been working for and with murderers and traitors. Would they have let him walk away, even *if* she had advised him? No. There was too much danger that he would then denounce them—they would have killed him. And she would have spent the last year or so consoling her children about their father's apparent suicide. Or traffic accident. Whatever method they used.

Things happened as they happened. Reuben accepted the hand dealt to him, and bet on it. Bet his life on it.

Whatever others may think of the choices he made, I know his heart. I know that he would and did sacrifice anything for the cause of freedom, in support of those he believed also fought for it. He took the long view of history. He cared about the world their grandchildren would inherit. He despised those who thought only of themselves, their immediate advantage. Whatever I might have advised him, he would have done what he did. I could not have changed him.

I wouldn't have tried.

So she shed tears over her work, but she kept working.

Reuben's jeesh came in and out of the Gettysburg White House, as the media were calling it now. She knew them all by their noms de guerre now: Cole, not Coleman; Load, not Lloyd. Mingo, Benny, Cat, Babe, Arty, Drew. Very young men when they first trained to be soldiers, but now men, seasoned veterans.

LaMonte knew an asset when he saw one. Eight extraordinarily good soldiers whose loyalty had already been tested. He turned them over to his National Security Adviser, and Averell Torrent used them for missions that required deftness, quickness. Seize this. Destroy that. In twos and threes they went out, sometimes in uniform, sometimes in civilian clothes, sometimes heavily armed in attack choppers, sometimes on domestic flights with no weapons at all.

They would find the agents of the Progressive Restoration and follow them to where their weapons or funds were stashed. The weapons were to be used to eliminate opponents of the Progressive Restoration in key states, as they had been used in the attempt to kill Cole, or to serve to defend states or cities that came over to the rebel side. The funds were to be used to bribe legislators, governors, mayors, and city councilors who needed a little help making up their mind.

Some of their small victories were kept secret; others, though, Averell Torrent went before the cameras to announce. Cessy soon realized that publicity depended on whether any rebels were killed who were not under arms. Take down a mech or blow up a hovercycle, and Torrent would go on the news, calmly and reassuringly telling the American people that an attempt had been made to assassinate a loyal American official, but the violent Progressive Revolution and its terrifying weapons had been stopped in their tracks.

But if the dead bodies were not men in body armor or ensconced in the new machines, then the event had no national significance. It was a matter for local law enforcement. If anyone noticed that the victims had been sympathetic toward the rebels' cause, the killing was assumed to be the work of local right-wing vigilantes.

The result was that LaMonte's administration retained its image of being infinitely patient, taking action only to protect American lives from the depredations of the rebels. And people got used to seeing Averell Torrent as the calm, reassuring voice of moderation, reluctantly taking action when forced to by the enemies of peace and freedom, but otherwise merely asking Americans to trust in the democratic process and not throw in their lot with the violence of the Progressive Restoration.

Meanwhile, the members of Reuben's jeesh would stop in and see her whenever they passed through Gettysburg. They all regarded it as part of their work, to help her decode the Farsi that Reuben had used for his notes. Words and phrases that were repeated, she would learn, but many phrases weren't in the dictionary, or at least not with the meaning he was using. Much of his Farsi was really the private language he and his comrades had developed—there was English slang in the Farsi, sometimes translated and sometimes transliterated, as there was also Arabic and Spanish and whatever other languages they happened to know.

It was all translated within a week, more or less. Then they helped her study the maps. She had threads that traced all the shipments, and as she learned whatever the FBI and DIA could find out for her about those shipments, she began to build up a clearer picture.

Meanwhile, she met with others in Gettysburg who were trying to figure out the Progressive Restoration movement—the rebels, as they called them now in the office. How much money would this all take? Who has that kind of money and can spend it without detection? Is the source of this foreign or domestic? They had to keep in mind the possibility that the Chinese were at the root of this. Or Al Qaeda. Even Russia. The joke inside Gettysburg was that it was really the French behind everything. They'd been secretly running the world since Napoleon, following an extraordinarily deceptive master plan that would eventually lead to conquering the world.

Jokes aside, it became clear to Cecily and those who agreed with her that a conspiracy like this had to be very tightly held or it would have been detected long before. Even true believers in a cause can be careless, but nobody had been. Nothing leaked. How?

The organization that Cecily imagined bringing this off consisted of only a handful of people, who then hired or encouraged others to do what they needed, but without telling them anything about what it was for.

But there were some points where they had to let larger numbers in on what they were doing. Somehow they had to recruit the soldiers who would run these machines, and the pattern was emerging: They must have recruited among groups of veterans who had turned against the war, the military, or the President. She had to assume it was the left-wing version of the way right-wing militias recruited. Find who's pissed off. Then find the ones who are angry enough to train to kill for the cause.

The bodies of those killed at Great Falls and at the Holland Tunnel established the profile, and now the investigators were tracking down others who had dropped out of sight in the past year or so.

Another place where they had to let outsiders in on the secret was weapons development. This wasn't something you did as a hobby. They had to recruit from among the experts—American experts, since nothing about the designs suggested European or Japanese concepts.

So the FBI worked on assembling a list of disgusted or disaffected researchers who had dropped out of sight over the years and could now be assumed to be working for the rebels. There were also some former automobile and aviation designers, computer engineers and hotshot programmers whose political views were far to the left and whose rage had seemed, to many of their coworkers, disproportionate. Some of them were found, having made perfectly innocent career changes. Others were not found at all. They went on the list.

The weapons themselves were still intimidating, but no longer baffling. With several mechs to study from the battle at the Holland Tunnel, the DOD experts had found nothing that couldn't be built using existing design theory. Excellent, creative engineers built these weapons, but not necessarily geniuses. Their work could be duplicated and countered.

Except for the EMP gun. The DOD people still had not duplicated the technology that kept the directed pulse coherent over such a long range. It was a serious problem that the rebels had an air defense system that kept military aircraft from overflying New York City any lower than satellite level. The DOD was working on systems that would momentarily shut down all electronics while the EMP blew through. But planes that depended on electronics to stay aloft were almost as damaged by the shutdown as by the EMP itself.

The U.S. was used to having air supremacy. Over loyal territory they still did. But that territory was shrinking, bit by bit.

Because in the absence of a firm military response, Americans who viewed the Progressive Restoration as heroes began to believe that they might just bring this thing off. Some worried that the leaders of the Progressive Restoration had not come forward—but the New York City Council insisted that *they* were now leading the movement to "restore Constitutional government" and the Progressive Restoration was obeying *their* orders. It put democratically elected officials at the apparent head of the movement, and for many people who sympathized with their views, that was enough.

In the first month, the legislatures of Washington State and Vermont passed resolutions joining themselves to the Progressive Restoration. In Washington the governor vetoed that action and mobilized the National Guard to make sure that no mechs or hovercycles showed up in Washington. The trouble was, he also asked President Nielson to keep U.S. forces from taking any "provocative military action." In effect, the state had declared itself neutral territory.

Meanwhile quite a few cities had passed or nearly passed resolutions declaring their recognition of the Progressive Revolution. And there were well-orchestrated movements in other states pressing for their legislatures to jump on the bandwagon.

There was no shortage of liberals, from moderate to radical, who also condemned the rebellion. This was the wrong way to go about it, they said. Nobody should have died, they said. If the Progressive Revolution has any links to the assassinations of Friday the Thirteenth, they should be tried and punished for the crimes.

At the same time, many voices that condemned the rebellion also argued strongly against taking military action. Cecily was not surprised to hear them call for negotiations. Having lived for years with a soldier-historian, she knew that negotiations only worked when you had something to offer or when the other side thought they had something to fear from you. It was hard to see what negotiations with rebels would accomplish except to give them time to build more and more support in the rest of the country.

Cecily could hear Reuben's voice in her mind, scoffing at all these people. If the states tolerate a takeover of the federal government by force, we'll never have peace again, he'd say.

The trouble was he wasn't here for her to argue with him, to tell him that if this rebellion was suppressed by military action against an American city, there would be no forgiveness for it. He would listen. He would realize that she was right, or at least that her views had to be taken into account.

Meanwhile, she worked at her investigation. The key was figuring out where all these shipments were controlled from, where the money flowed. When her information was complete, it could be combined with information from the other investigations and maybe they could figure something out.

She was glad she had *her* job and not LaMonte's. Because the country's split over how to respond to the war showed up in Congress. Party discipline was breaking down on both sides of the aisle. There were Democrats calling for military action against the rebels, and Republicans calling for a wait-and-talk policy. Each side of the debate saw only the worst possible consequences for the other side's view.

Which was a recipe for indecision and obstruction in Congress. No one there had declared for the rebels; no one had resigned, not even the Congressmen from New York City. All were calling for the Progressive Restoration to leave New York.

But that didn't mean that there weren't substantial numbers of Congressmen acting to slow down any kind of military action. Part of that was to hold up approval of President Nielson's appointments.

They approved George Sarkissian as the new Secretary

of State, though with a battle; Averell Torrent sailed through as National Security Adviser. However, there was such virulent opposition to former Secretary of State Donald Porter as the new Vice President—it was called a needlessly provocative action—that the acting Speaker of the House and the majority leader of the Senate refused to push through a vote on his confirmation even though they were of the President's party.

And there was no chance of getting a new Secretary of Defense through, regardless of who it was. The Republicans threatened to name one of their most radically right-wing members as Speaker of the House to replace LaMonte Nielson, making him the next in line for the presidency. But this was abandoned when legal experts in the law schools howled that even though it might be technically legal, the effect would be an end run around the Constitutional requirement that the new next-in-line to the presidency be approved by both houses of Congress. "It's just what you'd expect," said one of the sound bites, "given the reckless disregard for the Constitution shown by the Republicans from 2000 on." Once that became the story, the maneuver became politically impossible and the House continued with an Acting Speaker.

International reaction was predictable but maddening. The sworn enemies of the United States were quick to recognize the Progressive Restoration, declaring their U.N. ambassadors to be ambassadors to the United States as well, downgrading their ambassadors in Washington to mere consular status. But that sort of thing was expected from those nations, hardly worth noticing.

It was the wait-and-see reaction from supposed allies in NATO and elsewhere that infuriated LaMonte and Sarkissian. As Sarkissian said in one meeting, "Do our allies really want an armed rebellion controlled by unknown persons to get their fanatical little hands on the nuclear button?"

The worst was that President Nielsen's inner council was divided as well. Sarkissian and Porter argued for military action. Torrent argued for them to wait. And so far, at least, LaMonte was deciding things Torrent's way.

"You're right," LaMonte said to Sarkissian and Porter, more than once. "Our inaction is practically inviting other states to attempt to join with the rebels. But their resolutions have no legal force whatsoever. Passing a resolution doesn't give them military power. When we decide to take action, we'll take that action."

The longer we wait means the larger the portion of the country that will have to be treated like an occupied enemy when the war is over, they said.

But always LaMonte would say, "It's a struggle for hearts and minds. They *want* us to use military might. In their view, it proves that they're right about us. So we'll limit ourselves to very small military actions while we find out who these people really are. When we find out who's funding all this and who's giving the orders, then we can treat it as what it is—a police matter. We'll arrest the perpetrators, seize their military and financial assets, and then welcome everybody back to constitutional government with open arms and no grudges. That can only happen if there's no invasion, no bloodbath."

Cecily attended some of these meetings, though not as a participant, merely as an observer and a resource if someone should need her to answer a question. She knew that LaMonte did not come up with this plan himself. His adamant stand in favor of investigation-before-invasion was Torrent's plan.

But it was the right one. There was a reason why Reuben had respected the man so much. He was brilliant. He was completely nonpartisan. He always reasoned from practical principles: This might work, this certainly won't. And as he sent Reuben's jeesh out on missions that always worked, his stock rose higher and higher in the administration—and in Congress. He could speak the language of liberals to liberals and conservatives to conservatives, and yet his words to one group never antagonized the other. He was a living exemplar of what it might mean to be a moderate, if there were such things in American politics anymore.

It was also Torrent who heard from everybody working on the investigation. So it was hardly a surprise when he was the one who put it all together into some clear answers.

Not clear enough to announce anything, though. Because what he didn't have was proof of the kind that would overwhelm the media and the opposition in Congress.

"We can't build this like a legal case in corporate law," he explained to Cecily and the jeesh. "It isn't a judge we have to convince, it's the very people who are most committed to disbelieving everything we say."

"So who is it?" asked Cecily.

"We've known from the start who the most likely person behind all this is," said Torrent. "Aldo Verus."

"He's a clown," said Babe. "His birth name was Aldo Vera. A joke, like Armand Hammer."

"He's a straw man," said Drew. "The favorite bugbear of conservatives."

"Which is why we've worked so hard to find somebody else," said Torrent. "But Verus has been using his uncountable fortune to fund ultra-left-wing movements for years. His avowed purpose has always been to bring down the late President. He closely monitors every dime he contributes to front organizations to make sure it's being effectively used. He requires them to raise matching funds so he can husband his resources. He's a smart guy, he's grimly determined, and just because he *announced* his goal doesn't mean he can't be the one who's accomplishing it."

Torrent proceeded to enumerate the business holdings Verus had divested over the past two years. "He had plenty of money out of ordinary profits to fund the design of these weapons. But our weapons experts say that to get them from prototype to production, the big expenditures would have begun about two years ago. And that's exactly when he started selling off these companies."

"He can't outspend the Defense Department," said Cat. "Nobody has that much money."

"He's a better manager of his money than the Defense Department," said Torrent. "He doesn't have to maintain bases or pay the salaries of thousands of soldiers in Korea and Germany. He doesn't have to please Congressmen. And he doesn't have to match our military strength—he only has to have a credible enough force to cause us trouble."

Torrent gave them copies of the report on the probable cost of manufacturing the mechs and the hovercycles. "We've run the numbers. Assuming he pays his soldiers comparably to U.S. soldiers, and assuming that only one out of five of the mechs is internally manned, while the others are controlled by a computer operator at a remote location, and comparing that with the money we know he got from the sales of directly-owned assets, our estimate is that a possible force configuration is 250 mechs, a thousand hovercycles, and an additional thousand soldiers who run the focused EMPs and handle routine foot patrol."

"Don't forget that he might have plenty of funding that isn't his own money," said Cat. "There's all that Hollywood cash."

"That all had to be put into tax-deductible organizations. The only American money he can spend without public accountability is his own," said Torrent.

"But he might have tapped into Iranian money," suggested Benny.

"Possibly. Or Russian or Chinese. But I don't think so. If Verus accepted even a dime of foreign money, and it became known, then he'd lose vast amounts of his support. His cause can't look like it's sponsored by foreigners, period."

"Okay," said Cecily. "Let's just say *if* it's Verus, and he has the force you estimate, what then?"

"Satellite photos of the forces deployed in New York City indicate fewer than fifty mechs and only a couple of hundred hovercycles."

"A fifth of your estimate," said Drew.

"Exactly," said Torrent. "Where's the rest of it?"

Arty immediately said, "He's got stashes all over the

country. Look how fast mechs and hovercycles popped up when they were chasing Cole."

"Six mechs and a dozen hovercycles," said Torrent. "Near the nation's capital, at a time when they were needed to keep Major Malich's PDA from getting into our hands. But I don't think there are stashes all over, and you know why."

"Secrets are hard to keep," said Drew.

"Don't divide your forces," said Cole.

"Both," said Torrent. "Verus can't afford to have lots of hiding places, because these things are hard to hide. Especially the soldiers. It's hard to disguise garrisons, especially if you're training them to keep them in top form. And he doesn't want tiny forces scattered around where he might never need them. He needs to have most of them in one really terrific hiding place. A place from which he can disperse them as needed."

"Where?" said Cole.

"I don't know," said Torrent.

They all showed their disappointment.

"But you don't know it's Aldo Verus, either," said Cecily. "So where do you *think* it is?"

"That's why I had you bring in your map," he said. "Just as Verus is the obvious guy, the place is obvious, too."

Cecily lifted up the map and propped its frame on the end of the table. "I've been looking at it for weeks now, and it's not obvious to *me*."

"First, let's look at what he needs," said Torrent. "Rough terrain. A place where big things can easily be hidden. Which means forest or mountains. Or both. Iowa need not apply."

The soldiers nodded.

"Then he needs it to be close to where he'll need it. He isn't planning to conquer the whole U.S., he's going to try to win over and protect territories that are largely sympathetic to his cause."

"Blue states," said Drew.

"No," said Torrent. "Because you know that 'blue states'

and 'red states' are a lie. Most of the blue states are blue because the city vote overwhelmed the rural vote. But he can't hide these things inside a city, can he?"

Again they agreed with his reasoning.

"Then he needs isolation. Unsettled territory. Few neighbors. That practically rules out the whole East and Midwest, doesn't it? The land is too heavily settled, too constantly observed. Even in the wildest part of the mountains of New York State—ignoring how Republican those areas are—there are thousands of overflights and too much traffic on the roads."

"So he goes west," said Cole.

"Not California. Again, too populated and too many conservatives. There are only two states with wide open spaces, Progressive political dominance, and conservatives who feel so hammered they've practically given up."

"Ecotopia," said Mingo.

"Washington and Oregon," said Torrent. "That's right. *Now* look at Mrs. Malich's map."

Until that point, Cecily had seen it all as a web of shipments crisscrossing the country. But if you looked only at Oregon and Washington, Oregon was practically empty of endpoints. "It has to be Washington," she said. "But where? It's a big state."

"He needs to be near a major highway," said Torrent. "But he has to be in very rugged country."

"Most of the rugged country is on the west side, in the Cascades," said Cecily. "Which is also the most Progressive part of the state."

"It fits his recipe," said Torrent. "Assuming we're right."

"But haven't you already looked at the satellite photos?"

"Of course," said Torrent. "And there's nothing. But there's nothing anywhere in the world. Teams in the DOD have gone over the whole *world* looking for a place where these things might be built and stored."

"So you think he went underground," said Drew.

"We think that one of these mountains is probably riddled with caverns. Aldo Verus is smart enough to learn from Al Qaeda's tunneling. Only he'll do it on a larger scale, and totally high tech."

"What about the dirt?" said Mingo. "I've worked construction, man. I've dug tunnels. You get a shitload of dirt and it shows up on satellites, believe me."

"Not if it isn't on the surface either."

"You can't dig a hole and hide the dirt in the hole you dug," said Mingo. "Then it ain't a hole anymore."

"I thought of that," said Torrent.

"I'm not surprised," said Cecily.

"You dig the hole and hide the dirt underwater."

"So it's on the coast?" asked Arty.

"Somebody would have seen it if he were loading dirt onto boats and dumping it offshore. But Washington has a lot of lakes. Natural ones and artificial ones. Here's what I think. Verus used his funding of politically active environmental groups to get them to withdraw their opposition to building a dam somewhere. It just sails through. A dam in a canyon is going to form a really deep lake. So what if Verus owns a mountain right by the lake, and while the lake level is rising, his people are dumping rubble from their tunnel-building into the water? From the satellites, it just looks like the water level is rising higher and higher. Nobody's boating on it because the lake is still being filled. Nobody sees anything."

"Is Verus that smart?" asked Cole.

"Maybe not. Maybe it all happened in Russia or China. Maybe it isn't even Verus. But I think it *is* Verus and he *is* that smart. He practically owns the whole Progressive movement himself, it can't be anybody else because nobody does anything on the Left without his fingers in it. He's like Hitler with *Mein Kampf,* he announced it all right up front, only nobody believes he's serious, nobody believes it can be done. But look at what these rebels have accomplished. They've got New York, not only our largest city and probably the most Progressive, but the home of most of the news networks including Fox—which, by the way, he's smart enough *not* to censor *yet*. And with New

York they have the U.N. And they conducted this invasion in such a way that the city council endorsed it after the fact. These people are now the legally constituted police force of New York City so that technically they aren't even occupying the city, they're *part* of it. You think some *committee* of really sincere progressives brought this off?"

"I don't know, *we're* a committee," said Cole. "We're pretty smart."

"And we're thirty feet from the President's office," said Torrent. "Smart people don't form committees and send out mailings. They gravitate toward power so their ideas can be implemented."

"Brains and money," said Drew.

Torrent smiled. "One man with brains and money and ruthless ambition, all in service of a cause, so he feels completely justified in killing all kinds of people along the way, from Presidents to doormen. Doesn't all this sound like the same mind that played us all the way he did with Friday the Thirteenth and Major Malich's clandestine operations and . . . everything?"

He didn't need to mention General Alton's nearly successful attempt to involve Nielson in declaring martial law. He only had to look at Cole.

"I'm buying it," said Cole. "At least as a possibility. I assume you've already identified all the new dams and new lakes in Washington."

"Only two candidates for the job," said Torrent. "Right next to each other, part of the same power and water project. Lakes Chinnereth and Genesscret."

"Aren't those based on the Greek and Hebrew names for the Sea of Galilee?" said Cat.

They looked at him as if they'd never met him before.

"What, a black man can't study Hebrew?" said Cat. "Army taught me Arabic, Hebrew is the next language over. And I'm a lay minister."

"The lakes were named for a religious colony that was in the little valley just below where the dams are," said Torrent. "Nowadays nobody lives anywhere near there. All the surrounding land is national forest, leased by a bunch of lumber companies. I have no idea which of the two lakes was used for dumping dirt. Maybe both. The main thing is, they had no trouble getting their permits. Two lawsuits from environmental groups, but they were dropped."

"If it's really where the rebel garrison is, what can we do against two hundred mechs and eight hundred hovercycles?"

"Remember," said Torrent, "my guesses about what he's got could be in the wrong proportions. Maybe he's got twice as much equipment and half as many people. Every person they trained was a possible leak. Maybe Verus never had more than a couple of hundred soldiers. Now they might be scrambling to train volunteer soldiers from New York City. They might have hundreds of mechs lined up against walls with *nobody* to run them."

"Or maybe they have weapons we haven't seen yet," said Mingo.

"Or an army of thousands armed with standard weapons in addition to the troops that run their new machines," said Babe.

"I don't want you guys to make a frontal assault," said Torrent. "We need surgery here. We need *proof*."

"What constitutes proof?" said Cecily. "Half the people in the world don't even believe we landed on the moon back in '69. Why would they believe a bunch of pictures of mechs lined up in a cave when Hollywood CGI can create footage of racks of robots or crowds of soldiers?"

"But *your* video will be grainy and crappy-looking," said Torrent. "So people will believe it. Besides, what we really want is Aldo Verus and his top people, ready to confess to everything."

"Why would they talk?" said Cole.

"Are you kidding?" said Torrent. "Verus is a talker. It's *killing* him that he's had to keep this a secret. But he knows that if *he's* captured, it's all over for his particular campaign. No doubt he has visions of the Progressive Movement Worldwide going on without him. But this little war of his, beginning with Friday the Thirteenth, is over. At that point, what's to hide? He'll want to brag because he's a bragger. He doesn't just love his movement, he loves that it's *his* movement. He'll be eager to sign a book deal with Knopf and believe me, he'll write every word himself. Verus is the Unabomber—with money."

"You make it sound so easy," said Cecily. "But my husband couldn't even get out of the Pentagon alive. How are these guys supposed to go into an unscouted location and bring back a living prisoner with hundreds of troops shooting at them?"

"That won't be the situation," said Torrent. "If I'm right, then when we have possession of either Verus himself or Verus's dead body, right there in their fortress, the other guys will stop because what's the point?"

"They're true believers, that's why," said Cecily. "They're fanatics. They'll keep shooting."

"Some of them might," said Torrent. "But at the point you have possession of Verus and, I hope, his top people, *then* you call in the Army. You just have to hold out till they finish mopping up resistance and secure the rest of the prisoners."

"What if we can't find the installation at all?" said Cole.

"That's the thing," said Torrent. "It's all guesswork. And I certainly have no idea *where* in the area around the lake this place will be, *if* it exists. Or where, inside it, we'll find Aldo Verus."

"Why do you even think he's there?"

"Because on this one," said Torrent, "he's not going to let anybody else control it. He's micromanaging it, and he'll be right at the center of power. Trust me, if the place exists, and it's his, then he's there."

It dawned on Cecily. "You know him, don't you? You know him personally. You know him *well*."

Torrent looked surprised. "Of course. I assumed you all knew that. He's been to several of my seminars. He hates me, but he learns from me."

"Why does he hate you?" said Cecily. "You're no more a Republican than I am."

"Your example contains your answer," said Torrent with a smile. "You're no Republican, yet here you are. When I started consulting for the NSA, Verus accused me of being a whore and we stopped talking. Too bad, because he got it completely backward. Whores give out sex for money. Me, I'd give my advice for free. A chance to play with history? A chance to make a *difference?*"

Cecily had never seen Torrent be so candid about himself. And it fascinated her. "Good heavens, Dr. Torrent. You think you're Hari Selden."

"Who's that?" asked Drew.

Load and Babe both snorted as if Drew had revealed himself to be a complete idiot. "Asimov's Foundation trilogy," said Load.

"Guy who thinks he can shape a thousand years of human history," said Babe.

"Oh," said Drew disdainfully. "Science fiction. All those futures, with lots of little green men but no black people."

"That's Hollywood," said Babe. "Because they think black stars won't open sci-fi movies. The books are—"

"Please, boys," said Cecily. "You're preparing for an incredibly dangerous mission and you're arguing about movies?"

"You brought it up," said Load.

"Hari Selden," muttered Babe.

But after the meeting broke up, Cecily could not help but wonder how right or wrong she might be. It wasn't a bad thing to be Hari Selden, really. A man who manipulated history in order to save the human race from many centuries of misery and chaos. Hadn't Reuben come home from Torrent's class full of talk about what the Pax Romana meant to the world, and how miserable the chaos was afterward? And that was what Asimov's Foundation trilogy was about, too. *The Decline and Fall,* set in the future.

Now here was Torrent, getting to play in the sandbox of history. Getting to shape events.

Well, that was a good thing, wasn't it? A good thing he wasn't on the other side. If Aldo Verus was really the other side's mastermind, he was making Al Qaeda look like a bunch of Keystone Kops—both for cleverness and ruthlessness. America needed somebody like Torrent to balance the equation.

But it was still guesswork. Maybe it always came down to guesswork.

# SEVENTEEN

# BORDER CROSSING

Armies have spent a lot of time and effort training their soldiers not to think of the enemy as human beings. It's so much easier to kill them if you think of them as dangerous animals. The trouble is, war isn't about killing. It's about getting the enemy to stop resisting your will. Like training a dog not to bite. Punishing him leaves you with a beaten dog. Killing him is a permanent solution, but you've got no dog. If you can understand why he's biting and remove the conditions that make him bite, sometimes that can solve the problem as well. The dog isn't dead. He isn't even your enemy.

**GATHERED IN** a classroom at Gettysburg College, Rube's jeesh knew only two things: They were going to Lake Chinnereth, and they had to do it without anyone knowing they had entered the state of Washington on a military mission.

If they were caught, it would be taken as provocation. The governor had posted the National Guard at all the entrance points, with airplanes overflying the rest of the border, and boats patrolling the Columbia River.

As Drew said, "It plain *hurts* me to be looking at a map of part of the U.S.A. in order to figure out how we can get U.S. Army ordnance across a state boundary line undetected. This is just wrong. No matter who's President, we should be able to tell them to get their little National Guard boys out of the way, we're the American Army on American soil!"

The others could only agree.

But the job still had to be done, right away. "We can't enter from Canada," he said, "and I think we should avoid Oregon. We get spotted there, it's almost as bad as Washington itself—their legislature is debating a resolution right now."

"So," said Mingo, "it's Idaho or the Pacific Ocean."

"Idaho," said Arty. "I don't know nothin' 'bout boats."

"You want boats, send Marines," said Benny.

Most of them were looking at ordinary highway maps of the Idaho-Washington border. Load was flipping through a stack of U.S. Geological Survey maps. Drew had Google Maps and Google Earth up on his laptop.

"We've got to come in on a legitimate road," said Cole, "because once we're inside Washington, we need to carry our ordnance in regular trucks, not the kind of all-terrain military vehicles that could get in cross-country."

"We could come in with ATVs and then transfer to trucks."

"Any way to hide everything under, like, potatoes?" said Babe. "Coming in from Idaho the way we are?"

"Not bad," said Cole. "Let's find out how potatoes are shipped from Idaho to Washington. But look at the map. The most direct route is Highway 12. Gets us from Idaho right to Lewis County. National Forest Road 20 leads right to Lake Genesseret. Road 21 leads to the eastern lake, Chinnereth."

"Can't go up those roads," said Drew. "Probably the ones *they* use."

"No," said Cole. "We go in on National Forest Road 48 and then go a mile up 4820. Only a couple of us need to be with the truck. Everybody else goes in like birdwatchers or photographers, in rental cars, on different days, park in different places. We rendezvous here and then cross over the ridge."

"We're climbing *that?*" said Drew.

"You must have the vertical exaggeration set on 'two,'" said Cole. "The ridge isn't really that high."

"High enough," said Drew.

"So the guys with the truck," said Benny. "If they screw up and don't get there, then what?"

"Then the rest of you have binoculars and cameras," said Cole. "Take what pictures you can, email them in, and at least we know more than we did."

"Two trucks," said Drew. "Twice the chance of getting in."

"Twice the chance of getting caught," said Mingo.

"Either we can get in or we can't," said Cole. "We don't want one of the trucks to go in by the second-best route."

"And I bet you're with the truck," said Arty.

"We've been working together for a little while now," said Cole. "I don't care who goes in with the truck. There's nobody here I wouldn't trust for the job."

"But you *want* to go," said Arty.

"Don't *you?*" said Cole.

"No way," said Arty. "Trucks are great big targets. Trucks run over mines. Trucks get blown up."

"They haven't mined the roads," said Babe, disgusted.

"Not at the border," said Arty. "But the rebels? Up those National Forest roads they're using?"

"Start killing park rangers in jeeps," said Cole, "and somebody'd notice them. There are no mines."

"What ordnance are we taking, anyway?" said Cat.

"Separate discussion," said Cole and Drew at the same time. They laughed. "We're on border crossing right now," said Drew.

"Idaho and Washington got a lot of border," said Mingo.

"Route 12 comes across the border at Clarkston, Washington," said Arty. "Lewiston, Idaho, and Clarkston, Washington. Lewis and Clark. I feel like I'm in grade school again. We did a pageant about Lewis and Clark."

"What did you play, Sacajawea?" asked Cat.

"And we're headed for *Lewis* County," said Arty. "It's like a tour of American history."

"There's a road comes in just north of the river at Clarkston, so we aren't going right through town," said Mingo. "In case there's shooting."

"There won't be shooting," said Cole. "We're crossing into *Washington*, not Iran. If they stop us, they stop us, we don't shoot."

"And if they try to arrest us?" said Mingo.

"Then we're arrested," said Cole. "Let them take the heat for arresting United States soldiers. Better than us killing U.S. citizens. In or out of the National Guard."

"Those really the rules of engagement?" said Mingo.

"Absolutely," said Cole. "The only time we use our weapons is at Lake Chinnereth, and then only if we know they're definitely the rebels and we can't avoid shooting."

"Hell, the truck's all yours then," said Mingo. "Those are shitty rules of engagement. I'm not going to rot in some jail."

"It'll be an American jail," said Benny. "Cable TV."

"Okay," said Cole, "who's willing to go with the truck, under those rules of engagement?"

Everybody looked stonily forward. "We don't want to kill anybody," said Drew, "but we don't want *them* to be able to shoot, and us not."

"I don't want to do it alone," said Cole.

"It's just a U-Haul," said Mingo.

"No need two of us getting arrested," said Arty.

"I'd go with you," said Drew. "Except that's white man's country. Eastern Washington? Might as well be North Dakota. Black face with you in that truck, they're going to look extra hard at whatever you're carrying. They'll be looking for drugs."

"Come on," said Cole. What century *was* this?

"You never been black in the United States," said Cat. "Trust me on this. Drew and I travel separately or we're a gang. We come through Seattle airport, and we try real hard not to look like drug dealers."

"How's this," said Load. "The truck comes in from Genesee, Idaho, on this Cow Creek Road."

"That's a promising name," said Cole.

"Not exactly a major highway," said Arty.

"That's what we want, right?" said Benny.

"If they got nobody on it, then yeah," said Mingo. "But if they put somebody there, it's gonna be Barney Fife. Real eager to inspect *every* vehicle to count the bolts in the chassis."

"I look at the map and it looks like this goes nowhere," said Cole.

"No, you pick up Schlee Road to Steptoe Canyon Road and take that south to Wawawai River Road."

"Is that a real name?" said Arty. "Wawawawawawai?"

"What is this, the Grand Canyon?" said Cole. "Nothing crosses this river for miles."

"That's right," said Load. "You backtrack almost to Clarkston before you can cross the river. But we're not working to save gas, we're trying to go undiscovered."

"So what shows up more," said Cole, "a truck on main roads, or a truck driving on back roads? We have to remember they're watching by air, too."

"Maybe the guys with the truck go there and see what it looks like," said Mingo. "Play it by ear."

"There's no second chance," said Drew. "The first time you try is the only try you get. How can you see how it looks?"

"Cross in a car first?" said Arty.

"And then you decide that's a good place to cross, but when you come back with the truck, the guardsman recognizes you?" said Drew. "One shot."

"So whoever drives, decides," said Arty. "We can't decide it from here, looking at a map."

"Okay," said Drew. "Cole, when you're about to come through, you call me on your cell. If I don't hear from you in two hours that you got through, then we lay hands on whatever weapons we can buy inside Washington and go on without you."

"Okay," said Cole. "I'll do it."

"Of course you will," said Drew. "You're still active duty, so you're used to taking shit from everybody."

"It's the assignment I want," said Cole.

"Why?" asked Arty.

"When Rube and I came out of the Holland Tunnel, the National Guard saved our butts. They did their job and they went the extra mile. I want to be there to make sure we don't hurt any of them."

Arty rolled his eyes. Cat coughed.

"An idealist," said Drew.

"A pacifist," said Mingo. "Did you join the Peace Corps and get Special Ops by mistake?"

"Just teasing you," said Load. "None of us wants to hurt American soldiers. We all agree with you. But it's your job because you're the one most willing to do it. We trust you to bring us the tools of the trade."

"Of course, you got to change your appearance," said Mingo. "You went on CNN, people are gonna know you."

"I went on O'Reilly," said Cole.

"So even *more* people," said Mingo.

"How fast does your beard grow?" said Drew.

"Bleach your hair?" suggested Arty.

"Fake glasses?"

"Wax teeth?"

"You're getting silly now," said Cole. "I'll grow my beard, I'll dye my hair darker. It was a month ago. Nobody's going to remember."

Then they got down to the serious business of choosing their weapons. Torrent had opened the whole arsenal to them—including all the prototypes that were meant to counter mechs and hoverbikes.

"Guys, it's a candy store, I know," said Arty. "But we got to shlep these things through the woods and over a ridge that looks like it's, what, eight miles high."

"Vertical exaggeration," Drew reminded him.

"A hundred and fifty pounds on your back gives you all the vertical exaggeration you need," said Arty.

"Want to buy good backpacks in Washington?" said Drew. "Easier than trying to carry them through airports."

"Can we keep it after?" said Benny.

"If you pay for it yourself," said Mingo.

"Of course we're going to pay for it ourselves," said

Benny. "You think they're going to take a DOD purchase order?"

Cole shook his head. "They'll fill our ATM accounts with plenty of money. This is the United States government. Possibly the only entity with more money than Aldo Verus."

**SO IT** came down to Cole in a U-Haul. Everything they needed for a week in the woods—including rations, uniforms, backpacks, weapons, and ammunition. Covering it: a bunch of used furniture and boxes filled with old kitchen stuff. A Goodwill somewhere had been stripped of everything, it looked like.

If somebody just looked into the back of the truck, fine. If they pulled out a few boxes and looked inside them, fine. If they unloaded the first three layers, fine. But if the search got serious, Cole was toast.

He tried to picture the truck on the lonely back roads and he didn't like the picture. Oh, he had his cover stories—if he took the northern route, then he was moving from Genesee to Pasco, but he needed to pick up stuff from his mother-in-law's house in Colton on the way. If he went into Washington through Clarkston, then it was still Genesee and Pasco, only he could skip the mother-in-law. He even had the mother-in-law's name—a woman they knew would not be home, but who had a daughter the right age to be married to Cole. Just in case they got a guardsman who happened to be a local boy.

Still, once he got across the border near Uniontown, why in the world would he take that circuitous route on Schlee and Steptoe and Wawawai River Road? Obvious answer: He wanted to avoid crossing the border again. Maybe they'd buy it. But it was a lot of miles out of the way. If *I* were a patrolman and I heard that story, I'd unload the whole damn truck.

It had been a solitary drive. A few cellphone calls, but not too many, just verifying that Drew was in Washington and that there were more guards but they didn't seem particularly alert or hostile. Business as usual. Only . . . everybody in the airport watched the news. Baseball season, the Mariners were even in contention, sort of, but even in the bars, more people were watching CNN than ESPN or whatever game happened to be on.

"They care, man," said Drew. "I just don't know from looking which ones want the revolution to succeed, and which ones want it to fail."

"Probably most of them just want it all to go away."

"Don't see many people inspired by President Nielson, tell the truth."

"They inspired by the New York City Council?"

"The mayor's acting like he thinks he's the new President of the U.S.A.," said Drew. "People kind of laughed."

"Well that's a good sign," said Cole. "But we've talked long enough. Cellphones. Somebody might be listening."

"In D.C. I worried," said Drew. "Didn't know who was doing what, and everybody had all the tech. But out here? What, they're listening to *all* the cellphone calls?"

"Talk to you when I get in place," said Cole.

Well, now here he was on Down River Road in Lewiston. He'd picked a wide spot to pull off and pretend he needed to take a quick nap. Then he walked like he just needed to stretch his legs. Got to a place where he could see the crossing. Not bad. Two National Guard guys stopping everybody, but they were mostly just looking inside cars and passing people through.

Of course, that might just be people they knew. But this was the road that became Wawawai River Road at the border. There were a couple of trucks, too. And those got looked at more carefully. Backs got opened up. Anyplace big enough to hold—well, to hold the kind of stuff that Cole was carrying

Still, nobody was unpacking anything.

He should go north. That's what Drew and Load both told him. But last thing before he left, Mingo just said, "Barney Fife," and grinned.

I'm not the U.S. Army invading Iran. I'm not a terrorist

with a truck full of explosives to blow up a building or a city. I'm an American citizen crossing through a weird new security checkpoint where there didn't used to be one. What have I got to be afraid of?

It was too far to see the faces of the guards. If he showed binoculars, that would make him look suspicious. The crossing on Highway 12, right in town, that was a bad one. Lots of guys with guns, lots of traffic, six cars at a time, no way could he cross there. And from here, not too late to turn around, go north; if somebody noticed him, he could say he just pulled off to reset, decide whether to stop by his mother-in-law's house or not.

He sighed. Stretched. Sauntered back to the truck.

Hot hot day. That was the good thing about going in civvies. He could wear shorts and a T-shirt, sandals.

He got in the truck. It had done okay, crossing over the Rockies, driving more than twenty-five hundred miles. Good truck. Only three hundred miles to go.

He called Drew. This close to the border, they might be eavesdropping. So the call was circumspect. "Mom there?" asked Cole.

"Napping," said Drew.

"Well tell her I'm on the way."

Cole turned the key. Started up again. The air-conditioning kicked in. But he turned it off, rolled down the windows.

There was only one car ahead of him. The two guardsmen were looking in the windows. They waved the car on.

Cole pulled up to the portable stop sign. "I really got to do this to get to Washington now?"

"How it is," said the guardsman. "Air-conditioning broken?"

"Trying to save on gas," said Cole. "Moving is expensive enough."

"From where to where?"

"Heading for Pasco."

"Address there?"

Cole rattled it off. He was tempted to add chatty comments but decided against it. This guy looked serious. Young, but definitely Barney Fife-ish. Full of his authority, like a rookie cop. Didn't have to go the northern route to get that, after all.

"And where you from?"

"Genesee." He gave the address, but the guy wasn't listening.

"Open up the back, please."

Well, that was routine, he'd seen that from the top of the hill. He got out and headed for the back. Meanwhile, another car pulled up behind him.

The guardsman waved the other car around. "You take this one, Jeff."

So now it was just Cole and the man in charge. No use wishing it were the other way around. They couldn't have fit what they needed to carry inside a car trunk. Or even eight car trunks.

"Saw you up on the hill," said the guardsman.

Shit, thought Cole. "Yep," he said.

"Deciding whether or not you wanted to come through here?" asked the guardsman.

"I shut my eyes for a few minutes. Then I took a walk to stretch my legs." Cole let himself sound just a little bit defensive, because he figured a regular citizen probably would. But he didn't like the way this was going.

"Already tired of driving, just from Genesee?"

"I got up tired this morning," said Cole. "I loaded the truck yesterday and I'm still sore."

"Don't look like the kind of guy gets sore just from loading a truck," said the guardsman. "In fact, you look like you're in top physical condition."

"I used to work out," said Cole with a smile. But his heart was sinking. The one thing they hadn't taken into account was that even in civilian clothes, Cole looked military. And in shorts and a T-shirt, his utter lack of body fat was way too easy to see.

The guardsman leaned against the open back of the truck. "What am I going to find when you and I unload this truck?"

"Crappy furniture," said Cole. "Crappy stuff in nice new boxes. The story of my life."

The guardsman just kept looking at him.

"Why are you doing this to me, man?" said Cole. "I served my time in Iraq. Do I have to have uniforms hassling me now?"

"Am I hassling you?" asked the guardsman.

Cole sat up on the tail of the truck. "Do what you've got to do."

Another car pulled past them. So Jeff would be busy again for a minute.

The guardsman pulled out the ramp at the back of the truck and walked up, started untying the ropes that were holding the load in place.

And Cole remembered Charlie O'Brien, the guardsman at the mouth of the Holland Tunnel. That had been so much easier, soldier to soldier. They each had respect for what the other one was doing.

"You know," said Cole, "it's not like Washington is at war with the rest of the United States."

"I know," said the guardsman. A rope end dropped down across Cole's shoulders. "Sorry."

"It was the President and Vice President and Secretary of Defense of the whole United States that got murdered on Friday the Thirteenth. No matter what your politics were."

"I know that, too," said the guardsman.

"So . . . what if the guys who set the whole thing up— the assassinations—fed the information to the terrorists and then invaded New York. What if the U.S. Army had hard information that those guys were inside the state of Washington? What do you think they'd do?"

The guardsman stopped what he was doing. "I think they'd go in and get them."

"But the state of Washington says they aren't letting any

military in. Which means, if the bad guys are already *in* the state, the only people being kept out are the good guys. Assuming that you think the assassins are the bad guys."

"And the U.S. Army doesn't want to launch a big invasion," said the guardsman. "They just want something quiet. Something . . . Special Ops."

"Like that," said Cole.

The guardsman stood there awhile. "It'd make a difference, though, if those guys were gonna start shooting at guys like me."

"They'd be crazy to do that, wouldn't they? I mean, you're part of the U.S. Army, aren't you? What is this, a civil war?"

"I hope to God not," said the guardsman. "We'd get creamed."

"Nobody's going to be shooting at the Washington National Guard, I'd bet my life on that."

"Yeah, but can I bet *my* life on it?"

The question hung there.

"Man, think about it," said Cole. "If Special Ops sent a guy in, and he wanted you dead, you think you wouldn't be dead already?"

The guardsman's hand strayed to his sidearm. But then his hand went on. To reach for the rope end. Cole got it and handed it to him.

The guardsman started retying the knot.

"Thanks," said Cole.

"All that bullshit you told me, it was pretty good," said the guardsman. "But I saw you reconnoitering up there. I knew what I was looking at."

"And you made sure you were alone when you inspected my truck."

"Had to know how things were," said the guardsman. "But there was a guy on the news a month ago. He said, If somebody tells you to point your gun at a guy just doing his job, then *you* point it at the guy gave the order."

Cole felt himself blushing. Damn. Had the guy *recognized* him? A month later? With a stubbly beard and darker hair and in civilian clothes? Or did it just happen that Cole's words on O'Reilly made an impression that stuck with the guy, and he didn't recognize him now at all?

"Glad you watched that program," said Cole.

The knot was tied.

"Long way to go?" said the guardsman. "I'm betting it isn't downtown Pasco."

"A little farther than that," said Cole.

They pushed the ramp back up under the truck together. Then the guardsman held out his hand. "Appreciate your cooperation, sir."

"Thanks," said Cole. "Pleasure to know you."

Cole walked back to the cab as the guardsman went back to Jeff, who had just waved on a third car. "So you're not unloading it?" asked Jeff.

"I could see clear to the front," said the guardsman. "No reason to ruin this guy's day."

Cole started the engine and closed the door. He gave a little wave to the guardsman.

The guardsman returned a little hint of a salute and said, "Godspeed."

# EIGHTEEN

# APPOINTMENT

The problem with elections is that anybody who wants an office badly enough to run for it probably shouldn't have it. And anybody who does not want an office badly enough to run for it probably shouldn't have it, either. Government office should be received like a child's Christmas present, with surprise and delight. Instead it is usually received like a diploma, an anticlimax that never seems worth the struggle to earn it.

IT WAS a surprise press conference—only an hour's notice—and nobody in the President's staff knew what it was even about. He hadn't even told Sandy—or if he did, her slightly irritated shrug when Cecily shot her a questioning glace was a very convincing cover-up.

As President Nielson approached the lectern, Cecily remembered ruefully that one thing LaMonte had always been good at was keeping a secret. He subscribed to the old adage that once you tell somebody—anybody—it's not a secret anymore. She tried to guess what was going on by seeing who shared the stage with him in the auditorium, but since it consisted of all the cabinet members who were in Gettysburg at the time, plus the House and Senate majority and minority leaders, it was clearly a big deal. *They,* at least, must know what was going on.

Oh. There was Donald Porter. They must have reached an agreement on letting him be confirmed.

"Thank you for coming on short notice," said President

Nielson. "Yesterday my good friend Donald Porter came to me and we had a good long conversation. At the end of the hour, it seemed clear that I could not dissuade him from his decision to withdraw his name from nomination to be the Vice President of the United States."

LaMonte went on about Porter's years of service, but Cecily knew positive spin when she heard it. It was clear that the impasse with Congress over Porter's confirmation had become a serious barrier to getting anything done, not to mention a hazard to the country, since the United States was currently without either a Vice President *or* a Speaker of the House, making the eighty-four-year-old Senator Stevens the next in line. Nobody liked that situation, least of all Stevens himself, who had even less interest in acquiring the presidency than LaMonte Nielson had had.

So there had been a compromise, and it involved Porter walking away. From everything—since his successor at State, Sarkissian, had already been confirmed, and no SecDef nominee could get past Congress, there was no government job open to Porter at the moment, and little likelihood that he would be confirmed even if there were. So he had suddenly acquired a strong wish to retire from public life, possibly to write and teach.

The real question, though, was whom President Nielson would tap as his new Vice Presidential nominee. He must have discussed it with the leaders of both parties, and they must have agreed, or they would not be sharing the podium right now. Was it somebody on stage, or someone waiting in the wings? It was hard to imagine any of the cabinet officers being acceptable. Was it one of the majority leaders?

"As you know, this office was thrust upon me by the Constitution and the action of enemies of this country. I did not seek it. I had spent my public career as a strong partisan, willing to compromise with members of the opposition party, but always aware of which side I was on.

"What America needs right now is not to take sides. Not a Republican or a Democrat, but a Vice President who can symbolize and represent national unity—America at its best, without division, without rancor, and with the full support of both parties in Congress.

"That naturally means reaching outside the two-party system, outside of the ranks of those who have sought public office. Over the past three years, starting as a frequent consultant to the National Security Adviser, then a full-time aide, and finally for the past month as the National Security Adviser, Averell Torrent has established a brilliant record of public service in a time of national crisis.

"I have never asked him if he was a Republican or a Democrat. I have never needed to. He is a loyal servant of the Constitution and of all the people of this country. I have come to rely on his wise counsel. It is no disrespect to the others who have held the office of the Vice President of the United States to say that it is my firm belief that it has never been held by a person of such wisdom, such intellect, and such a vast breadth and depth of knowledge.

"In some ways, the vice-presidency is a thankless office. But under recent Presidents, the Vice President has been relied on more and more to oversee ever-more-important aspects of government. It is with the full and, dare I say, enthusiastic approval of the leaders of both parties in both houses of Congress that I assure you that I will continue that practice and expand upon it. When he is confirmed, Averell Torrent will be a part of every decision I make as President—in fact, he already is—and he will have far-reaching authority of his own, under my direction of course—in fact, he already does."

With that, President Nielson beckoned Torrent up to the lectern to make a short statement of acceptance—he said almost nothing, keeping his demeanor grave and managing to wear an expression of benign puzzlement, rather like someone who has been given a very lavish gift but didn't really need it and has no idea where to put it.

Then the party leaders in Congress came forward and they started taking questions. Torrent was deferent—his answers were brief and almost invariably referred the questioner to the President or to the Congressmen.

But to Cecily, it looked like a tour-de-force performance. He wasn't playing to the room, he was playing to the camera. His voice was quiet and steady, his face calm, his expression pleasant enough, but full of dignity.

He's running for President already, thought Cecily. He's creating an image that the voters want to see. He could not have placed himself better. The consensus choice of both parties in Congress. Appointed in order to bring all factions of the country together. Young but not too young. Attractive, intelligent, but not bookish or aloof. Look at him laugh at LaMonte's little jest. Natural, easy laughter, his whole face involved in the smile. The twinkle in the eyes. But not so handsome he doesn't look real. Not so brilliant he doesn't look approachable. He's never run for office but he knows how to create an image and he's creating it.

Was it even possible for him to run? Of course it was. It was nearly August, but both political conventions had been postponed in the wake of Friday the Thirteenth. The Democratic convention would be first, in mid-August; the Republican convention right before Labor Day. The Democrats had their likely candidate, who had been about to announce her choice for vice-presidential nominee when the assassinations happened; she had held off since then because it was hard to know, until things settled down, how people would perceive candidates who were strongly identified with the progressive movement within the Democratic Party. She might need to reach for a more moderate running mate than she would otherwise have chosen.

No one had locked up the Republican nomination. And now there was a real chance that the nomination might go to Averell Torrent. Everyone in that room knew it. President Nielson had practically said it—what the country needs right now is someone to bring people together. A moderate, a nonpartisan. If that was so good a trait for the Vice President, it would be ten times more important for the President who would be chosen in November.

No one knew what the political fallout of Friday the Thirteenth and the Progressive Restoration's takeover of

New York would be. Up till this moment, President Nielson had looked confused and powerless—because, up till
this moment, there had been no good choices available and
no power he could exercise without potentially devastating
consequences. At a stroke, his nomination of Torrent, and
its acceptance by both parties in Congress, made Nielson
look far more effective and struck a blow to the heart of the
Progressive Restoration's charge that the Republican administration was a bunch of fanatics who had trashed the
Constitution.

In short, if Torrent was the new face of the Republican
Party, would state legislatures be so eager to follow along
with the push to join with the Progressive Restoration?

Of course, everything depended on how well Torrent
stood up to the scrutiny the media would now put him
through. His life would be researched and dissected. It
helped that he was married to a shy but lovely woman and
had two attractive sons and a pretty daughter, all in their
teens—the family would be splendid as an image of stability. Even though Torrent had long traveled the country lec-
turing and giving seminars, there had never been a breath
of scandal about sexual peccadilloes. He had inherited a
little family money but lived rather simply and while his
speaking and teaching fees were respectable, they were not
exorbitant. He was not, by any modern standard, rich. It
would take fifty Torrents to make an Oprah, by Cecily's
rough estimate.

Cecily liked LaMonte, and felt a great loyalty to him. So
she was also a little sad. This appointment made it absolutely clear that LaMonte had no desire to run for President himself. He would go down in history as a caretaker
President. And Cecily knew that was exactly what he
hoped for—he would want to be remembered as a man
who executed the office faithfully, and walked away from it
as soon as he had done his job.

In all likelihood, he would probably return to the House.
The new laws of presidential succession did not necessarily require that he resign his House seat, and Cecily tried to

remember if he had or not. She didn't think so. In such a time of crisis, nobody was agitating for a by-election in Idaho yet. Or maybe he had already quietly let it be known that his name *would* be on the ballot in November— running again for Congress. Nobody would dare to run against him or try to replace him.

So everybody was happy, really. The country was better off. LaMonte had quite possibly changed the momentum and the direction of the national mood.

Now all that was needed was for Rube's jeesh to find the smoking gun—the place where all these Progressive Restoration weapons had been made, where their soldiers had been trained. And maybe, just maybe, proof that the rebels had been ready to take advantage of Friday the Thirteenth because they had planned it. Right now that charge was a staple of the far-right pundits, but it was dismissed as absurd by nearly everyone else. Cecily knew that because the traitors obviously had to have contacts inside the White House and the Pentagon, it was easy to assume that the treason came from the Right, not the Left—the opposite camp from the Progressive Restoration.

But she knew better. The lurid details of Reuben's murder by his secretary had gone through the normal media nonsense—claims that his secretary had probably killed him because they were having an affair, or because he had backed out of their treasonous conspiracy at the last moment and tried to save the late President. Cecily did her best to ignore such things because they would only make her crazy and she could do nothing to stop them.

She knew that the FBI had turned up the fact that while DeeNee had never done anything illegal or even questionable—or she could never have been cleared to work where she did in the Pentagon—her friends from college remembered her as being a fervent radical of the Left, even by the standards of American university English departments. The FBI found no links to any particular movements—DeeNee had not been a joiner—but there was no way to pretend that there was much chance that whatever conspiracy she had been a part of was of the Right. But since the report on Reuben's murder was now tied up in the report on the Friday the Thirteenth assassinations, nothing had been made public. She had found out only because LaMonte told her.

"I'm not going to make it public and I hope you'll respect that decision," LaMonte had said. "If it leaks that she was a campus leftist, it will be interpreted as an attempt by my administration to blame the Left, which means the Democrats, for Friday the Thirteenth. It would only be more divisive. When we get the full answer, then we'll publish it and damn the consequences. But until then, Cecily, let them babble on the television and don't let the nonsense bother you. The truth *will* come out in due time, and your husband *will* be recognized as the hero and patriot and martyr that he was."

But LaMonte would probably not be in office when the final report was ready. Someone else would be. If it was the Democratic candidate, Cecily had little faith in her letting a report that implicated anyone from the Left ever see the light of day. Maybe it would be Torrent. But would he allow a divisive report to be issued, given that he would be trying to hold the factions together?

Then again, he was bold enough to use Reuben's jeesh as a fighting force to make surgical strikes to work against the rebels wherever one of their minor strongholds had been found. Maybe he would be wise enough to regard the provable truth as the best road toward reconciliation.

Cecily pinned her hopes on Cole and Reuben's friends. If Torrent was right, and these lakes in Washington were the stronghold of the rebels, maybe they would find there the proof that would reveal who was responsible for Friday the Thirteenth—and for Reuben's murder. Reuben would be completely exonerated. Their children could grow up without a taint of treason attached to their father, but could take pride in him.

The press conference was over. But Cecily's thoughts had taken her down an emotional road she usually stayed away from. All she could think about was Reuben.

Sandy came up to her after the reporters rushed out to file their stories or do their standups in front of the "Gettysburg White House." She saw Cecily's attempt to hold back tears and said, "My dear, I know you aren't moved by Torrent's appointment."

"No, no," Cecily said. "It's Reuben, that's all."

"You've hardly given yourself a chance to grieve."

"Work is the cure," said Cecily. "I was just thinking about our kids and how the world would view their father as they grew up."

"The world will honor him, or the world can go hang," said Sandy. "Meanwhile, give yourself a break. Nobody's going to get any serious work done today anyway, it will all be buzz and whisper and speculate. It's a field day for the pundits, in and out of the President's staff. Go home and come back tomorrow."

It was good advice. But when Sandy said to go home she meant one thing. To Cecily it meant another.

She could hardly go "home" to the little house where Aunt Margaret was looking after the kids—the last thing they needed was to see their mother as an emotional wreck.

So she got in her car and drove out of the secured area and drove down U.S. highway 15 to Leesburg, and then down Route 7 through the familiar sights of Loudoun County. She had been so immersed in the war they were fighting that she had almost forgotten that most of America didn't know they were fighting a war. People might be keenly aware of and troubled by the fact that New York City and the state of Vermont were not under the active authority of the U.S. government, that Washington State was neutral at best, that other states might join the rebellion—or the "restoration"—and they no doubt had strong feelings about it. But they were still going to work and doing their jobs, shopping at the malls, eating at the restaurants, watching the phony reality shows of summer, or going to the summer blockbuster movies. Cecily wondered briefly whether current events had helped or hurt one of her and Reuben's favorite series, *24*. Did it now seem too close to painful reality for people to enjoy it? Or was its sometimes far-fetched plotting now completely vindicated by events that were even less probable than the conspiracies on the show?

By the time 24 went back on the air, people would no doubt have calmed down about Friday the Thirteenth. The show would still be a hit. *American Idol* would still find hordes of people waiting to humiliate themselves for a chance to be on television. The World Series would still be more important to a lot of Americans than the presidential election. One of the great things about democracy was that you were also free to ignore government if you wanted to.

The house was locked. Undisturbed. She had arranged for her mail to be forwarded to her office in Gettysburg and she had paid all the bills—the air-conditioning was running and the water was still connected.

No, not undisturbed after all. The bedroom had been entered by someone who—no, she knew why the closet and several drawers were open. Cole told her that the Secret Service agents had sent people here and to Cole's apartment to get uniforms and underwear and toiletries for him and Reuben that last night of Reuben's life. The Secret Service agents who had been willing to die to protect her husband, and who nearly had—both severely injured in the fighting, but both now out of the hospital and, presumably, back on the job, at a desk no doubt until their recovery was complete. She had visited them in the hospital once and thanked them for trying to save her husband, and for saving Cole, but she could see that they were still ashamed of having been caught flat-footed by DeeNee and her .22.

Cecily pulled down the covers of the bed, took off her shoes, and crawled between the sheets. She had heard that sometimes the scent of a loved one would linger in their sheets, their clothing, but either time had erased any smells or they were simply too normal for her to recognize them. She had a good cry over that. But she would have had a good long cry if the smells had still lingered there, too. It was about time she cried, she told herself even as she wept. And then she was done with weeping, for the moment, anyway. She got up and went downstairs to the kitchen and began cleaning out the dead food in the fridge. Here there was no shortage of odors, and she got the garbage bags out of the house and into the big plastic cans behind the garage. She expected the cans to be full of reeking garbage, too, but some neighbor must have taken them to the curb on garbage day and brought them back. She hesitated to put these bags in the cans because she had no intention of being here on garbage day—but maybe the neighbor would check. Or maybe not. Better to leave the garbage here than stinking up the kitchen.

Hadn't the children's bikes been out on the lawn? No, she made them put them away in the garage before they left. Didn't she? She checked, and they were there, so she must have—the neighbors didn't have keys to get in and put things away. It wasn't that kind of neighborhood. Cecily had been one of the few mothers who was home during the day.

I want to be home with my children again, she thought. And then whispered it. "I want to be home again."

But not yet. Not until she had finished with the work she was doing. There was still more evidence to gather. More pieces to fit into the mosaic.

Which made her think of the "office"—a room in the finished half of the basement where they kept their financial records and all of Reuben's books and papers from school. Nothing classified or secret, not in print and not on the family computers. The laptop in the office was more hers than his. It's where she kept track of the family finances and paid bills online.

She walked into the room and switched on the light. Someone had been in here, too. The laptop was gone.

Well, that was hardly a surprise. They wouldn't have pursued Cole so relentlessly for the PDA without also looking for any other place where Reuben might have kept his data. But she had to commend the thieves for their tidiness. If they had gone through the rest of the papers or searched through the whole house, they had put everything back neatly enough that she couldn't tell.

And maybe it was the Secret Service that took the computer. Maybe they had it and would give it back to her so she could update her financials.

She opened the file cabinet that contained Reuben's papers. Not many in recent years—everything was so secret there was no chance he'd keep things at home. But his student work was all here. The papers he had written for classes. His dissertation, of course. And all his notes from all his classes, written in Farsi and neatly filed.

His notes had always looked both beautiful and forbidding. Because Farsi used the Arabic alphabet, it was written from right to left, with words that looked virtually the same—it was a script-only language, so each letter flowed into the next one, and many important distinctions consisted entirely of the dots and marks surrounding the letters. To someone who didn't know the alphabet, it looked more like art than language. But now Cecily had learned the Arabic alphabet and knew many words of Farsi on sight.

Enough, in fact, that she could identify which class each folder of notes was from. They were headed by subject and teacher name. The teachers' names were often written in roman letters, but sometimes not. She quickly realized that those written in Farsi were the names that were also words that could be translated. No doubt Reuben got a kick out of thinking of professors by the Farsi translations of their names.

"Torrent" was a word. Which of these was Torrent's class? She had no way of knowing—the word "torrent" wouldn't have come up much in Reuben's records on his PDA. She didn't actually speak Farsi. What she had mastered was more like a graduate student's version of a foreign language—exactly what was needed to read a particular set of documents and not a speck more.

But she wanted to know what Reuben had written about

Torrent's class. And when the boys got back from Chinnereth and Genesseret, they could help her by translating it.

If they got back.

She couldn't think that way. They were soldiers like Reuben had been. They were careful, highly trained, and very hard to beat. They could only be killed by treachery, the way Reuben had been.

"Treachery." A strange word, she thought. What is a treacher? How do you treach? Of course the real words were "traitor" and "betray," but what an odd word, that looked like it ought to function like "teacher." Those who teach are committing teachery, she thought. While those who commit treachery are treachers. Do they go to college to get their treaching certificate? Do they belong to the treaching profession? She chuckled at her own humor, then realized that with Reuben gone there was no one to tell it to. He would have laughed and probably would have reversed the joke, dropping the *r* in *treason* words to refer to teaching. "Our kids have got some mighty fine taitors in school this year. They'll be carrying out their teason in our children's classrooms. They plan to betay our kids."

It would have become a family joke word. "What did they betay you in school today?" "None of my teachers would be convicted of teason, Dad. Lack of evidence." And on and on for years.

But not now.

Her eyes again filled with tears, she pulled out all the folders that didn't have the professors' names written in roman letters and took them with her out to the car. She'd find out what Reuben learned from Torrent. And, knowing Reuben, he would have written his opinions of his professor as well.

Only as she drove back out toward the Leesburg bridge did the connection of treachery with Torrent emerge to the level of consciousness.

At first she dismissed it. And then she didn't.

Wasn't it because of Torrent that Reuben was first recruited to work on his clandestine projects with Phillips? Torrent was already well connected in Washington, even then. She remembered Reuben talking to her about how the guys recruiting him were probably the ones Torrent had hinted about. But she distinctly remembered the "probably" in what Reuben said. Nobody had actually identified themselves as coming from him. Reuben talked about that because Torrent had told him that they *would* mention his name. He even said that he meant to check with Torrent to see if these guys were the ones he had been talking about.

Did he? Or did he decide not to bother the Great Man? Or did he try, but Torrent didn't bother to answer?

Even if Reuben's contact with Phillips originated with Torrent, that didn't mean that Torrent had anything to do with their activities. Somebody might have said, we're looking for a good man who can be trusted to do this and this and this, and Torrent simply recommended Reuben.

Treachery, though. Treachery was on her mind. DeeNee was on her mind. Working with Reuben for years, knowing his secrets, helping him keep his clandestine work secret. How far did this conspiracy reach?

The information on the PDA had been part of the data that Torrent used when he deduced where Aldo Verus's secret garrison had to be. But what if it wasn't mere deduction. What if Torrent was part of it all along?

How could he be? He had been sending the jeesh out on missions that involved taking out guys on hovercycles and taking down mechs and trying to find EMP weapons. Working against the rebels.

Or was that part of Torrent's game plan? Make it plain that he's definitely on the side of the Constitution, so that he can get exactly where he is—Vice-President-to-be, with a strong possibility of being nominated for President?

No, no. That's too twisted and deep a game. Torrent showed them the reasoning that led him to those lakes in Washington.

Showed it to them. Demonstrated it. Made the trail clear.

He knew where it was all along, but couldn't tell them until they had gathered enough information that he could *show* them a rational path leading to the conclusion.

No proof. Probably not true. *Probably.*

But if it *was* true, then what mission were Cole and Load and Benny and Mingo and all the rest on, what were they really doing? Was it a wild goose chase? If Torrent was honest and he really had deduced the location the way he showed them, then in all likelihood it was simply wrong and they'd find nothing there.

If it *was* real, though, and Aldo Verus—or somebody—had an arsenal and a garrison underground in those mountains, then was he sending the jeesh into a trap? Had he used them for his purposes and now no longer needed them? Was he planning to have them killed and the incident made public to discredit President Nielson and swing more of the country toward the Progressive Restoration?

No, it couldn't be that. Because Torrent had just thrown in his lot with President Nielson. Not that he'd become a Republican, necessarily—he was still noncommittal about that—but he had declared for the Constitution and against the rebels. Plus, if the mission to Chinnereth led to a public relations disaster, it would be a disaster for Torrent, too. His fingerprints were all over the mission.

Her mind leapt to another connection. Was it possible that both Torrent and General Alton were agents provocateurs, secretly part of the rebel conspiracy, with a mission to destroy the constitutional government by embarrassing it and providing justification for the Progressive Restoration?

It put everything in a new light. Or perhaps into a new darkness. It was too convoluted. So many things could go wrong with such a plan. You don't pin your revolution on the actions of people who are, essentially, actors.

Not actors. Moles. Espionage services do it all the time.

Still, she could not believe Torrent was some sacrificial lamb playing a part. As Cole told about it, General Alton had been so obvious that he was almost certainly putting on an act—that's what they all assumed now. His mission was to try to get LaMonte to commit the folly of imposing martial law, without the support of the Army but thinking that he had that support. Was Torrent also putting on an act?

Was he so self-sacrificing that he would bring himself into a position to play for the presidency *exactly* at the time that he was launching the incident that would bring this government to disaster?

Well . . . yes, maybe. Who knew? Being the newly appointed Vice President would make his sponsorship of the provocative incident in Washington all the more damaging to President Nielson and to the Constitutionalists in general.

Her hands were trembling on the wheel. I don't know any of this, she thought. It's not true. It's absurd. Torrent is brilliant. He's also very full of his own views and opinions, and has the books to prove it. He is simply unbelievable as the self-sacrifice of somebody else's ambition.

Unless he's a true believer in the cause. DeeNee certainly never gave a clue of her deep hatred of all things military and/or conservative. Then again, DeeNee kept it a secret by never talking about herself or her views on anything. Torrent talks all the time. Has it *all* been a lie? Starting when?

Not possible.

Okay, possible, but hard to believe.

And it's not as though she could go and ask him. By the way, are you a treacher? Are you going to treach my husband's loyal friends, these fine soldiers?

If he was part of the conspiracy, then he had performed brilliantly. He had fooled everybody. If he was part of the rebel movement, then part of his act had been to send out missions that led to the deaths of many of the rebel soldiers and the thwarting of many of their plans.

She might as well imagine that Cole and the others were part of the conspiracy too, and didn't really kill anybody, but rather faked the battles and planted the evidence and . . .

That way lies madness. She knew better. She knew these guys, and how Reuben had met them, and there was no double-dealing there.

And Torrent was no doubt exactly what he seemed to be—a brilliant professor of history who had been entrusted with the chance to help shape history during a time of national crisis that he had nothing to do with causing.

But as she drove northward toward Gettysburg, she began to lay out her own plan. She wouldn't wait—she'd get a Farsi speaker in Gettysburg to identify the notes from Torrent's classes and translate them for her right away. Maybe she'd learn something from Reuben's notes that would either set her mind at ease or give her leads to follow up, the way his PDA records had.

And she would research Torrent's own life. Find out whom he knew. Who had taken his classes. Who had sponsored and attended his lectures. The press would be involved in exactly this research, but she knew something about the laziness of reporters, about their tendency to find only what they were already looking for. She couldn't count on them turning up anything, whether it was there or not. She would find it herself.

# CHIПΠERETH

Concealment and active defense are not compatible strategies.

**BEFORE THEY** got close enough to Chinnereth and Genesseret to need to cut off cellphone use, Load briefed them all on what he saw during his first driveby. Both National Forest Roads 20 and 21 had been gated off because of the dam, with electronic keycards required for entry. But not road 48. "Which is odd," said Load, "because it switchbacks up the mountain and 4820 cuts off and skirts around it, way above Chinnereth. Overlooking it. Nothing you do at Chinnereth wouldn't be completely visible to somebody on 4820."

"Doesn't sound odd, if there's nothing going on there except a couple of dams," said Cole.

"Except that they had to build awfully high and expensive dams to contain the amount of water those lakes can hold," said Load.

"Either they aren't there," said Cole, "or they think their concealment is so good they've got nothing to fear from being observed."

"Or," said Load, "they've got patrols up there to make sure nobody sees anything and lives to tell the tale."

"So what do you think?" said Cole. "Go in at night, dark? Or still play tourist like we planned?"

"Your call," said Load.

"Why me?" said Cole. "It's *our* mission, not *my* mission."

Load didn't answer.

"We've all led missions."

"You're active duty," said Load. "And you're the one Rube picked."

"He didn't even know me," said Cole. "Three days."

"But we know you now," said Load. "We voted you our *abun*."

It meant "father" in Arabic, but it had come to mean "boss-man" among the Special Ops troops that went in-country in the Middle East.

Cole didn't waste time arguing when he was only talking to one guy anyway. "I think we go in dusk," he said. "Some daylight, but gone before we unload the truck. The seven of you come in with only two cars. We rendezvous low on 48. To unload the ordnance. We don't want it to look like a parking lot, and we don't want to try to take this U-Haul up a winding mountain road. You go in first, Load, and pick the spot, out of sight from the valleys with the lakes."

"And you come in right before dusk?"

"With no lights, once I'm on the road."

"Anybody asks you," said Load, "you're going up to Hager Lake and Jennings Falls."

"With a truck full of furniture and dishes?" asked Cole.

"Tell them your friends have the fishing tackle and cameras."

"My plan is not to get challenged," said Cole.

"Go with that one," said Load. "Better plan."

Cole's timing went well enough. The sun sank below the ridgeline fairly early, but there was still light in the sky when he found the entrance to road 48 and pulled off. Other cars were using headlights, but it wasn't particularly odd that he wasn't yet.

He was a little bothered by the sign warning about a dangerous, narrow, unpaved switchback road. But with any luck, he wouldn't have to negotiate any of the tight turns.

He was half right. The truck ground along in low gear to

the first switchback, and there was Load, greeting him like an old fishing buddy. But there *was* the tricky maneuver of going straight when the road curved, backing up the higher part of the switchback, and then making a scary little hairpin turn to get the truck pointing down the hill and the back of it pointing into the trees. Several times it felt like the truck was going to tip over, which would have been inconvenient. But finally it was done.

They used the last shreds of daylight to load the furniture and boxes off the truck, take out the weaponry, and conceal it in the trees. Then, with only one lantern inside the truck, and with a bit of cursing, they loaded all the furniture and boxes back onto the truck so it wouldn't be *so* obvious to a curious forest ranger or rebel scout that the important stuff had been taken out of the truck and nobody cared what happened to the furniture.

Then, in the dark, they changed into their camo and put their civilian clothes in big Ziploc bags. They put on their vests and packs, loaded and hefted their weapons, and then started up the road, picking different spots to conceal their civvies and then memorizing the spots.

"Just in case we return alive," said Arty cheerfully.

"Sometimes your sense of humor is actually funny," said Benny. "I hope I'm there next time it happens."

After that they were quiet, except for the occasional low click of the tongue to draw their attention to something—a turn, an impediment in the route. They stayed close to the trees. There was light enough from a sliver of moon to see where they were going, but that meant enough light for them to be seen. But they stayed with the road, since in the dark all they could do among the trees was crash around. Flashlights were out of the question. If there were sentries anywhere, flashlights would alert them like the blinking lights on airplane wings.

At the third switchback, a track led off to the southwest—road 4820. They followed it around the mountain for a little over a mile. In the stillness of the evening, they could hear a waterfall below them, though the trees were too thick for them to see down to the surface of the lake they knew must lie below them. Then there were a couple of switchbacks. When they came to a third one, they finally left the road and proceeded only a few dozen yards into the trees between the legs of the hairpin turn.

The ground sloped; they found the most level spot. Cole, whose alarm watch was already on vibrate, assigned Mingo and Benny to the first watch, Mingo upslope, Benny down.

Three hours later, Cole's alarm woke him. In turn, he woke Drew, and they went together to relieve Mingo. Leaving Drew where Mingo had been, Cole and Mingo went to relieve Benny. Cole remained on watch while Mingo and Benny went back to the main camp to sleep.

Another three hours. There was only a faint breeze now and then, but it was a chilly one—this far up in the mountains, July didn't mean what it meant down in the lowlands. But they had dressed for it.

There were things to be seen and even smelled, but mostly Cole listened. He had to learn the natural sounds in order to be able to distinguish unnatural ones. Animals aren't as quiet as most people think. Humans don't hear them because the din they make themselves masks all smaller sounds. But squirrels are not silent as they move through brush or leaves. The stooping of an owl; the screech of small prey; the padding of an animal's footsteps through the night.

Something larger. Probably a porcupine, thought Cole. Whatever it was, it got close enough to catch Cole's scent; then it hustled away in another direction.

His alarm went off again. Summer nights were short at this latitude—about nine hours—but it was still dark. It hadn't taken them all that long to walk up the road.

Cole returned to the camp and wakened Cat and Babe. Tonight Arty and Load got the full night, though Cole knew by now that for Arty, sleep was never all that deep. Babe once told him that Arty spent most of his nights reliving dark passages through Al Qaeda tunnels in Afghanistan. He never woke screaming, but he slept with a constant alertness, as if in his sleep he still knew he could find an enemy lurking in crevices anywhere.

"First light," he reminded Cat and Babe. They went up and relieved Drew first; Cat stayed and Drew went with Babe to the downhill post before he returned to camp.

Their watch was less than an hour long. First light meant the first glimmer of lightening in the eastern sky. But Cole had used the time to catch more sleep. Soldiers learned how to sleep whenever the opportunity presented itself. Like any other people, they needed eight hours or more to be at peak. But in the presence of the enemy—which, for all they knew, they were right now—adrenalin made up for the lack of sleep. Besides, even at half of their peak alertness, Cole knew these soldiers were sharper than most people. Sharp enough to still be alive despite all their enemies had thrown at them in the past.

They created a weapons cache a hundred feet from the road, leaving the heavier weapons there. Cole assigned Drew and Babe to stay with the cache. Each of the others carried sniper rifles and sidearms, rations, ammunition, and other supplies.

They also wore the infrasound transceivers Torrent had obtained for them. They used a digital signal, but it was carried on sound waves too low in pitch to be heard by human ears. It was like the shout of a giant. Elephants used sounds that low to communicate with each other from miles away. The receivers were on; they didn't turn on the transmitters until the carrier signal was actually needed. No need to be blasting low-pitched tones all over the mountains except at need. Besides, the captured mechs had a variant on this technology. The best guess was that their equipment operated at such a different pitch from the Army's new system that they wouldn't be able to pick up the jeesh's transmission tone. But there was no certainty of that.

They spread out, never so far that they couldn't keep track of where the man in front of them was, but never so close that a trap could be sprung on all of them at once.

There was a ranger tower atop the ridge between the lakes, but it seemed to be unoccupied. It might hold cameras, however. Cole and the others knew enough not to let themselves be seen from that angle—but not to assume that it was the only observation point, either.

The slope and the trees were such that from their side of Lake Chinnereth, they could observe the opposite shore but not their own. Certainly the other side of the lake offered nothing interesting. If the trees had been cut right to the maximum waterline, then the lake level was about three feet below full—about normal for summer here. Once the turbines started running to generate electricity, though, the lake would drain steadily but slowly all summer, and it didn't seem to Cole as though the watershed here would be large enough to replenish the lake waters if there was a constant drain.

This reservoir didn't make sense. The slope of the canyon was so steep that the dam had to be very high in order to hold enough water to make a lake of any size. Yet the lake was only about four miles long on one branch, three and a half on the other. He knew from the map that Lake Genesseret was even smaller—two miles long.

It was a boondoggle. The federal government had paid for this project, and it would never pay for itself. Nor would it generate that much electricity if it was also supplying some town somewhere with water. This was exactly the kind of project that environmentalists loved to kill. It should have been easy to do, because the dam was indefensible.

Yet there was no sign of any kind of development here beyond the lake itself. The original route of road 21 was under water, and if a new road had been cut it must be on this side of the lake, since it could not be seen on the other.

Their travel today would go much faster if they climbed down to the clear-cut slope between the waterline and the trees, but there they would be completely visible to any observers. The idea was not to be detected. So they would move slowly through forest, going miles around Lake Chinnereth, then moving up to the ridge between the lakes and again going down to look at Genesseret and go far enough around it to inspect all its shores.

And then back again to the cache and, if they found nothing, then pack it all up and come home again.

There was an island in the middle of Lake Chinnereth, which must once have been the rounded top of a low hill. There Cole could see the only human structure beyond the dam itself that was visible here. It was a cabin that might once have been a ranger way station or, conceivably, somebody's small summer cabin. It looked like it had probably been made from local timber, laid down like Lincoln logs. It was impossible to tell whether it pre-dated the dam or was thirty years old. It certainly wasn't much older than that, and might not be abandoned—there was still glass in the windows.

Down near the waterline, there was a small dock with a short swimmer's ladder. And not a floating dock—it made no allowance for changing water levels. It's as if the builder expected the lake always to be full.

The dock had to have been built after the dam, or there would have been no point. But the cabin didn't look like it could hold a serious number of mechs, even in the basement. And even if it *could* contain such things, how could they be loaded onto barges from that tiny dock?

Even stopping frequently to listen and observe, they made good time through the woods; they took turns walking point and tail, and now and then they could talk in low voices to each other and pass observations and orders up and down the spread-out line. Each man controlled his own eating as he walked—there was no need to stop for meals.

When they reached the end of the east fork of Lake Chinnereth, Cole split Load and Arty off to go out to the point of the peninsula between the lakes and observe what they could. If they hadn't heard from Cole to the contrary, they were then to go back around to rejoin Drew and Babe at the cache.

So now there were only four of them proceeding overland to the west fork of Chinnereth and then up the ridge between the lakes. There were a few signs of hikers, but none of the litter was new and the few campsites were covered with layers of pine needles. Again, no way to tell if there had been hikers through here since the lake was formed.

Cole sent Mingo and Benny around to the west side of Genesseret to reconnoiter the eastern shoreline. They didn't need to go all the way to the dam. As soon as they had observed and photographed the whole eastern shore, they should come back around and, again, if Cole had not told them otherwise, round both lakes and return to the cache.

Only Cat was with Cole now, moving together near but not on the crest of the ridge between lakes. Occasionally they would cross over the ridge and move down the other side, since they were observing the far shores of both lakes now.

They were near the peak of the ridge now, approaching the observation tower. Now they moved even more stealthily, moving slowly and methodically toward the tower from two different directions. There was no sign of any kind of wiring, though that hardly proved that there *was* no wiring. Nor was there any sign of cameras—but, again, that might simply mean that the cameras were very small and well concealed.

In the southwest, clouds were building. A summer thunderstorm? That would be potentially disastrous—lightning could do worse things than an EMP gun. Even fog would be irritating, forcing them to wait till it cleared to complete the mission.

Cole crept back away from the cleared area around the tower; he knew Cat was doing the same. They would move slowly around to two other vantage points and inspect the other two sides of the tower.

It was in the midst of this maneuver that Cole's receiver vibrated. He immediately began backing farther away from the tower. He pressed the go-ahead button.

"Mingo here," said Mingo. He was talking softly, but articulating very clearly. "Come down to the area twenty feet above the clear-cut zone. Right where you are, just go down. No structures, no sign of tunneling, but something you need to see."

Cole pressed the go-ahead button again, requesting more information without having to speak aloud.

"If you don't see it, then we're crazy," said Mingo. "I'm not going to predispose you."

Cole pressed the code for Cat, knowing he had heard. Cole whispered, "Down to Genesseret."

It took only fifteen minutes to move, relatively noiselessly, to the zone twenty feet or so above the clear-cut zone. Whatever they were supposed to see, Cole couldn't see it.

And then he could. The ground was suddenly wet underfoot.

Cat noticed it, too. He moved toward Cole and when they were near enough, said in a low voice, "Somebody ran the sprinklers this morning."

The ground was sodden, as if it had been heavily watered. From about fifteen feet above the waterline, the pine needles no longer carpeted the forest floor in a natural way. They had been carried downward as if by receding water, hanging up on tufts of grass, roots, rocks, any obstruction, the way floating pine needles would when the water drained away.

Cole switched on his transceiver and coded for Mingo. "Is this about even with the top of the dam?"

"From what we can see," said Mingo, "it *could* go ten feet higher. But the line is absolute. Everything below it soaked, everything above it as dry as normal. Benny has me for ten that this lake has been fifteen feet higher within the last twenty-four hours. Which is impossible and/or weird."

"You bet against him, though."

"Somebody had to," said Mingo. "It's how he pays for food."

"Anything else on our side?" asked Cole.

"Nothing."

"And we've seen nothing on yours. Anything near the dam?"

"Just the old road 20, where it dives down under the water. The new road's on our side, but it's already overgrown with grass and saplings. Nobody's using it."

Cole sat and thought for a while. This obvious change in the water level was weird, but it was hard to see what the point of it would be. Why would they have released so much water, so rapidly? The lake was small, as reservoirs go, but it was still millions of gallons of water. By now Mingo had probably figured out approximately how much. He asked.

"If it was all released in a single flow, it would be enough to cause flooding downstream," said Mingo. "The valley floor is populated. The neighbors would complain. Cole, this water was here, no more than a day ago. It went somewhere."

Mingo was a civil engineer and it was his business to be able to make guesses that were worth something.

"Any sign of it draining right now?" asked Cole.

"No," said Mingo. "In fact, it's at the *usual* waterline right now. Where the vegetation changes. The high level seems to be the rare condition."

"Heavy rainstorms here lately?"

"No," said Benny. "Dryish summer for this area."

"Rain heavy enough to raise the water level this high, you would have seen it on the news. 'Washington State washed out to sea,' that would have been the story."

"Somehow they're raising and lowering the water level of the lake by massive amounts," said Cole, "and I can't think of a single reason why."

"I'm still trying to think of how," said Mingo.

"Anybody get close enough to the shoreline on Chinnereth to see if it does the same?" asked Cole.

"Drew here. We reconnoitered the shoreline while we were waiting. Nothing like what you describe. The shoreline was the first wet area. No flooding higher up."

"Load here. Ditto. If the water level rose fifteen feet on Chinnereth, it would flood that cabin."

Cole sat and thought for a long moment.

"Maybe they dumped a huge amount of rubble in here," said Mingo. "That would raise the level. But that wouldn't explain why it went back down."

"No roads where they could dump the rubble," said Benny.

"While we're complaining about what they don't have here," said Load. "I don't remember seeing any power lines running away from this dam."

"No, there were power lines," said Benny.

"And a power station? Lots of transformers? Where?"

"No. Nothing like that," said Benny. "But definitely power lines. No, wait. They ran along Highway 12. But I never saw them link up with the dams. Sorry."

"This was officially a hydroelectic project," said Cole. "There are turbines in the dams."

"So maybe they use the power right here," said Cat. "In their vast system of underground factories and training facilities."

"Cat and I are going back up to the observation tower to check whether there's any kind of vent up there for an underground system."

They all switched off their transmitters. It was harder going uphill. But not slower. That's what all the stairstepping and rock climbing were for.

Now Cole knew what to look for, he climbed a tree well back from the cleared perimeter and scanned for some kind of pipe or vent hidden in the tall grass.

Bingo. There were about two dozen small pipes, sticking up only a few inches above the ground before they bent over to keep water from coming in. At ground level you couldn't see them for the grass.

Cole pointed his soundcatcher toward them and was able to pick up a difference between the pipes and the surrounding area. They were connected to something that was actively producing noise.

He climbed back down the tree and backed away from the cleared area, heading down the Chinnereth slope this time. Cat was soon near him, though they did not talk and remained fifty feet apart as they made their way down the slope.

Near the cleared edge of the woods, but not close enough to be seen, they stopped and Cole approached Cat. Across the water, the cabin sat on its little island. It had a chimney, which might very well contain vents for more underground structures.

It might also contain something else. An entrance.

"I think I'm going for a swim," said Cole.

"I was having the same thought," said Cat.

Cole switched on his transmitter. "We're on the west shore of Chinnereth, just west of the cabin. Cat and I are going to swim across to see if there's an entrance there."

"Water's gonna be cold, *abun*," said Babe. "You two gonna have little tiny dicks when you get there."

"Least I'll still have one," said Cat.

"We won't go for another half hour," said Cole. "Drew and Babe, bring the SMAW down near the waterline in case we need some backup. Load and Arty, you get to Chinnereth shoreline nearest to the cabin. Benny and Mingo, you can't get here in time to be useful. So go north, get to Highway 12, but stay in infra range. If we confirm that this is the place, get to where you can make contact with Torrent so he can send in a strike force."

"I don't know what you just figured out," said Babe.

"That's because you're in public relations," said Mingo, "and I'm an engineer."

"Thought that meant you drove trains," said Babe.

"There are standpipes in the tall grass under the observation tower," said Cole. "There's machinery operating underground."

"And the water," said Mingo. "Only place where it could go is from one lake into the other. Anything else would be too obvious. They must pump it out of Chinnereth, uphill, into Genesseret, using all that electricity they've stored up.

Genesseret rises, Chinnereth falls. Exposing their doorway. They go in or out, whatever, and when they're done, they seal the watertight entrance and let the water flood back downhill to fill it back up. Genesseret drops back to normal, Chinnereth rises."

"You can't *know* that," said Babe.

"No other possibility," said Mingo. "Word, man."

"The ultimate moat," said Drew.

"That's a lot of water to move," said Babe.

"The federal government paid for the whole thing," said Benny. "Your tax dollars at work."

"So why are you going out to the island?" asked Arty.

"We're almost sure," said Cole. "But are we sure *enough* to call in a strike force yet?"

"They got to have a back door," said Mingo. "Can't drain the lake every time somebody's got to go outside to smoke."

"Boat," said Cat.

They switched their transmitters off.

A small motorboat was coming up the lake from the area of the dam. Heading for them or for the island? Had their chatter been detected? Even if they couldn't decode the scrambled signal, they'd know somebody was there.

But the boat pulled up to the little dock on the island.

And waited.

And waited. The driver of the boat didn't seem particularly alert. Like a cabdriver waiting for a fare.

The door of the cabin opened. Four men came out.

"Is any of them Verus?" asked Cole.

Cat looked through his binoculars. "No," he said. "You recognize any of them?"

Cole took the binoculars. The men wore suits. He thought he might have seen one of them on television. The news, probably, since he didn't look like an actor. But he didn't remember who or when.

The men got into the boat and it pulled away from the dock. The boat headed on down the lake.

Cole took off his pack. He quickly inflated the floats on

it and attached his weapons and boots to the top. The floats were widely spaced enough for it to be stable, at least on smooth water. Top-heavy, but it wouldn't tip. He attached the towline to it and shrugged on the harness. Cat was doing the same.

"Never much call to use these in Afghanistan or Sudan," Cat said.

"Nice to get a chance to test out all the equipment," said Cole.

"Glad you're so white," said Cat. "Easier target on the water."

Cole just grinned at him.

Then he moved swiftly down the slope and into the water. It was cold, but he didn't hesitate. His body went into that momentary shock and he trembled a little, but as soon as he had laid the miniraft of his pack down on the water, he immersed himself and began swimming in long, steady strokes, dragging the pack behind him. He broke water as gently as possible. But if someone was watching, there's no way he wouldn't be visible on the calm surface of the water.

Having their main entrance hidden under water explained why they didn't have a lot of patrols. Patrols would be seen. Encounters with civilians would leave memories.

Of course, so would letting a civilian see the lakes drain. It was so easy to get here. Hikers might do it at any time.

Easy? Not so easy. They had moved very cautiously. They had made little noise and made sure to stay out of sight. Maybe regular hikers *were* detected, and either they didn't drain the lake until they had passed or they'd send somebody out dressed in a ranger uniform to send them on their way.

It was so *cold*. He could feel his body reacting to it, struggling to stay warm. But they were most of the way to the island now. Not much longer. He glanced around to see Cat was only a little bit behind him.

Cat pointed toward the island and started swimming faster.

The island was rising.

Which meant the water level was falling.

Just a little way below the waterline, the island stopped being a hill. It was a thick pillar, solid concrete. Of course. There wouldn't be an island here. They had built it.

The dock was now hanging in midair; the pillars of the dock were actually resting on steel beams jutting out from the concrete wall of the island. Under the dock, there was a ladder rising up to the level of the beams. From there, it looked easy enough to get to the short wooden swimmer's ladder.

What was going to be hard was climbing that ladder without being seen.

Cole and Cat got to the base of the ladder at about the same time. The water was still sinking. But it wasn't getting warmer.

"Can't stay in this," said Cat.

"Can't climb," said Cole. "They'll see us."

Back on the shore they had come from, only about a hundred yards closer to the dam, a heavy concrete wall was being revealed. Huge steel doors looked like they could withstand the water pressure just fine. But once the water sank low enough, and those doors opened, anybody coming out of them would have a clear shot at anybody climbing the ladder.

Cole clung to the ladder with his legs as he worked the pack back onto his shoulders. It was hard—his fingers were numb and he was shivering. Cat was having the same amount of trouble.

"Just leave the packs?" asked Cat, shivering.

"We'll want our weapons if we make it up top."

"Big if," said Cat.

In answer, Cole started to climb. It was hard to keep his grip. And cold numb wet bare feet weren't as stable to climb with as well-fitting boots. But he had to keep moving. Maybe he could still get to the top before the doors opened.

Cat was keeping up with him, nice steady progress up the ladder.

The big steel door started opening. A couple of men in rebel body armor came out and scanned the area. It didn't take them two seconds to see Cole and Cat, and another two seconds to start shooting.

They missed.

"Their marksman training not as good as our marksman training," said Cat.

"Fine with me," said Cole.

A bullet came much closer.

"Getting the range now," said Cat.

"I'm nearly there."

Cole noticed the whooshing sound behind him and to the right. A moment later, the entrance of the tunnel erupted in flames.

"Good shot with the SMAW," said Cat.

"Inappropriate weapon," said Cole. "Rifles would have been enough."

"Either way, I think we lost our element of surprise, *abun*."

Cole knew that Drew and Babe would be moving the SMAW to a different position now.

"Wish I knew what was waiting for us at the top of this ladder."

Rifle fire from directly behind them didn't result in any bullets striking near them. It was sniper work—*ping*. Wait. *Ping*. That would be Load and Arty, firing past them at someone on top of the island.

And now there was returning gunfire from directly above them, shooting out across the water.

"I just hope Drew and Babe don't try to use a mortar," said Cole. "I don't want them to blow up that cabin."

"Don't stop to put on your infra, *abun*."

"Wasn't going to."

They were now on the steel beams that supported the dock. But there was gunfire coming from inside the huge doors again, and from men fanning out along the shoreline. Correctly, Load and Arty were only shooting at targets on top of the island, so that Cole and Cat would have a chance to get up and onto the surface without getting their heads blown off the moment they raised them above the level of the dock.

Cole got out his handgun and swung out to climb the swimmer's ladder.

"Such a baby," said Cat. He clambered directly onto the dock from the other side.

There were two bodies—in ranger uniforms, not armor—lying on the ground. But Cole was aware—from the sound, from motion—that there were others inside the cabin now, and a pair who had moved off into the brush beside the cabin. He flattened himself on the ground. He was immediately aware of every rise and dip in the surface and arranged his body to present the hardest possible target, even as he looked into the brush and found a target. A flurry of motion told him that he had at least come close.

He crept over to the nearest body and used that slight cover while he got his pack off. It would be like a howdah on an elephant to carry that around with him during this. He pulled his rifle off the pack. This was sniper work now.

# TWENTY

# TRAP DOOR

If your soldiers can't fight at least as well as the enemy's soldiers, it doesn't matter how good a commander you are. Training is the foundation of everything.

**THE TWO** dead bodies had been disguised as park rangers. The guys they were facing now wore body armor.

Whatever training the rebel troops might have had, it wasn't at Army Ranger level. They relied too much on their armor. It made them feel invulnerable. So they constantly revealed themselves. And they shot carelessly—too quickly, without stability. They also didn't learn from their own bad shots. They'd overshoot the first time, and on the next shot they'd do it again.

Even undertrained soldiers can kill you with a lucky shot, though. Cole had no intention of dying because he had contempt for his enemy.

Their pistols were mostly for noise and show. The rebels dodged the bullets—they didn't trust their armor enough to overcome their reflex to flinch.

Cole reached up and detached the M-24 sniper rifle from his pack. It fired a heavier round than the pistol—that's why he brought it. Testing had shown that at fairly close range, it penetrated the rebels' body armor at certain key points. Like the faceplate.

Two shots. Two rebels down.

"Good work," said Cat. "Now it's time for Minimi."

Cole fired into the cabin window, shattering glass, as Cat scrambled up the slope and got into position against the cabin wall, just beside the window. It was an obvious time to toss a grenade into the cabin, but they both knew they couldn't risk damaging whatever mechanism concealed or locked the passage down into the tunnels. So Cat reached down and pulled up a lump of turf and tossed it through the window as if it were a grenade. It would take the guys inside a split second to realize it *wasn't* an explosive device. During the split second, Cat raked the inside with automatic fire from his Minimi.

They both reached the door of the cabin at the same time. It was open. They came in low, Cole first, and found three rebel soldiers, two dead, one trivially wounded in the left arm.

"I surrender!" the wounded guy said.

"How are we supposed to take you captive?" said Cole.

Cat walked over to the guy

Terrified, the rebel said, "I'm an American, you can't kill me."

"Tell it to the cops you guys killed in New York," said Cole. "And the apartment building doorman."

"You guys are all murderers!" shouted the rebel. "You love to kill!"

Cat reached down and broke the guy's right arm.

The guy screamed, staring at his arm. When he could speak, he groaned, "I'm an American!"

"American with a broken arm," said Cat.

"He might be left-handed," said Cole.

Cat broke the other arm. The guy screamed again. "Threat neutralized," said Cat.

"Torturers," the rebel gasped.

"Look, you said not to kill you," said Cole. "Which do you want, pain or dead?"

Cole gave the guy a dose of morphine. "I think he wants us to surrender to *him,*" said Cat.

The cabin didn't have any obvious elevator doors. Hardly a surprise. Nor was there any visible trap door in the wooden floor, or anything that looked like a passageway inside the fireplace.

"You'll never find the entrance," said the rebel.

"Kick his arm," said Cat. "He'll tell us."

"Torturers!" shouted the rebel.

Cat picked up the clod of dirt and grass that Cat had tossed inside as a fake grenade. He pushed it into the rebel's mouth. The rebel sputtered, spat. But he wasn't talking.

Then, using his sniper rifle, Cole shot downward into the floor. Methodically he crossed the room, shooting straight down. Obviously there was concrete under the wood. Right across the room, no change. He moved over closer to the fireplace, put a new magazine in his M-24, and started firing downward again. Concrete. Concrete. Steel.

The steel section lined up with the fireplace. Cole could now see that the wooden floor extended under the stone of the hearth.

"It slides under the fireplace," said Cole. Stepping out a couple of paces, Cole could see how the floor planks, while they didn't all end in a straight line, had a slightly wider separation from the abutting boards.

"No doubt they've turned off whatever switch runs this from up here," said Cole.

"Think there's a way to open it by hand?" said Cat.

"Probably. From below."

Cole thought about how the trap door worked. It slid under the fireplace. The hearth wasn't deep enough to hold the entire trap door. So there had to be a projection on the outside of the house to hold the rest of the trap door.

"Going out back," said Cole.

"I'll stay here and make sure nobody comes upstairs."

Cole went outside. On the way around the cabin, he couldn't resist going near enough to the edge to look over.

There were mechs and hoverbikes coming out of the big doors now and swarming up into the woods. Cole knew that if Arty and Load could get back around the eastern arm of the lake to the cache, they'd be fine—they had weapons designed to counter both vehicles. Machines weren't so good in the deep woods anyway. And seeing how the footsoldiers—only about twenty of them—fanned out, they were clearly not trained at all for rough-country combat. Urban warfare, that's what these guys were ready for. The other guys would be fine. And the more rebels they kept busy out here, the better it would be for Cole and Cat.

If they could even get down inside.

This was too much like a frontal assault. Two guys, and even if they got through the trap door, what would they do, ride the elevator and get blasted when they hit bottom? Or go down the stairs, where a flamethrower or a grenade could kill them before they had a chance to get off a shot?

At the same time, the longer they waited here, the better chance the rebels had of killing them. And what if Mingo and Benny couldn't get to a phone? What if President Nielson decided not to send a strike force?

The best chance of success here would come from moving forward. Pushing. But . . . carefully.

There was a concrete road running from the huge doorway out toward the dam. It was under water the whole way till it got near the dam. There it looked like a paved marina ramp as it rose up to the usual waterline. Clever disguise. They could bring trucks in and out of here without anything looking like a highway.

Cole jogged around to the back of the cabin. Sure enough, under the grass behind the chimney brick, there was a concrete projection. Totally enclosed. No easy way in.

Cole pulled the pin on a grenade and laid it down in the corner where the brick joined the concrete. Then he threw himself to the other side of the concrete projection and rolled down the slope.

Boom.

Cole got up and ran back. Some damage to the concrete. Not a lot.

He unpinned another grenade, set it right where the most damage was, and leapt and rolled. Another explosion. More damage.

After the fourth grenade, he had a hole.

He ran back to his pack, carried it up to the hole. He pulled out the crowbar and the flashlight. He could have used a sledgehammer, but that wasn't something that he had wanted with his gear when he was hiking.

With the flashlight, he could see the mechanism that pulled the trap door into the concrete sleeve. Not really a complicated machine. He didn't want to damage the tracks where the trap door would slide. Just the lever that pushed the trap door closed.

It was sweaty, frustrating work, because he didn't have great leverage. He also had to make sure he didn't drop the crowbar, because there'd be no getting it back, and he was the only one who had brought one.

Eventually, though, he popped the lever out of its socket. Now it was dangling free.

Taking the crowbar, the flashlight, and his pack, he ran back around the cabin and went inside. Cat had poured himself some coffee from the percolator. "Good stuff," he said. "Lots of caffeine."

"No thanks," said Cole. "You can go out and get your pack now."

Cat jogged out. The broken-armed rebel glared at Cole. He was sweating with pain and looked so miserable Cole almost felt sorry for him. "I notice nobody came out to see if you're all right," he said.

The guy didn't say anything.

"I guess they knew we were going to beat the shit out of you," said Cole. "You know, before people start wars, they ought to make sure they know how to win."

"We don't have to win the war," said the rebel. "We just have to keep you guys killing people till public opinion turns completely against you."

"Same strategy as Al Qaeda," said Cole.

"We're not terrorists, *you* are."

"Since you're terrified and I'm not, I suppose you're right," said Cole. He worked his knife into one of the spaces between floor planks, slicing away bits of wood to make a gap wide enough for the crowbar. "You're guilty of treason, but maybe they'll let you off because we broke your arms. Military brutality and all that."

"I'm not the traitor, you are."

"I'm a sworn soldier of the United States of America, performing my duties according to orders," said Cole. "You're a hired goon of Aldo Verus, functioning as his private army in order to subvert the United States. Besides, you guys are the ones who killed the President."

"Not *my* President," said the rebel.

"That's my point," said Cole. "He was President of the United States, but he wasn't *your* President. What does that make you?"

"We didn't have anything to do with killing him. Terrorists did that."

"It was your guys who stole the plans the terrorists used."

"No way," said the rebel. "It was your guys who *wrote* those plans."

Cole couldn't deny that. "Only so we could plan to counter them."

"And yet," said the rebel, "you hadn't gotten around to countering them, had you?"

"And when the President died, you guys were right ready to move."

"We've been ready for months," said the rebel.

"Waiting for Friday the Thirteenth."

"Waiting for a right-wing coup to give us an excuse," said the rebel. "We never thought that asshole in the White House would be dead."

Cole set his anger aside and thought about what he'd said. Was this just the line they fed their own troops? Or was it possible that Aldo Verus hadn't arranged the assassinations? Could it be that he was waiting for General Alton to get his phony coup under way, and they only seized on Friday the Thirteenth as an opportunity after the fact?

The evidence in Rube's PDA only dealt with his clandestine work for Phillips in the White House, helping move

Verus's ordnance around the country. It had nothing to do with the plans that were leaked to the terrorists.

DeeNee, though. Wasn't she the link proving that they were all working together?

"Got to you, didn't I?" said the rebel.

Cole ignored him. DeeNee was dead. She assassinated Rube and then she died. So nobody could ever ask her who she worked for. The guys who chased him were after Rube's PDA. But was it possible that they *weren't* in league with DeeNee? That they had simply staked out the Pentagon parking lot, waiting for Rube to show up?

Cole remembered back to that Monday morning, June sixteenth. There was shooting inside the building, but nobody shot at him out in the parking lot. The security forces inside the Pentagon had killed three bad guys inside. Was it possible that that was *all* of the guys who were with DeeNee? That the guys who followed him out in the parking lot were a different team, and that's why *they* didn't shoot as soon as they saw him? It took the guys outside a while to realize that Cole, not Rube, had the PDA now. That's why they didn't shoot him down, or even follow him immediately.

Absurd. Too complicated. They simply lied to their soldiers. They couldn't very well announce, "We're going to kill that evil right-wing madman in the White House and then take over America." You get a whole different kind of recruit when you announce *that* as your purpose.

"What were you blowing up out there?" asked the rebel.

"You know, for a guy who was afraid to die, you sure do test our patience."

"If you were going to kill me, I'd be dead," said the rebel.

"That's right," said Cole. "We chose not to kill you. We put up with your shit. And yet you still believe we're murderers and torturers."

"You broke my arms."

"So you couldn't shoot us in the back, idiot. Use your brain. Or have you turned that over to Aldo Verus, too?"

"I think for myself."

That was twice that Cole had mentioned Aldo Verus's name, and neither time had the rebel denied knowing anything about him. But he *had* denied having anything to do with the assassination. So Verus *was* his boss of this army and the soldiers knew it.

"Guys like you are so angry that they can lie to you about guys like me and you believe it," said Cole. "You can't even conceive of the idea that maybe a guy becomes a soldier because he loves his country and is willing to die to keep it safe. No, you have to believe that guys like me are murderers looking for an excuse to kill. And yet *you* put on a uniform and *you* took up arms."

"I'm nothing like you," said the rebel.

"Right," said Cole. "Because *I* trained to do my job right. And because *I* recognize that even my enemies are still human beings. Assholes, but human ones."

Cat came back into the cabin. "Nothing else on this island. Nobody even bothered to shoot at me. I think they think we can't get through their door."

"Maybe we can't," said Cole.

"You can't," said the rebel.

Cole pushed on the crowbar. The wood splintered a little, but it also moved. The trap door had slid about a half inch.

Which meant it would probably slide farther. Far enough for the door to open.

"The question," said Cole, "is this. Do we open it enough to toss a grenade down and kill anybody waiting for us? Or do we hope they trusted their mechanism here so much that they aren't even bothering to defend it?"

"We throw a grenade and they aren't there," said Cat, "the grenade tells them we made it through and they come running."

"On the other hand, we open this and they *are* there, they just toss a grenade up here and *we're* dead."

Cat pointed his thumb at the rebel. "One consolation is, he's dead, too."

"Collateral damage," said Cole. To the rebel he said,

"But your team doesn't believe armies should *ever* cause collateral damage, don't you?"

The rebel just glared at him.

"Safety first," said Cole. "I'll shove, you toss."

Cat got out a grenade.

"Of course, I'll be right here where the blast will still hit me," said Cole.

"Well, don't be there," said Cat.

"I can't open the trap door if I'm standing on it," said Cole.

"You could *try*," said Cat.

Cole went over to one of the dead rebels and dragged his body over to the set of slight gaps marking the end of the trap door. Cole shoved the crowbar under the body and lodged the angled end of the crowbar into the gap. Then he stepped over the body and started pushing on the other end of the crowbar. "Is it moving?" he asked.

"Are you pushing?" asked Cat.

Cole pushed hard enough that his feet slid on the floor.

So he tipped over a table and ran it up against the far wall. By bracing his feet against the end of the table, he kept himself from sliding. And now the trap door started to move.

"Anytime you feel like it," said Cole.

He pushed farther. The trap door began to move smoothly.

A burst of machine-gun fire from inside the trap door shuddered the dead body in front of him and shoved it back into Cole's face.

Cat flipped a grenade down the gap.

It exploded. There was no more firing.

Now the two of them opened the door the rest of the way. It went rather easily.

Steep stairs led down into a small concrete room with an elevator door on one side and the top of a spiral staircase on the other. There were pieces of body armor scattered on the floor, some still containing fragments of flesh and bone. The pieces didn't come out even, so some of them must have blown off the edge and down the spiral stairway.

They went back up into the cabin and put on their packs. Cat quickly finished his coffee. "Shouldn't drink this," he said. "I'll just have to pee later."

"You didn't put on your catheter?" said Cole with mock surprise.

"Can't find any that fit me," said Cat.

Cole turned to the miserable-looking rebel. "We probably won't come out this way, so . . . I'll see you at your treason trial."

No smart remarks. The guy just looked away.

Down on the elevator landing, Cat pushed the button for the elevator.

"Oh, come on," said Cole.

"Ain't gonna ride it, man," said Cat. "Just want to see if it comes when I call."

They waited, weapons trained on the door. It opened. The elevator was empty.

"We could put that guy inside and send it down," said Cat. "Then it's friendly fire that'll kill him."

"Being an ignorant jerk who believed a lot of lies shouldn't get you the death penalty," said Cole.

"Not even sometimes?" Cat was holding the elevator door open.

Cole leaned close to him and whispered. "Push the button for the bottom floor and let's go down the stairs."

Cat pushed the button and scrambled back out of the elevator before the doors closed.

Then, as quietly as they could, they started down the stairs.

# TWENTY-ONE

# COMMAND AND CONTROL

Anybody who thinks that the dread of shame isn't stronger than the fear of death has only to consider how many Roman senators, generals, and traitors preferred to fall on their swords or open their veins rather than live through humiliation. But it's not just humans. Wounded animals try to hide till they're dead, rather than let their predators eat them alive.

**THEY WERE** about halfway to the bottom when the rebel in the cabin shouted, "They're coming down the stairs!"

Should have killed him, thought Cole.

No. We should have closed the trap door from the inside.

Fortunately, there was a good chance nobody at the bottom could understand what he was yelling.

They heard gunfire below them.

The elevator door must have opened. But the sound was muffled. They must have built a heavy door between the stairway and the elevator landing at the bottom.

But now that they knew Cole and Cat hadn't come down the elevator, they were bound to think of the stairway. If it was a grenade they tossed, Cole and Cat should stay high on the stairs. But if they opened the door and fired, they should be down there to shoot back.

Cole didn't remember seeing any of the rebels armed with grenades.

He sat on the railing, leaned a hand on the center pole,

and slid down. As he neared the bottom, he tipped himself off the railing and out of Cat's way. He landed on the floor, and flung himself into the corner, his rifle pointing at the door just as it opened. He shot once, hitting the door and knocking it farther open.

Cat hit the bottom of the stairs with the pin already pulled on a grenade, rolled it on the floor through the gap in the door, then pulled the door shut. It went off.

A moment later they had the door open, and this time there was no attempt at conversation—everybody they saw in that space, alive or dead, they fired at quickly. Then started down a bare concrete tunnel—which, from its placement, could only be a tunnel leading under the lakebed toward the mountain where Verus's arsenal was.

"I hope that grenade didn't weaken the concrete of this tunnel," said Cat. "Don't want all that water coming in."

"Too bad," said Cole. Because at that moment water *did* start coming in. But not from any damage caused by the grenade. The rebels were flooding the corridor themselves, water gushing through a two-foot-diameter tube at the other end.

They could either go back and climb the stairs to the cabin and wait for reinforcements, or charge straight into the gushing water and try to get above the level of the tunnel before it completely flooded.

Cat didn't hesitate, so Cole followed him.

They stayed to the edge of the tunnel where the force of the thick stream of water wasn't so strong. But the tunnel was filling rapidly—knee level, then hip level by the time they forced their way past the stream and realized they were on the wrong side—there was no door here. Cole could just make out the door shape on the other side *through* the thick gush of water.

"Swim under?" said Cat.

"No time to go back," said Cole.

"Get my weapon all wet," said Cat.

Cole took the Minimi out of his hand as Cat shrugged

off his pack. Cat swam under the stream. Cole threw his pack over the gush of water, then his weapon. Cat caught them both.

Now Cole threw his own weapon and his own pack. But the water was shoulder height. Harder to dive low enough to get under the stream. He felt it sucking at him, churning him out away from the door.

Then he felt Cat's hand catch him under the arm, drag him back.

Their packs were floating on top of the water; their weapons were on top of the packs.

"Door's locked," said Cat.

Cole grabbed Cat's Minimi, leaned his back against Cat, and walked his legs up the door. When Cat was holding him above the level of the water, he fired a burst down between his legs at the thick glass of the window in the door. It took two bursts before the glass crazed and broke.

It wasn't a very big window. Cole kicked out a few shards of glass, pulled out his pistol, and went through first, because his feet were already high enough. It was the base of a spiral staircase, just like on the other side, and there was nobody there.

He looked up. Still nobody.

Cat was pushing through the weapons. Cole picked them up and set them on the stairs, out of the water.

The packs wouldn't fit through the window in the door. Cat, who was floating now, kept pulling watertight ammunition packages out of packs and pushing them down through the broken window. Cole put them on higher stairs, out of the water. Then Cat's feet came through. Cole pulled. Cat was bigger in the shoulders than Cole was, and he got stuck.

At that moment, something dropped down from the top of the stairs. Grenade, thought Cole. They've got grenades after all.

But he kept his concentration, marking where the grenade had fallen into the water without letting up on pulling Cat.

Cat slid through. Cole dived for the grenade. Fumbled. Found it. Pushed it into the torrent coming through the window and pushed it down, knowing it would go off any second and take his hand off.

He let go of it and yanked his hand back.

It exploded, making the door tremble and allowing water to spray in around the edges. Cat had already gathered up all the ammunition for his weapon and some of Cole's. He handed it to Cole and started up the stairs as Cole got his weapon and stuffed ammunition into his pockets.

Another grenade dropped. Another. Cole grabbed one of their grenades and, knowing it was insanely dangerous, threw it spiraling almost straight back up, like the highest forward pass he ever threw in his life. If it went off when it was passing Cat, he would be killing his own man. But if Cat got to the top with a bunch of guys there training automatic weapons on him, he'd be dead anyway.

Meanwhile, there was a second grenade in the water near him. Cole raced up the stairs. Both grenades went off almost at once. The one below him splashed water all over the inside of the stairwell, like the first spurt when you turn on a blender. But the stairs themselves, being steel, shielded Cole from most of the blast. He stumbled, but he kept going.

The upper grenade apparently hadn't killed Cat—his footsteps were still heading up.

Somebody was still alive up there, but it was Cat's Minimi that kept firing, the other weapon that fell silent.

He reached the top to find Cat lying on the floor using an armored body as his shield, exchanging bursts with somebody who was some distance away, where Cole couldn't see. Cole stayed on the stairs and got his rifle out, then inched forward until he could see into the room that Cat was firing into.

It was a narrow, high-ceilinged cavern with steel bracing extending up to the roof. The walls were lined with mechs, squatting on the floor like they were all taking a dump. Cole had always thought that the mechs would hang like suits, with their legs dangling. But then how would any-body get inside?

Cole pushed himself forward a little farther and found a target—a guy running for one of the mechs. Being in a good position, his shot was clean and he took him down. Slid farther in and took out another.

They stopped trying to get to the mechs. Instead, they fled the room. "Idiots," said Cat softly. "They should have been *in* the mechs before we made it up here."

"Maybe some of them already are," said Cole. "Playing possum."

"They that smart?"

"I just don't want to walk down between those rows."

Which was fine. There were corridors leading off to the left and right. Cole chose the one to the left for no better reason than that he was on that side already.

He tried to imagine the architecture of this place. It wouldn't be like a building, with rooms one after another, divided only by thin walls. They had a whole mountain on top of them. So each room would have plenty of rock be-tween it and the next one, with only corridors connecting them. The really tall corridors would be for mechs to walk along. Stay with the low, man-sized corridors, and they'd be more likely to face opponents that weren't armored like tanks.

The cavern architecture also meant that corridors could be long and could lead anywhere. This one was sloping up-ward and turning. The turn made Cole uncomfortable. It meant he couldn't see all the way ahead.

Then it looked like the corridor ended.

No. As he rounded the last bit of curve he could see that it took a sharp turn to the right. No door this time. No rea-son to put a lot of doors in here, when you were above the water level and nobody could get in here anyway.

But now Cole had to wonder: What was their mission now? They had headed for the cabin only to reconnoiter. They hadn't meant to assault the place. Each step along this road, after the firing started, was oriented toward survival. Except . . . when there *had* been a choice about which way to run in the flooding tunnel, Cat had chosen to go toward the enemy, not away. And Cole had gone along without a second thought.

They had proof enough that this was where the bad guys were. One of the guys outside had to have taken pictures of the mechs and hoverbikes coming out of those huge doors in the mountainside. Video, too, of the rebels shooting at Cole and Cat on the ladder up to the cabin.

With no one actually shooting at them, Cole gave a hand signal for Cat to wait and keep watch. Then he switched on his transmitter.

"You think that's still working?" asked Cat.

"Light still comes on," said Cole. "And it's supposed to use the ground as a conduit." Cole coded for Drew first.

And got an answer. "Drew here. You guys okay?"

"Mingo and Benny get through to Gettysburg?" asked Cole.

"Don't know yet," said Drew. "But everything and everybody's coming through those big front doors."

"More guys looking for you?"

"We killed two mechs with rockets and then they all headed back for home. Trucks are coming out now, driving up and over the dam. Looks to me like they're evacuating the place."

"Just cause two guys got inside?" said Cat. "Big babies."

"They've got to believe we're just the preliminary team," said Drew. "If they believe we're just an advance team, and you actually got inside, I think they took that as a bad sign."

"Besides," said Babe, "these are the guys who decided *against* a military career."

Evacuating, moving to a different location. Why? Because they intended to make this one unusable themselves. "I think they're planning to flood this whole place," said Cole. "Genesseret is higher than this whole complex. Run water through it all, ruin everything."

"Doesn't eliminate the evidence that it exists," said Drew.

"If they're planning to flood this, I want to get a little higher up," said Cat.

"Tell us when Mingo reports that a strike force is coming," said Cole. "Make sure you have a radio ready to tell them about the ordnance and personnel that are getting away. Capture it all on the road." Then he signed off and turned off his transmitter.

Cat slid down the wall to a squatting position. "How long will it take a strike force to get here?"

"I don't know," said Cole. "If they come from Nevada or Montana, at least an hour."

"Carrier off the coast—the Marines might get here fastest."

"I don't mind getting my ass saved by the Marines," said Cole. "Long as they save my ass."

"If the bad guys are evacuating—"

"In order to flood the whole place?"

"I've done enough swimming," said Cat.

"So—before we move on, what's our goal here?"

"Stay breathing," said Cat.

"We could have stayed at the cabin," said Cole.

Cat thought about that for a few seconds. "Well, we want higher ground if they're going to flood the place. And my guess is, if we try to go out the front door, they'll be waiting for us there. Why hunt us down if they know we've got to come to *them*?"

"So we want to go up. If there's any place high enough in here to stay out of the water."

"And I was thinking," said Cat, "maybe Aloe Vera's here somewhere. Course, he'd be crazy to be here where he couldn't deny knowing about it."

"Maybe he doesn't want to deny it," said Cole. "Maybe he's proud of it."

"Here's where the ordnance is coming from," said Cat. "Maybe the orders come from here, too. Guy builds this army, don't you think he'd want to run it?"

"So we're looking for Verus?"

"Hell no," said Cat. "We're looking for command and control. Wipe it out in advance of the main assault."

It was elementary. Wipe out enemy command and control—it's what Special Forces were supposed to do in advance of an attack. But he'd never been in an invasion. He'd always worked on hearts-and-minds, recon, small-group assaults. Cat, however, had been there for Iraq in 2003. Different experience, so different stuff comes to mind in a crisis.

Still, thought Cole: I should have thought of it.

"If we do happen to find him," said Cole, "we need him alive. For the cameras."

"I think his dead body does the same job," said Cat.

"Better to pull him out of a hole."

"Like Saddam."

"Meanwhile," said Cole, "I wonder what's waiting around this corner. You got any grenades left?"

"In my pack," said Cat. "Floating in that tunnel."

Cole dropped to the floor and rolled out into the corridor, keeping his weapon pointed down the hall.

There was nothing there. Just more ramp going up and another turn.

"Goes up," said Cat behind him.

"Just the direction we wanted to go." Cole got up and ran up the slope. Cat followed him.

The next jog wasn't into a corridor, it was into a large, heavily braced cavern. This was one of the factories. Not a fully automated assembly line—the volume wasn't great enough to justify that. It looked like they used teams to assemble the pieces into finished hovercycles, one bike per team, six teams working, plus carts loaded with parts.

But nobody was assembling anything right now. Which went along with what the guys were seeing outside. Everybody evacuated.

On the wall, there was a map of the place with two escape routes marked. One led to the huge front door, the other to the tunnel connecting to the cabin.

"I don't believe this map," said Cole. "I don't think

they'd build this place without an escape hatch that didn't require that the lake be drained."

"They didn't expect the tunnel to be full of water," said Cat.

"But they flooded it themselves. Their defense is flooding the front door, too. No way are they so stupid they get trapped if both entrances are flooded."

"So there's an escape route didn't quite make it onto the map?" said Cat.

"One that trucks can't use," said Cole.

"But Aloe Vera can."

Studying the floorplan, though, there was nothing conveniently labeled "Command and Control."

"I'll keep watch," said Cole, "you look at this."

Cat looked. "Not like a regular building. Nice rectangular tower, you can spot the gaps when they leave stuff off the floor plan."

"So if you were in charge of this place, where would *you* put the command center?"

"Up high," said Cat. "They got three levels higher than this one. Not a lot of routes leading there."

"I bet Command and Control is four levels up," said Cole, "since the floorplan only shows three."

"Bet you're right," said Cat.

"So which way up you want to use?"

Both he and Cat had memorized the map while studying it—part of their training, to be able to memorize maps so they didn't have to carry them around.

"Not the ones that lead toward the front door," said Cat. "Let's avoid the crowds."

They ran into only three people on the stairs they took—all civilians, from their clothing, and two of them women. One of the women cried and shrank away, but the other armed herself with her shoe, brandishing it at them as they passed her and moved on up the stairs. "You can holster that shoe now," said Cole as he passed her. She didn't seem to think it was funny.

The stairs ended at the top level on the map. But this

level was smaller than the others. There were plenty of offices on this level, mostly in the form of cubicles. Every computer's cpu had been blown up by a small enough explosive that it was contained entirely inside the case—but smoke was coming out of many of them and most were splayed out or otherwise deformed. Not much data was going to come out of those computers now, but you never knew what a hard drive was going to live through. Might still be something retrievable. Unless they were heat bombs, and then all the plastic inside would be melted. That's what I'd use, thought Cole. So that's probably what Verus used.

His infra vibrated. Somebody calling him. "Cole here."

It was Benny. "As soon as we gave the word, they took off from Montana," he said. "By now they're probably only fifteen minutes away."

If the Progressive Restoration had observers with the forces in Idaho, which was likely enough, then that would explain why they started evacuating this place when only a couple of soldiers had penetrated it. Cole thanked Benny and signed off.

"You see any controls for that big front door?" said Cat. "Or for flooding that tunnel we were in?"

"We didn't see controls for opening the trap door in the cabin, either," said Cole.

"And there's got to be a control for sending water from one lake into the other."

"What do you want to bet," said Cole, "that wherever those controls are, Verus is sitting there waiting to raise the water level of Chinnereth just as our attack force is moving through the big front door."

"That would be mean," said Cat.

"And then he'd use the secret back door that isn't on any of the maps. The one that's camouflaged and opens up on the slope of the mountain somewhere on the Genesseret side."

"That would be smart," said Cat.

"Well, only semi-smart," said Cole. "Smart would be to

give himself up peacefully and denounce us for violating Washington's neutrality."

"Nobody's gonna buy that now," said Cat.

"Come on," said Cole. "People buy any lie they want bad enough to believe. We're the U.S. Army. When we screw up, everybody thinks it's on purpose and some of us should go to jail. Even when we *win,* they think we screwed up. What Army were you in, anyway?"

"My bad," said Cat.

"One level up from here," said Cole. "Gotta be a stairway somewhere."

"Maybe not," said Cat. "Maybe just a closet door."

"Leading into Narnia?"

"Leading to a stairway."

There weren't all that many doors, but all of them were locked. In the movies, people always shot doors open. But shooting a deadbolt lock didn't withdraw the deadbolt from the socket. And these were heavy doors, with lots of metal. Bullets could ricochet. Shrapnel could fly. You could kill yourself shooting at doors like these. Not to mention they didn't want to scare Verus into jumping down his rabbit hole—if he had one.

"Desks," said Cole. He headed back for one of the rooms full of cubicles and opened drawer after drawer, lifting up papers and feeling around inside.

Sure enough, he found a key that looked like it might do the job. Somebody forgot he had a spare in his desk. Happened all the time.

It wasn't a master key, but it did open two of the first three doors they tried. Naturally, Cole assumed that the one it *didn't* open was the one they wanted, but the third door opened to reveal a normal flight of stairs going upward.

And up and up. It wasn't just one story up, it was *way* up. Maybe not all that far from the observation tower on top of the mountain between the lakes.

They ran up at a measured pace—didn't want to be caught out of breath at the top, just in case somebody had a weapon waiting for them.

There it was. Command and Control. A single room full of screens and computers and control panels and gauges. These computers hadn't been blown up, because these didn't contain incriminating data, they just controlled the local machinery.

Cole moved into the room. Now he could see another door, labeled "Restroom." Standing near it were two men. One of them was Verus, in slacks and an open-collared short-sleeved white shirt. The other man was wearing a business suit and holding an AK-47.

"Just go back down the stairs," said the man with the gun. "Nobody has to get hurt."

Cole shot him in the head. He dropped like a rock.

"Calm down now," said Verus.

Cat moved into the room behind Cole and began scanning the controls. "Here's the control for the doors," said Cat. "Still open. There are still trucks going out. And the tunnel—flooded. Hey, thanks for that, Aldo. We're still not dry."

"You had no right to come here," said Verus.

No point in arguing with him about who had a right to attack New York City and kill the cops, or chase Cole through DC and Maryland to get Reuben's PDA.

"And here's the lake levels," said Cat. "One shaft is already open, pouring water back in from Genesseret."

"Can you close it?" asked Cole.

It was Verus who answered. "You can't close the upper gate until the Genesseret water level falls to normal."

"How many shafts?" asked Cole.

"Six."

"So it's refilling at one-sixth of the maximum rate," said Cole. "Still too fast. Close it."

"But he said—" And then Cat realized that he had been taking the enemy's word for how the thing worked. Why wouldn't he? It was an American telling him. "Bastard's probably got a *secret* set of controls all primed to flood everything and somewhere there's an LED display counting down the seconds."

"You watch too many movies," said Cole.

"You're Bartholomew Coleman," said Verus.

"Sorry I didn't let your guys kill me in D.C."

"Too bad you were brainwashed by the right-wing extremists," said Verus. "I could have used someone as resourceful as you."

"What about me?" said Cat. "I'm resourceful, too."

"*This* time we get to put John Wilkes Booth on trial," said Cole.

"I didn't have anything to do with killing that pathetic joke of a President," said Verus.

"You just happened to be all set to invade New York two days later," said Cole.

"We were going to move on July Fourth," said Verus. "General Alton's coup was going to be our provocation."

"So Alton *was* yours," said Cole.

"Then he decides to improvise and recruit *you*," said Verus. "Idiot."

"You want it done right, you got to do it yourself," said Cat.

"So am I under arrest, or are you going to murder me?" asked Verus.

"You're under arrest," said Cole.

"Either way I win," said Verus. "Excuse me while I take a leak." He turned and pushed his way into the restroom, slamming the door behind him before Cole could grab him.

Cole knew immediately that the restroom was not just a toilet. Before he could finish saying "Son of a bitch," he was at the door, opening it.

Just an unoccupied restroom with a closed toilet stall. Cole immediately dropped and slithered under the stall door. Inside there was a low doorway leading to a sloping ladder going upward. He could hear Verus climbing rapidly. Cole unlocked the stall door as Cat came in. "I think I got the flow stopped," said Cat.

"He went up here," said Cole, ducking into the ladderway. "I can see him."

"Just shoot him," said Cat.

"We want him alive," said Cole softly. "And he knows it."

They raced up the ladder after him. It was easy to overtake him. Verus was physically fit, but he was also in his sixties.

There was no reason to stop him, though, and risk having him fall and injure himself on the ladder. Cole just reached up and tugged on his pant leg a couple of times, to let him know he was right behind him.

Near the top, Verus slapped his hand against a button on the wall and a trap door opened automatically. If he had visions of closing it before Cole could get out, he was disappointed—Cole was out almost before he was, and grabbed him by the arm as he tried to run away Verus fell to the ground, pulling free of Cole's grip. At once, Cole pointed his rifle at Verus.

Cat came out of the trap door behind him. Only then did it close.

"Shit, we walked right by this and didn't see it," said Cat.

They were only a dozen yards from the cleared area around the observation tower.

There was a helicopter approaching from the northwest. Not the direction any task force would come from—but just the right direction for a chopper planning to take Verus to Seattle.

"No wonder the clearing around this tower's so big," said Cole.

Cat got his Minimi into position and fired a burst toward the chopper. It didn't burst into flames, but the pilot got the message all the same. The chopper swerved away.

Verus got to his feet, watching the chopper fly away.

When he turned around, he was holding a pistol, which he pointed right at Cole.

"Go ahead," said Cole. "Let's have the video of Aldo Verus shooting a United States soldier in the performance of his duties. Let's have that at your treason trial."

Verus lifted the gun toward his own head.

Cole shot him in the hand. It was a big heavy bullet and his hand exploded in blood. Verus screamed and fell to the ground, holding his hand and writhing.

"I'm a sharpshooter with the U.S. Special Forces," said Cole. "You're not getting away with *shit*."

"More choppers," said Cat. "Good guys this time."

"Your transceiver still working?"

Cat switched it on. "Seems to be. Even wet. Cool."

"Tell whoever's doing liaison with the attack force that most of the people they want are in trucks out on Highway 12. And we have Verus."

Cat made the call.

"Lie down on your belly and put your hands behind your back," said Cole.

He frisked Verus, then started field-dressing his hand. The bones were pretty messed up inside. That hand would never work right again. Cole knew it was petty, but it made him feel a grim satisfaction. That's for Rube. That's for a bunch of cops and a doorman in New York. I hope it hurts you every day of your life.

Meanwhile, he got the bleeding stopped and the wound bound before one of the Blackhawks landed in the clearing to take Verus into custody.

# TWENTY-TWO

# LINKS

History is never proved, only supposed. No matter how much evidence you collect, you're always guessing about cause-and-effect, and assuming things about dead people's motives. Since even living people don't understand their own motives, we're hardly likely to do any better with the dead.

Keep testing your guesses against the evidence. Keep trying out new guesses to see if they fit better. Keep looking for new evidence, even if it disproves your old hypotheses. With each step you get just a little closer to that elusive thing called "the truth." With each step you see how much farther away the truth is than you ever imagined it to be.

**IN ONLY** a few minutes, Cole told the colonel in charge of the task force everything pertinent that he knew, and Colonel Meyers assured him in return that they had already intercepted the convoys heading both directions up and down Highway 12.

"Good job capturing the command center intact," he said. "And Verus alive. News teams already have him on film."

"Broadcasting?" asked Cole.

"No way to keep it secret when we went across the border. Lots of uproar on the news about it. So Torrent preauthorized us to allow the embedded news teams to broadcast live *any* evidence that we had taken the right place. I decided Verus's face qualified. Along with those rows of mechs still inside. And the convoys."

"I look forward to watching the coverage," said Cole.

"You've got no time for that," said Colonel Meyers. "Torrent wants you to go straight back to New Jersey."

"Jersey?"

"He wants you with the cops who go back in to accept the surrender of the city."

"They've surrendered," said Cole.

"Not yet," said Meyers. "Which is why you've got time to get there."

"But I have a prisoner," said Cole.

"No, sir, I'm sorry. *I* have a prisoner. You have other orders." Meyers put a hand on his shoulder. "But you trust these other guys of yours, right? They can stay right with Verus all the way to Montana. We'll treat his wound and get him back to Andrews and they're with him, all right?"

Cat grinned at him. "I want to hear him say 'owie owie' when they treat his hand."

"They don't need me in New York," said Cole.

"True," said Meyer. "I think Torrent wants you there for the cameras. Last American soldier out of the city, first one to go back. It's all for the cameras, guys. We want to get the message out—this is one country, with one Constitution. Your face is part of that. Like it or not."

Cole was escorted to the chopper that was taking him back out of the battle zone. In the air, he found out that Averell Torrent had been confirmed by both houses of Congress as the new Vice President of the United States, and took the oath of office in the Senate chamber. But it was still Torrent's operation, and during his few minutes on the ground in Montana before boarding an eastbound military transport, he was given a cellphone whose number Torrent had.

Four and a half hours later, he was standing at the entrance to the Holland Tunnel. Captain Charlie O'Brien was there to greet him. So were the cops that Cole and Rube had led out of the city a month ago.

By now, Torrent had briefed Cole by telephone. "The city council has assured President Nielson that all their previous actions and statements were made under duress. They would welcome liberation by United States forces. They ask us to be careful to avoid bloodshed."

"I'd like to arrest their asses," said one of the cops. "Nobody minded them killing *us*."

"I believe," said Cole, "that one of the sacrifices you're being asked to make is to pretend that you weren't stabbed in the back. Just remember that the cameras will show you coming back into the city as the lawful police force— what's left of it. It's your show. I know you'll do it with class."

That was Cole's own decision—that the cops would lead the way. Torrent had tried to persuade him that he and Charlie O'Brien should be the point men, but Cole refused. "This isn't the U.S. Army or the New Jersey National Guard entering New York, it's New York's own. New York's finest."

Torrent conceded the point.

So they got into Humvees and headed on through the tunnel until they were thirty yards from the entrance. An advance team had already ascertained that there was no ambush waiting for them.

O'Brien and Cole followed the uniformed policemen up to the tunnel mouth, where the news cameras from inside the city were waiting for them.

Cole couldn't hear what was being said—but he knew the message well enough. Because the police force had been nearly destroyed during the invasion by the traitors, they had deputized members of the New Jersey National Guard and U.S. Army as auxiliaries to the New York City police. They were there to help arrest those traitors who laid down their weapons and surrendered, and to kill any who resisted.

The moment was carried live on all the networks and news channels. It was not known how many of the Progressive Restoration would refuse to surrender. In the end, only one mech operator fired at them and was immediately killed. A few of the rebel soldiers were apprehended trying to escape. No doubt some *did* escape.

Everyone else surrendered.

The Second American Civil War was over. By far the largest group of casualties were New York City policemen and firemen. The second largest group consisted of rebel soldiers killed by Cole and his comrades in Washington, D.C., and, later, at Lake Chinnereth.

The only U.S. military personnel killed or injured in the war were Major Reuben Malich and one of the military police who protected Cole's escape in the Pentagon on the sixteenth of June, and then the men who died in their vehicles on MacArthur Boulevard.

Every one of them, on both sides, an American.

After Cole and O'Brien were photographed with the policemen they had helped to save, they were piled into a car and taken back through the Holland Tunnel.

"You ever get your car back?" asked Cole.

"Oh, yes," said O'Brien. "You owe me a tank of gas."

"I owe you more than that," said Cole.

"Hey, how many guys actually got to blow up one of those mechs during this little war?"

"Damn few," said Cole, "and thank God for that."

The car dropped O'Brien off in his unit's staging area, where the same car was parked. Then Cole was driven on to Gettysburg, where the rest of Rube's jeesh had already been brought. Again, partly for the cameras. But also to be debriefed by Torrent.

During the debriefing, President Nielson came in to Torrent's office, waving his hand downward for them to stay seated and continue. He listened as Torrent asked his questions. Soon after Nielson, several others came in. Including Cecily Malich.

It was Mingo who interrupted Torrent in the midst of thanking them and bringing the debriefing to a close. "Excuse me, sir, but there's a member of our jeesh who didn't live to make this fight. His wife just came in."

Torrent turned around, noticing Cecily for the first time.

All the members of the jeesh stood up and saluted her

She rose slowly to her feet, crying a little, and saluted them back.

There weren't any cameras in the room. So the picture the world saw was the eight of them, still dressed for combat, lined up behind President Nielson and Vice President Torrent at the press conference.

When it was thrown open for questions, Cole tried to get Babe, who was, after all, a public relations professional, to serve as spokesman. But Babe refused. "I didn't go inside, man," he said.

So Cole and Cat stood at the podium, with the President and Vice President looking on. The questions were what you'd expect. Sure, they were heroes. But the press was still the press.

"How many Americans did you kill on this mission?"

"As many as necessary to protect myself and my men, and to accomplish our mission," said Cole. "And not one more."

"Why did you obey an order to enter a state that had closed its borders to military operations?"

"With all due respect, sir," said Cat, "all our operations took place inside the United States of America, under orders from the President of the United States. We did not cross any international boundaries."

"Weren't you afraid that your attack would lead to more bloodshed within the United States?"

Cole took that one, forcing himself to stay completely calm. "I was in New York City when this rebellion began. I saw the dead bodies of policemen and firemen and one uniformed doorman on the streets of that city, before I fired a single shot in this war. I believe our actions today put an end to the bloodshed that the rebels started."

"Do you feel you have avenged the deaths of the President and Vice President on Friday the Thirteenth?"

"We're not in the vengeance business," said Cat. "We're in the business of defeating those who wage war against America."

Cole added, "We know these people were behind the attack on New York, because that secret factory in Washington State was where the weapons they used were manufactured. But whether they had anything to do with the prior assassinations remains to be seen." Cole could see the President's staff visibly relax. They didn't want anything that could be used by Verus's lawyers to claim he had already been tried in the media.

"Some reports say that you shot Aldo Verus after he was arrested."

Cole smiled at the reporter. "After I told Mr. Verus that he was under arrest, he attempted to flee. We overtook him. He then drew a weapon. I did not shoot when he pointed it at me. I shot Mr. Verus in the hand only when he pointed the pistol at his own head. I wanted him alive for his treason trial. Since I was fifteen feet away, a bullet to the hand was the only way I could prevent him from taking irrevocable action."

Cat added, "We didn't believe we had time to negotiate the surrender of his handgun."

A lot of people laughed. A lot of them were reporters.

After the press conference, Cecily came up to Cole. "I can't get over the questions they asked you. Like you were criminals."

"It was a game," said Cole. "Didn't you notice? The guy who asked me about shooting Verus after he was arrested—he was from Fox. He was setting me up for the answer I gave. Bet you that'll be the sound bite that runs everywhere tonight on the evening news."

"And *not* a headline saying, 'Soldier accuses Verus of assassinations.' Okay, I see." She took his hand in both of hers. "Cole, have you called your mother yet?"

"No, ma'am," said Cole.

"So she's going to learn about all this by watching the news?"

"Probably not," said Cole. "She doesn't watch the news."

"So you can still call her."

He nodded.

"You can use my phone." She led him out of the room.

Her office —which she shared with four other staffers—was empty. She led him to the desk and he sat down to make the call.

"Before you dial," she said. "And before I leave you alone to talk to her, I just want to ask you. Will you come see me—soon? There's something I want to talk to you about."

"What is it?" She looked worried. What could be wrong *now*? They had the rebel arsenal. They had New York City back.

"When you come visit me," she said. "Call your mom." Then she left.

But when he called for an appointment the next day, she wasn't in. And the day after, she called him and said, "Look, I was probably wrong. It was just stupid. Come see me and the kids anyway—at home. And I mean really home—the President is moving into the White House now, and I'm taking my kids back home to Virginia."

Cole could imagine how it might be for her to enter the house she had shared with Rube. "Would you like company when you go back home for the first time?"

"I've already been back," she said. "I'm okay. But thanks for offering."

He figured that was that. They'd worked well together, even liked each other, but whatever confidence she was going to share, she had changed her mind. And that was fine. Her privilege.

**VERUS HAD** asked to see Torrent, and Torrent accepted. They did not notify the press. Verus was being held under guard at Andrews Air Force Base; Torrent arrived in a limo and was hustled directly to Verus's room.

Verus's arm was in a sling, his hand thickly bandaged.

Torrent sat down without waiting to be asked. "How is your hand?" asked Torrent.

"My own doctor got to examine it and approved of the

work they did. As a starting point. There'll be more surgeries. I'll probably never get full use of it, but people have suffered worse than that in wars."

"I thought you hated war."

"I hate wars that are fought to advance fascism," said Verus. "I didn't invite you here to argue with you."

"Really? Then why am I here?"

"Because you're the reason I fought this war," said Verus.

"I didn't realize I had made you so angry with me. In fact, I thought you enjoyed my seminar."

"Your lectures spurred me to action," said Verus. "I realized that it wasn't enough to lobby against fascists. Bayonets could only be stopped by bayonets."

"But Aldo," said Torrent. "If you really believed that, you and General Alton wouldn't have had to fake up a right-wing coup attempt."

Verus smiled thinly. "You think I don't know what you are?"

"We know *you're* a traitor, and definitely *not* a pacifist. What am I?"

"You're the devil, Torrent," said Verus. "And we all do your work."

Torrent rose to his feet. "You could have faxed me that message."

"I wanted to say it to your face. I just want you to know. This war isn't over. Even if you kill me or keep me in chains, your side will be brought down in the end."

"My side?" said Torrent. "I don't have a side."

With that, he left the room.

**CECILY MOVED** her children home. Aunt Margaret stayed with them for a while, and when she went home to New Jersey, Cecily came home from the White House. "I was just transitional," she told LaMonte. "My children lost their father. They need me. But I needed the work you gave me to do. So I thank you for that."

It was hard, especially because many of her friends—
*most* of her friends—seemed to regard the death of her husband as something that made her too sacred to actually talk
to. She got notes. There were flowers. A few visits, with the
standard words, "Well, if there's anything we can do."

But no calls from girlfriends inviting her to dinner or the
movies.

Then, about a week after she moved home, Cat and Drew
came by right after dinner, bringing ice cream. They sat
around the kitchen table with Cecily and the kids, and told
stories about Reuben. What he did in the war. What he did
in training. What he did when he was on leave with them.

A week later, it was Mingo and Benny. Same thing, with
pictures this time. They'd made a scrapbook and they left it
with them.

Babe came alone a few days later. He had made a DVD
of a slide show about Reuben. It was really funny. And
sweet. At the door, as he was leaving, she asked him, "Did
you guys draw lots? Take turns?"

"Oh, did the other guys already come? Have we been
pestering you?"

"No, no," she said. "I love you guys for this. Reuben
never talked about his work, not with the children."

"Before he was a martyr," said Babe, "he was already a
hero many times over. I think when kids have lost their dad,
they need to know who he was and why it's important that he
did the things that made it so he can't come home anymore."
He smiled a little. "I *know*. My dad died in the Gulf War."

Eventually they all came. And came back. Along with
other friends of Reuben's from the military. And she began
to get visits from military wives that she'd known on various assignments.

But Cole didn't come.

At first she wondered why—was a little hurt, even.

Then she realized that Cole might have fought with
these guys, but he didn't really feel like part of the group.
He had been added in.

And then she remembered telling him she wanted to talk to him, and then changing her mind. Maybe he interpreted that as my having changed my mind about wanting to see him.

Or maybe he's busy.

I'll call him.

But she knew that he *was* different from the other guys. Because he had been with Reuben those last three days. When the President died. In New York. And in the Pentagon, when DeeNee shot Reuben down. If he came over, she would tell him. Even though she couldn't prove anything. She'd tell him because she had to tell somebody.

But not yet.

She watched the news assiduously, as she always had.

All the movements to recognize the Progressive Restoration died with the arrest of Aldo Verus. Vermont's legislature didn't bother rescinding their resolution because, as their attorney general assured everybody, it had no binding legal force anyway.

America watched with Cecily and her children as the Progressive Restoration forces in New York surrendered peacefully after two days of dithering—and after the city council voted unanimously to declare them to be traitors and request them to leave their territory.

And more and more evidence came out, exposing Aldo Verus's network of influence and financial control. Many organizations dissolved themselves; others repudiated the financing they had received from Verus and pretended they hadn't known where it came from and that it certainly shouldn't be taken as any link between them and Verus's abortive revolt.

Verus himself waited in a special prison as his hand underwent repeated reconstructive surgeries and he was kept on continuous suicide watch.

The children lost interest. The war was over.

But Cecily kept watching, with special interest in Averell Torrent.

She wasn't all that unusual. Torrent was enormously

popular. Almost movie-star popular. And he was handling it all so brilliantly. There had been talk right from the start about giving the Republican presidential nomination to Torrent, though there were also grumblings about how nobody even knew where he stood on abortion, on marriage, on taxes, on immigration, on *anything* except defense.

But whenever reporters asked him if he was seeking the Republican nomination, he'd answer, "I'm not a member of any party. I'm not seeking any nomination." And then he'd walk away.

Then, in an interview on Fox News, O'Reilly said, "All right, Mr. Vice President, I'm going to ask you point-blank. Remember, this is the no-spin zone."

"I never forget that, Mr. O'Reilly."

"If the Republicans nominate you, will you accept the nomination and run for President?"

"No spin," said Torrent.

"And no evasions, please."

"Here's the thing. I believe in democracy. Hard-fought elections. But right now—this country's been on the brink of war. No, we were over the brink. Shooting had begun. And what was it about? The same divisive, vicious, hate-filled rhetoric that has dominated our elections for the past—what, fifteen, twenty years? I'm sick of it. I don't want to be part of it."

"I hear that, Mr. Vice President. But you still haven't answered my question. Am I being spun, sir?"

"I'm being as clear as I know how," said Torrent. "The only way I'd run for President is if I were nominated by *both* parties."

O'Reilly laughed. "So the only way you'll run is if you run against yourself?"

"I know I wouldn't smear my opponent and he wouldn't smear me," said Torrent.

"So are you asking the Democrats to nominate you, too?" asked O'Reilly.

"I'm asking people to leave me out of all the hatred and bitterness, all the lies and all the spin. I accepted the office

I hold now in order to end the impasse in Congress and help return this country to some kind of normality. I expect to step down when my successor is sworn in in January. After that, I'll see if some university will take me onto the faculty."

O'Reilly smiled and said, "The gauntlet is down, Democrats. It happened before, back in 1952, when nobody was sure whether Eisenhower was a Democrat or a Republican. Both parties wanted to nominate him. He picked one of them. But Vice President Torrent refuses to choose between them. The Democrats have the first convention. Will they stay with their current front-runner, who just happens to have the highest negatives of any candidate who ran this year? Divisiveness? Or healing? But I give you the last word, Mr. Vice President."

Torrent smiled gravely. "I miss the classroom. I look forward to teaching again."

"In other words, you think there's no chance you'll be nominated."

Torrent only laughed and shook his head, as if the idea was ridiculous.

But he didn't say no.

And despite the front-runner's most desperate efforts, she couldn't block Averell Torrent's name from being presented at the Democratic convention. Too many delegates were announcing that they would switch to him on the first ballot, regardless of what they had pledged back in the primaries.

As one of the delegates said on camera, "A lot has happened since the primaries. If we didn't have a responsibility to think for ourselves, there'd be no reason to have living delegates come to a convention, they could just tally the primary votes and make the announcement."

Leading Republicans fell all over themselves to announce that if the Democrats nominated Torrent, they'd nominate him, too.

It's really going to happen, thought Cecily.

And . . . I have to talk to somebody or I'll go crazy.

So she went to look for Cole's number, and realized: She didn't know it. She had only the numbers of cellphones that he had long since discarded. And of course his office number at the Pentagon, where his assignment had evaporated when Reuben was killed.

Finally she called Sandy in the White House.

"If you want your job back," said Sandy, "the answer is hell yes what took you so long."

"I don't," said Cecily, "but it's nice to know I've been missed."

"I don't miss you, I just have jobs for you to do," said Sandy. "So what *do* you want? Because I'm so busy I don't have time to scratch my butt."

"Bartholomew Coleman's phone number."

"You call me to get a phone number?"

"Captain Coleman," said Cecily. "The soldier who was with Reuben when . . ."

"I know who he is, I see him every day," said Sandy. "Home phone? Cell? Office?"

"You see him every day?"

"He's assigned to the Vice President as his top aide on military affairs. He's at all the briefings."

"I didn't know." Cecily was dismayed. Had Cole climbed into bed with Torrent? Then she couldn't talk to him.

"So don't you want the numbers now?"

"Sure, of course," she said. "I just didn't know—yes, all the numbers."

She could write them down. She just wouldn't use them. And she didn't.

But that night, he showed up at her door at nine o'clock.

"Cole—Captain Coleman. I didn't know—I didn't expect—"

"Sandy said you called," said Cole. "And then when you found out I worked with Torrent, you suddenly didn't want to talk to me."

Sandy was way too observant.

"But I've kind of been waiting for you to call," said Cole. "When you sort of backed off from talking to me a few weeks ago, I figured you wanted to wait. Or something. But . . . you know I really liked your kids. I don't want to lose contact with you. I only knew Rube—Major Malich—for a few days, but . . ." He took a deep breath. "Look, I was hoping there'd be cookies."

She laughed and ushered him into the kitchen. Mark and Nick were still up and they remembered Cole and practically tackled him and dragged him to the floor. Well, Mark did. Nick just watched him, but Cecily saw how his eyes glowed. Cole had made an impression on her sons.

They didn't talk about Reuben. They didn't talk about world affairs. Instead Cole asked the boys about things they were doing. They ate ice cream. Cole demonstrated how cupcakes don't actually have to be bitten into, you can jam a whole one in your mouth at once. Then he made a show of choking before he swallowed it all. "The bad thing," he said, "is when you cough icing out of your nose."

At ten o'clock Cecily sent the boys to bed.

"I'll go now," said Cole. "It's late for you, too."

"No," she said. "Stay. I do want to talk to you."

He answered softly, so the boys wouldn't hear. "It's about Torrent, right? I'm not married to him. I'm *assigned* to him."

"His request?"

"He's vetting the White House staff and the Pentagon. Working with the FBI to isolate the ones who *should* be under suspicion so the rest can breathe easy again."

"That sounds like an awfully controversial job for somebody who claims to be against divisiveness," said Cecily.

"That's just the point. He's the one that everybody will accept as being impartial and not politically motivated. He doesn't have a *history* with anyone."

"Actually," said Cecily, "he does."

They went down into the basement. Into the office. There she laid out the translations of Reuben's class notes. "First things first," she said. She handed him a paper with one paragraph circled.

"Augustus Caesar," he said. "So?"

She handed him another.

"Augustus again."

And another.

"He's a history professor," said Cole. "Augustus is his tory."

"Three different classes, Cole," said Cecily. "Only one of them even vaguely dealt with Rome."

"You're building a case, I see," said Cole. "So . . . build it."

"Read what Reuben said right *after* that paragraph."

Cole read it aloud. " 'Roman Empire an obsession? Especially Augustus and Trajan'—you didn't show me any Trajan notes."

"Keep reading."

" 'Heroes of his. Guy watches two sides fight it out in civil wars. Then steps in, puts a stop to it, Rome hails him as hero who brings peace and unity. Shows great respect to Senate, republican form of government. Modesty. But rules with iron hand. Torrent suffers from empire envy? Always says American empire can't fall because we're still in republic phase, not an empire yet. Wishing he could play Augustus and start one?' "

Cole set down the paper and leaned back in the chair. "So you think Torrent—what, set up a civil war just so he could come in and be the great conciliator?"

"I've read a lot about Augustus and Trajan, since getting these notes translated," said Cecily. "They were great emperors. Not cruel. They really did seem to want to maintain stability within the empire. Bring Rome to its true destiny. Improve life for everybody."

"So they were decent guys."

"But they were dictators, Cole. They played up to the people. To the army. To the Senate. They kept themselves popular. They also had their opponents murdered. They stayed in office till they died. And once you've got an emperor, even a good one, you can't be sure the *next* one will be an Augustus or a Marcus Aurelius, or a Trajan or a Hadrian."

"Could be Nero," said Cole. "Caligula."

"Then I keep thinking—am *I* being Brutus? He and his friends were worried about Julius Caesar becoming dictator, and so they conspired to murder him to save the republic. But his death just launched the civil wars that brought Octavian to power, that renamed him Augustus and put an end to democracy."

"Such as it was, in Rome."

"It was a lot, for those days," said Cecily. "And it's a lot for us, too. They're going to nominate him, Cole. You know they are. Both parties. He's going to run unopposed."

"The two-party system isn't going to die in one election."

"If we *have* another."

"Come on."

"Oh, he'll allow another election, and another, and another. Augustus kept all the *forms* of the republic. He just made sure that nobody was nominated that he didn't approve of. He kept control of the army."

"Torrent doesn't have *that,* I can assure you."

"I know. I'm just worried about nothing. Except."

"Except what?"

"What if Torrent's benign image is just that? Just an image?"

"You said he had a history. What?"

"He's been teaching a long time. And he's a noted teacher. His books are very popular. So all of this might be coincidence."

"All of what?"

Cecily handed him a list of names.

The first name on the list was Aldo Verus. He had attended two seminars of Torrent's, years ago—seminars called "History for Future-minded CEOs." Cole hadn't heard of most of the rest of the people, but Cecily provided a description of their activities along with their link to Torrent. They were all prominent in the Progressive organizations that were tied to Verus.

"He had a lot of students," said Cole.

"I know. I said so, didn't I? But the thing is, he *did* have *these* students." She handed him another sheet. It contained only two names.

Reuben Malich and Steven Phillips. "I've talked to Phillips."

"He's not in jail?" asked Cole.

"Nobody can prove that he knew any more than Reuben did what was being shipped and to whom and from whom. I'm not inclined to press it with him, because then people might press it with Reuben, and I *know* he didn't know."

"Me, too," said Cole.

"Phillips says that Torrent asked him if he'd be interested in being approached for some extra assignments. Just like Reuben."

"But Torrent didn't actually give him any assignments."

"He just asked if he'd be interested. He said the people would use his name. But when the approach came, they *didn't* mention Torrent. Same with Reuben. So Phillips—and Reuben—were never sure if these people had been sent by Torrent or not."

"But they took the assignments."

"Because they thought the assignment was from the President. And because . . . because it was secret and exciting and . . . these are *men,* Cole. And in the back of their mind, they thought it probably was from Torrent, and they knew he was such a brilliant guy, everything must be on the square."

"As if brilliant equals good."

"Exactly," said Cecily. "But we still don't know if he had anything to do with it. And we don't know who the people who approached Reuben and Phillips even were. Phillips doesn't know, anyway, and Reuben never said and never wrote down anything."

"So Torrent may or may not be involved with Verus."

"No, that's *not* the point," said Cecily. "I'm almost sure he's *not* part of Verus's operation. Verus was in control of everything about his operation. People reported to him, and he reported to God. Or history. Whatever he believed in. *Not* to Torrent. And can you imagine Torrent reporting to *him*?"

"Maybe. It's possible."

"I don't think so," said Cecily. "You met Verus."

"I didn't see him at his best."

"But can you imagine that if Torrent worked for him, Verus would sit still for Torrent being nominated by both parties? Essentially *handed* the presidency?"

"Of course he would," said Cole. "If it means he wins after all."

"Okay, maybe," said Cecily. "But I don't think so. Because of this."

She handed another sheet of paper to Cole. It had only one name on it. DeeNee Breen. Took a class with Torrent as an undergrad at Princeton. Got an A.

Cole felt sick. "But it was just a class."

"From Torrent. At Princeton. Coincidence. Lots of students took classes from him. Not all of them murdered a major in the U.S. Army, but I know I'm reasoning backward. It's no proof of anything. It's just . . . I had to tell somebody. I had to show somebody or I'd go crazy, watching Torrent do this—this rocket ride to supreme power."

"Who would keep a secret like this?" said Cole. "This conspiracy would be too—"

"Cole," said Cecily, "who would believe Verus could bring off his conspiracy? Anyway, I don't know if it *was* a conspiracy. It might have been more like some kind of evil Johnny Appleseed. Torrent might just have gone around planting seeds. Who knows what he said to Verus that maybe provoked him. Like, 'You talk about how committed you are, Mr. Verus, but you don't do anything. You took the name of a Roman Emperor, but you act like a lobbyist.' That's the way he talked. Challenging. Goading. He goaded Reuben. Called him 'soldier boy' all the time. It made Reuben all the more eager to prove himself to Torrent."

Cole remembered that day when Torrent led them through the reasoning process that pointed to Chinnereth and Genesseret. "You're saying that he already knew where Verus's operations were?"

"No, no, that's the beauty of it. He goads Verus. Makes him read history books that will point him to certain courses of action. But he isn't actually *in* on it. I think he really did figure out where Verus was exactly the way he showed us. Maybe he had some scrap of inside information—after all, he was NSA, he had access to intelligence reports that he wouldn't necessarily share with us. But he wasn't in on it, any more than he was directly in on what Reuben and Phillips were doing."

"And DeeNee?" asked Cole.

"That's different. The men who were waiting to ambush you—they're dead. We can't question them. Did they know she was planning to kill Reuben? Were *they* planning to kill him, or just subdue him and get the PDA? Did they work for Verus or Torrent or some third party we don't know about? It's all so murky and I don't know. But she was a student of Torrent's."

"Were the guys who were with her?"

"No. Nobody else."

"I don't know, Cecily. I just don't know."

"I don't know either. I'm not accusing him. I'm really not. But this stuff just won't go away."

Cole nodded. "I guess it's like having a song on your mind. You can't get rid of it. You *hate* the song. So you sing it to somebody else, and now we've *both* got the song on our minds."

"I'm so sorry!" she said. "You'll notice that I *didn't* call you, you just came over."

"Absolutely," said Cole. "And I'm glad you told me. Really. No lie. I'm glad you told me and nobody else."

"Because they'd think I'm crazy?"

"Because word might get around and somebody might kill you," said Cole.

She was rocked by that. "Come on."

"If it's true," said Cole. "*If* it's true. Then you're just begging to be murdered. To shut you up."

She reached over to the papers, turned on the shredder beside the desk, and turned them into confetti.

"Very dramatic, but they're on disk, aren't they?" said Cole.

"Not for long," she said. "And yes, I do know how to overwrite files so that they are truly and completely erased."

"But you know and I know," said Cole. "And we're both going to keep watching, aren't we?"

"I don't know," she said. "I didn't think of this as something *dangerous*."

"Yet you didn't talk about it to anybody."

"I thought they'd think I was crazy. Everybody talks about Torrent like he's God."

"The savior of America," said Cole. "But it might not be assassination. Declaring you mentally unfit and taking your children away would do the same job, wouldn't it?"

"You're scaring me," she said.

"I'm sorry. But I'm not joking. You've planted the seed in my mind. I'll watch. I promise you. I love this country. I don't want a dictator. But I don't want you to talk to anybody else about this. And I don't want you to do any more research. You had to call people to get this information. You had to go to websites, you had to write to people, correct?"

She nodded.

"So you might already be on a list somewhere. Even if it's only inside Torrent's head. For what it's worth, though, I think there's a good chance you're completely wrong. Which means you're safe. But then it's just as important not to say these things out loud to anyone else because if Torrent's innocent, then this is . . . really kind of vicious slander."

Cecily nodded again.

"Cecily, let's both watch him. Let's see how things play out. What he does with real power, when he gets his hands on it."

"All right," she said.

"Meanwhile," said Cole, "I really have missed you guys.

I really do like your kids. Can we be friends? Paranoids together, yes, but also friends?"

"Mark and Nick adore you."

"And vice versa," said Cole. "I'll visit now and then, and sometimes we'll watch Torrent on the news and exchange knowing glances. With any luck, we'll laugh about what we were thinking tonight."

"Were we thinking it? Or was *I* the only one?"

"Oh, you've got me thinking it, all right. You got the song on my mind, too."

They left the office. Cole insisted on rinsing the ice cream dishes and putting them in the dishwasher. "First time I've done dishes for anybody who wasn't my mom," he said. "I mean anybody I *liked* who wasn't my mom."

"I'll have cookies for you next time."

"Good, because it's my life's ambition to be fat."

She gave him a hug at the door and he hugged her back. "I can't help it," she said. "I feel better now, because somebody else knows."

When he was gone, she locked the door, went downstairs, got all the confetti from shredding those papers, and ran them down the garbage disposal in the kitchen.

**AT THE** Democratic convention, Torrent was nominated for President on the second ballot.

A week later, at the Republican convention, he was nominated by acclamation.

He became the first President since Washington to be elected with all of the electoral votes. And the largest popular vote in history, of course, since it was only divided with a handful of fringe candidates. But there was a huge turnout at that election. As pundits delighted in pointing out, if Torrent had gotten only *half* the votes he got, he still would have had the largest vote total of any presidential candidate in history.

People believed in him. They were ready for peace. They were ready to be united.

And in a house in Potomac Falls, Virginia, the Malich

family watched the election returns with Bartholomew Coleman as their guest of honor. There was no suspense. But the TV stayed on, filling the sound clips of cheering crowds and excited newsmen.

Now and then, Cole and Cessy exchanged knowing glances.

When the polls closed in California, President Nielson appeared on camera. He had been reelected to Congress from his Idaho district in a landslide of his own. He seemed genuinely happy as he said, "I am pleased to announce my resignation from the presidency, effective tomorrow at noon. I was never more than an emergency President, and the emergency is over. There's no reason for Averell Torrent not to start right away doing the job you chose him to do."

Cecily broke down in tears. Just for a moment. "That's just like LaMonte. Have we ever had a President who truly didn't want the job?"

"Besides Warren Harding?" said Cole.

"Who?" said Mark.

"A dumb guy who got chosen to be President once because he looked presidential and all the people who actually wanted the job had too many people who hated them," said Cole. "But your mom is right. Nielson did a good job as long as he was needed. And he chose his successor." He grinned at Cecily. "Just like Trajan and Hadrian and Antoninus Pius and Marcus Aurelius."

"And you claim you're not a historian," said Cecily, wiping her eyes, but laughing ruefully.

Thirty minutes later, Torrent came on the screen.

"I am honored beyond measure by the trust the American people have shown in me. I'm glad that so many people have come to the polls to show they share my dream of a nation united, a single people who sometimes disagree, but always remain friends and fellow-citizens. I will live up to your trust to the best of my ability.

"I am moved by the generosity and humility of my good friend, President LaMonte Nielson. Not only did he raise me to national prominence, but also he trained me for the job that you have voted to give me. His willing resignation from the presidency is in the spirit of Cincinnatus, the great Roman leader who, having saved his city, resigned all his offices and returned to his farm to continue his life as an ordinary citizen."

"A Roman reference," said Cole.

"But not an emperor," said Cecily.

Torrent was still talking. "There is nothing ordinary about LaMonte Nielson, however. He will continue to serve in Congress, and he will continue to hold a place in the hearts of the American people, in gratitude for his excellent service during our deepest national crisis since the Civil War."

"Exactly the right thing to say," said Cecily.

"Tomorrow I will be sworn into office as the second *appointed* Vice President to succeed to the presidency because of the resignation of his predecessor. In January, I will be sworn in again, for the term you just elected me to. But I have not forgotten that last June, on the thirteenth day, foreign terrorists murdered the elected President of the United States, the Vice President, the Secretary of Defense, the Chairman of the Joint Chiefs, and other dedicated servants of the American people in the performance of their duties.

"This was an offense to the entire American people. During the turmoil of the past few months, we have had our minds on problems within our borders. But the outrage committed against us has not been forgotten. Our response will be measured. It will be just. It will be thorough. It will be inevitable.

"But throughout the world, let every nation look to America for friendship. If you live at peace with your neighbors, if you provide fundamental human rights to your citizens, then we will join hands with you in perpetual partnership. We will show you that America longs for peace. We will have it within our own borders. We will help maintain it wherever it is threatened.

"And here at home, we will look at ourselves, not as groups arrayed against each other, quarreling over endless divisive issues, but as a single society, linked together by a shared culture, a shared history, and a shared future. Let's build that future together, day by day, as neighbors, with respect, as you have joined together tonight in this great exercise of democracy."

That was it. He was done.

There was no cheering crowd, because he had not given his speech at election headquarters. There was no election headquarters. He had not campaigned. Instead, he had gone from city to city, state to state, wherever the local candidates would agree to appear with him together, on the same platform, and each pledge to support their opponent if he should win. It was as if he were running an anti-campaign.

And now, his acceptance speech was given quietly, while sitting in his living room, with a single camera crew. Behind him, shelves of books. Beside him, his family. The perfect image of what Americans would like to think their Presidents are—intelligent, loving, kind, modest, and surprised by their good fortune.

"I wonder," said Cole, "if he'll remember that Cincinnatus speech four years from now."

"He won't have to," said Cecily, "if he's reelected."

"He seems like exactly the President I've wished for," said Cole.

"Me too," said Cecily.

"Hope it's true."

"Me too."

Cole got up from the sofa and stretched. "Let's have cookies."

# AFTERWORD

**THE ORIGINATING** premise of this novel did not come from me. Donald Mustard and his partners in Chair Entertainment had the idea for an entertainment franchise called *Empire* about a near-future American civil war. When I joined the project to create a work of fiction based on that premise, my first order of business was to come up with a plausible way that such an event might come about.

It was, sadly enough, all too easy.

Because we haven't had a civil war in the past fourteen decades, people think we can't have one now. Where is the geographic clarity of the Mason-Dixon line? When you look at the red-state blue-state division in the past few elections, you get a false impression. The real division is urban, academic, and high-tech counties versus suburban, rural, and conservative Christian counties. How could such widely scattered "blue" centers and such centerless "red" populations ever act in concert?

Geography aside, however, we have never been so evenly divided with such hateful rhetoric since the years leading up to the Civil War of the 1860s. Because the national media elite are so uniformly progressive, we keep hearing (in the elite media) about the rhetorical excesses of the "extreme right." To hear the same media, there *is* no "extreme left," just the occasional progressive who says things he or she shouldn't.

But any rational observer has to see that the Left and

Right in America are screaming the most vile accusations at each other all the time. We are fully polarized—if you accept one idea that sounds like it belongs to either the blue or the red, you are assumed—nay, *required*—to espouse the entire rest of the package, even though there is no reason why supporting the war against terrorism should imply you're in favor of banning all abortions and against restricting the availability of firearms; no reason why being in favor of keeping government-imposed limits on the free market should imply you also are in favor of giving legal status to homosexual couples and against building nuclear reactors. These issues are not remotely related, and yet if you hold any of one group's views, you are hated by the other group as if you believed them all; and if you hold most of one group's views, but not all, you are treated as if you were a traitor for deviating even slightly from the party line.

It goes deeper than this, however. A good working definition of fanaticism is that you are so convinced of your views and policies that you are sure anyone who opposes them must either be stupid and deceived *or* have some ulterior motive. We are today a nation where almost everyone in the public eye displays fanaticism with every utterance.

It is part of human nature to regard as sane those people who share the worldview of the majority of society. Somehow, though, we have managed to divide ourselves into two different, mutually exclusive sanities. The people in each society reinforce each other in madness, believing unsubstantiated ideas that are often contradicted not only by each other but also by whatever objective evidence exists on the subject. Instead of having an ever-adapting civilization-wide consensus reality, we have become a nation of insane people able to see the madness only in the other side.

Does this lead, inevitably, to civil war? Of course not—though it's hardly conducive to stable government or the long-term continuation of democracy. What inevitably arises from such division is the attempt by one group, utterly convinced of its rectitude, to use all coercive forces available to stamp out the opposing views.

Such an effort is, of course, a confession of madness. Suppression of other people's beliefs by force only comes about when you are deeply afraid that your own beliefs are wrong and you are desperate to keep anyone from challenging them. Oh, you may come up with rhetoric about how you are suppressing them for their own good or for the good of others, but people who are confident of their beliefs are content merely to offer and teach, not compel.

The impulse toward coercion takes whatever forms are available. In academia, it consists of the denial of degrees, jobs, or tenure to people with nonconformist opinions. Ironically, the people who are most relentless in eliminating competing ideas congratulate themselves on their tolerance and diversity. In most situations, it is less formal, consisting of shunning—but the shunning usually has teeth in it. Did Mel Gibson, when in his cups, say something that reflects his upbringing in an anti-Semitic household? Then he is to be shunned—which in Hollywood will mean he can never be considered for an Oscar and will have a much harder time getting prestige, as opposed to money, roles.

It has happened to me, repeatedly, from both the Left and the Right. It is never enough to disagree with me—I must be banned from speaking at a particular convention or campus; my writings should be boycotted; anything that will punish me for my noncompliance and, if possible, impoverish me and my family.

So virulent are these responses—again, from both the Left and the Right—that I believe it is only a short step to the attempt to use the power of the state to enforce one's views. On the right we have attempts to use the government to punish flag burners and to enforce state-sponsored praying. On the left, we have a ban on free speech and peaceable public assembly in front of abortion clinics and the attempt to use the power of the state to force the acceptance of homosexual relationships as equal to marriages. Each side feels absolutely justified in compelling others to accept their views.

It is puritanism, not in its separatist form, desiring to live by themselves by their own rules, but in its Cromwellian form, using the power of the state to enforce the dicta of one group throughout the wider society, by force rather than persuasion.

This despite the historical fact that the civilization that has created more prosperity and freedom for more people than ever before is one based on tolerance and pluralism, and that attempts to force one religion (theistic or atheistic) on the rest of a nation or the world inevitably lead to misery, poverty, and, usually, conflict.

Yet we seem only able to see the negative effects of coercion caused by the other team. Progressives see the danger of allowing fanatical religions (which, by some definitions, means "all of them") to have control of government—they need only point to Iran, Saudi Arabia, the Taliban, or, in a more general and milder sense, the entire Muslim world, which is oppressed precisely to the degree that Islam is enforced as the state religion.

Conservatives, on the other hand, see the danger of allowing fanatical atheistic religions to have control of government, pointing to Nazi Germany and all Communist nations as obvious examples of political utopianism run amok.

Yet neither side can see any connection between their own fanaticism and the historical examples that might apply to them. People insisting on a Christian America simply cannot comprehend that others view them as the Taliban-in-waiting; those who insist on progressive exclusivism in America are outraged at any comparison between them and Communist totalitarianism. Even as they shun or fire or deny tenure to those who disagree with them, everybody thinks it's the other guy who would be the oppressor, while *our* side would simply "set things to rights."

Rarely do people set out to start a civil war. Invariably, when such wars break out both sides consider themselves to be the aggrieved ones. Right now in America, even though the Left has control of all the institutions of cultural power and prestige—universities, movies, literary publishing, mainstream journalism—as well as the federal courts, they feel themselves oppressed and threatened by traditional religion and conservatism. And even though the Right controls both houses of Congress and the presidency, as well as having ample outlets for their views in nontraditional media and an ever-increasing dominance over American religious and economic life, they feel themselves oppressed and threatened by the cultural dominance of the Left.

And they *are* threatened, just as they are also threatening, because nobody is willing to accept the simple idea that someone can disagree with their group and still be a decent human being worthy of respect.

Can it lead to war?

Very simply, yes. The moment one group feels itself so aggrieved that it uses either its own weapons or the weapons of the state to "prevent" the other side from bringing about its supposed "evil" designs, then that other side will have no choice but to take up arms against them. Both sides will believe the other to be the instigator.

The vast majority of people will be horrified—but they will also be mobilized whether they like it or not.

It's the lesson of Yugoslavia and Rwanda. If you were a Tutsi just before the Rwandan holocaust who did not hate Hutus, who married a Hutu, who hired Hutus or taught school to Hutu students, it would not have stopped Hutus from taking machetes to you and your family. You would have had only two choices: to die or to take up arms against Hutus, whether you had previously hated them or not.

But it went further. Knowing they were doing a great evil, the Hutus who conducted the pogroms also killed any Hutus who were "disloyal" enough to try to oppose taking up arms.

Likewise in Yugoslavia. For political gain, Serbian leaders in the post-Tito government maintained a drumbeat of Serbian manifest-destiny propaganda, which openly demonized Croatian and Muslim people as a threat to good Serbs. When Serbs in Bosnia took up arms to "protect themselves" from being ruled by a Muslim majority—and were sponsored and backed by the Serbian government— what choice did a Bosnian Muslim have but to take up arms in self-defense? Thus *both* sides claimed to be acting in self-defense, and in short order, they were.

And as both Rwanda and Bosnia proved, clear geographical divisions are not required in order to have brutal, bloody civil wars. All that is required is that both sides come to believe that if they do not take up arms, the other side will destroy them.

In America today, we are complacent in our belief that it can't happen here. We forget that America is not an ethnic nation, where ancient ties of blood can bind people together despite differences. We are created by ideology; ideas are our only connection. And because today we have discarded the free marketplace of ideas and have polarized ourselves into two equally insane ideologies, so that each side can, with perfect accuracy, brand the other side as madmen, we are ripe for that next step, to take preventive action to keep the other side from seizing power and oppressing our side.

The examples are—or should be—obvious. That we are generally oblivious to the excesses of our own side merely demonstrates how close we already are to a paroxysm of self-destruction.

We are waiting for Fort Sumter.

I hope it doesn't come.

Meanwhile, however, there is this novel, in which I try to show characters who struggle to keep from falling into the insanity—yet who also try to prevent other people's insanity from destroying America. This book is fiction. It is entertainment. I do not believe a new American civil war is inevitable; and if it did happen, I do not believe it would necessarily take the form I show in this book, politically or militarily. Since the war depicted in these pages has not happened, I am certainly not declaring either side in our polarized public life guilty of causing it. I only say that for the purposes of this story, we have *this* set of causes; in the real world, if we should ever be so stupid as to allow a civil war to happen again, we would obviously have a different set of specific causes.

We live in a time when people like me, who do not wish to choose either camp's ridiculous, inconsistent, unrelated ideology, are being forced to choose—and to take one whole absurd package or the other.

We live in a time when moderates are treated worse than extremists, being punished as if they were more fanatical than the actual fanatics.

We live in a time when lies are preferred to the truth and truths are called lies, when opponents are assumed to have the worst conceivable motives and treated accordingly, and when we reach immediately for coercion without even bothering to find out what those who disagree with us are actually saying.

In short, we are creating for ourselves a new dark age—the darkness of blinders we voluntarily wear, and which, if we do not take them off and see each other as human beings with legitimate, virtuous concerns, will lead us to tragedies whose cost we will bear for generations.

Or, maybe, we can just calm down and stop thinking that our own ideas are so precious that we must never give an inch to accommodate the heartfelt beliefs of others.

How can we accomplish that? It begins by scorning the voices of extremism from the camp we are aligned with. Democrats and Republicans must renounce the screamers and haters from their own side instead of continuing to embrace them and denouncing only the screamers from the opposing camp. We must moderate *ourselves* instead of insisting on moderating the other guy while keeping our own fanaticism alive.

In the long run, the great mass of people who simply want to get on with their lives *can* shape a peaceful future. But it requires that they actively pursue moderation and reject extremism on *every* side, and not just on one. Because it is precisely those ordinary people, who don't even care all that much about the issues, who will end up suffering the most from any conflict that might arise.

# ACKNOWLEDGMENTS

**MY FIRST** and greatest thanks must go to Donald Mustard and his team at Chair Entertainment, who began developing the videogame of *Empire* and yet held off on committing to any storyline so that I would be free to let the characters, situations, and events of this novel develop organically. Their development work provided the premise of a new American civil war, the mechs and the hovercycles, the falling and rising water level in a lake in the state of Washington, and the hero whose life ends, leaving others to carry on to victory. These were potent seeds to nurture in a story that is otherwise my own.

Over the past few years, as my novel *Ender's Game* has been more and more widely read and discussed within America's military communities, I have had opportunities to meet many soldiers and have been deeply impressed, not just by the standard military virtues of courage, commitment, and loyalty, but also by the level of intelligence, education, open-mindedness, initiative, tolerance, patience, and wisdom that are not just the virtues of individuals, but the virtues admired and striven for within a surprisingly vibrant and healthy portion of American society. Our military is, of course, not immune to the diseases that afflict all such institutions throughout the world, but they are aware of those potential problems and many brilliant and dedicated officers and soldiers constantly seek to avoid them in their service to our country. I salute them.

However, I do not name them, mostly because I would not want any of them to be blamed for the many errors I am bound to have made in this book. I have never served in the military, and when trying to depict a complex and long-lived society, no amount of research can compensate for lack of membership in it. The mistakes here are my own. To those who have helped me achieve such understanding as I managed to achieve, I give my thanks. You know who you are. Godspeed to you.

During the writing of this book I relied, as never before, on the Internet. When I make up a fantasy or science fictional world, or work in a historical period, the Internet is usually quite useless. I am relying either on my imagination or on historical information so arcane and detailed that it can only be found in books. With *Empire,* however, I was working in the very near future, and so contemporary information was essential.

The website usmilitary.about.com provided me with information about the specific weapons that my characters would be carrying into combat. Google Maps took me moment by moment through chase scenes and combat in Washington, D.C., and New York City and helped me find Cole's route into Washington State; Google Earth gave me two imaginary reservoirs behind impractical dams in the stretch of land near Highway 12 between Mount Saint Helens and Mount Rainier.

As always, I relied on my team of pre-readers. Since they have lives of their own, I sometimes churn out chapters when they can't take time to read them. Thus over the progress of a novel, I will be helped now by this reader, now by another. Early in the writing of this book, Aaron Johnston and Erin and Phillip Absher gave me quick and valuable responses; later on, the burden shifted onto Kathryn H. Kidd and Geoffrey Card, who kept me alert to problems and possibilities. Errors were also caught by members of the online forum at my Hatrack.com website, including Alexis Gray and Marc Van Pelt.

Of course Donald Mustard, who was creating the game

right along with my writing of the novel, saw every chapter and responded helpfully. In particular, I owe to him and his brother Jeremy some of the closure in the last two chapters.

And I was much encouraged by the observations of my friend and colleague Lynn Hendee, on whose judgment I have long relied.

As with all my books, every chapter was seen first by my wife, Kristine, who as always caught many errors and alerted me to problems that no one else noticed. Until she is pleased, the chapter is not done.

And my editor, Beth Meacham, not only gave me excellent suggestions at key points in the writing process, she also set aside other work to read the chapters the moment they were written. Because of that, and her heroic labors on behalf of the book when it took longer to develop the story than I had anticipated, we were able to meet the deadline to get this book published in the fall of 2006, a mere four months after I finished writing it.

I also appreciate the rest of the staff at TOR who have gone the extra mile to make up for my lateness and to compensate for my errors. I'm proud of how you made this book look and how you brought it before the public.

And to my publisher, Tom Doherty: Thank you for betting on a pig in a poke and trusting me to deliver. That you do not have an ulcer is entirely not my fault.

Barbara Bova, my agent, is both my protector and provocateur—it's been an exciting thirty years, hasn't it?

And to Zina Card, who spent hours watching episodes of 24 with Kristine and me so I could keep in mind the rhythms and energy of an effective thriller, thank you for your delightful company and your patience with my need to make you visit Washington, D.C., twice this summer. Now you get your normal family back—at least until the next book.

A new collection of short fiction from one
of SF's most beloved and popular writers,

# ORSON SCOTT CARD

## KEEPER OF DREAMS

This massive new volume collects nearly all of Orson
Scott Card's short fiction published since the release of
the earlier *Maps in A Mirror*. Twenty-four stories, plus
new introductions and commentaries by the author, make
this collection a definitive retrospective of the short fiction
career of the writer the *Houston Post* called "the best
writer science fiction has to offer."

"[Card] demonstrates his talent for shorter
  fiction.... Detailed introductions and afterwords
  reveal insights into the thought processes of
  one of the genre's most convincing storytellers.
   An important volume."
                    —*Library Journal* on *Maps In A Mirror*

978-0-7653-0497-1 • 0-7653-0497-X
IN HARDCOVER APRIL 2008

www.tor-forge.com